HOTSHOT

A SAM BLAIR MYSTERY, BOOK 1

GENE PECK

To: Jane

"Undeniably great is the mystery of devotion . . . ."
1 Timothy 3:16

PHOTO CREDITS

Above Photo: "United States Attorney Maurice M. Milligan Taking the Oath of Office as he commences his Second Term, February 1938. Pictured: U.S. Attorney Maurice M. Milligan; Assistant U.S. Attorneys Thomas A. Costellow, Otto Schmid, Richard K. Phelps, and Sam C. Blair; First Assistant Randall Wilson; and U.S. District Judge Merrill E.

Otis." *United States Department of Justice*, February 26, 2015, www.justice.gov/usao-wdmo/historical-resources/snapshot-history-maurice-milligan.

Cover Photo: courtesy of Missouri Valley Special Collections, Kansas City Public Library, Kansas City, Missouri.

1

JUNE 17, 1933, 7:17 A.M

A rhythmic clink came from across the Transit Hall. Looking that way, I saw seven plainclothes men with a shackled prisoner in their midst coming up the stairs from Platform Ten. Anyone reading the papers would have recognized the man in chains. He was Frank "Jelly" Nash, a recent escapee from Leavenworth Prison.

The "Jelly" moniker was hardboiled for nitroglycerin. That was Nash's favorite tool for blowing safes. And even though he wasn't as famous as John Dillinger or Baby Face Nelson, Nash had knocked off more banks than anyone in U.S. history.

That achievement had put him at the top of Hoover's Public Enemy list. And it also made him of interest to me. I was a new Assistant U.S. District Attorney, and that meant I might get a chance to prosecute Jelly someday. But right now, that was purely academic. He wasn't back behind bars yet, and this *was* Kansas City.

KC's known as "Crime Capital USA," and for good reason. Just take murder for instance. The town's per capita homicide rate is nearly twenty percent higher than Capone's Chicago. And it's the same for every category of crime.

Why is the crime so bad? The local machine and the mob are in bed together. And the crooks have rolled out the welcome mat for their pals. That means anyone on the lam can hole up here for a while, and the cops will look the other way. It's sort of a professional courtesy extended by Boss Tom Pendergast.

What that means, of course, is that there are plenty of gunsels hanging about. You know the kind of guys, who for a few bills will try anything. And that includes springing prisoners passing through town. I shook my head. Some rookie must have planned the Nash transfer—to have routed it through Kansas City.

I lit a cigarette while keeping an eye on the detail. It shuffled its way through the crowd toward the Transit Hall's four-hundred-foot center aisle. As they went, the guard behind Jelly kept a tight grip on his belt. Reaching the aisle, the detail formed into a wedge with Jelly in the middle.

While they were getting situated, a reporter in a pork pie hat ran up to the lead man in the detail and started firing questions at him. The lead guy waved the news jockey off. But the fact he was there was worrying. It meant Nash's itinerary had leaked.

I sized up the detail's armament. Everyone but the lead man was carrying. Two cradled shotguns and the others had revolvers in their hands. Still, I'd been a lot happier, if one of them had been holding a Thompson.

Any crook will think twice before taking on a Tommy gun. It can spew eight hundred rounds per minute. And a Thompson's forty-five caliber bullet, drum magazine, and fore grip give it deadliness, staying power, and accuracy.

The lead man gave a wave, and the wedge set out. They

trooped down the center aisle past rows of pew-like benches lined with waiting passengers. The guards scanned the crowd as they went.

Middle-aged and bald with a beaked nose, Jelly wasn't much to look at. But a hotshot grin was plastered on his face. And despite the chains, he still managed to swagger.

I let the detail go by, then followed them. They went down the center aisle and through an arch into the Grand Hall. A clock was suspended from the top of the arch. Its six-foot dial read 7:22 a.m.

Continuing across the black-and-tan marble floor, the detail's measured pace echoed off the ninety-foot-high coffered ceiling. An unmanned travelers-aid desk stood in the center of the Hall. A uniformed copper was lolling on its counter. But he was too busy eyeing a pert redhead to notice the detail going by.

As they neared the exit, Jelly and his guards bore to the left of the semi-circular array of ticket windows set against the station's south wall. They passed through a shaft of sunlight shining through a ninety-foot-high tombstone window. It was one of three built into the front of the station.

Reaching the eastern bank of doors, the detail marched through them exiting toward the parking lot beyond. I halted, finished my cigarette, and stepped on it. Then I heard a familiar voice behind me.

"Well, if it isn't Memory Man."

It was Ken McIntire, of course, unimaginatively known as "Mac." He'd tagged me with that label shortly after we'd met. And sure enough, when I turned around, he was standing there twirling a palm-straw fedora. We shook hands.

Mac and I had a lot in common. We were nearly the

same age, with small-town upbringings, recent law degrees, and less than a year in our current jobs. Mac was with the Bureau of Investigation.

Raising a finger, he said, "Okay, Blair, got one for you."

"Shoot."

"How many times did Babe Ruth beat the single-season home-run record before 1925 and in what years?"

"Three times," I said, "And in consecutive years, 1919, 1920, and 1921."

"Okay," he said. "Got another one. How tall is the Empire State Building?"

"From sidewalk to roof, 1,250 feet."

Mac's mouth dropped open, "Jeez, how do you do that?"

I smiled and replied, "If you really want to know, I'll tell you sometime." Then jerking my head in the direction of the prisoner detail, I asked, "You with the Nash transfer?"

With a frown, Mac looked toward the eastern bank of doors. "Nope. Still, I couldn't resist coming down this morning for a look-see."

"Where're they headed?"

"The Big House."

That was con-speak for the U.S. Penitentiary in Leavenworth, Kansas thirty-five miles to the northwest.

"Going by car?"

"I expect. Safer than waiting around here for the Leavenworth local."

I nodded in agreement.

Then Mac gave me a double-take and broke into a grin. Pointing to my left cheek, he snickered, "Who you been smooching with? There's lipstick all over you."

Flushing, I rubbed at the spot he'd pointed to. "Just my older sister, Dolores. Put her on the express to Jeff City to see the folks."

"Well, you'd better get it off before you get to the office." Still grinning, Mac popped on his hat and headed towards the newsstand. Over his shoulder, he said, "Got to get some smokes. Catch up with you."

"You bet," I replied turning towards the eastern bank of doors.

A yellow weight-and-fortune machine stood by the exit. I glanced in its mirror and saw that there was still a red smudge on my cheek. Pulling out my handkerchief, I licked a corner and rubbed at the spot until it was gone.

The oval face in the mirror had a straight nose, hazel eyes, and square chin. Auburn hair showed under the Panama. It was clipped short on the sides but left long on top. A latticework of faint white scars marred the right cheek, where the smudge had been.

I stood on tiptoe to check my outfit in the mirror. I was wearing a gray, summer-weight three-piece suit, with a powder-blue shirt and burgundy tie. It was seasonal and smart without being too snappy.

"Okay, kiddo," I said, speaking to the guy in the mirror. "Let's see if you can do something really tough—like getting to work on time." Turning toward the exit, I slipped into an easy lope. Weaving my six-foot frame through clumps of passengers, I passed through a propped-open door.

Emerging from the station's dimness, the bright June sunlight blinded me. And I nearly collided with a redcap wheeling luggage inside. Then looking east toward Main, I slowed to a walk seeing no up-town streetcar in sight.

Glancing back at the station, I admired its temple-like façade, which hinted at the role transportation had played in the city's history. In steamboat days, the Town of Kansas had been founded on the southern bank of the Missouri River, where a limestone ledge had served as a natural landing.

With statehood, Kansas City, as it was now known, became a jumping-off point for the country's westward expansion. Local entrepreneurs made their fortunes outfitting wagons crossing the prairie to California, Oregon, and Santa Fe.

When the railroads came, the city fathers successfully lobbied Congress for the exclusive right to build a permanent railway bridge over the Missouri. The bridge, along with the city's central location, had put KC on the direct route to the Eastern markets from the developing West. The resulting rail traffic had led to the construction of this massive Beaux-Arts terminal, which was the third busiest in the country.

With still no northbound streetcar in sight, I scanned the area in front of the station for Jelly and his guards. I was hoping they had already left for Leavenworth. KCPD's Hot Shot, a four-door with gun ports and plating, was parked in the yellow zone outside the western bank of doors. But Jelly and his detail were nowhere near it.

Then I saw them. They were just to my right, in the parking lot's first row of cars. Jelly and three of the guards were already inside a dusty sedan with Nebraska plates. The remaining four stood outside talking and smoking. One of them tossed his cigarette and started around the front of the car heading for the driver's door.

As he reached it, three men sprang up from behind the second row of cars. Two of them were carrying Thompsons. As they ran towards the dusty sedan, they pointed their guns at the lawmen shouting, "Up, up, up!"

At first, it looked like the lawmen might comply. Then a shotgun went off, and everyone cut loose. Machine guns clattered. Pistols popped. And once again, a shotgun roared.

Everyone around me scattered. But I had an urge to run

straight into the shooting. Then someone gave me a shove. I hit the sidewalk face-down, and my Panama went flying. Bullets hammered the wall above me.

Twisting my head, I saw the back of a man in a brown suit lying on the ground beside me. He must have been the one who'd pushed me. I was glad he had.

Raising my head to look over him, I could see the sedan with Nebraska plates. It was rocking from machine-gun fire. There were at least three bodies on the ground around it. One of the shooters started circling the car, trying to flush a lawman hiding behind it.

Holding his arm, the lawman made a break for the station doors. Bullets chased him as he ran. I ducked as more lead raked the wall above.

Then the shooting stopped. And a gravelly voice shouted, "They're dead!" This was followed by the sound of running. With that, the man in the brown suit slowly got up. And I did the same.

The uniformed policeman I'd seen lolling on the traveler's aid desk charged out of the station. He emptied his revolver at the three fleeing men. One of them slumped and gripped his shoulder. The shooters piled into an already running Chevy. It squealed away swerving onto Pershing, heading west toward Broadway.

I ran to the shot-up sedan. Its windshield was a web of cracks—pocked with holes. Shards of glass were scattered across the hood. Kneeling by a man lying face down, I felt for a pulse. There was none. Standing up, I peered through the open window on the driver's side.

The sweet-metallic scent of fresh blood hit me. Jelly Nash was alone in the front seat. His mouth gaped, and the back of his head was missing. Three others were slumped over in the rear. One of them was clearly dead, but another was moaning.

I silently prayed a *Requiem aeternam* and made the sign of the cross. Turning away, I stepped on something and nearly fell. Under my right foot was a steel ball, a third of an inch in diameter. Pocketing it, I backed into the murmuring crowd.

Staring at the shot-up car, all I could think of was my sister, Midge. She'd been gunned down too. It'd happened ten years ago in Jefferson City. We'd been walking home from school when robbers had burst out of the Exchange National Bank. One of them had shot her.

The police had asked me to describe her killer. But for some reason, I couldn't. There are parts of that day I just can't remember. And there's something else too. I've been a bumbler ever since. Usually, it's small stuff like tripping and knocking things over. But every so often, something more serious happens.

I jumped back as two police cars squealed to a stop behind the shot-up sedan, their sirens winding down. Uniform bulls spilled out taking control of the scene. They moved the crowd away from the car. A plainclothes detective was with them. He had a hard look and wore flashy clothes for a cop. He also had a mouthful of protruding teeth.

Walking over to the man, whose pulse I'd checked, the detective prodded him with the toe of his spectator shoe. When there was no response, he went around the back of the car to take a closer look at two more of the dead. They had fallen together, on their backs. One was cradled in the arms of the other.

Squatting down, the detective methodically emptied the dead men's pockets. He placed their personal effects into his open handkerchief, wiping his hands on their clothes when he was finished. Rising, he knotted the handkerchief and slipped it into his pocket.

Plucking a kitchen match from his vest, the detective stuck the wooden end into his mouth. Chewing on it, he surveyed the scene—hands on hips. With his suit coat pulled back, I could see a narrow leather sheath on his belt. It had an ice pick in it. That seemed to be an odd thing for a cop to be carrying.

After a moment, the plainclothes man went over to the driver's door and opened it. A spent shotgun shell rolled out onto the running board. Picking it up, the detective sniffed it. Then he pulled back the front seat and spied another one at the feet of a slumped-over man. He stuffed both shells into his pocket.

The plainclothes man must have felt my eyes on him. He turned and gave me a flat hard stare. "What're you looking at, bub?"

His voice was cold, and his jutting teeth gave his words a sibilant hiss. When I didn't reply or look away, the detective started walking toward me. His eyes got harder as he came.

At that moment, a couple of wise guys strolled out of the station. One of them whistled through his teeth at the plainclothes man. The other one called out to him by name, "Hey, Rayen!"

The plainclothes man pulled up short. He turned to look back at the two men. Giving me one last hard look, the detective plucked the match from his mouth and flicked it at me. It bounced off my chest. Then he pushed his way through the crowd and went over to the Hot Shot. There he and the two wise guys put their heads together.

I hadn't meant to provoke the detective, but I hadn't

been able to take my eyes off him. There was something about the guy. But I couldn't put my finger on it.

Looking back at the shot-up car, I saw that the newshounds had arrived. And the cops were letting them do whatever they wanted. A photographer picked up a bloody Panama and placed it on a fender. Then he waved the crowd away from the front of the car.

Another photographer positioned the patrolman, who had fired at the fleeing gunmen, between two eyewitnesses. He grouped them so that the two dead lawmen lay at their feet. Then he motioned for the crowd behind the car to come forward—to fill in the frame. After snapping their pictures, the photographers raced into the station. When they were gone, the cops once again took over the scene.

I heard sirens in the distance. The ambulances were coming. It didn't look like there would be much for them to do.

Someone tapped me on the shoulder. It was the reporter in the pork pie hat. His breath stank of burnt coffee and too many cigarettes.

"Jim Wetzel, *Journal Post*," he muttered. "See the shooting?"

I nodded still trying to take it all in.

The reporter leaned into me. "How many gunmen?"

"Three."

"You sure?" he countered. "Others are saying four."

"I only saw three."

"How many Thompsons?"

"Two."

"What was the third man carrying?"

"An automatic."

"See one with a shotgun?"

"No."

"You're certain?" he asked, challenging me again.

"Yeah," I said starting to get fed up.

"Recognize any of them?"

"No."

"You didn't see Harvey Bailey or Pretty Boy Floyd?"

"No. But I was keeping my head down, so I can't be sure."

"Name?"

"Sam Blair."

"Occupation?"

Reluctantly, I told him, "Assistant U.S. District Attorney."

At that, his eyes widened, and he crowded me. "So, what's the D.A.'s take on the shooting?"

That did it. "Look, buster, he's the one who'll be talking to the press—not me. And don't use my name." With that, the reporter smirked and turned to the person next to me.

The plainclothes man with the overbite was still talking to the two wise guys. Not wanting to be around when he came back, I hunted up my hat. Remembering the guy in the brown suit, I looked around for him. But I realized, I hadn't gotten a good look at his face.

I did see Mac though. He was talking to a police sergeant by the eastern bank of doors. After finishing his conversation, Mac ran into the station. He was probably calling in a report.

My gaze returned to the shot-up car. This was going to cause one helluva stink. It was like giving the middle finger to the Bureau of Investigation, some of whose agents had to be among the dead.

Then my thoughts shifted to the killers. I wondered who they were—hired guns or hoods from the local mob? And what had they wanted—to spring Jelly or to silence him? And if Jelly had been their target—why had they killed him?

But I stopped myself right there. This was none of my

business. And since I was the least experienced Assistant D.A., the chances of this case being assigned to me were nonexistent. Glancing at my watch, I swore. It was ten till eight. Turning, I raced toward the streetcar stop.

LUCK WAS WITH ME. I managed to snag a downtown trolley, just pulling away. Soon, we were rumbling past 1908 Main—where Tom Pendergast had his office. As usual, there was a line of petitioners on the sidewalk out front.

Boss Tom wasn't your typical politician. He wasn't interested in making fine speeches or basking in the spotlight. No, all Tom wanted was power. And he knew that the best way to get it was to elect a whole slate of candidates, who were beholden to him, rather than hanging his hat on his own candidacy.

And once Tom had acquired power, he knew how to use it. Five mornings a week, starting at 6:30 a.m., he held court at his private office. There, he dispensed favors to those who were worthy and listened stonily to those who were not.

Loyal supporters shared in the largess, which could range from free loads of coal in winter to well-paying civic jobs, which required no work. Alternatively, opponents found their water inexplicably cut off or their property tax doubled. And the only way to right such wrongs was to go hat in hand to the Boss at 1908 Main.

And Pendergast knew never to let a crisis go to waste. When the Depression hit, cities everywhere had tightened their belts until their economies had wilted. But not Pendergast. He had thrown open the city's coffers and kept the local economy afloat with municipal cash.

As a result, stores had remained stocked, and there were

few commercial vacancies. But the Boss had also known that this was just a temporary fix. So, he'd proposed an ambitious public-works program called the Ten-Year Plan. And in 1931, the voters had approved it with a whopping forty-million-dollar bond issue.

Municipal Auditorium had been the Plan's first project. And a new City Hall, County Court House, and Police Headquarters had followed. The use of excavation equipment had been kept to a minimum in the construction of these buildings. So that more out-of-work laborers could wield picks and shovels.

Initially, the Ten-Year Plan had received rave reviews. Even the President had spoken highly of it. And it was said that FDR had expressly modeled his Works Progress Administration on the Pendergast Plan. But when the bids were accepted on the city's first project, a troubling fact had emerged. Either the Boss or one of his cronies had been awarded every one of the bids.

Called out for this impropriety, Boss Tom had been typically unrepentant. "What's wrong," he'd growled. "Isn't my concrete as good or better than any?" That, of course, wasn't the point. But as usual, his aggressiveness had served to deflect his detractors.

Despite such unsavoriness, it had to be admitted that the city had benefited from the Boss's program. Not only had it created sorely needed jobs, but the resulting civic structures were neither ugly nor poorly built. They were, in fact, Art Deco masterpieces. The kind of buildings local citizens could take pride in—as long as they didn't look too closely at their cost.

It also had to be admitted that Pendergast was a man who knew how to get things done. He had a knack for reconciling the seemingly irreconcilable. And he seemed to instinctively know how a bargain could be struck. But with the Boss, there was always the same problem. As ingenious as his solutions might be, the means he employed were invariably corrupt. And what's more, his example inspired others to go and do likewise. So, it wasn't long before nothing could be done in the city without a bribe or a kickback.

And whenever the Boss was criticized for this shady dealing, his supporters would leap to his defense. "So what?" they'd bluster, "Every big city has its graft." As if that, somehow, excused it.

Oddly enough, even though his hand was in their pockets, most Kansas Citians were proud of their Boss. They liked his hard-nosed politics and sharp deals—when they were directed at someone else. And they admired the way he'd put their city on the political map.

Of course, Pendergast's power wasn't all political. His association with the local mob had given the machine real muscle. Interestingly, the idea of a mob-machine merger hadn't come from the Boss. In a surprise move, Johnny Lazia, the mob's youthful *cumpari*, had deposed the Boss's lieutenant, who ran the city's North Side. But instead of trying to dethrone Pendergast, Lazia had proposed an alliance. And Boss Tom had realized that, with the mob behind him, he would be unassailable. So, he'd readily accepted Lazia's offer. And with that, KC had become a town where anything goes.

Not long after my move to Kansas City, a hand-written note had landed on my desk. It was in red pencil on Jackson Democratic Club stationary. The note had said, "Come see me," and it was signed, "T. J." That was short for "Thomas Joseph," and it was what Pendergast's friends called him. I was curious, so I went.

With all his power, you might have thought the Boss would have had a swanky office. But you would be wrong. It was nothing more than a second-floor walk-up in a pokey, two-story building on the southern edge of downtown.

In response to Boss Tom's summons, I'd gone to 1908 Main and taken my place in the line out front. As it grew shorter, I'd climbed the narrow stairs between the Southwest Linen Company and the Ever Eat Café. I'd expected to find a lot of down-and-outs at the top. But instead, the waiting room was a cross-section of the city. Bankers rubbed shoulders with day laborers, struggling widows with members of the bridge-and-martini set.

When my turn came, I was ushered into a low narrow room. It was sparsely furnished with a roll-top desk, side chair, and corner safe. There were only two things on the Boss's desk, a Jackson Democratic Club notepad and a red pencil.

Boss Tom stood when I entered, and we shook hands. At five eight and two-hundred-and-thirty pounds, Pendergast was round, but there was nothing fleshy about him. His grip was firm, his grey eyes unwavering.

As soon as we sat down, the Boss told me he was glad I'd come. "I want to know everyone in town," he'd said in rumbling tones, "Especially anyone with the Government." Then he'd begun talking about the city and his vision for it. It was a vision, he implied, a man like me would surely share.

The image he sketched was of a place of health and prosperity. Where there was ample work, and the populace lived productive lives amid impressive public structures, spacious parks, and quiet neighborhoods. Here, they were free to enjoy themselves and seek their pleasure—without excessive governmental meddling.

Making all this happen was a tight-knit "organization," which was only political out of necessity. It was more like a brotherhood, efficiently ordered to public service. This organization, as was only fair, shared in the prosperity of the city, which it governed. Fixing his eyes on me, T. J. had added, almost offhandedly, "We're pretty full-up, but there's always room for another good man."

For a moment, a vision had hung in the air. In it, I was the U.S. District Attorney sitting behind a massive desk shrewdly evaluating cases while giving instructions to my staff as they waited deferentially upon me. Then I'd shifted in my seat, and the vision had vanished.

"No thanks," I'd said.

In response, the Boss had cocked his head. His tone had changed. "At the bottom, Sam, politics is give-and-take. You may not like it but that's the way it is." Then he'd added, "No one gets a job like yours just because he's good at what he does."

That stung. Of course, I owed my job to my Father, and the Boss knew it. But that didn't mean I could be bought and sold. Once the Boss realized I wasn't on offer, I'd been shown the door.

That was the only time I'd met with the Boss. And it was the only time I'd been in his office. Only later, did I begin to wonder, if that safe in the corner, was where this story had all begun?

2

JUNE 17, 1933, 8:10 A.M

I bounded up the steps of the Federal Courthouse, passed the art-deco lamps, and strode across the white-marble lobby. It was ten after eight. Squeezing into an elevator, I rose with one stop to the sixth floor.

Arriving there, I opened the gold-lettered door of the U.S. District Attorney's Office. Thankfully, the reception was still empty. I turned right down a long hallway.

As the fourth Assistant D.A., out of a total of four, my office was at the end of the corridor. It was an institutional green square with a pebbled window. The latter opened onto a ventilation shaft, and pigeons cooed on the ledge outside. As I'd come down the hall, I'd noticed that none of the other Assistant D.A.s were in their offices. I wondered why, so I went looking for them.

I found everyone gathered in the open work area where the typing pool was located. Everyone that is, except for the Chief, who had yet to arrive. Not surprisingly, they were talking about the Union Station shootings.

Thomas Costellow was the Assistant D.A. with the longest tenure. He had the floor. In his mid-forties with grey-flecked brown hair, Costellow came from the kind of money that made politics irrelevant. His right hand held an elevated cigarette; his left was inserted into his suit-coat pocket.

"Half-a-dozen gangsters armed with submachine guns mowed down the police this morning—right in front of Union Station. There are more dead than in the St. Valentine's Day Massacre."

"That's what I've heard too," moaned Mrs. Wilkes. "There are heaps of dead—both bystanders and police." Mrs. Wilks was forty-ish and proper. She was the senior member of the typing pool.

"Oh-h," oozed Ginny Oaks, her eyes wide. Ginny was the receptionist, who also ran the switchboard. She was a full-figured redhead in her early thirties, who favored dresses with large floral patterns.

"Probably just kids shooting off firecrackers," scoffed Otto Schmid. The office contrarian, Schmid was in his mid-thirties with an acne-scarred face. He was another of the Assistant D.A.'s.

Raised in a West Bottoms' tenement, Schmid had beat the odds by going to Notre Dame and then Harvard Law School. It had all been paid for by machine scholarships. So, it wasn't surprising that Schmid was a Pendergast man.

When the conversation lagged, I spoke up. "I was at Union Station this morning." Everyone's eyes turned to me.

"Did you see the shooting?" asked Audrey Baxter, her eyebrows lifting.

I nodded.

The newest member of the typing pool, Audrey was twenty-two with amber eyes and golden hair. Slight, but pleasingly ample, her lips were peach, and her skin pale rose. She was the office heartthrob.

Audrey and I had gone out several times after work. But we'd had to be careful. There was a strict prohibition against office relationships, and we could get the sack if we were caught.

"What did you see?" asked Phelps.

Richard Phelps was the last of the Assistant D.A.'s. In his early fifties with receding black hair, Phelps was married with six children. He was a former schoolteacher and state representative, who was our resident expert on legal research and citation.

"Three gunmen jumped a prisoner detail in the parking lot," I replied. "A couple of them were carrying Thompsons."

"Who was the prisoner?" asked Schmid no longer trying to hide his interest.

"Jelly Nash," I replied.

"That was fast," said Charlie Meeks, the office boy. "He was only arrested yesterday in Hot Springs, Arkansas."

Despite his baby face, Charlie was almost thirty. He was the office boy not for any lack of ability, but because jobs were scarce. Charlie was the one to go to if you wanted the skinny on anything. Heck, he probably already knew about Audrey and me.

"Were they trying to free Nash?"

This came from First Assistant Randall Wilson, the office's second-in-command. Short and pear-shaped, Wilson was a stickler for rules. During the Great War, he'd been made a Major. But contrary to his Army rank and behind his back, he was known as "the Skipper." It was a title he detested.

"Well, if they were," I said, "They weren't successful. Nash was killed."

Mrs. Wilkes gasped.

"Anyone else?" asked Wilson.

"At least four lawmen . . . maybe more."

This was met by silence.

After a moment, Wilson asked, "Recognize any of the gunmen?"

"No—I was too busy keeping my head down."

Flicking the ash from his cigarette, Costellow lifted his chin. "Sounds like you're a material witness, Blair. If you haven't already—you'd better let the Bureau know."

I nodded, amazed I hadn't thought of that myself. Stepping back, my elbow grazed a can of newly sharpened pencils on the edge of Audrey's desk. They tumbled to the floor.

I flushed and knelt to gather them up; Audrey joined me. One of the pencils rolled away under her desk. In reaching for it, I instead grabbed one of Audrey's fingers. She stifled a laugh.

"Ahem!" said Wilson.

Startled, I leapt up banging my head on Audrey's desk. "Damn it!" I said rubbing the sore spot.

"Language, Mr. Blair," said Wilson.

Then I saw that he was looking at Audrey. And that his glance had swung back to me. I hastily put the No. 2's I'd gathered into the righted can. Thankfully at that moment, the Chief arrived. And everyone dispersed in a charade of busyness. I headed toward my office, but Wilson cut me off.

"Late again, Mr. Blair?" He said it with a raised eyebrow.

I swallowed, "Yes, Mr. Wilson."

"I'll have to mention it to Mr. Vandeventer if it happens again."

"Right," I replied.

Thirty minutes later, I was in the men's room drying my hands on the roll-up towel. Costellow came through the door. When he saw that we were alone, he marched over to me and stuck a finger in my face.

"Don't ever do that again, Blair." He was flushed, and his voice was tense.

Surprised, I wondered what he was talking about? Then I got it. He thought I'd intentionally tried to embarrass him. The stuffed shirt! He'd embarrassed himself—by shooting off his mouth before getting his facts straight.

I grabbed Costellow's finger and bent it back until he was kneeling on the floor, his face contorted in pain. Thanks to Sister Agnes, everyone who'd attended Holy Cross Elementary knew how to do a finger lock. She'd called it the "Bully Bend."

When Costellow had had enough, I let go. Cradling his finger, he glared up at me. I stepped around him and went out. Putting a finger lock on Costellow had probably been a bad idea. He could cause me plenty of trouble. But it was too late to worry about that now.

Around eleven, U.S. District Attorney William Vandeventer buzzed me to his office. When he did, I frowned. I sure as hell hoped the Chief wasn't going to grill me about Audrey.

The D.A.'s office occupied the southwest corner of the sixth floor. I knocked and entered. The high-ceilinged, mahogany-paneled room had two sets of double windows. One set looked south over Ninth Street, and the other, west, along Grand Avenue. The Chief was sitting behind his oversized desk—lighting his pipe.

In his late fifties, Vandeventer was rangy and going thin on top. When not in court, he favored tweeds, and that was what he was wearing today. I came to a stop in front of his desk. He didn't motion for me to sit.

The Chief held a flaring match to the bowl of his billiard

pipe while sucking vigorously on the stem. Smoke spewed from the corner of his mouth. Shaking out the match before it could burn his fingers, he spoke without looking up.

"What's the status of the Lazia investigation?"

I relaxed. It wasn't about Audrey.

For over two years, Treasury had been trying to assess thirty-seven-year-old Johnny Lazia's actual income in the hopes of indicting him for tax evasion like they had Capone in Chicago. I gave the Chief the short answer. "I've reviewed the file and have a meeting with Treasury Agents Sharp and Beach on Monday."

"That means you don't think they have enough for an indictment?"

"That's correct."

"What's missing?"

"The money needs to be directly tied to Lazia."

"And it isn't?" asked the Chief.

"Only circumstantially."

"What more do we need?"

"Fact testimony—putting the money into Lazia's hands."

"That's a tall order."

"It is," I admitted. "But without direct evidence, the jury is unlikely to convict."

"Why not?"

"You know the drill, sir. They'll be getting death threats —anonymous letters under their doors, calls late at night. Even with solid evidence . . .," I shrugged.

Vandeventer did not immediately answer. Instead, he opened the middle drawer of his desk and took out a brass tamper. After pressing down on the tobacco in the bowl of his pipe, he replaced the tamper and closed the drawer. Then he spoke.

"Do what you have to do, Mr. Blair. But we're going to file that indictment."

"Yes sir."

The Chief struck a fresh match and, once again, drew heavily on his pipe. Lifting his eyes to mine, he muttered, "That'll be all."

I turned and left, shutting the door carefully behind me.

Like most of downtown, the U.S.D.A.'s workweek included Saturday mornings. As we prepared to shut down at noon, I ran into Audrey in the corridor outside my office. Her arms were full of olive-and-red case reporters, which she was returning to the courthouse library.

With a twinkle, she asked, "How's your head?"

I grinned and checked to see if we were alone. Seeing that we were, I whispered, "Lunch at the Liberty Bell?"

She nodded. "I have to finish a brief first," she whispered. "But it shouldn't take long,"

"Great."

Wilson appeared at the end of the hall. Audrey quickly turned and walked briskly back to reception. I strolled into my office intently studying the letter I was holding.

THE LIBERTY BELL was a half-pint diner located three blocks east of the courthouse. It was cheap and good. Plus, it was rarely frequented by others in the office.

The Liberty Bell had a narrow counter with eight stools that ran its width and a single two-person table shoehorned into a corner. Its owners were a middle-aged couple named Hank and Lucille. Hank was a short wiry guy in a long white apron and square cap. He manned the grill. Lucille took orders and served up the food. She was a bosomy redhead with pencils stuck in her hair.

I snagged the table and ordered a black coffee. Since it was Saturday afternoon, there were only two other customers in the place. One of them was a beat cop on his lunch break. The other looked like a cab driver between fares.

It wasn't long before Audrey joined me. I ordered the fifty-cent special—chop suey. She had an egg-salad sandwich with a glass of water.

Once Lucille had our orders, I leaned over to Audrey and asked, "Can I get your home number?" I inhaled Audrey's warm fragrance; she smelled like butterscotch. Our knees inadvertently bumped under the table. She didn't shy away when they did, and I liked that.

"Sure, it's Atwater-5308," she said. "But don't be put off if dad answers."

I leaned in even closer, "Why, does he bite?"

Toying with her fork, she said, "Not usually. But I do!" And she stuck her fork into my encroaching arm.

"Ouch!" I said rubbing it while making an anguished face.

Audrey giggled.

"So, what does your dad do?" I asked.

Her face clouded over. "Not much—now."

"Sorry." Just when things were going well, I'd stepped in it.

"It's all right," she replied. Which meant, of course, that it wasn't. I waited to give her time to say more if she wanted.

"He used to be with the KCPD."

Ah, that was it. After Boss Tom had gained control of the city, he had appointed Johnny Lazia as "police liaison." And all the up-and-up cops on the force had either resigned or been fired. Then Lazia had replaced them with his boys. It was also said that he'd expunged the criminal records of anyone who'd been with the mob.

Not surprisingly, Audrey's dad was one of the good guys. And his firing explained not only her enmity towards Johnny Lazia but also the Pendergast Machine. Still, the lawyer in me couldn't resist probing.

"So, what did your dad do for the police?"

"Chief of Detectives," she said, "But let's talk about something else."

"Sure thing."

Our food arrived, and we ate for a while in silence.

Then Audrey asked, "What were you doing before you came to the D.A.'s office?"

"Working with my two older brothers in Jefferson City."

"What was that like?"

I shrugged, "The usual civil practice, some litigation, contracts, wills, and trusts."

"Sounds pretty good."

"Yep, slow and steady. You'd think I'd have been happy just to have a job. But—I wanted to be a prosecutor."

"That's because of Midge, isn't it?" she said.

I nodded. It was my turn to be silent.

"So how did you end up in Kansas City?" she asked.

"Well, dad could see I wasn't happy."

"What does he do?"

I paused before answering, "He's a Justice on the Missouri Supreme Court."

"Ah," she replied.

"Yep, I'm just another sausage out of the patronage pork barrel."

"Well, that's how you get government jobs," she said rising to my defense.

"I know. But I still don't like it."

"Oh, I almost forgot," said Audrey digging in her purse. "I've heard back from Menninger's."

After she'd found out about Midge's death, and how it had affected me, Audrey had asked a million questions. Then armed with my answers and the help of a local librarian, she had looked for clinics where I might get treatment. And she'd found one of the best in Topeka, Kansas, which was only about fifty miles west of Kansas City. But Audrey hadn't stopped there. She'd written to the Menninger Sanatorium asking them if they would take me as an outpatient.

Audrey pulled a crumpled letter from her purse and smoothed it out on the table. "Here it is." Finding the part she wanted, she read it aloud:

> Having evaluated your description of Mr. Blair's condition, we would like to schedule an appointment with him to conduct a preliminary assessment. Please have Mr. Blair contact Dr. Karl Menninger at this address to arrange a mutually agreeable time.

I was moved by her efforts and reached for her hands. "Thanks, Audrey, I . . . ."

She reddened and quickly stopped me. "I just want you to get better," she said leaning forward, her eyes softening. I squeezed her hand and let go.

The bell above the door jangled, and two men stepped inside. Hank glanced around. Seeing them, he frowned. Lucille turned and stood staring at the two men.

Feeling the tension, the cop at the counter turned and looked over his shoulder. He made eye contact with the shorter of the two men then turned back around and resumed eating. No one spoke.

From their flashy clothes and thuggish look, the two were Lazia's boys. The one in front was short and square with a round fleshy face. He was smiling—showing his teeth. The one behind him, standing just inside the door, was tall and bullnecked. He was sullen and menacing.

Then through the front window, I saw First Assistant Randall Wilson; I grabbed Audrey's arm. She glanced around, and we both ducked, as the bell jangled. The door swung open hitting the tall goon in the back. He twisted around and scowled at Wilson.

Speaking through the gap, Wilson said, "Excuse *me*!"

The tall man's face darkened. He slammed the door in Wilson's face, twisting the deadbolt and flipping the sign to the "Closed" side. Wilson fell back then immediately stepped to the front window and put his face against the glass, shielding his eyes with his hands to see inside.

Audrey and I twisted in our seats keeping our backs to the window and hunkering down even lower. The tall thug strode over to the window. He hammered on the glass, jerked a thumb at the First Assistant, and shouted, "Scram!"

Out of the corner of my eye, I could see Wilson stepping back. For a moment, I thought he was going to try the door again. But instead, he stalked away.

"Whew!" I exhaled.

"Did he see us?" Audrey asked biting her lip.

"I don't know," I whispered. "But that's the first time I've been glad to have a couple of Lazia's goons around." Audrey giggled nervously.

Oblivious to our discomfort, Hank was having trouble of his own. He spoke in a low tone to Lucille. "Mind the grill, Babe."

Walking over to the cash register, Hank hit the "No Sale"

key. He took an envelope from beneath the cash drawer. Then circling the counter, he held it out to the smiling man.

The thug took the envelope, opened it, and thumbed the contents, counting. "You're twenty short," he said. His smile broadened; he was enjoying himself.

Hank frowned and started to say something. Changing his mind, he turned back to the register. Opening it, he took out all the bills and three rolls of change.

Hank walked back to the smiling man and put them in his outstretched hand. The man slowly counted the money and slipped it into his pants pocket. The envelope went into the inside pocket of his suit coat. Without a word, the two turned and left, leaving the door standing open.

Hank shut it, flipping the sign to the "Open" side. Then he went back to the grill. There he and Lucille had a whispered, agitated conversation.

"Those guys make me sick," said Audrey.

"Yeah," I said eyeing the beat cop at the counter. "But when the cops and the goons are on the same side, you've got to be careful. Besides, we've got problems of our own."

"I know," she groaned twisting her napkin.

I sure hoped Wilson hadn't spotted us. I didn't want Audrey to lose her job. And I didn't want to lose mine either. Draining my cup, I thought about the Lazia indictment. Weak or not, I sure hoped I'd be able to file it.

3

JUNE 17, 1933, 7:35 P.M

It was dusk. I was sitting in the kitchen of my bungalow reading the evening edition of the *Kansas City Star*. I shook out the paper and turned back to the front page. The headline read, "FIVE SLAIN AT STATION." I re-read the article under it.

Of the four Bureau agents present at Union Station this morning, only one, Raymond Caffrey, had been killed. He was the man, lying face down, whose pulse I'd checked. Surprisingly, another agent, Frank Smith, had managed to emerge from the backseat of the shot-up car, unscathed.

The lawman, who had been sheltering behind the car during the shootout, was Reed Vetterli. He'd been the lead man in the detail and was Special Agent in Charge of the local BI office. Vetterli had escaped with a flesh wound.

Joe Lackey, who'd been sitting beside Smith in the backseat, had been hit three times in the back. While one of the bullets had been removed, the other two had been left in place. They were too close to the spine. Lackey's condition was rated serious, but stable.

Besides Caffrey and Nash, three others had died: Otto

Reed, an Oklahoma Police Chief, who'd helped arrest Jelly in Hot Springs, and the two Kansas City police detectives, who'd been providing a local escort. They were William "Red" Grooms and Frank Hermanson. Reed had been sitting in the backseat next to Smith, while Grooms and Hermanson had been standing outside the car.

The article said that there was still some question about the number of gunmen involved. As the reporter, Wetzel had said, some eyewitnesses had seen three gunmen—others, four. And forensic evidence had also suggested the presence of a fourth gunman.

Eyewitnesses also confirmed that two of the shooters had been seen carrying Thompson submachine guns, a third had had a forty-five automatic in his hand. But three of the dead—Nash, Caffrey, and Hermanson—had died from shotgun wounds. That had led the authorities to believe that a fourth shooter had been present, armed with a shotgun.

And something else was puzzling. Grooms and Hermanson hadn't been carrying their department-issued Thompson submachine gun. Normally, the Hot Shot, to which they were assigned, had one clipped to the passenger door. And the detectives had routinely carried it during prisoner transfers—to serve as a visible deterrent.

This morning, however, the Thompson was missing, and the detectives had proceeded to the station without it. The paper had said that Director Higgins had determined that the machine gun's absence was due to an "administrative error." I wondered what that meant.

The article also quoted from a press release that had been issued by City Manager, Henry McElroy. One of its sentences caught my eye: "It has definitely been established that no Kansas City gangster had anything to do with the shooting this morning." I snorted when I read that.

Those words had to have come straight from the mouth of Johnny Lazia. And there were similarly self-serving statements from Director of Police, Otto Higgins, and Mayor Bryce Smith. In my experience, such disclaimers usually meant that the opposite was true.

After all, Johnny Lazia had to have been at least tacitly involved. It was common knowledge that anyone planning a crime in Kansas City had better clear it first with the mob boss. If that hadn't happened, then either the shooters were rank amateurs, or the mob itself had been behind the ambush. And now, the politicians were now closing ranks to protect Lazia.

There was one more item of interest in the article. Director of Police, Higgins, had changed his tune from an earlier edition. He was now no longer saying that Nash had been deliberately murdered. Instead, he now thought Jelly had been killed "by mistake." The paper did not say what had changed Higgins's mind.

Folding up the *Star*, I glanced at the sorry remains of my dinner of sardines, saltine crackers, and a glass of milk. I got up and put my dishes on top of others already in the sink. Deciding I couldn't put it off any longer, I turned on the tap and added some soap. As I scrubbed the dishes, I longed for a shot of bourbon to rinse the fishy taste from my mouth. But that wasn't going to happen anytime soon.

In March, FDR had signed the Cullen-Harrison Act, once again legalizing the manufacture and sale of three two beer. It was widely expected that the Eighteenth Amendment would be repealed by the end of the year, but it was going to be some time before legal liquor was flowing again.

And considering my position, if it wasn't legit, I wasn't drinking it.

Prohibition had been an exercise in coerced virtue. And like all coercion, it had failed. Instead of banning alcohol, the Volstead Act had made it a forbidden fruit. And it had also unintentionally created a booming market for enterprising criminals. Now, it was hoped that, by making drink legal again, the bootleggers' flow of cash would be cut off, and crime would fall away.

There was a rap on the screen door. Wiping my hands on a towel, I went to see who it was. Mac was standing on the front porch, hands in his pockets.

Unlatching the screen, I asked, "What's up?"

"Got a moment?"

"Sure," I answered.

"It's about this morning," Mac's voice trailed off.

I opened the door for him, and he stepped inside.

"Oh, yeah," I said. "I should've given you a statement this morning. Didn't think about it until later."

"No problem," he answered. "Drop by the office on Tuesday—after lunch. We'll do it then."

"Okay," I replied. But when Mac made no move to leave, I figured he had something else on his mind.

"Want to sit down?" I asked.

He nodded, came in, and took one of the armchairs by the fireplace. Mac shook out a cigarette and lit it. So, I sat down across from him and lit up too. We smoked in silence, as the room grew darker.

Finally, Mac began to talk. "When I joined the Bureau, they said there'd be risks. But saying's one thing and seeing's another."

Images from that morning came to mind. I saw bodies

on the ground and the back of Jelly's head. I could almost smell the blood again.

"And when it's people you know," he continued. "It's just not what you expect."

Images of Midge's body replaced those of the riddled lawmen. Thinking he wanted reassurance, I said, "You'll get them."

"Oh, sure," said Mac. "Hoover will see to that."

I said nothing in response. Once again, we lapsed into silence. And only the ends of our cigarettes glowed in the darkness.

I sympathized with Mac. The newly reorganized Bureau of Investigation was still sorting itself out. During its first fifteen years, the BI had been known more for corruption than for solving crimes. And by 1924, the country had had enough. A Senate investigation had forced the resignation and indictment of both the Bureau chief and the sitting U.S. Attorney General.

Many had figured the BI was finished, but the new A.G., Homer Cummings, had other ideas. He thought the country still needed a federal police force. So, he'd named a like-minded, twenty-nine-year-old bureaucrat as Director and instructed him to clean house. The bureaucrat's name was, of course, J. Edger Hoover.

Hoover took the A.G.'s directive to heart and fired all but a handful of agents. In their places, he'd hired young men fitting a certain profile. They were all between the ages of twenty-five and thirty-five. All had law degrees; all were clean-cut and eager.

Only a couple of items were missing from Hoover's employment criteria: one, experience in solving crimes and, two, in arresting criminals. But for J. Edger, just having his

G-men look the part was enough. He figured they could learn anything they lacked through on-the-job training.

So, by 1929, Hoover had three-hundred-and-thirty-nine new agents in place. And Ken McIntire was one of them. But with all their inexperience, it was a real question whether the Bureau's agents were up to the task. And now, it looked like their first real test would be the Union Station Massacre.

I stubbed out my cigarette and switched on a lamp. Then I asked Mac the question that had been nagging me. "Think the gunmen were trying to free Jelly?"

"Not likely," said Mac.

"Because they used Thompsons?"

He nodded. "Too hard to control."

That's what I thought too. "Higgins thinks Jelly was killed by accident."

Mac shook his head.

"But then why was he killed?"

"Afraid he'd talk," said Mac, "When we got him back to Leavenworth."

"Yeah. But about what?"

"Don't know. But whatever it was. It had to be big."

After Mac left, I climbed the narrow stairs to the attic. At the top, I snapped on a light that hung from a cord and sat at a desk pushed against the wall. A framed picture of Midge was on the desk. The black-and-white photo didn't do justice to her auburn hair and blue eyes. But it had captured her generous grin.

On the desk beside Midge's picture were two manila folders. One contained some newspaper articles, which had covered the Exchange National Bank robbery and her death. Inside the second was a summary from the Jefferson

City police report describing the events surrounding her death.

Above the desk, was an oversized map of the Midwest. It was dotted with colored pins. They marked towns where bank robberies had occurred during the last fifteen years. String traced the routes of the most notable sprees.

Under each pin was a slip of card stock with a reference number printed on it. Each number matched a three-by-five card summarizing that robbery. The cards were stored in an old library catalog, which stood to the right of the desk. They were cross-indexed using a keyword system.

I'd begun my investigation immediately after the Jefferson City police had given up on theirs. But for many years, I'd made little progress. During that time, I'd learned that, if I was going to find Midge's killer, I would need hard facts—like fingerprints, ballistics, and blood types. I'd also realized that I would have to be able to trace the past movements of criminals of interest. That meant I would have to have access to law enforcement files. And it was getting my hands on these files, which had first led me to consider becoming a lawyer, and then a prosecutor.

When I joined the D.A.'s office, I'd started mining its files for everything it had on bank robbers. And I'd been pleasantly surprised. It turned out that First Assistant Wilson had an interest of his own in the subject. I don't know why. But because of it, there were meticulous files on every crook who had robbed a bank in the Midwest during the past twenty years.

I'd begun my suspect list with three individuals, which the Jefferson City Police had identified at the time. Not surprisingly, none of them had panned out. But my file search turned up other, more likely, candidates. And it wasn't long before I'd put together a shortlist of viable names.

Big-time bank robbers like Floyd, Dillinger, or Nelson were avidly followed by the press. As a result, the dates and locations of their heists were known. Because of this, I'd quickly determined that no famous bank robber, except for one, could have been in Jefferson City on the day Midge had died. Interestingly, that sole exception was Frank Jelly Nash.

Before Midge's death, Nash had been hiding out in Kansas City. Shortly afterward, he had turned up in Arkansas. The precise timing of his relocation, and the route he'd taken, were unknown. So, it was possible that Jelly could have been in Jefferson City on the day when Midge had died.

And that wasn't all. One of the suspects in the Exchange National Bank robbery had been approximately Jelly's height and weight. Nash's hair and eye color were also like the robber's. And even though the stick-up man in the Exchange National Bank robbery was said to have had a full head of hair, Jelly often wore an expensive toupee.

Of course, most of the witnesses had thought that the Exchange National Bank robber had been younger than Nash at the time. But not all the witnesses had agreed. So, I'd kept Jelly on my list. The fact he was dead was irrelevant. Until he was ruled out, Jelly would remain a suspect.

The other individuals on my list were also there because their known movements had not ruled them out. And of course, because they had robbed at least one bank in their career. Their names were, Ferris Anthon, Maurice "Blondie" Denning, Jack Gregory (or Griffins), Earl Keeling, "Little Nuggie" LaPalma, Thomas Limerick, William "Billy Boy" Pabst, and William Weissman.

While five of the eight were still living in Kansas City,

Keeling, Limerick, and Pabst had moved to Omaha. It was also noteworthy that Anthon, Griffins, and LaPalma were Joe Lusco's boys. While Denning and Weissman worked for Lazia.

Of course, I'd realized that Midge's killer might not be a career criminal. There were plenty of amateur bank robbers out there. And my recollection of the robbery gave some credence to that theory. The man, whom I believed had shot Midge, had been wearing a red bandana mask, and most career criminals did not wear masks.

But even if Midge's killer had been an amateur, that didn't mean I couldn't find him. I hoped that at least one of my suspects had either been a participant in the Exchange National Bank robbery or had knowledge of it. And even if that individual hadn't killed Midge, he might know who had.

So, using my position as an Assistant D.A., I'd put out the word to police across the Midwest. I'd listed my eight suspects and told them that they were persons of interest in an old murder. And I'd asked them to contact me if any of the eight were arrested.

I'd also said that all I wanted was to ask a few questions. And that I'd like to be able to ask them myself. If that wasn't possible, I would forward the questions to them. That was all I could do. I didn't know where my private investigation might lead me. And since it was outside my professional remit, I'd kept my cards close to my vest. I hadn't even talked to Mac about it.

The phone started ringing downstairs. I looked at my watch. It was eleven forty-five. When I picked up the receiver, a familiar voice was on the other end of the line.

"Sam?"

"Yes, dad."

Never one for chitchat, my father immediately launched into the reason for his call. “Did you know Dolores is engaged?”

“What?”

“Yes, surprised us too. But that’s not the half of it. She’s going to marry that local gangster of yours.”

“Who?”

“Johnny something or other.”

“Not Johnny Lazia?”

“That’s him. Hardly the son-in-law we were hoping for. Dolores is on her way back to Kansas City. Could you try talking some sense into her?”

Fat chance, I thought. But instead, I said, “Sure, Dad, I’ll try. But Dolores’s engagement is going to cause you plenty of trouble.”

“I know. I’ll have to recuse myself from every case even remotely tied to Pendergast, his machine, or the Kansas City mob.”

“You think it’s a setup? After all, you are a law-and-order judge.”

Chuckling, dad said, “I think that’s too byzantine, even for Boss Tom. No, I suspect it’s just another of your sister’s wrong-headed decisions.” After a pause, he added, “More than anything, I’m worried she’ll end up a young widow.”

It was then that it hit me. Sis’s engagement was going to cause me problems too. I could be taken off the Lazia case. Or worse, Vandeventer might fire me.

Dad began signing off. “Well, let us know what Dolores says when you talk to her.”

“Will do, dad.”

“Bye, son.”

Why was Dolores marrying Lazia? It couldn’t be for love. She wasn’t the type. Just as puzzling, was why Lazia was marrying her. He was a gangster, for Pete's sake. They never married outside the mob.

And unlike dad, I smelled a rat. To my mind, Dolores's engagement had all the earmarks of a Pendergast ploy. If you can't buy them—compromise them.

I couldn't settle down, so I went out onto the front porch for some air. The moon was full, and crickets creaked in the shadows. Despite the lateness of the hour, someone was playing dance music on a radio down the street.

I recognized the program. It was the "Nighthawks Frolic." That's WDAF's after-midnight broadcast featuring bands from the local clubs. Tonight, it sounded like Andy Kirk and His Clouds of Joy. They were playing their theme song, "Cloudy."

I sat on the porch rail and lit a cigarette. Above the dark outline of the trees were the glittering shapes of the Northern Cross and Hercules with his heel on the head of Draco. Mine were the only lights still on in the neighborhood.

It wasn't long before the radio switched off. And even, the crickets fell silent. Taking one last drag, I flicked my cigarette into the air. It arced out over the street and hit the pavement with a shower of sparks. Glowing briefly, it went out.

4

JUNE 18, 1933

It was Sunday morning in the octave of Corpus Christi. Wearing a white-and-gold chasuble, Father Moriarty chanted, "Ite, missa est." And the altar servers responded, "Deo gratias." Following the Prayer to St. Michael the Archangel, the organ surged, and Visitation Church began discharging its congregation onto the sidewalks along Main. Genuflecting, I pocketed my rosary and joined the exiting crowd.

Father Moriarty was greeting parishioners as they left. The priest was only five-four and, like many religious, of an indeterminate age. Despite his diminutive stature, he had a booming voice.

Besides running a parish, Father was the Diocesan Vicar General. He also taught theology at the local seminary. As such, he was as knowledgeable as they came about the faith. Father took my hand and clapped me on the shoulder.

"Great to see you, Sam."

"It's my pleasure, Father."

Coming out of the double doors, I was surprised to see Dolores up ahead. She had a sharp dresser with her, who had to be Johnny Lazia. So, I decided it was time to meet Dolores's fiancé.

I caught up with the two of them, as they were getting into the back of a long black Packard. Just as I started to speak, someone behind me grabbed my shoulder and spun me around. I staggered and nearly fell.

A chunky moon-faced man thrust his chin at me. "Get lost, *Stupitu!*"

I'd seen the mug before. His name was Charlie Carrollo; he was Lazia's minder. Even though he was bigger than me, I didn't like being manhandled. And so, I stood my ground. Seeing I wasn't backing off, Carrollo's jaw hardened, and he raised a balled fist.

"Hold it," a voice said. And although Carrollo froze, he glared at me.

The mob boss climbed out of the Packard. Even though he was only the size of a welterweight, Johnny Lazia carried himself with the confidence of a much larger man. He was wearing a sharply tailored, navy three-piece suit. His peaked ivory pocket square matched his immaculate shirt and cocked homburg. And a silk canary tie completed his ensemble.

Placing a hand on my upper arm, Lazia asked, "You all right?" Sunlight glinted off his glasses, as he looked up at me. Despite the empathy in his voice, the eyes behind the wire rims were unreadable.

"Sure," I answered straightening my coat, still trying to check my anger. "I'm fine." Over Lazia's shoulder, I could see Dolores peering at us through the open door of the Packard. She was frowning.

"Sorry," said Lazia. "Sometimes, Charlie comes on too strong." He said it indulgently like he was talking about an unruly dog. And as if, Carrollo wasn't still standing there scowling at me.

Then Lazia flashed a smile and stuck out his hand. "You're Dolores's younger brother, aren't you? I'm Johnny Lazia." The guy was nearly forty, but there was a boyishness about him that made the "Johnny" work.

Not wanting to be rude, I took his hand. "Please to meet you," I said coolly. "Sam Blair." Our eyes locked, and I tried to keep my gaze neutral. But Lazia was better at this than I was. His smile broadened, as he continued to shake my hand.

There was a commotion. A crowd was rushing down the sidewalk at us. They were waving placards and chanting. One sign read, "Dump the Boss," another, "Nix Voting Fraud." And the chant sounded like, "Clean House."

A banner in front identified the group as with the National Youth Movement. There were reporters too and a photographer. The latter skirted the crowd, kneeling he snapped a picture of Lazia and me.

Then I saw Audrey. She was in front holding the banner. When Audrey saw me shaking Lazia's hand, she dropped the banner, and pushed her way back through the crowd. I started to go after her, but Lazia stopped me.

"I wouldn't do that," he said.

It was then that I noticed some in the crowd were shaking their fists. As they surged forward, Lazia and I backed against the Packard. Dolores slid over, and Lazia pulled me in after him. Some in the crowd yelled at us through the open door. Others pressed their placards against the windows and beat rhythmically on the roof.

Carrollo stepped between us and the crowd closing the car door with his back. A young man thrust a placard in his face. Carrollo ripped it in two, and the youth swung at him.

Deftly dodging the blow, Carrollo punched the young man in the stomach—winding him. With that, the crowd fell back, but the shouting grew louder.

Circling the car, Carrollo slipped behind the wheel. As he closed his door, the crowd again surged forward. This time, they pressed against the car shouting at us through the glass. The Packard's V-12 throbbed into life. As we slowly nosed our way through them, they fell away.

On the other side of the crowd was a line of advancing police. They were smacking their nightsticks rhythmically against their palms. The line parted for us to pass through it. Then it reformed and continued its advance.

Glancing at me in the rearview mirror, Carrollo asked, "Where to?"

I gave him my Brookside address. Then I glanced over at Dolores. She was sitting on the other side of Lazia staring out at the passing houses. Now also silent, Lazia sat forward on the seat beside me. He glanced at Carrollo and nodded.

Slowing at Fifty-First Street, Carrollo kept the car in second and turned down the hill. Up ahead, was a man walking down the sidewalk; his back was to us. Even though the suit was a different color, I knew that broad back. It was the man from Union Station. I tried to get a look at him as we went by, but he tugged down on the brim of his hat.

It was seven a.m. on Monday morning—two days after the Massacre. Dolores and I had met for breakfast. We were in the Forum Cafeteria at the corner of Twelfth and Walnut.

Taking a bite of toast, I took a long look at my sister. Dolores could have been a fashion model if she'd wanted. She was a smoky blond with wide-set green eyes and a snub nose. There was a little gap between her front teeth. But I thought that made her more interesting.

Sis was busy adding a dollop of brandy to her coffee. Then she lit one of those red-tipped cigarettes that aren't supposed to show lipstick stains. I put down my toast and took the plunge.

"Look, sis—the guy's a grade-A hood."

She wrinkled her nose like I'd dropped something smelly on the table.

"Mind your own business," she replied.

"We're family, your business *is* my business."

"Then you'll be on the business end of something you won't like."

"Now, you're giving me the business."

Dolores's face took on a sly look. Leaning over, she whispered, "I know who killed Midge,"

It was always the same. Whenever I got under Dolores's skin, she would throw Midge's murder in my face. And it always worked.

"Aw, cut it out," I said.

Then just when she had me off subject, *she* started talking about Lazia. Who knew?

"He's told me about prison," she said.

"That was when he was just a kid. Now he's all grown up and head of the local mob."

Dolores rolled her eyes, "Johnny's in the soft-drink business."

"And Pendergast's a concrete salesman."

"Oh, leave Boss Tom out of it."

"Why?"

"Cause, unlike the rest of the country, KC's doing just fine. And you can thank T. J. for that."

"Oh yeah? And should we thank him for all the rotgut, con games, and floosies too?"

"Why not? He's just giving people what they want."

"There are laws against it—that's why," I growled

"Only cause of snoots like you," she snipped stubbing out her cigarette. "You don't get it, do you? People want to do what they want."

"So, robbing, kidnapping, and murder, that's okay too?"

"Who made *you* God?" she snapped.

"O-oh, so now He exists," I fired back. I should have known better. My right hand clipped my coffee cup. And it spilled.

Dolores chortled, as I tried to stem the brown tide with my napkin. A waitress rushed to my aid. But even after she'd finished, there was a huge stain on the tablecloth.

Trying to get my moxie back, I said, "Well, one thing's for sure . . .."

"What's that?" said Dolores ready to pounce.

"You're way too tall for him."

That got a genuine laugh. Dolores had four inches on Lazia. Score one for my side.

We held fire while the waitress refilled our cups and handed me a fresh napkin. When she left, I made another run at it.

"Come on, sis, how can you stand the guy? He's got blood on his hands."

Giving me a level stare that told me to drop it, Dolores took a sip of her refilled cup. Making a face, she again slipped the flask from her purse and doctored her coffee.

I leaned back in my chair, "Okay—so when?"

"Soon as we jump through all the hoops," she said.

"Where?"

"Visitation," she answered.

I was surprised. Even though I'd seen her at Mass on Sunday, Dolores hadn't been a churchgoer for years. I'd expected her wedding to be at the city clerk's office—with maybe Pendergast officiating.

But it made sense when I thought about it. The Boss was a daily communicant, and the mob was also known for its religiosity. Of course, most people thought they were a bunch of hypocrites. But I wasn't so sure. After all, it's the sick who know they need a physician, not those who are well.

"Where's the reception?" I asked.

"Cuban Gardens. Johnny's booked the Bennie Moten Orchestra." Moten's was the top dance band in town. Closing her eyes while rhythmically tapping the table, Dolores hummed a few bars of the "Moten Swing" with its infectious four-beat pulse.

I was about to give it another go, and Dolores must have sensed it. Glancing at her watch, she grabbed her purse. "Got to go."

"Come on," I pleaded.

But she was already in motion. After kissing the air in the vicinity of my cheek, she was gone. I tossed my napkin on the table.

Later while waiting for the cashier, I wondered what I was going to say to dad. Then another thought hit me. I still hadn't figured out what was I going to tell Vandeventer about Dolores's engagement. Oh, Brother, it had better be soon—and it had better be good.

5

JUNE 20, 1933

After lunch, I headed for the Bureau's offices in the Federal Reserve Bank Building at 9th and Grand. I was going to give Mac my statement on the Union Station Massacre. But when the elevator doors opened, he was standing in the corridor talking to two men I didn't know.

Mac introduced me to KCPD Detectives Floyd Thurman and Lew Hart. Thurman was the senior of the two. He was six-foot with a square build and a boxer's lumpy face. Hart was pale and slight, with a dimpled chin and black hair. He was one of those guys who look like they always need a shave.

Since BI agents lacked statutory authority to make arrests, they often worked with local police. Knowing the KCPD was one with the mob, I was careful whenever I encountered them. But I figured Thurman and Hart must have passed the smell test, or the Bureau wouldn't have been partnering with them. At least, I hoped they had.

When introductions were over, Mac asked, "What's up?" He had forgotten our appointment.

"Coming to give you my statement."

"Oh yeah. Sorry, no-can-do. Got a lead to follow up." Then tapping me on the chest, he said, "Tag along. It's about the Union Station dust-up."

That got my interest, so I decided to join them.

Thurman left us when we reached the street. We walked to Hart's car, which was parked at an expired meter on Ninth. It was the Hot Shot—KCPD's fast-pursuit sedan.

The new Plymouth was pretty slick with a high-powered V-8, armored plating, and a bulletproof windshield. I stepped back and took a long look at her. The Hot Shot's streamlined shape and special fittings made it sleek and menacing. Like Saturday's paper had said, there was a Thompson clipped to the right front door. And there was a corresponding gun port in the windshield on the passenger's side.

Hart wasn't much of a talker, but we managed to pry out of him that the Hot Shot had been formerly assigned to Grooms and Hermanson. They were the two KCPD detectives killed at Union Station. And I remembered seeing the Hot Shot parked under the canopy outside the western bank of doors on the day of the Massacre. Since Thurman and Hart were now the senior detectives on the force, it had been re-assigned to them.

We got in and drove south on Gillham. It was a fine June day, and it felt good to be out of the office. Soon, we were winding through the fading mansions of Hyde Park. Enjoying being in charge, Mac leaned over the front seat filling me in on where we were going, and why.

At the Bureau's request, the Bell Telephone Company had worked up a trace on calls from Nash's known associates in Hot Springs, Arkansas. The inquiry had been limited to calls made after Nash's arrest and before his scheduled transfer to Leavenworth. It turned out that all the calls made to Kansas City had been to the same number. The listing was for a Mr. and Mrs. Vincent Moore, who lived at 6612 Edgevale Road on the city's South Side. Mac explained that that was where we were heading.

It had now been three days since the Massacre, and Mac said that the powers-that-be figured the Edgevale Road address was probably vacant. But just in case it wasn't, we were to proceed with caution. Mac's orders were simple. Scout out the neighborhood, see what could be learned about the Moores, and "don't break any eggs."

Our destination was in the Armour Hills neighborhood. It was a white middle-class subdivision built ten years earlier in a mix of architectural styles. Like a lot of J.C. Nichols's developments, it favored meandering streets, landscaped islands, and faux statuary. The 66th block of Edgevale Road was a short one. There were only three houses on it. And 6612 was the house in the middle.

We cruised by the white California Bungalow with a pillared porch, tile roof, and stone chimney. There was no car in the drive. And while the sashes were up on the front windows, all the shades were drawn. We rounded the corner and pulled to the curb on East 66th.

The Tudor house, neighboring 6612 on the north, faced the corner of East 66th Street and Edgevale. Anyone approaching its front door couldn't be seen from 6612. We decided to try that one first. Hart strode up the stone walk and used the knocker.

A dog started barking in a backyard a couple of houses to the west. To the northeast, a gray-uniformed postman with a peaked cap and shoulder bag plodded from house to house. No one answered at the Tudor.

Since the Hot Shot was so distinctive, we decided to

drive around the block to avoid passing in front of 6612 again. We did so and parked on East 66th Terrace. The house, next to 6612 on the south, was a two-story Dutch Colonial. It faced Edgevale Road. Anyone approaching its front door would be visible from 6612, but only from two windows on the southwest side.

It was Mac's turn. He crossed the lawn and mounted the steps turning his back to 6612 when he got there. He pushed the doorbell. We could hear it buzzing through an open window. But even after pushing it a second time, he still got no answer.

When Mac returned to the car, we sat for a while discussing our options. The dog on East 66th continued to bark, but he was losing interest. The postman had moved on to the block to the east.

We had used up our two best options. A third, less ideal, remained. On the other side of the street was 6623; it faced the intersection of Edgevale and East 66th Terrace. If we crossed Edgevale Road, we would be able to approach 6623 without being seen, until we reached the front stoop. This time, however, we would be visible from the south and southeast-facing windows of 6612. Not wanting to return empty-handed, we decided to give it a try.

It was my turn. The Federal-style house was a two-story redbrick with white trim and black shutters. As I approached, I heard the promising sound of a vacuum running on the ground floor. Beyond the screen, the inside door was standing open. I waited until the vacuum switched off, then rapped lightly.

At first, there was silence, then footsteps. A trim woman in her fifties came to the door smoothing out the wrinkles in her housedress. Her brown hair was bound-up with a scarf.

"Yes?"

Giving her my best boyish smile, I touched my brim and asked, "Do you have a moment, mam?"

She was friendly but firm, "If you're selling something . . . ."

Shaking my head, "No mam, just a few questions . . . it's about one of your neighbors." The last bit was the dangling bait.

A curious look came into her eyes, "Really, . . . what about?"

I held out one of my cards by thumb and forefinger, so she could read it through the screen.

She read it aloud, "Samuel C. Blair, Assistant U.S. District Attorney. Well, Mr. Blair, you'd better come in." She unlatched the screen door.

"Thank you, mam." I took off my hat and stepped into a polished hallway.

With a bob of her head, she introduced herself, "Mrs. Earl Smith."

We didn't shake hands. Mrs. Smith was a woman who thought shaking hands with strange men was neither necessary nor proper. She gestured toward the living room. It was furnished with a camelback sofa facing the fireplace, matching club chairs, and the latest Zenith console radio.

"Can I get you something? Coffee? Soda?" she asked.

"No, thank you, mam. Wouldn't want to trouble you."

"Lemonade?"

Realizing she wasn't going to take no for an answer, I nodded and said, "Thank you."

Mrs. Smith took my hat promising to return shortly. I sat on the sofa. Glancing around, I could see that the living room window on the northeast offered an unobstructed view of 6612.

When Mrs. Smith returned, I started to rise. But she

shushed me down and handed me a glass of lemonade. Then she placed a plate of coconut macaroons on the coffee table in front of me, before taking a seat herself.

"Thank you, mam."

I took a sip of lemonade and nibbled on a macaroon making sounds of approval. Then I began, "It's about your neighbors at 6612 Edgevale Road."

"We wondered about them," she said.

"About whom, mam?"

"The Moore's."

"Can you describe them—generally?" I reached for another macaroon.

"Man and woman in their mid-to-late thirties, smart dressers, . . . little girl about eleven. Moved in about three months ago."

"What did you wonder about them?"

"Well, they had lots of visitors, . . . at all times of the day and night, . . . taxis, out-of-state cars. Never sat on their front porch, . . . kept their shades down even in this heat. Whenever we tried to talk to them, they never had much to say. Even the little girl was tight-lipped."

"Have you seen them lately?"

"No."

"When did you see them last?"

"Sunday afternoon. They were leaving in their car," she said.

"All of them?"

"Yes."

"Any activity since then?"

"Just the moving van."

"When was that?"

"Yesterday," she said.

It sounded like the powers-that-be were right. "Would it

be possible for you to come downtown and give us a statement?" I asked.

Mrs. Smith was suddenly flustered, "Well . . . I suppose I could if you think it necessary. Of course, I'd like to talk to my husband first."

"Of course," I said.

Before long, Mac and Hart had joined us, and it was arranged that Mrs. Smith would go to the Bureau later that afternoon.

When we returned to the car, Mac said, "Sounds like they've already skipped. Couldn't hurt to have a look-see."

"I'm game," Hart growled. He plucked a kitchen match from his vest and stuck the wooden end into his mouth.

I heard myself saying, "Why not?"

We left the car and fanned out. Then I realized Hart was probably the only one of us who was armed. Just the other day, Mac had told me that internal Bureau policy discouraged agents from carrying firearms—except in extraordinary circumstances. Of course, he'd added, that policy was under review following the Union Station Massacre.

As we crossed the street, I found myself hoping no one was home at 6612. I remembered the bodies lying on the ground around the shot-up car at Union Station. And I didn't relish coming up against any kind of firearm at close range.

Nevertheless, not wanting to appear skittish, I marched up the bungalow's steps at Mac's side and crossed the porch to the front door. We waited there, giving Hart time to circle around back. Then Mac opened the screen and rapped on the front door. Getting no response, he rapped again.

When there was still no reply, Mac put his hand on the knob. It turned. So, he pushed on the door. And it swung open, all the way. As we stood there, I realized we were perfect targets—silhouetted against the bright afternoon sunlight.

Something flew at us out of the darkness. A cat shot between my legs and disappeared down the steps. Exhaling, I realized I had been holding my breath.

Unfazed, Mac stepped through the doorway and into the dark house. Turning, he told me to go around back and tell Hart he was inside. I nodded and gladly headed for the rear of the house.

Hart was standing beside the back door, flat against the wall, his revolver in his hand. Hart's eyes watched me as I approached. I ducked under a window and came up behind him. Just as I whispered, "Mac's inside," the back door swung open. It was Mac.

"Seems empty," he said in a low voice, "But . . .." And Hart nodded.

We stepped into a white kitchen. A foot of yellow broomstick held the unplugged fridge's door open. And a dozen empty beer bottles stood by the sink.

Jerking his thumb at the bottles, Mac whispered to Hart, "Remind me to have them dusted for prints." Hart nodded.

Newspapers were spread on the linoleum where a kitchen table had stood. My nose curled. The cat had been using them.

Mac pointed to the cellar door. It was ajar. Gun in hand, Hart opened the door with his foot and disappeared downstairs. Returning, he shook his head and then held out an open hand. In it were five galvanized roofing nails.

"Bucketful down there," he whispered.

I looked at Mac.

"Bank-robber ploy. Toss them out when the cops chase them. To cause blow-outs."

I nodded.

We pushed through a swinging door into a blue-and-white dining room. A shattered floral plate lay on the floor. Through an open archway, we could see into the living room. We walked towards it.

Mac raised a shade on a front window. The sunlight revealed an empty living room with chocolate woodwork and walls covered with roses-on-aqua paper. A candlestick phone sat in a corner, on top of a curled directory. To our left, a narrow hallway ran to a tiled bath. There were three doors along the hall, all opening onto empty bedrooms.

That left only the attic. Still holding his gun, Hart climbed the dark stairs. We could hear him moving around overhead. He called for us to join him.

In the attic, sunlight glimmered dimly through a dormer window. So, Mac switched on a dangling bulb. By its swaying light, we could see exposed rafters and unfinished tongue-and-groove flooring.

Hart walked to an alcove to the right of the stairs and looked down. We joined him. There were marks on the floor. Something with hard narrow wheels had been rolled about, possibly a bed. Holstering his revolver, Hart pointed to a corner. In it was a wad of rust-colored bandages. And next to the bandages, a chrome syringe gleamed in a white-enamel pan.

LATER THAT AFTERNOON, I tapped on Vandeventer's door. Hearing a muffled, "Come in," I entered.

The blinds were drawn against the afternoon sun. The light that filtered through them had turned the room the color of vellum. The Chief was at his desk, signing a stack of letters. He looked up when I stopped in front of him.

"We have fact testimony to support the Lazia indictment," I announced.

"Who's the brave soul?" he asked.

"Raymond Edlund, a cashier at Merchants Bank."

"What will he say?"

"Cashier's checks worth thousands of dollars were either cashed by Lazia or deposited into his account every week."

"Sounds good. What about the sources of the money?"

"Edlund has first-hand knowledge of Lazia's business dealings at Cuban Gardens and the local greyhound track. He says the cashier's checks were given to Lazia by freelance gamblers at both places. They were his percentage of the take."

"What did you have to give Mr. Edlund in return?"

"A *nolo* on banking fraud and conspiracy charges, if he stays the course."

"Any other inducements?" he asked.

I hesitated. Then by way of explanation, I added, "Edlund often went to the Chesterfield Club."

The Chief lifted an eyebrow, "Ah, . . . where the waitresses wear only a smile." Then he added, "I suppose there are photographs you mentioned might be of interest to his wife?"

I said nothing.

"Quite right, Mr. Blair, best for me not to know."

Then he added, "Think he'll stay the course?"

"If they don't get him first," I answered.

"And what have you done to prevent that?"

"Edlund and his family are under round-the-clock Bureau protection."

"I assume you're telling me this because we're on track to file the indictment?"

"Yes sir."

"Good."

As I turned to go, the Chief said, "Just a moment, Mr. Blair."

"Yes?"

He reached under his blotter and tossed a glossy eight-by-ten across the desk at me. I picked it up. The black-and-white shot was sharply focused, and the figures in the foreground were unmistakable. In it, I was shaking hands with Johnny Lazia, in front of Visitation Church.

When I glanced up, Vandeventer's lips were thin. "Give the Lazia file to Mr. Costellow." Then he looked down at the letters in front of him.

"I'd like to explain."

"Not now."

"It's not what it looks like. There's something you need to know. It won't help me, but you need to know it anyway." I swallowed and threw it out there.

"My sister's engaged to Johnny Lazia."

It was like dropping a match into a gas can. Vandeventer's face went dark, and a vein stood out on his temple. He opened his mouth to speak. But before he could, I charged on.

"I just found out myself on Saturday." Pointing to the photo, "And that was taken Sunday morning—at church. It's the only time I've met the guy. I swear it!"

Still not giving him a chance to speak, I kept going. "I know it looks bad. And I should have told you sooner. You know how much I hate crooks like Lazia—and you know why. I'd never sell out to him. Never!"

The Chief threw his pen onto the desk and stood up.

I was begging now. "I can't control what my sister does. I don't know why she's marrying Lazia. And my job—it means everything to me. Please, sir."

The Chief strode to the window and snapped open the blinds. Hot sunlight spilled into the room casting a barred shadow onto the floor. After glaring down at the traffic on Grand, Vandeventer swung back to me.

His face was livid, and when he spoke, his voice pulsed with anger. "I *should* fire you. And I *will* fire you. If there are any leaks—whatsoever. Understood?"

I nodded.

"Your name will be scratched from the pleadings. And Costellow will take your place. But you're not off the hook!"

He pointed a finger at me like a gun. "You're going to do every bit of research on this case. The motions and briefs too—all solo! You damn well better give your best, Mr. Blair. Or else! Is that clear?"

"Yes sir," I said quietly. Then I added a heartfelt, "Thank you."

He waved me away, "Get out of here! I've got work to do." Gesturing at the letters on his desk, he added in a quieter voice, "And tell Meeks to come and get these."

I nodded and slipped out the door.

AT NOON ON THURSDAY, June 22, I was sitting glumly at the counter of the Liberty Bell. I was nursing a black coffee while mulling over the current state of my life. In the space of a few days, everything had gone down the toilet.

The "Blue-Plate Special" I'd ordered, two fat dogs and a pile of kraut were sizzling on the grill. A haze of grease floated in the air. As I took another sip of coffee, Mac slid onto the stool beside me. We shook hands, and I could see something was up.

Pushing back his hat with a thumb, Mac said, "Remember Mrs. Smith?"

"Sure."

"She and her husband both gave statements."

"That's swell."

"Yeah," he grinned, "Here's what they knew." He ticked each point off on a finger. "Name of the store, which delivered the Moore's groceries, name of the removal company that took away their stuff, name of the town in Minnesota where the little's girl's grandparents live." Grabbing the last two fingers, "Hell, they even had license plate numbers for most of the out-of-state cars."

I whistled. "Get an ID?"

He nodded, "Picked Moore out of the booking photos." He paused dramatically.

"Well, spit it out," I said.

He smiled enjoying himself, "Hard guy, by the name of Vern Miller. A war hero, if you can believe it, and a Sheriff in South Dakota before going bad. Spent a couple of years in the Pen up there. Worked with the Harvey Bailey gang."

"And it gets better," Mac added. "Miller's handy with a Thompson. Said to be able to sign his name with one. Oh, and Nash worked with Bailey the same time Miller did."

It all fit. "So where is Miller?" I asked.

"We don't know—yet . . . but we will," said Mac rubbing his hands.

6

AUGUST 11, 1933

July passed with nothing new in the Union Station case. Then just after dinner on Friday, August 11, Mac called. He asked if I was interested in helping him follow a lead. Naturally, I said yes.

Mac pulled to the curb at nine, and I climbed into his gray Desoto coupe. Then we headed north on Main. As we drove, Mac filled me in. We were going to meet a guy at the Hey Hay Club. He would be wearing a maroon tie with a white orchid on it. The guy was said to know who Miller's accomplices were at Union Station. Mac cautioned that it might be something, or it might not.

As we crested the hill on Main, the stepped silhouette of the three-square-mile business district came into view. It sat on a bluff overlooking the river. Sixty-five high-rises were clustered there ranging from ten to thirty-six stories. Kansas City had the eighth tallest skyline in the country.

Bustling during the day, downtown was dead at night. Only an occasional car traveled its solitary streets, and its wide sidewalks were empty. But it was a different story just a little to the east. There, between downtown and Troost, south of 12th and north 18th was a fifteen-square-block area of one-and-two-story brick buildings, which pulsed with light and music. It was locally known as the "entertainment district," and that was where we were headed.

In this area was the largest concentration of open illegality in the country. As Edward Murrow, editor of the *Omaha Herald* had put it: "If you want to see some sin, forget Paris and go to Kansas City. With the possible exception of such renowned centers as Singapore and Port Said, Kansas City has the greatest sin industry in the world." And he was right.

KC's entertainment district had over three hundred bars that never closed. All of them thumbing their noses at the Volstead Act. Scattered among them were illegal gambling establishments offering nonstop poker, roulette, blackjack, and craps as well as the racing wires. With the latter, you could wager on any horserace in the country. Then there were the brothels; fifty or so operated along both sides of 14th Street. The "girls" sat in open widows displaying their wares while bantering with potential customers on the sidewalks.

And if liquor, gambling, and girls weren't enough, Kansas City had one more attraction. And this one was even legit—Swing. The Depression had hit big-band musicians hard, and they'd been drawn to the city looking for work in its twenty-four-hour clubs. The competition had been stiff, and it had spurred innovation. A distinctive Kansas City sound had emerged. It was marked by a bluesy 4/4 beat with effortlessly riffing sections and serial solo improvisations.

There were thirty or forty Swing clubs in the entertainment district. They had names such as the Reno, Spinning Wheel, Subway, and Hi-Hat. They signaled their presence with neon. And propped open their doors to let the music do the talking.

Of course, like the rest of the country, Kansas City was segregated. That meant, the only Negroes allowed inside white clubs were the performers. The Reno was the sole exception to this rule probably because its owner had paid a hefty bribe. But even in the Reno, the races were separated by a waist-high divider.

The Negro part of town had its Swing clubs too. They were located around 18th-and-Vine, in the black business district. Three of note were the Yellow Front, Street's Blue Room, and the Cherry Blossom. The latter was where Count Basie got his start. The Negro clubs had some of the best music, so whites often went to them. But except for the Reno, the opposite wasn't permitted.

And there was one more thing about the entertainment district. You needed to be wary if you went there. It was mob-run after all, and it was easy to get fleeced—or worse, even if you were careful. Some folks thought this added to the excitement. But they were only half smart.

Mac and I eased to a stop outside the Hey Hay; an overflow crowd was jiving on the sidewalk. And the ropey smell of hemp hung in the air. We worked our way inside to look for our guy and to get a couple of beers. But the place was so crowded it was impossible to tell if anyone was wearing a tie—much less what was on it. So, we decided to take our beers outside hoping to have better luck by the front door.

When we got there, I saw a fresh dance bill was pasted to the bricks. It was advertising tonight's band, the George E. Lee Orchestra. On it was a shot of George and his sister, Julia. She had a husky come-to-momma voice and had made a name for herself singing songs such as "Don't Save It

Too Long" and "Come on Over to My House Baby, Nobody's Home but Me."

After Benny Moten's, Lee's was the city's most popular dance orchestra. As we got our mugs refilled, the band began playing Mary Lou Williams's "Froggy Bottom." And the dance floor was shoulder to shoulder. After that, came the rumble of the dirty blues number, "Snatch and Grab it," with Julia at the keys. Most in the audience sat that one out clapping and cheering as Julia did her stuff.

Mac and I never did see anyone wearing a maroon tie with a white orchid on it. And about one, we threw in the towel. As we climbed into the Desoto, I remembered that Mac had just moved. So, I asked where he lived now.

Mac told me that he had an apartment at the Cavalier, which was on Armour, between Troost and Forest. He told me it was a bachelors-only establishment, and several guys from the Bureau lived there. When I still wasn't familiar with it, Mac said, that he would drive by and show me where it was.

The night had cooled off. And I twisted the wing-vent until the air was blowing directly on me. We drove south on Cherry, east on Admiral, and then south again on Troost. We pretty much had the streets to ourselves.

As we rounded the corner of Troost onto Armour, shots rang out. And they were close. Snapping off the headlights, Mac swerved to the curb and killed the engine.

Peering over the dash, we could see four silhouettes. They were standing on the sidewalk across the street, on Armour's south side. A couple of them were bent over, looking at something on the ground.

Mac whispered, "They're in front of the Cavalier."

The group suddenly scattered. Two of them jumped into a new Buick idling at the curb. The other two pelted east down the sidewalk away from us. Grinding into gear, the Buick pulled into the street and also headed east.

One block away, a Franklin touring car swung off Forest onto Armour. It squealed to a stop diagonally, in the middle of the street. Two men leaped out. One carried a double-barreled shotgun, the other a revolver. Although the car was unmarked, the men handled themselves like lawmen.

Intent on escape, the Buick sped up and snapped on its high beams. The passenger leaned out of his window and began firing at the men in the street. One of them took cover behind a parked car. But the one with the shotgun stood his ground.

When the Buick was nearly upon him, the man discharged both barrels into the windshield of the on-coming car. The Buick wobbled, as the man leaped out of the way. Then it slammed into the side of the touring car.

The man holding the shotgun ejected the spent shells and began reloading. His eyes shifted to the men running down the sidewalk. One of them, still running, veered out into the street and opened fire on him. But the gunman's companion thought better of it. He disappeared down a dark alley to the south. The lawman, who'd been sheltering behind the parked car, leaped up and pursued him.

As the shotgun clicked shut, the man in the street slid to a halt. He dropped to his knees, tossed his automatic onto the pavement, and raised both hands.

"Don't shoot!" he shouted, "Don't shoot." I'm a friend of Johnny Lazia!"

For a moment, it looked like the man with the shotgun might fire anyway. But then he lowered his gun. Walking over to the man kneeling in the street, he flipped the man's hat off with the barrel of the shotgun. Then he leaned down and peered into his face.

Now that the shooting was over, lights came on in the apartment buildings around us. People in robes and slippers poured out, and a chattering crowd gathered in front of the Cavalier. Sirens wailed in the distance.

As we got out, I asked Mac, "Who's the guy with the shotgun?"

"Sheriff Tom Bash," he said.

I'd had heard of Jackson County Sheriff Bash; he was said to be no friend of either Pendergast or the mob. And from what I'd seen, he also had a cool head. We walked toward Bash. The Sheriff's deputy emerged empty-handed from the alley and began handcuffing the man kneeling in the street.

An older gent in striped pajamas broke off from the crowd in front of the Cavalier and trotted over to Sheriff Bash ahead of us. We could hear them talking as we approached. The man said that he was the Cavalier's manager. There was a body on the sidewalk in front of his apartment building. It was one of his tenants—Ferris Anthon.

Anthon was one of the eight suspects on my list. And not long ago, I'd gone through his file as part of my investigation into Midge's murder. Anthon was originally from Chicago, and he had come to KC in the early twenties.

Anthon had started as a bank robber, but then he'd gravitated to bootlegging. He was one of Joe Lusco's boys. Lusco was a mid-level gangster with big ambitions. The word was that he was trying to horn in on some of Lazia's rackets.

While waiting to talk to Bash, we glanced at the kneeling man. He was lanky with a hard narrow face and a head of black curly hair. He glared back at us.

Mac whispered, "Gargotta."

Charlie Gargotta's nickname was "Mad Dog." It suited

him because he was vicious and unpredictable. Gargotta was Lazia's top enforcer. He'd been arrested over forty times for murder, rape, kidnapping, and other crimes, but nothing had ever stuck. It was testimony to the machine's grip on the local state courts.

Once Bash was free, Mac stepped forward and introduced us. The Sheriff was a bluff, broad-shouldered man. He had a round open face and a thatch of unruly black hair that stuck out from under his pushed-back Panama.

After some awkward pleasantries, Bash strolled over to the touring car. We followed him. He opened the back door and helped a middle-aged woman and a fourteen-year-old girl up off the floorboards. They were pale and shaken. The woman was Bash's wife, and the girl was a family friend.

Bash explained that they'd been on their way home from guarding the cash box at a charity social when they'd heard shots and turned off to investigate. As soon as he saw the getaway car, Bash had ordered his wife and the girl to lie on the floor. They were lucky not to have been hurt.

Just then an unmarked Model-A Fodor glided to a stop followed by a squad car and taxi full of press. Bash excused himself. The reporters quickly surrounded the Sheriff. I noticed that Wetzel from the *Journal Post* was among them.

Three patrolmen got out of the squad car, and two detectives from the unmarked sedan. One of the plainclothesmen was the flashy dresser with the overbite from Union Station. I'd forgotten his name.

There was another detective with him. He was short and nondescript also wearing snappy duds. The two detectives squatted down beside the forty-five Gargotta had dropped. One of them shined a flashlight on it while the other made out an evidence tag. They put their heads together as they did. I pointed them out to Mac and asked if he knew them.

Making a face, Mac said, "The one with the flashlight is Jeff Rayen. He's Chief of Detectives. Steer clear of him. And watch out for his partner, Claiborne, too."

"Why?"

Mac sidled over to me and whispered, "After Gargotta, Rayen's the mob's clean-up guy. And Claiborne's his wheelman." Giving me a significant look, Mac added, "Rayen's known as 'the Iceman.'"

"Huh?" I said not getting it.

Mac gave me a how-dumb-can-you-get look. Then he explained, "He likes to use an ice pick—okay?" When he saw that the penny still hadn't dropped, Mac added in exasperation, "You know—like Murder Inc. in New York City?"

Finally, I got it. Murder Inc's signature method was to stick an ice pick into their victim's brain—through an ear. Death was instantaneous and left no visible marks. More importantly, from the killer's perspective, even an experienced pathologist had difficulty determining the cause of death. I didn't ask any more questions after that.

We got the nod from Bash's deputy. And we gave him our statements. When we were done, he said we could go. But before leaving, we strolled over to the Cavalier. The ambulance boys were just putting Anthon's body on a stretcher.

Like Nash, even though he was dead, Anthon would stay on my list of suspects. But that left only six who were still alive. And I was starting to worry that they might all get killed off before I had a chance to question any of them.

Mac remembered something he wanted to tell Bash. So, I waited for him on the sidewalk near where Anthon had died. The crowd was gone now. And everything was dark and quiet.

I lit a cigarette. As I stood there watching the ambulance pull away, I felt a sharp prick in my back. I froze.

A lazy voice whispered in my ear, "That's right, Bozo. Don't move." Then the speaker jabbed the pick in, a little deeper. I winced and dropped my cigarette.

"You're a nosey little bastard, Blair. And know what happens to nosey little bastards?"

Realizing that he wa*d*s expecting an answer, I shook my head.

"They end up—dead!" And he shoved the pick into my back.

I cried out and staggered forward. But when I whirled around, Rayen was gone. Only the blood sticking to my shirt was evidence of what had happened.

Feeling the wound, I was relieved it wasn't as deep as I'd feared. And I felt stupid for getting caught off guard like that. I decided not to say anything to Mac about it. So, I crossed the street and got into the Desoto.

On the drive home, Mac suddenly snorted. "What are the odds of stumbling onto a murder like that?"

I shook my head. "Just shows how bad things have gotten."

"Yeah. And Anthon would have to die on my doorstep," he said glumly. "I may have to move again."

After a moment, Mac chuckled, "And what a goat's rodeo. Two of Lazia's boys were shot dead, and another one was caught red-handed. The 'men of honor' aren't going to like that. No siree."

"The men of honor?" I asked.

"Yeah, the guys who run the mob. That's what they call themselves—in Sicilian."

"I thought Lazia ran the mob."

"Naw, Lazia is just the frontman. The men of honor are the ones really in charge." He gave me a sideways glance, "To look at them, you'd think they're just a bunch of geezers.

But watch out, if you ever come across them. They're plenty dangerous."

"Who are they?"

He shrugged, "We only know three for sure. There are two brothers, Joe 'Scarface' and Pete 'Sugar House' DiGiovanni. Then there's a guy by the name of Jim Balestrere. The three of them came from Sicily in the teens. Brought the *omerta* with them."

I'd heard of the *omerta*. It was part of a code of conduct, which had evolved in Sicily under centuries of foreign occupation. Originally, the code had been about loyalty, family, and manhood. According to the code, men did not concern themselves with others' affairs. And if they had a grievance, they took care of it themselves. The worst thing a man could do was go to the authorities.

Over time, the code had become a way of life. And since those who followed it did not respect the law, they felt no compunction about living by unlawful means. And the *omerta's* injunction of silence was used to shield their activities.

"Considering how much the mob must take in, the men of honor must be loaded," I said.

"Naw," said Mac shaking his head. "Only the young guys are interested in the money. For the men of honor, it's more about respect and tradition."

Then picking up on what Mac had said earlier, I asked, "So what's been going on that the men of honor wouldn't like?"

"Foul ups, like tonight. And like the Union Station Massacre. They hate the spotlight."

"Think they'll do something?"

"Hard to say. If something happens to Lazia, you'll know for sure."

When I got home, I examined my back in the mirror. I washed the blood from the wound and put a band-aid on it. Even though my shirt was ruined, I might still be able to wear the coat.

The next morning, there was front-page coverage of the Anthon shooting. And Sheriff Bash was given the Hollywood treatment. As part of its spread, the *Star* ran pictures of the two men Bash had killed. Their names were Sam Scola and Gus Fasone.

I recognized them when I saw their pictures. They were the two guys, who'd shaken down Hank and Lucille at the Liberty Bell. Even though Sam and Gus had helped Audrey and me duck Wilson that day, I wasn't going to be pining for them.

7

SEPTEMBER 1933

In early September, a grand jury was empaneled before Judge Merrill Otis in downtown Kansas City. Vandeventer, assisted by Costellow and Phelps, presented the jury with our evidence. Since the grand jury had multiple matters to consider, we knew it would be a while before we learned whether they would take up the Lazia indictment.

While waiting for their decision, I'd busied myself with other cases and tried to be patient. Still doubtful of my integrity, Audrey had remained distant. And not surprisingly, since word of the indictment had leaked, Dolores had also stopped speaking to me. And then there was Costellow. He gloated over my fall from favor, and I knew he was just waiting to trip me up.

On September 16, the grand jury handed down the Lazia indictment. And I couldn't believe it. We'd gotten all four counts we'd asked for, two misdemeanor failure-to-file and two counts of felony tax evasion. The trial was set for early February.

Vandeventer, Costellow, Phelps, and I immediately met

to discuss trial strategy. What that meant was that they brainstormed while I scribbled down the projects they came up with. Here, unlike in most cases, the Chief told us a plea deal was off the table. We were going all out for a conviction.

Soon, my desk was overflowing with draft briefs and motions. The latter when finished were funneled to Wilson, for him to assign to the typing pool. Mrs. Wilks, Audrey, and the others were kept busy trying to handle my increased output as well as the usual office business.

I had worried that Wilson would be difficult to deal with, but I was wrong. The First Assistant seamlessly fed project after project to the burdened typists. Not surprisingly, he had a sharp eye for typos, as well as errors in grammar and punctuation.

But Wilson didn't stop there. He recommended improvements in logic and argumentation. Changes that I had to admit made the briefs tighter and clearer. More surprisingly, he delivered his comments with patience and insight. And he often provided a gloss as to how the proposed revisions might play out in the larger context of the trial.

Once my research and drafting were well underway, Vandeventer and I began meeting in his office after work. He'd stride up and down throwing out possible lines of attack that might be used by the defense to undermine our witnesses and evidence. Then he'd challenge me to come up with the best argument to counter each one of them. And after every session, he would add more items to my lengthening project list. Soon, we'd done everything we could think of to get ready for trial.

In mid-November, I took a day off to travel to Topeka for my appointment at Menninger's. I'd booked an early train to be on time for my nine o'clock appointment. And I was looking forward to forgetting about the Lazia trial for a day.

After Audrey had located Menninger's, I had done some research of my own. The clinic wasn't your stereotypic loony bin. They didn't put people in straitjackets or do electric-shock therapy or frontal lobotomies. They simply asked questions about your problems trying to unearth the causes. Often, they said, when those came to light, things began to sort themselves out.

I knew I would have to make a clean breast of it to Dr. Menninger. I'd have to admit that, after Midge's death, I'd not only become a bumbler, but I'd had other symptoms too. One of them was the reoccurring dream of a face. While I was dreaming, I knew whose face it was, but not after I awoke. And yet, even after I was awake, I knew that the face belonged to Midge's killer.

Then there were the urges. They'd told me to harm myself. Not that they used words exactly. But I knew that's what they meant. Usually, I could resist them. But twice now, they'd nearly killed me. And even more troubling, other people had been hurt too.

I'd never told anyone about the dreams or the urges—not even Audrey. They'd have put me in a straitjacket if I had. But eventually, I'd been forced to admit that my symptoms were happening for a reason. And that, since they'd started after Midge died, her death must have something to do with them.

I'd figured Dr. Menninger would think so too. And that he would ask me about what had happened on the day of Midge's death. So, I had brought along the manila folder containing the summary prepared by the Jefferson City

Police. It laid out everything that had happened that afternoon.

Although I had read the summary many times, I wanted to read it again, just to refresh my memory before talking to Dr. Menninger. So once the train was rolling, I flipped the folder open and began to read.

FACTUAL SUMMARY OF ALLEGED CRIME(S)

1. General Description, Date, Time, and Location of the Alleged Crime(s): All of the following are believed to have been committed by the same three individuals. Crime One: Sometime between 10:00 p.m. on October 15, and 6:00 a.m. on October 16, 1925, a 1923, black Hudson four-door sedan was stolen from the lot in front of Heisinger's Motors at 426 Brooks Street, Jefferson City, Missouri. This vehicle was subsequently used in the armed robbery of the Exchange National Bank (hereinafter known as the "ENB"). Crime Two: At fifteen minutes before closing, or approximately 3:45 p.m., on Tuesday, October 16, 1925, three armed men entered the ENB located at 132 High Street in Jefferson City, Missouri, and committed an armed robbery. Crime Three: In the course of committing the armed robbery of the ENB, a girl bystander was shot and killed.

2. Specific Crime(s) Allegedly Committed: Auto Theft, Armed Robbery, First-Degree Murder.

3. Description of Alleged Perpetrator(s): The three men were in their early to mid-twenties. Two of them were not wearing masks during the robbery of the ENB, but they were not known to anyone in the bank. All three men were armed with revolvers. Suspect One was approximately

5’10” tall and weighing 145 lbs. with dark brown hair and eyes. He was last seen wearing a charcoal, pin-striped three-piece suit with a matching grey fedora. Suspect Two was around 5’9” tall and weighing 150 lbs. with light brown hair and hazel eyes. He was last seen wearing a white shirt with a brown tie and plus-fours with matching black-brown-and-tan argyle knee socks. He was also wearing a brown newsboy cap. Suspect Three was estimated to be 5’11” tall and weighing about 130 lbs. He had unshorn, grey hair, and light-colored eyes. This individual had on an ill-fitting navy three-piece suit with a grey fedora, and he was the only one of the three to wear a mask during the robbery. The mask was a red bandana. (The above descriptions are a composite drawn from statements given by the two customers and four employees who were inside the ENB at the time of the robbery. Their names, addresses, and individual statements can be found in Appendix C). Additional details have been added from the descriptions given by two witnesses outside the ENB, Mrs. Margret L. Stanford and Mrs. Louise T. Harf. (Their statements can be found in Appendix E).

4. Description of the Crime(s): Crime Two: Upon entering the ENB, the three robbers ordered the two customers and four employees to lie on the floor. The employees and customers immediately complied. Suspect Three stood guard at the bank’s front door throughout the robbery. Suspect One approached the bank president, held his gun to his head, and demanded that he open the safe. The president complied.

Once the safe was open, Suspect One filled one of the bank’s canvas moneybags with approximately $11,000 in cash. After that, the three robbers backed out of the bank keeping their guns trained on those inside. Suspect Three led the way as they left. He was followed by Suspect One. Suspect Two was the last to leave. The robbery lasted no more than fifteen minutes.

Crime Three: Two local youths, Samuel C. Blair, age 18, and Midge S. Blair, age 16, were on the sidewalk outside the ENB when the robbers emerged. The two are children of the Right Honorable James Thomas Blair, a Justice on the Missouri Supreme Court, and his wife, Grace Marie Blair. At the time of the incident, the two youths were on their way home from Jefferson City High School. (Samuel C. Blair's statement can be found in Appendix D. Midge S. Blair died before she could give a statement.)

Upon encountering the two young people outside the ENB, Suspect Three pointed his gun at Samuel. Samuel has said that he experienced a memory lapse of approximately twenty seconds at this point. And as a result, he has no recollection of what transpired during this interval.

Two women, Mrs. Stanford and Mrs. Harf were conversing on the sidewalk across the street from the ENB when they heard a shot. Looking in the direction of the bank, they saw four individuals (two men, a boy, and a girl) standing together on the sidewalk in front of the ENB. They also saw a third man backing out of the bank's front doors.

The women have stated that one of the men, standing with the boy and the girl, had a red bandana around his neck. (At this point, Suspect Three's mask had slipped from his face.) Suspect One was standing between Suspect Three, and Samuel. All three were staring at Midge Blair, who was staggering backward holding her chest.

Mrs. Stanford and Mrs. Harf have both stated that, even though they were not looking in the direction of the ENB when the shot was fired, they believe that Suspect

Three fired the shot. However, neither can explain why. The two women also stated that, even though they could see Suspect Three's exposed face, the distance was too great for them to accurately describe him. (The statements of Mrs. Margret L. Stanford and Mrs. Louise T. Harf can be found in Appendix E.)

Following the shot, Suspect Three again pulled the mask up over his face. At the same time, Samuel rushed to the aid of his wounded sister. And the three robbers fled to their car parked at the curb and sped off. The get-away car was the stolen 1923, black Hudson four-door referenced in Section 1. There were no license plates on the car.

5. Related Developments: The get-away car was reported stolen on the day of the ENB robbery by Mr. Claude K. Heisinger, owner of Heisinger Motors. It was recovered the day after the robbery in downtown Kansas City, Missouri. According to the Kansas City, Missouri Police Department (hereinafter known as the KCPD), the car contained no fingerprints or other physical evidence when it was recovered. (See Appendices F and G respectively for the statement from Claude K. Heisinger and the KCPD Recovered Auto Report.)

On November 16, 1925, a state clinical psychiatrist, Dr. Homer K. Mather, examined Samuel Blair. According to Dr. Mather, the boy had likely experienced an episode of stress-related amnesia. Such conditions, he stated, are not uncommon in life-threatening situations. The doctor rated the likelihood that the boy would recover his lost memory at fifty-fifty. (The psychological evaluation of Samuel C. Blair by Dr. Homer K. Mather can be found in Appendix H.)

During the six months following the ENB robbery, the Jefferson City police contacted the KCPD on three sepa-

> rate occasions seeking information on possible ENB robbery suspects. In each instance, the KCPD stated that they had nothing in their files related to any of the individuals in question (See Appendix J for the names and details of the suspects and the specific outcome in each instance). All leads were followed up, and all suspects were eliminated from the inquiry.
>
> 6. Status of this File: Two years after the date of the robbery, the JCPD removed this file from active status due to the absence of new developments in over a year. Two years following that, the case was marked "unsolved," and the file was sent to cold storage. On the same day that the file was shipped to cold storage, and at their request, a copy of the case file was provided to the Blair family.

I CLOSED THE FOLDER. Reading about Midge's death always reminded me of the humiliation I'd felt when I'd had to admit to the police that I had no memory of what had happened a few minutes before. And I'd never forgotten the disbelieving looks on their faces.

Oddly enough, it was this experience that led me to learn memory techniques. Secretly, I'd hoped that, if my memory improved, I might recover those forgotten seconds. But of course, it doesn't work that way.

The desire to recover my lost memories was one of the reasons I'd wanted to go for treatment. Naturally, I'd also wanted to get over the clumsiness, recurring dreams, and urges too. But for some reason, it was the memory lapse that had bothered me the most. And I'd had the feeling that, if I could just remember who had shot Midge, everything else would fall into place.

THE MENNINGER SANATORIUM turned out to be a rambling, three-story stucco building on the western edge of town. Dr. Karl Menninger was waiting for me when I stepped out of the cab. He was a quiet, bear-like man in his early forties with old-fashioned pince-nez glasses and kindly eyes. He led me to his office.

Dr. Karl began by describing what we were going to do. He said that the process was called the "talking cure." He told me that all I had to do was to say whatever came into my mind and to talk as long as I wanted. His job was to listen and take notes. Then he had me lie on a couch while he sat behind me at his desk. He asked me to begin, starting wherever I wanted.

It took a while for me to get going, but when I did, I was surprised by how much I had to say. I began by telling Dr. Karl about growing up in Jefferson City with my two brothers and two sisters. Even though it's the state capital, Jeff City is in many respects a small town. It has shady tree-lined streets and neighborhoods of white frame houses.

My earliest memories are of running with a neighborhood gang. It was a mixture of boys and girls of elementary school age. We climbed trees, played pranks on each other, and invented elaborate games. In my memory, it was a time of sunlit days and long evenings where we sat on the front porch and chatted with the neighbors.

This was before radio. And like sing-alongs, reading was what everyone did for fun. Our family especially enjoyed reading aloud. Three of dad's favorites were the Bible, Malory's *Le Morte d'Arthur,* and the works of Shakespeare.

When dad read to us from the Bible, he often chose the Gospel of John. He especially liked the part where Jesus appeared to Doubting Thomas after the Resurrection. I can still hear dad intoning, "Put your finger here and see my hands, and put your hand here into my side. And don't be unbelieving but believe."

Another of dad's Bible favorites was the calling of Samuel. As a child, Samuel had been given to God by his mother to fulfill a vow she had made. And he'd served the high priest Eli in the temple at Shiloh sleeping near the Ark of the Covenant. Awakening to God's voice calling him in the night, Samuel had replied, "Speak, Lord, your servant is listening."

While I loved it when our family read aloud, the Saturday matinee was the highlight of my week when I was a boy. That was when the dime serials ran at the Capitol Theater. *Sherlock Holmes,* starring William Gillette, was my all-time favorite. Runner up was King Baggot's spy thriller, *The Eagle's Eye.*

Midge was the sibling I was closest to. She was two years younger than me. Quick and fun-loving, she knew how to give as good as she got. Midge and I had a lot in common. Besides the dime serials, we loved puzzles, poetry, and stargazing.

My two brothers are several years older. And so, we didn't spend much time together growing up. But that's changed now. We're all lawyers and enjoy talking shop and Missouri politics.

Then there's Dolores. My older sister has always been difficult. One night over dinner, right after she'd turned twenty-one, Dolores had declared that Man had created God—not the other way around. God, she'd said, was no more real than the Tooth Fairy or the Easter Bunny. She'd also dismissed the Church as "bunk."

Now my mother, Grace Marie, is French Canadian, and in her family, Catholicism runs deep. Dad is a convert, and like many converts, he's also keen on his faith. That's why he's always insisted that we kids know what we believe.

As for me, a Creator is the simplest and most probable explanation for Life on this planet. I don't see how we could have randomly and spontaneously arisen from some sort of primordial soup. After all, even if the relevant elements had been there, where did the spark of life come from? And how can anyone look at the wonder of creation, and think there is no God?

As for the Church, it's the only human institution I know of that has survived pretty much unchanged for over two thousand years. And that's despite being constantly split by dissent and hit with persecution. But the Church's best argument is her saints. And if you've ever met one, you know what I mean.

Anyway, it wasn't long before Dolores had announced that she was moving out. She'd said that she needed room to breathe. And at the time, I'd thought that maybe that was a good idea. But as soon as Dolores had moved to Kansas City, she'd started hanging around with crooks. And it was a real disappointment for all of us.

It was then that I'd run out of steam. So, I'd stopped talking. And Dr. Karl had asked me to tell him about the day when Midge had died.

"Well, I'm not sure I've got all the facts straight," I'd replied. "But I've brought a file with me." And I'd started to get up for it.

But Dr. Karl had stopped me. "Don't worry about that, Sam," he'd said. "I'm more interested in your thoughts and feelings than in the facts. Just tell me how you felt when it happened, and what you were thinking."

"Okay," I'd said not sure of where to begin.

So, I'd just launched into it. I told him that it had been a crisp October afternoon and that Midge and I had been walking home from school. She was giggling and telling me about something Hank Blevins had done. He was the class clown and her beau. Midge had been so tickled; it'd made me laugh too. We were still laughing when we reached the bank. At that moment, three robbers had burst out. And one of them had raised his gun and pointed it at me. We were so close, that there was no way he could miss.

I was about to tell Dr. Karl that this was the point where my memory failed. But then, something new came to me. The new memory was so vivid and intense that it caused me to quit talking. In it, I could see the hand that had held the gun. It had long, pale fingers. Then my eyes had traveled upward, and I'd looked straight into the gunman's eyes. But I was puzzled by what I saw there. The eyes were wide and ambiguous, full of something I couldn't read.

Then my memory skipped like it always did whenever I tried to remember that day. And it had picked up with me sitting on the sidewalk holding Midge after she'd been shot. But this time, the intensity of my recollection was so strong that it was like I was reliving that day, all over again.

Midge's head was in my lap. And as I gazed down at her blood-smeared face and fading eyes, all the hopelessness and frustration welled up inside me again. Tears spurted from my eyes, and I began to sob.

Then I realized that I was no longer sitting on the sidewalk in Jefferson City, but I was on the couch in Dr. Karl's office. And he was standing beside me with a reassuring hand on my shoulder. It had taken me some time to compose myself.

After that, we'd taken a break, and Dr. Karl had given me a tour of the Sanatorium. He'd explained that they were set up for residential care. And he'd shown me the living quarters, library, dining room, and solarium. There were plenty of patients staying there too.

After lunch, we'd gone back to Dr. Karl's office, but this time we hadn't resumed the talking cure. Instead, we'd discussed my history of clumsiness. Dr. Karl asked whether anything more serious than bumbling and tripping had ever occurred? And I'd told him about the house fire in law school, and the time I'd crashed into the roadhouse restaurant just outside of Jefferson City.

I'd explained that the fire had happened during my first semester of law school. It'd been my turn to fill the heating stove in the boarding house where I'd lived. I was in a hurry to get back to studying and had accidentally sloshed kerosene onto the hot stove. The house had caught fire and the place had burned down. Fortunately, everyone had gotten out alive.

I'd explained to Dr. Karl that the fire had happened during finals at the end of my first semester. At the time, I'd been afraid I wouldn't do well. I'd kept thinking that, if I was ever going to find Midge's killer, I needed to be at the top of my class. That would give me the pick of prosecutors' jobs. Turned out, I needn't have worried. Despite the fire and losing all my books and notes, I'd still ranked third in my class that semester.

The roadhouse accident had been more serious. And to this day, I still don't know quite what happened. It had been a bright September afternoon. The pavement had been dry, without sand or gravel. I guess I'd just been going too fast.

In the crash, I'd fractured an arm, a leg, and my collarbone. I'd also been pretty badly cut by broken glass. That's where the scars on my left cheek come from. Five others had been hurt too, all of them much worse than me. Fortunately, though, no one had died.

I'd told Dr. Karl that the crash had happened upon my return to Jefferson City after law school. My dad had insisted that I take my place in the family firm instead of applying for prosecutor's jobs as I'd wanted. I was frustrated, but I'd done what he'd asked.

At the time, I was making zero headway on Midge's case. And I knew that I would never catch her killer where I was. I'd even complained to my parish priest back home about it. I'd told him I was praying, but that it wasn't doing any good.

The priest had laughed and said, "It's not like pulling a lever or spinning a wheel, Sam. God's a person too. He's got ideas of his own." And I'd told Dr. Karl that it had turned out that the priest was right.

Following the accident, dad had realized just how unhappy I was. That's when he'd done the unthinkable and asked for a political favor. At the time, I'd never even considered the U.S.D.A.'s office in Kansas City, even though it had everything I was looking for. So, my prayers had been answered after all.

While I was describing both the fire and accident, Dr. Karl had just listened, and he'd let me blather on. But at the end of each episode, he'd asked whether there was there anything else I wanted to tell him? Both times, I'd just said, "No."

After that, Dr. Karl switched subjects. Out of the blue, he'd asked, if I'd had any reoccurring dreams? I was bowled over. And I'd told him about the dreams of the face.

He'd asked me whether the face in my dreams was "disembodied?" Again, I was surprised. I'd told him that it was. Then he'd asked whether, during the dream, the face would grow, in size? Astounded, I'd said that it had. It grew until we were eye-to-eye and nose-to-nose. He'd described my dream exactly.

Next, Dr. Karl had wanted to know whether the face in my dream was a "familiar" one? And I'd told him that I was certain it was the face of Midge's killer. But I didn't know how I knew that. Then he'd asked me to describe the face. And I'd told him that, even though I knew whose face it was when I was asleep when I awoke, I could neither describe the face nor say whose it was. He'd just nodded.

With that, we'd ended our session and gone for a walk on the grounds. Dusk was coming on, and it was colder. Ice crystals floated in the air. Coming to a boarded-over cistern, I'd leaned against it and lit a cigarette. Dr. Karl had stopped beside me and was cleaning his glasses.

"You understand, Sam, we're just at the beginning of your treatment," he said.

"Sure, but—can you give me some idea of what's wrong with me?"

"Ever read stories of fighter pilots during the war?" he asked putting on his glasses.

"You bet. Like most boys, I read whatever I could get my hands on."

"Heard of Charles Nungesser?"

"Wasn't he the French guy trying to beat Lindbergh across the Atlantic?"

"That's right, he was a French ace; forty-three confirmed kills. He joined an escadrille in 1915 when the life expectancy for a new pilot was less than two weeks. And he survived the War."

"Sounds like one lucky guy."

"Yes and no," replied Dr. Karl. "Nungesser acquired lots of injuries. Some were the result of combat. These included multiple fractures of his arms, ribs, and legs as well as breaking his upper and lower jaws. He also received several bullet wounds including one to the mouth and a shot-away ear."

"I guess he wasn't that lucky," I said trying to make a joke.

Dr. Karl went on as if he hadn't heard me. "Most fighter pilots were superstitious. They relied on lucky charms and propitiatory rituals to cope, but not Nungesser. He flouted the taboos. His personal insignia was a black heart. Sketched in white, on the heart, were a skull-and-cross-bones, two candles, and a coffin. Nungesser had that insignia painted on every plane he flew."

Dr. Karl continued, "Injured or not, Nungesser insisted on flying. Once when both of his legs were broken and in plaster casts, he'd ordered his ground crew to carry him to his plane so he could get back into the fight."

"So, what are you saying?" I asked.

"There are competing forces within us, Sam. One is the life instinct as most clearly seen in Eros, sex, and pleasure. It's a tendency towards survival, creativity, and propagation."

"Opposed to it is the death instinct or what Freud called the 'death drive.' It's an urge towards barrenness, aggression, and self-destruction. In a healthy person, these two forces are balanced."

When he remained silent, I said, "And you think, they're out of whack in me?"

Dr. Karl said nothing to that. He took off his glasses again and wiped them with a cloth.

When he still didn't say anything, I asked, "So—how did I get this way?"

"I suspect it has something to do with the death of your sister, Midge."

"So, I'm not accident-prone?"

"No. The clumsiness is just a symptom."

After that, we walked back to the house in silence. A cab was waiting for me in the drive, its engine ticking over. It was darker now and colder. I put my hand on the door handle but hesitated.

"What about my dreams?"

At first, it didn't seem like he was answering me, just picking up where he'd left off. "During the War, many fighter pilots had recurrent dreams, one of the most common was described by an American ace, Reed Chambers. It's been discussed in the psychological literature."

"In Chamber's dream, a disembodied face would appear. At first, it was vague and distant. Slowly, it would draw nearer until it was nose-to-nose. Then he would awake with a start. The face haunted Chambers. He kept wondering whether it was the face of someone he'd killed—or the face of the man who would kill him."

Dr. Karl put his hand on my arm, "Come stay with us, Sam, so we can get to the bottom of this."

"I—can't right now. I've got a major trial soon. Maybe, after it's over."

Dr. Karl nodded as if he'd expected this, "At the moment, your symptoms are relatively minor. However, you've had two major episodes."

"But they were some time ago."

"Proximity in time isn't always a factor."

Then he went on speaking carefully, "I don't want to alarm you, but if you do nothing, the next major incident will likely be more serious—even fatal—to you or someone close to you."

Then we'd shaken hands. I'd mumbled my thanks and gotten into the cab. As it started rolling, I lowered my window.

"What happened to Nungesser?"

Dr. Karl cupped his hands to his mouth to call after me, "Took off to fly the Atlantic—and hasn't been seen since."

As the cab traveled through the dark, I kept going over what Dr. Karl had said. I wasn't sure why he was telling me about Nungesser. But one thing was certain. My dream and Reed Chambers were alike.

And there was something else. I hadn't been completely candid with Dr. Karl. I'd meant to tell him about the urges. They'd been really strong when I was refilling the heating stove. And when I was speeding toward the roadhouse restaurant. After each incident, I hadn't been sure what had happened.

I knew I should have told Dr. Karl about the urges. And I'd promised myself that I would—next time. But as soon as I got home, I'd put Menninger's out of my mind. There was just too much going on, to worry about that now.

8

JANUARY 1934

Thanksgiving came and went. Then Prohibition ended on December 5; it was celebrated with riotous partying. But the only festivities I'd had time for was a day trip to Jefferson City for Christmas. And I'd rung in 1934 at my desk toasting the New Year with a cold cup of coffee. The shimmering summer heat was a memory, and snow had already covered the courthouse steps twice.

As the trial drew near, Vandeventer's imagination became more heated. And he feverishly spun out more ideas for motions and briefs. I was close to my limit. But I strove to keep pace with his requests remembering his demand for top-quality work—or else.

Then there was Costellow. Not surprisingly, he'd taken every opportunity to show me up in front of the Chief. These had ranged from pointing out a citation error in the argument for our felony tax-evasion claims, which Phelps, Wilson, and I had somehow collectively missed, to a draft brief that had vanished off Audrey's desk before she'd had a chance to type it.

Costellow had had the nerve to suggest that I hadn't

written the brief at all. And that I was claiming it had been stolen to cover up for this fact. I'd been furious at the suggestion, and I was certain that Costellow had taken the brief himself. But then something had happened, that changed my mind.

Mrs. Wilks came to my office one morning fiddling with her wedding ring. She walked right in without knocking, which wasn't like her. And before I could say anything, she launched into a story.

"When I came in this morning," she said, "I gathered up all the motions and briefs I'd typed for you yesterday. And as I always do, I double-checked them against my project log. It was then that I noticed one of the briefs was missing. So, I immediately went to Mr. Wilson and informed him of this fact."

"Of course, I knew that a brief had gone missing last week, and how much trouble that had caused. And I was worried it had happened again. But when we came back to my desk and went through the stack a second time—the missing brief was there."

"Could you have overlooked it the first time?" I asked gauging her reaction.

"I'm quite certain I did not," she said firmly.

Now, Mrs. Wilks was a meticulous typist. She averaged over seventy words per minute, and rarely made mistakes. In addition, her grammar was superb, and she often made corrections on the fly. Although I'd never admitted it to Audrey, if I'd had my druthers, Mrs. Wilks would have typed all of my projects.

The senior typist continued, "Mr. Wilson said that I should come and tell you about the mislaid brief. And he also thought that I should tell you something else that I have observed."

"What's that?" I asked.

"Mr. Schmid has been spending considerably more time than usual in the typing area." She gave me a significant look. "And yesterday, I caught him looking at one of your briefs on Miss Baxter's desk while she was away. I thought that this might be of interest to you."

"It is," I confirmed.

Rising, I said, "Thank you, Mrs. Wilks. I very much appreciate you coming to me with this." And at that, she gave a bob of her head and disappeared.

Since our case strategy was still evolving, not much harm had likely been done by Schmid's snooping. But the Chief, Wilson, and I decided to take steps to prevent him from doing so in the future. Apart from the obvious need to keep all work product under lock and key, we toyed with the idea of using Schmid to feed misleading info to opposing counsel, who were the obvious recipients of his intelligence. But frankly, we just didn't have the time to bother with that. More than anything, though, it was a warning that the Lazia team would stoop to anything to win.

One evening, just after six, I was returning to my office after picking up a couple of draft motions that the Chief had okayed, when I happened to glance into the reception area. There, I saw a young man with wavy brown hair helping Audrey on with her coat. They shared a secret smile and left arm in arm.

It was like someone had punched me in the stomach. I'd remembered seeing the same young man hanging around the office recently. But I'd thought that he was just another of Ginny's serial boyfriends. What a dope—I'd been too busy to put two-and-two together.

I knew I had no right to think of Audrey as my girl. And because of the Lazia misunderstanding and the busyness of trial prep, I hadn't taken the time to mend our relationship. Now, it looked like I was too late. All fear of the Chief's wrath evaporated. And I snapped off my desk lamp and headed home.

It was cold and dark when I pulled into the drive. I eased to a stop in front of the garage and got out. With an effort, I slid the door open on its icy rail and put the car away. Crunching through the snow, I paused to stamp my feet clean on the front walk.

Mounting the steps, I let myself into the house. As I reached for the light switch, something hit me—behind my left ear. I went down hard and fell into a darkness that had no bottom.

WHEN I CAME TO, I was face-down on my living room rug. My eyes gradually focused on a pair of brown shoes. They were thick-soled and scuffed. I moaned and rolled over onto my back.

That was a mistake. Pain arced like lightning between my temples. I kept my eyes tightly closed until the pain went away. Then I opened an eye. A light was on in the room. It was coming from the floor lamp by one of the armchairs. That was also where the shoes were.

I raised my hand and felt behind my left ear. The hair was matted and sticky. And I winced when I touched the wound. This time, after the lightning, there was nausea. And I didn't move again for a long time.

After a while, though, I realized I had to get up. So, I rolled gently over onto my hands and knees. I wavered there trying to get the hang of it. Then whoever was in the room stood up and walked into the kitchen. I heard the water running from the tap. Inching towards an armchair, I slowly pulled myself up and into it. After I was settled, a large hand thrust a glass of water at me.

"Here—take small sips," a gruff voice said.

Clasping the glass in both hands, I did as instructed. And I raised my eyes to look at the man standing in front of me. He was short, broad, and solid. A rumpled fedora was pushed back on his head revealing closely cropped grey hair. Washed-out blue eyes peered at me from a furrowed face.

He didn't seem like the one who'd hit me. Rather, he was like a passerby at an accident. Even so, I wondered who he was. And why he was here in my house.

"You've been sapped," he said. Like it was a common occurrence. And maybe it was in his world. Then he sat down in the armchair across from me.

I took another sip of water.

And the man said, "Your father asked me to keep an eye on you and your sister—after you moved to town." Making a face, he added, "Although, it didn't go so good tonight."

With that, the tumblers in my head slowly began to turn. In my current state, it took longer than usual. But one by one, they eventually fell into place.

"You were at Union Station," I said remembering the broad back in the brown suit. "On the day of the Massacre."

He nodded.

"And at Visitation, the day—I met Johnny Lazia."

He nodded again.

"You work for my father?"

He nodded a third time.

"So, what are you?" I asked, "Some kind of minder?"

He shook his head.

I groped for other options. "A gumshoe?"

He made a face.

"Then what?" I asked.

"Ex-detective—KCPD."

Oh, like Jack Baxter, I thought.

I extended my hand and said, "Sam Blair."

He smiled and put out a hand twice the size of mine, "Budge Reno."

I took his hand. "Budge?"

"What I go by."

"Nice to meet you—Budge," I said giving his hand a shake.

We sat for a while just looking at each other. My head ached, and I rubbed my brow. Then I said to no one in particular, "Wonder who?"

"Lazia I'm guessing," said Budge. "Or at least, one of his boys."

"But why?"

"Could be Johnny's been giving you a pass—because of your sister," he said. "But he doesn't want you to think you've got him buffaloed. So, he has one of his guys give you a tap—just to let you know."

"Or," said Budge still spinning out the possibilities. "It could be someone else. Been poking around in something somebody wouldn't like?"

I immediately thought of Rayen. But if he had come after me tonight, he wouldn't have used a sap. And I probably wouldn't be here now talking to Budge. So, I figured it had to be someone else.

"You're probably right about Lazia," I said.

Then I had another thought. I reached into my vest pocket and pulled out the metal ball I'd been carrying around since the day of the Massacre. "Can you tell me what this is?" I asked.

Budge took it between thumb and forefinger. “Where’d you get it?” he asked.

“Union Station, on the day of the shootings. It was beside the shot-up car.”

“That’d be double-ought buckshot,” he said dropping it back into my palm.

“Buckshot?”

“Yeah, there are three categories of shotgun loads, from the smallest to the largest: birdshot, buckshot, and slug.”

“I thought this was too big for buckshot.”

“Nope. They’re about nine of those 33-caliber balls in a 12-gauge, special-load shotgun shell. During the War, we Marines favored them in ‘trench sweepers:’ pump shotguns with short barrels. We’d jump into a Hun trench and let fly.”

He warmed to his subject. “If you hold the trigger down on a sweeper, the gun fires every time you pump it. With its short barrel, a sweeper is better than a machine gun in a tight space. Although they can be plenty dangerous if you don’t know what you’re doing. Krauts lost so many men to sweepers they lodged a formal complaint under the Geneva Convention,” he continued. “Said using them was a war crime.” Then he snorted, “As if poison gas wasn’t.”

“Think somebody had a—sweeper at Union Station?” I asked.

“Could be. Heard a couple of shotgun blasts. And from what I saw, someone in the backseat had fired one.”

“Backseat? Of the shot-up car?”

“Sure—windshield glass all over the hood,” said Budge. “Then there was Jelly.”

I looked quizzically at him.

“Back of his head,” said Budge pointing with his thumb.

I swallowed remembering what I had seen. And then I recalled the spent shotgun shells. One had rolled out onto the running board when Rayen had opened the driver's door. And then when he'd pulled back the front seat, there'd been a second one on the floor in front of the slumped-over lawman.

"You think a lawman shot Jelly?" I asked incredulously.

"Looked like it," said Budge. "I'm not saying it was intentional."

I tried to think it through. If someone had fired a shotgun from the backseat that would explain not only how Jelly had been killed, but also how Caffery and Hermanson, both standing outside the car, had died from shotgun wounds. And it would also explain why there had been no fourth gunman.

But such a scenario would fly in the face of the Bureau's official narrative. And it would mean that Vern Miller and his accomplices had only killed two of the dead and that the other three had been blown away by one of the lawmen. I could imagine how Mac and Hoover would take that suggestion.

"Oh, yeah, I almost forgot," said Budge.

Picking up something from the table beside him, he held it out to me in the palm of his hand. "Found this on the floor behind your front door."

It was a wooden kitchen match with a blue tip and a freshly chewed end.

"Mean anything to you?" he asked.

I shook my head. "Think my visitor dropped it?"

"Could be," he said.

Seeing the match in his hand stirred a distant recollection, from the day of Midge's death. It wasn't one of my lost memories. But it was something I'd forgotten.

There had been a chewed kitchen match lying on the

sidewalk at Midge's feet on the day she'd died. I'd pointed it out to the Jefferson City cops at the time. But they'd said lots of people chewed matches, and that it didn't mean anything. I hadn't been so sure. But I'd forgotten all about it, until now.

THE NEXT DAY, I was sitting at the counter of the Liberty Bell when Mac slipped onto the stool beside me. I put down my corned beef sandwich, and we'd shook hands. It had been a while since we'd talked.

"Ever catch Miller?" I asked.

"Sort of," he said.

I gave him a quizzical look. So, he went on.

"Over the summer, we tracked him to New York City then the Greenbrier Hotel in West Virginia, and, after that, to the Hialeah Racetrack in Miami. He was having a high old time and didn't bother disguising himself. But he always kept a couple of steps ahead of us."

"We finally got a break and located his sweetie, Vi Mathias, aka, Mrs. Vincent Moore. She was staying in an apartment in Chicago. Turned out, the Moores had dropped the little girl off with her grandparents in Minnesota and then split up. We got word they were going to meet in Chicago at the end of October."

Mac paused, and I could tell he was deciding how much to tell me.

"What happened?" I asked prodding him.

Ticking the items off on his fingers like he was fond of doing, Mac said, "One, placed a BI agent and his wife just down the hall from Vi; two, tapped the phone to her apartment; three, brought in two squads of Chicago police and

replace him. But there did seem to be something funny about the timing. And it was common knowledge that Pendergast had been pulling every political string he could, to derail the Lazia case.

One afternoon, when Charlie was dropping off the mail, I'd asked him what he knew about it. He'd stepped out into the hall and checked that it was clear before answering me.

"Maurice Milligan is replacing the Chief," he said.

"What's the scoop on him?"

Leaning on the mail cart, Charlie rattled off the salient points in the life of Mr. Milligan. "Brainy as a kid, he studied law as a hobby. Got one of the top scores on the state bar exam one month after graduating from high school. Decided he was too young to practice, so he went on to get a B.A. and law degree from the University of Missouri."

When Charlie stopped, I nodded for him to continue.

"Practiced briefly in Richmond, Missouri before leaving to fight in France during the War. When he returned, he was appointed probate judge for Ray County where he has served for fifteen years."

"A probate judge," I sniffed. "Must have good connections."

Charlie nodded, "Milligan's younger brother, Jacob, is in the U.S. House of Representatives. Senator Bennett Clark's his mentor."

Now I got it. Bennett Clark was a household name in Missouri but not as big a name as his father Champ Clark had been. If a Clark was behind Milligan, he'd been a shoo-in.

"Didn't Jacob Milligan run for the Senate during the '34 primary?" I asked.

"Yep," said Charlie. "But he lost to Harry Truman. And of course, Truman went on to win the election."

I remembered Truman. They'd called him "Haberdashery Harry," because he'd once run a men's clothing store that had gone bust. Truman was a slight, bespectacled man known for his salty talk. During the War, he had acquitted himself well commanding an artillery battery in the AEF. There was only one problem with Senator Harry Truman. He was a Pendergast man.

"Boss Tom have anything to do with Vandeventer's replacement?"

"It's no secret he tried," said Charlie. "He wrote a letter to Jim Farley, the Postmaster-General, and FDR's former campaign manager, complaining about the Lazia investigation and trying to get rid of Vandeventer."

"Is that why the Chief is leaving?"

"I'm not sure."

"Thanks, Charlie. Any idea when Milligan will start?"

"Soon."

As Charlie started to leave, I cleared my throat. Then I asked, as casually as I could, "Oh, anything on that other matter I mentioned to you?"

"I wondered if you were going to ask," said Charlie giving me a knowing look. "The guy's name is Chandler Brown. He's studying sociology at the University of Kansas City and is a genuine card-carrying red. Writes a monthly column in *The Proletarian*."

"Despite his bolshie views, Brown seems likable enough. No known crimes or misdemeanors. He'll probably turn out fine—once he grows out of his pinko phase."

That was all I wanted to know. And I signaled to Charlie that that was enough. But Charlie didn't work that way. If you asked him to look into something, you were going to get the whole scoop—whether you wanted it or not.

"Even though you're not asking, Brown's been seeing a

certain someone for about three months now. Met at a Reform Movement Rally. They've been stepping out two or three times a week. And it seems pretty serious. She's even taken him home to meet her folks."

My face had fallen by the time Charlie had finished. But he acted like he hadn't noticed. I thanked him, and we never spoke of it again. I felt like a heel for having snooped around in Audrey's private life. And I vowed never to do that again.

But I had to face it. Audrey was serious about Chandler Brown. Still, that just made me more determined to get her back. And I promised myself that, once the Lazia trial was over, mending our relationship would be my sole priority.

As usual, Charlie's info on Vandeventer was correct. The Chief stepped down just days before the Lazia trial was due to start. And Milligan's swearing-in took place in the D.A.'s office with Judge Otis presiding. They even took a picture of it. All of us Assistant D.A.'s were there.

Afterward, Milligan spoke to Vandeventer alone. We figured he was getting the lay of the land. Turned out, that was only part of it. Milligan took the opportunity to ask Vandeventer to stay on as a special prosecutor—just to handle the Lazia trial. His official title would be "Special Assistant to the Attorney General." Not surprisingly, Vandeventer had agreed.

From one angle, it made perfect sense. The trial was just days away, and it would have been difficult for Milligan to get up to speed in time. But why replace Vandeventer, if you were going to try Lazia anyway? I didn't get it.

Whatever the reason, it suited me fine. Throwing his concerns out the window, Vandeventer had made me second chair. And he told Milligan not to expect a plea deal. As we'd planned, we were going for a conviction on all four counts.

9

FEBRUARY 5, 1934

The trial began at nine on Monday morning, February 5, 1934. It was right upstairs in Judge Otis's courtroom. And it was an intense eight days that I'll never forget. In my memory, it is one long blur.

Out of necessity, much of our evidence had to come from Lazia's criminal associates. We knew they'd show up because we'd subpoenaed them. But that didn't mean they'd be helpful. Combined with a handful of government witnesses, we hoped their testimony would be enough to make our case.

Frank Walsh was Lazia's attorney. Two inches shorter than his client, he was a politically connected, highly regarded criminal defense lawyer out of New York City. Walsh was savvy and tough. So, we knew our government witnesses were in for a rough ride.

In his opening statement, Vandeventer laid out our case. He explained that Lazia was not on trial for illegal gambling or bribery, even though there would be evidence of both. The Chief stated that the evidence would show Lazia had earned more than enough to file tax returns in both 1929 and 1930 but had not filed a return for either year. This was why the indictment contained two misdemeanor failure-to-file counts.

The two felony counts related to numerous cashier's checks Lazia had received from his gambling associates in both years. Lazia had denied that the money from these checks was "taxable income." Vandeventer stated that the evidence would show that this was incorrect. And that Lazia had, "deliberately and intentionally," not paid taxes on this money.

When Vandeventer was finished, Frank Walsh rose and reserved his opening statement until after we had rested our case. So, we immediately began calling our witnesses. Our first two were Treasury Agents Sharp and Beach. I conducted their direct examinations. Both testified as to their role in the Government's investigation into Lazia's finances, and what they had found. Despite Walsh's aggressive cross, we got in everything we needed from them.

Next, we began to call Lazia's criminal associates. Chambers and Ellison testified about their roles in the acquisition and running of a greyhound track and a casino nightclub. The latter was known as "Cuban Gardens." During Sharp and Beach's investigation, Lazia had admitted on the record that he'd made a "sizable" but unspecified financial stake in both enterprises.

On direct examination, Chambers and Ellison both testified that the track and nightclub had generated large sums daily. They'd been almost cocky about how much money they'd made. Not surprisingly, Walsh had downplayed these numbers on cross. Chambers and Ellison had readily followed his lead and agreed that "maybe they had overstated" the amount they'd made.

We then called Arthur McNamee. McNamee was a long-time Kansas City gambler. He testified that, before 1929, he had agreed with Lazia to operate both the casino nightclub and dog track.

"Did you have an agreement with Mr. Lazia as to the division of profits?" asked Vandeventer.

"Yes, after we'd covered the operating expenses and the costs of the building, furnishings, and equipment, we'd each take fifty percent."

"And was one of your operating expenses $500 a week to a Mr. Crummett?"

"Yes."

"And why did you pay that money to Mr. Crummett?"

"To take care of the locals."

"What do you mean by 'taking care of the locals?'"

"Well, so we wouldn't be molested."

"By the 'locals,' do you mean the local police, Mr. McNamee?"

"Yes."

"Is that what you call 'a fix,' Mr. McNamee?"

"Some people call it that."

"And the money you paid Mr. Crummett, was it from income that you received from Cuban Gardens?"

"There was no income from Cuban Gardens. You see, we hadn't got our original investment back yet."

"What was the amount of your original investment in Cuban Gardens?"

"I couldn't say."

"Can you tell us approximately?"

"I couldn't say. Mr. Lazia took care of that part of it. We just had a gentleman's agreement."

"By that you mean, you didn't have a written contract with Mr. Lazia?"

"That's right—just a gentleman's agreement."

On cross, Walsh once again elicited from McNamee that, despite the substantial daily receipts he had testified to on direct examination, he'd been "exaggerating quite a bit" and neither the dog track nor Cuban Gardens had "actually made any money." In fact, following Walsh's lead, he'd said that both had incurred heavy losses in 1929 and 1930.

Then Walsh asked McNamee if he had "bought out" Lazia in 1931. McNamee said that he had.

"Did you pay him in cash?"

"Well, cash or cashier's checks, I don't recall which."

"Is it customary among gambling men to use cashier's checks just like cash?"

"It is."

"Regardless of endorsement?"

"That's right."

"And sometimes the checks aren't endorsed at all, correct?"

"Yes, that sometimes happens."

"They're passed around just like dollar bills, aren't they?"

"They are."

"And that goes for cashier's checks in the amounts of hundreds or even thousands of dollars?"

"Yes."

Arthur Slavin was our next witness. Slavin was an intermediary between the owners of Cuban Gardens and several gambling syndicates. He was well-schooled in the art of evasion.

"Did you purchase cashier's checks for use at Cuban Gardens?" asked Vandeventer.

"Yes."

"How many cashier checks did you buy from Merchants Bank?"

"That's impossible for me to say. I didn't keep a record of what I bought."

"How often did you go to Merchants Bank to buy cashier's checks?"

"Most mornings, although I missed some mornings."

"And every time you went to Merchants Bank did you buy cashier's checks?"

"I can't say that I did."

"Did you ever buy more than one cashier's check at a time?"

"It's possible."

Next, we called Ray Edlund, a cashier at Merchants Bank. This was the bank where Lazia had an account and did most of his financial business. Originally, Edlund was going to be our star witness. He'd assisted Lazia in many of his business dealings. But Edlund had gotten cold feet shortly before trial and had limited the number of subjects he was willing to testify about.

Fortunately, Edlund still gave us what we needed regarding the amounts and activity in Lazia's account during 1929 and 1930. We also used him to get bank records into evidence. And there was one more thing Vandeventer wanted from Edlund.

At the end of the teller's direct testimony, the Chief pulled a cashier's check from the stack already admitted into evidence. "Mr. Edlund, I'm handing you a cashier's check for $5,000 from Merchants Bank. What's the number on that check?"

"The number is 65644."

"Is there an endorsement on the back of that check?"

"There is."

"In whose name?"

"Johnny Lazia."

"Is that Mr. Lazia's signature?"

"No."

"Do you know whose handwriting it is?" asked Vandeventer.

"Yes. It's mine." There was some murmuring from the gallery at this point.

"You signed Mr. Lazia's name on the back of that check?" Vandeventer asked.

"I did," Edlund confirmed.

"Did you often do that?"

"Well, I have several times."

"Do you routinely endorse cashier's checks for other customers at Merchants Bank?"

"No."

"So, why did you endorse this check for Mr. Lazia?"

"Because he asked me to."

"Just to be clear, Mr. Edlund. Mr. Lazia handed you this cashier's check and asked you to endorse it—in his name?"

"Yes," said Edlund.

"Did you ask Mr. Lazia why he wanted you to do that?"

"No."

"He could have endorsed the check himself?"

"That's right."

"And once you endorsed this cashier's check in Mr. Lazia's name, what did you do with the money from that check?"

"I deposited it into Mr. Lazia's account."

"Can you verify that?"

"Yes, the bank's records will show the deposit."

"So even though the check didn't have his signature on the back, Mr. Lazia received the money from it?"

"He did."

"You've said that this wasn't the only cashier's check you endorsed for Mr. Lazia?"

"No, he asked me to endorse cashier's checks for him quite a few times."

"Let me hand you Government Exhibit Number 33. Please identify it."

"This is the list that I prepared of all the cashier's checks that I endorsed in Mr. Lazia's name during the years 1929 and 1930."

"And what did you do with the money from these cashier's checks?"

"Occasionally, Mr. Lazia would ask me to cash one and give him the money, but usually he would just have me deposit the funds into his account."

"Just to be clear, is it your testimony that Mr. Lazia either received cash from the checks on this list or the money was deposited into his account?"

"That's correct."

"Did you ever endorse a check for Mr. Lazia and keep the money yourself?"

"No."

"Did Merchants Bank, at the Government's request, audit Mr. Lazia's account for the years 1929 and 1930?"

"It did."

And did the bank find any shortages in Mr. Lazia's account for either of those years?

"No."

"Thank you, Mr. Edlund. No further questions, Your Honor."

Walsh declined to cross-examine the teller, and he left the stand.

10

FEBRUARY 8, 1934

So far, our evidence had gone in well, and Walsh hadn't dinged our witnesses too much. Of course, on cross, Lazia's associates had tried to walk back much of the favorable testimony they'd given us on direct testimony. But we'd expected that, and overall, we thought that the result had been to reinforce the credibility of their prior statements.

As I'd suspected, we'd needed someone to put the money into Lazia's hands. And despite his waffling, Edlund had managed to meet our expectations. He'd shown that, despite Lazia's efforts to obscure the money trail, by using fraudulent endorsements, the cash had either been deposited into Lazia's account or had been paid over to him. And the bank records had proven this.

So, we were hopeful as we neared the end of our case. But evidence at trial is never as strong in court, as it is when you're arguing it to your colleagues back in the office. And so, I tried to restrain my optimism.

Our final witness was Harry Riley, an IRS accountant. Riley had investigated all of Lazia's publicly known financial transactions during the years of the indictment. This had included not only his business dealings at Cuban Gardens and the greyhound track but his personal finances as well.

Riley had then conducted a cash-flow analysis of Lazia's known income. The latter was primarily based on bank records from Lazia's accounts especially his principal one at Merchant's Bank. Subtracting Lazia's expenditures from his income, Riley had determined that Lazia had made more than thirty times the statutory minimum required for filing a tax return.

The Chief then asked Riley if any of Lazia's income had come from cashier's checks? Riley had responded in the affirmative. Concerning 1929, nearly $83,000 worth of cashier's checks had passed through Lazia's account at Merchant's Bank. In the following year, the amount had been nearly $98,000.

To put that kind of money into perspective for the jury, Vandeventer had asked Riley what the average annual wage had been in 1930? Riley had said that it had been $1,970. Then the Chief had asked, what the average cost of a new home had been in that year? Riley had responded that it was $7,145. And finally, he'd asked for the average price of a new car. To this, Riley had replied that it had been $640.

Vandeventer then changed subjects. He asked Riley if, in his work for the IRS, he'd ever studied how gamblers use cashier's checks? Riley had responded that the methods gamblers used, to avoid the detection of their income, was an area he'd specialized in.

"Do gamblers do anything unusual when buying cashier's checks?" asked the Chief.

"They often purchased them in someone else's name."

"Why would they do that?"

"To make it difficult to trace the money back to them."

"Have you come across that practice in your investigation for this case?"

"Yes. Here in Kansas City 'Arthur Slavin' is kind of a gambling trade name. While Mr. Slavin certainly purchases cashier's checks, many gamblers use his name, instead of their own, when buying them."

"Is it common for gamblers to make and pay off bets using forged cashier's checks?"

"Yes, particularly when large sums are involved."

"Why would they do that?"

"So, they can later claim they did not receive the money from those checks."

"And in your opinion, what is the purpose of that?"

"To avoid paying taxes on it."

Next, Vandeventer had asked Riley if, during his investigation into the finances of Cuban Gardens and the greyhound track, he had found any evidence of lost income? Riley had responded that he had not. He had been unable to locate any financial records for either enterprise. And without financial records, Riley had said, business losses were impossible to verify.

Profits, however, were more readily ascertainable, he'd said. And his research had indicated that Cuban Gardens and the greyhound track had operated well in the black during both years of the indictment. Riley had concluded by quoting Arthur McNamee, the well-known Kansas City gambler, who had earlier testified for the prosecution. According to McNamee, both Cuban Gardens and the greyhound track had been "real cash registers."

During cross-examination, Walsh had stuck to hypotheticals. But all of them had boiled down to the same question. If the business losses sustained by Cuban Gardens and the greyhound track had been of such and such a magnitude, wouldn't they have been sufficient to outweigh any "alleged income" Riley had found?

In each instance, Riley had conceded that, if the numbers were as great as Walsh had stated, it was "theoretically possible" that they might have offset such revenues. But he had also gone on to state that he had found nothing to indicate that this was the case. And further, that such a conclusion was "inconsistent" with the totality of the evidence. Following Riley's testimony, we rested our case.

It was then that Walsh gave a brief opening statement.

"Ladies and gentlemen of the jury, the Court will instruct you that it is not simply the amount of money that a man takes in nor the amount in checks that pass through his bank account, that is taxable. Rather, what is taxable is the gain or profit a man acquires from his labor and capital. Business losses of any sort must enter into this calculation. And for the Government to prevail, it must show that Mr. Lazia willfully evaded paying taxes on any gain that he might have received. It is not sufficient for them to merely show that a sum of money passed through his hands or his bank account."

Walsh called Lazia as his first witness. Johnny came groomed for the occasion in an ill-fitting charcoal suit and a brown tie. Even so, he sauntered to the stand, nodded familiarly to the judge, and flashed a smile at the courtroom. He just couldn't help himself.

After entering Lazia's name, age, and address into the record, Walsh asked his first substantive question. "Mr. Lazia, were you convicted of a felony when you were only seventeen years old?"

"I was."

"And did you receive a prison sentence for that offense?"

"I did." Then Johnny leaned forward and volunteered with a smile, "And I was later pardoned."

Next, Walsh took Lazia through the details of his acquisition and ownership of both the greyhound track and Cuban Gardens eliciting from him that, during 1929 and 1930, he'd "never gotten a dime in profit" from either. The only money he'd received, Johnny said, was in partial repayment for his "original investment." Further, he claimed, both enterprises had suffered heavy losses during those years.

Lazia also asserted that the cashier's checks, which had passed through his account, were taken solely for the purpose of "making change" for his associates at the dog track and Cuban Gardens. He explained that these friends of his had experienced "liquidity problems" due to the stock market crash and subsequent Depression. And that he had converted the cashier's checks into cash just "to help them out."

Further, Lazia explained, the money he had exchanged for the cashier's checks had come from his portion of the daily receipts from either the dog track or Cuban Gardens. He maintained that the transactions with his associates were strictly "a wash." And he denied that he had made any profit from them.

On cross, Vandeventer had asked whether Lazia had kept any accounting records for either the dog track or Cuban Gardens? Lazia said that he hadn't. But he knew that there had been "big losses" in both years.

The Chief then shifted ground. And he asked Lazia to state the total amount of his "investment" in both Cuban Gardens and the dog track.

To this, Lazia had replied, "I couldn't say."

"Then how were you going to know when you had recouped the money from your investments?"

"Well, once the mortgages were paid off, the construction, furnishings, and equipment costs had been met, and we were covering our operating expenses, then we would have known we were in the black."

"So, you were relying on the holder of your mortgages and the contractor who'd built these facilities and the sellers who'd provided you with both the gambling equipment and the furnishings to tell you when you had paid off your original investment?"

"That's right. You see we all had a gentlemen's agreement."

"So, you have no idea how much money you spent on building and setting up Cuban Gardens and the dog track?"

"Correct."

"Can't you give us even a ball-park estimate, Mr. Lazia?"

"Sorry."

"Are we talking thousands of dollars or hundreds of thousands of dollars?"

But Lazia wouldn't be drawn. "I couldn't say."

Here, Vandeventer raised a sheaf of affidavits in his hand. "You know, Mr. Lazia, it's curious. When we asked your contractor and your suppliers how much you paid them to build and furnish Cuban Gardens and the dog track, they also say they don't know?

"Really?"

"And when we ask them who does know, they all say, you do?"

Unfazed, Lazia simply shrugged, "Don't know why they'd say that."

Once again, the Chief shifted ground. "Okay, Mr. Lazia, I'm handing you a cashier's check, Government Exhibit Number 19N, already in evidence. That is check, Number 65644, correct?

"Yes."

"And your signature is on the back?"

"It's my name—but it isn't my signature."

"So, you didn't endorse that check?

"That's right."

"But you asked someone to endorse that check for you, didn't you?"

"Why would I do that?"

"Just answer the question, please."

"No."

"Mr. Edlund, a teller at Merchants Bank, has testified that you asked him to endorse cashier's checks in your name on multiple occasions."

"That's nuts."

"So, you're saying he lied?"

"Sounds like it."

"You didn't receive the money from this check?"

"Nope."

"Now, let me hand you Government Exhibit Number 23, which is also already in evidence. What is it?"

"Some sort of bank record," said Lazia.

"It's a record for the year 1929 of withdrawals and deposits for a particular account at Merchants Bank, correct?

He shrugged, "Guess so—but I'm no expert."

"That's your account number at the top, isn't it?"

"Yeah."

"And if you turn to page two, there's an entry for cashier's check number 65644, correct?"

"Uh-huh."

"Is that a Yes?"

"Yeah."

"So, this document shows that the money from that check was deposited into your account, right?"

"I don't know that it does. Like I say, I'm no expert."

"Well, if you didn't receive the money from this check, who did?

"I think that teller guy, Edlund, took the money himself."

"You're saying Mr. Edlund stole the money from this check?"

"Yeah, that's what I think. And he dummied up the records to cover for himself."

"So, you're denying that you received the money from check number 65644?"

"I am."

"And you're also denying that this bank record is correct?"

"That's right."

"Now, let me hand you Government Exhibit Number 33, which is already in evidence. This is a record of all the cashier's checks presented by you to Merchants Bank in 1929 and 1930, which Mr. Edlund has testified under oath that he endorsed for you in your name."

"Okay."

"Is it your testimony that you did not receive the money from any of these checks?"

"Yeah—that's right."

"And if I were to tell you Merchants Bank audited your account for the years 1929 and 1930 and found no discrepancies for either of those years, would your testimony still be that the bank audit was wrong?"

"You bet."

"Turning to another matter, Mr. Lazia, you've admitted you were convicted of armed robbery, right?"

"Yes." The smile returned.

"And that was a felony conviction?"

"It was." He seemed proud of it, and maybe he was.

"You were sentenced to twelve years in prison, correct?"

"That's right."

"But you were paroled after serving only nine months of that sentence, right?"

"I was." The cockiness had returned.

"A condition was attached to your parole, wasn't it?"

"Yeah." His smile slipped a little.

"You were paroled on condition that you would join the U.S. Army, right?"

"That's right. But you see . . .."

Holding up his hand, Vandeventer stopped him, "Just answer the question."

Here Lazia frowned. He glanced at the Judge who looked over his glasses at him.

Vandeventer continued, "And you were paroled in 1917, correct?"

"Yeah."

"We were at war with Germany at that time, right?"

"We were." The smile was gone.

"But when you were released from prison, you didn't join the Army, did you?"

"No."

"You returned to Kansas City and resumed your, uh—former activities?"

"That's right."

"No further questions, Your Honor."

After Vandeventer sat down, Walsh took Lazia through a brief redirect. "Why didn't you join the Army in 1917, Mr. Lazia?"

"My father was out of work. And my Mom and the younger kids had no means of support."

"And did you bring this to the attention of the draft board?"

"I did."

"And did they grant you a deferment from military service?"

"They did." Here Lazia shot Vandeventer a glance. It said, "Gotcha!" And at this point, Walsh entered Lazia's draft card into evidence.

When I'd checked with the draft board before trial, they'd had no record of a Lazia deferment. That had changed. When we examined Lazia's draft card, the entry in the deferment section was "economic hardship," and the signature of the granting party was smudged.

Charlie Carrollo was Walsh's second and final witness. Lumbering to the stand in a tailored pinstriped suit and garish floral tie, Carrollo testified in his capacity as "President of the North Side Financial Company." He also improbably described himself as Lazia's "financial advisor."

The North Side Financial Company was an entity that had not surfaced during our investigation. Subsequent checking with the Missouri Secretary of State showed North Side Financial to be a company of recent existence but apparently in good standing. The records also stated that Charlie Carrollo was its President.

Carrollo testified that the North Side Financial Company held the "mortgages" on both Cuban Gardens and the greyhound track. Anticipating our likely cross-examination, Walsh elicited from him the amounts of these mortgages. They were about ten times greater than the going rate for comparable property in the county where these businesses were located.

Walsh then asked Carrollo about the amounts of Lazia's monthly mortgage payments. Carrollo explained that the payments were "large" because Lazia had intended to pay off the mortgages early. Carrollo also testified that Lazia had asked him to "keep the daily accounts" for both the dog track and Cuban Gardens during the years 1929 and 1930.

This was news to us. We had turned up no evidence of any such accounting during our investigation, and no mention of it had been made, so far, at trial. Vandeventer shot to his feet. He strenuously objected and asked for a sidebar.

Standing before the Judge, but out of hearing of the jury, Vandeventer had berated Walsh for springing this new evidence on us at the eleventh hour. Walsh had just shrugged. Then he'd said it wasn't his fault it our investigation had been "incomplete and incompetent."

The Chief had pleaded with the Judge, "Your Honor, we've been ambushed. We've never seen these alleged records before, and we need time to thoroughly evaluate them. We're requesting an adjournment of two days to do so."

But Judge Otis wasn't having it. He was itching to get the trial over. Giving Vandeventer an exception for the record, he allowed the new evidence to come in. He then gave us thirty minutes to review the ledgers before the trial resumed.

When we finally got a chance to examine the accounting ledgers Walsh had admitted into evidence, the numbers were, not surprisingly, consistent with Lazia's defense. The losses, which they claimed had been suffered by the dog track and Cuban Gardens conformed almost exactly to the hypotheticals Walsh had proposed to Riley during his cross-examination. We'd been had.

Following the recess, Carrollo again took the stand. He testified that his accounting records showed that both the dog track and Cuban Gardens had endured heavy losses during 1929 and 1930. He said, the greyhound track had gone out of business shortly afterward, and around the same time, Lazia had been forced to sell his interest in Cuban Gardens to Arthur McNamee.

When the time came for cross-examination, it was my turn, and I went to the lectern.

"Mr. Carrollo, in 1931 you pled guilty to a felony, correct?"

Carrollo scowled, "No, I didn't."

"Are you sure?"

"Yeah, I did pay a fine, but it wasn't for no felony."

I handed a document to the clerk and then passed copies to Walsh, the Judge, and Carrollo. I identified the document for the record. It was a certified photo-static copy of a page from Volume 5 of the criminal record of the U.S. District Court for the Western Division of the Western District of Missouri dated September 24, 1931.

"May I read the document into the record, Your Honor?"

After glancing at Walsh, who did not object, the Judge said, "You may."

"*United States of America vs. Charles Carrollo*, Case Number 10839, this day Charles Carrollo appears in person with counsel and waives formal arraignment and enters a plea of guilty to the indictment herein charging felony conspiracy to violate the National Prohibition Act."

"Mr. Carrollo, did I read the document correctly?"

"Yeah."

"Does that refresh your recollection that on September 24, 1931, you pled guilty to the charge of felony conspiracy to violate the National Prohibition Act?"

"Yeah—but what I pled to wasn't a felony."

Next, I turned to Carrollo's "accounts" for the greyhound track and Cuban Gardens. Holding up the ledgers, I asked,

"Mr. Lazia gave you the numbers you put down in these books, didn't he?"

"Yeah, Lazia, gave me the numbers."

"And he gave them to you orally, correct?"

"I put them down just like he said."

"He didn't give you any written records or receipts to verify those numbers, did he?"

"All the numbers are right there in those books just like he said."

Glancing at the Judge, I said, "Your Honor."

Judge Otis leaned over and made eye contact with Carrollo. "Answer the question," he said sternly.

Rolling it all into one, I asked, "You don't have any contemporaneous written records or receipts to back up the numbers in these accounting ledgers, do you Mr. Carrollo?"

"No."

"All of these numbers were given to you orally by Mr. Lazia, correct?"

"Yeah."

With that, I sat down. Walsh chose not to redirect Carrollo, and the defense rested. It was time for closing arguments. But since it was just after noon, Judge Otis adjourned for lunch.

11

FEBRUARY 13,1934

During the recess, we learned that a carload of Lazia's men had shadowed the jurors, as they had walked to the nearby Pickwick Hotel. This was where the jurors had lunch when the court was in session. Despite the cold weather, the Packard had crept along beside the jurors with its windows rolled down. And as the car had rolled along, the occupants had talked loudly among themselves. They'd made a point of referring to the jurors by name, stating their home addresses, and even mentioning the names of their spouses and children.

But that wasn't all. As the jury was returning to the courthouse, a newsboy, with a single newspaper under his arm and waving another over his head, had dashed past them down the courthouse steps shouting, "Extra! Extra! Jury Does its Duty! Acquits Lazia!"

When we learned of these efforts at jury tampering, we considered asking for a mistrial. But we quickly realized that, if we won the motion, Vandeventer wouldn't be around to try the case when it again came up. And if we didn't take our shot at Lazia now, we might not get another one. So, we decided to go forward anyway.

Procedurally, the prosecution gives its closing argument first. I was going to give ours. Vandeventer, in turn, would give the rebuttal, after Walsh's closing. Theoretically, my job was simple: summarize the evidence and show that we had met the elements of our case. But it was the first time I'd ever done it, and I only hoped that I wouldn't embarrass either Vandeventer or myself.

Costellow had joined us at the counsel table to help with the handling of exhibits. I was at the end of the table, closest to the jury box. Vandeventer was sitting in the middle, between us.

When the Judge was ready, he gave me a nod. I rose, picked up my notebook, and walked around the back of the counsel table. As I passed behind Costellow, through no fault of his, my right foot somehow hooked the leg of his chair. And I stumbled.

All would have been well if Costellow hadn't chosen at that moment to extend his left foot. He was clever about it. He just stuck it out far enough to catch mine, as I was about to regain my balance. The result was dramatic. My arms wheeled. My notebook flew into the air. And I fell flat on my face.

There was a collective gasp. This was followed by some tittering, which ended when Judge Otis glared from the bench. I immediately jumped up, retrieved my notebook, and went to the podium. My face was hot, as I tried to focus on my notes. But at first, the words were incomprehensible. Eventually, I was able to decipher the opening phrase. I squared my shoulders and began.

I started by reminding the jury that, despite some of the testimony they had heard, this was not a case about illegal gambling or bribery. It was about tax evasion. And that was why our evidence had focused on Mr. Lazia's income during the years 1929 and 1930.

I noted that Mr. Lazia had testified that he'd kept no financial records for either Cuban Gardens or the greyhound track. And this had been corroborated by the testimony of his associates, Chambers, Ellison, and McNamee. And yet, Mr. Carrollo, the defense's final witness, had somehow produced accounting ledgers for those businesses. Further, he had claimed to have kept those records for Mr. Lazia during the years of the indictment.

"Now, you may think it curious that these records were not uncovered during the Government's two-year investigation. They were not mentioned by anyone until Mr. Carrollo took the stand. Of course, the law permits you to weigh the truthfulness of his testimony in light of the large losses claimed as well as the credibility of Mr. Carrollo himself, who is a convicted felon."

Next, I turned to the teller's testimony. "Mr. Edlund has stated that Mr. Lazia frequently asked him to endorse cashier's checks in Mr. Lazia's name. Mr. Lazia has denied this. He claims that Mr. Edlund stole the money from these checks. However, bank audits for both 1929 and 1930 did not find any money missing from Mr. Lazia's account."

"Now, which is more likely?" I asked. "That Mr. Edlund embezzled over one hundred and eighty thousand dollars from Mr. Lazia's account—contrary to the bank records. Or, that Mr. Lazia received the money from those checks, but now wants to claim that he didn't?"

I then summarized the testimony of Treasury Agents Sharp and Beach as well as Riley's investigation into Lazia's finances. I said that this evidence had shown that Lazia had income beyond the minimum statutory requirement for filing tax returns in both 1929 and 1930. Despite this, Lazia had not filed in either year.

Then I took up the two felony counts, which required a finding of "willfulness." I explained that the Judge would instruct the jury that, in lay terms, the word "willful" meant that the evidence must show that Lazia acted "on purpose," in not paying his taxes.

I reminded the jury that, during the trial, they had seen Lazia minimize and deny the amount of his income on multiple occasions. I stated that they could take this behavior into account in assessing his "willfulness." And I ended by urging them to find Lazia guilty on all counts.

With that, I carefully walked back to the counsel table and sat down. Vandeventer was unaware of Costellow's contribution to my spectacular fall. He leaned over and, with a wink, said, "Neat trick you used at the beginning—to get everyone's attention." I smiled wanly back at him.

Then I looked beyond Vandeventer at Costellow. He was staring straight ahead, but he was wearing a self-satisfied smile. I decided it was time to wipe that smile off his face—once and for all—when we got back downstairs to the office.

I turned my attention back to the trial. Walsh was striding to the podium. The diminutive defense attorney stood there, saying nothing until the courtroom became completely silent.

When all eyes were on him, he launched into his closing argument using his best folksy manner. "Now, ladies and gentlemen of the jury, the Government has gone to great lengths to tell you that this case isn't about illegal gambling. Well, you and I both know that's hogwash. Of course, this case is about illegal gambling." That got some genuine chuckles, and I couldn't help smiling myself.

Then holding up an index finger, Walsh continued, "But

there's something you may not know. Even though it's illegal, the laws of the United States still classify gambling as a source of taxable income. In fact," looking meaningfully at the jury, "the Internal Revenue Code tells us that a gambling man can use his gambling losses to offset his gambling gains. So, under the laws of this country, money from illegal gambling is taxable. And the U.S. Government wants its share of it. Further, gambling losses are just the same as any other business losses."

Walsh went on, "Now, that we've got that clear, I want to raise one more matter with you. The fact is my client is an admitted gambler. I know it. You know it. We all know it. Some of you may not like it. It may even be against your religion. But I know that you won't let that stand in the way of rendering him a fair and just verdict. You swore to do so when we selected you. And I know I can count on you to hold to that promise now."

Then Walsh launched into the substance of his closing. He said that from start to finish, Sharp, Beach's and Riley's investigation had been "incomplete and incompetent." Had they done the "bare minimum," they would have located Carrollo's accounting records, and in all probability, this matter would never have come to trial.

Further, the missing evidence had "hopelessly skewed" the Government's case. The clearest example of this was Riley's audit of Lazia's business dealings, which had completely overlooked all evidence of business losses. The time had come, Walsh said, for the jury to see what the "real" evidence was.

Turning to a chalkboard, Walsh tabulated the amounts of Lazia's income and losses using the evidence that was most favorable to his client. According to his calculations, Lazia had not made sufficient income in either 1929 or 1930 to meet the statutory minimum for filing a return. Walsh conceded that Lazia had not filed returns in either year, but he insisted that this was because Lazia hadn't needed to.

Next, Walsh focused on the willfulness standard. He argued that there was no evidence Lazia had intentionally or deliberately tried to evade his taxes. During 1929 and 1930, "like a lot of people during the Depression," Lazia had suffered financial hardship. He had lost heavily on his investments in the greyhound track and Cuban Gardens. The dog track had gone under. And he had ended up being forced to sell his stake in Cuban Gardens.

To "stimulate" these businesses, Lazia had, "maybe unwisely," taken gamblers' cashier's checks to "make change" for them. But in this way, he had hoped to enhance their cash flow, and by helping them, to help himself. Through "no fault of his own," these efforts had failed.

Shifting ground, Walsh turned to the possible rationale for the Government's case. "Why I ask you, would two local agencies of the Federal Government choose to misinterpret what Mr. Lazia had done? Why would local elements of the U.S. Treasury and U.S. District Attorney's offices want to claim that cashier's checks, which had merely passed through Mr. Lazia's hands, were 'taxable income?'"

"You may find it of interest," said Walsh, "That as a Hoover appointee, Mr. Vandeventer is a life-long Republican!" This comment drew a sharp objection from Vandeventer and a rebuke from the judge. Unfazed, Walsh made a perfunctory apology to the court and carried on with his argument.

"So, what is the purpose of this case? Is it to recover back taxes from Mr. Lazia? No. Its goal is to put him behind bars! And why?" asked Walsh, "Why? That's the obvious question. Why would they want to punish a man, who is essential to the Democratic Party's administration of this city?" For a moment, the specter of a politically motivated prosecution hung in the air.

I could sense Vandeventer's ire. And I thought he might object. But he let it pass, choosing not to draw further attention to defense counsel's bogus claim.

Walsh ended, as nearly every criminal defense attorney does, by focusing on the burden of proof. He claimed that we had not established Lazia's guilt "beyond a reasonable doubt." And since we'd failed to meet our burden, there could only be "one just outcome," an acquittal on all counts.

When his turn came, Vandeventer appeared to ignore Walsh's political gambit. He opened by pointing out that the defense had not disputed that Lazia hadn't filed tax returns in either 1929 or 1930. And as such, this fact was established.

Then he began writing over Walsh's numbers on the chalkboard, replacing the defense's evidence with ours. These were the "real numbers," Vandeventer asserted. And they showed that Lazia had made enough income, in both years, to file a return. Then he wrote across the top: "Counts 1 & 2, GUILTY."

Vandeventer then went on to assert that only one matter was in dispute: Had Lazia "intentionally and deliberately" tried to avoid paying his taxes? He quickly summarized the large amounts from the cashier's checks that had either been cashed by Lazia or deposited in his account. Flipping over the chalkboard, Vandeventer wrote down the totals for both years and underlined them.

"And now," he said, "We've come to the smoke-and-mirrors part of this case. How cashier's checks and gentlemen's agreements are used to hide taxable income. First, falsely endorsed cashier's checks are used to obscure the money trail. Ask yourselves, why did all the cashier's checks that Mr. Lazia either converted into money or deposited into his account carry false endorsements? The answer is simple. So, that he could later claim that he did not receive the money from them."

"Second, oral agreements are used, instead of written contracts, to hide the amount of money that has been put into a business. Notice that no one knows how much Mr. Lazia invested in either the dog track or the casino night-club. Not even Mr. Lazia himself. And if the amount of his investment is unknown, then no one can calculate any profit that he may have made. And if his profits can't be calculated, then neither can his taxes."

Here Vandeventer paused and his tone changed. "Returning to the falsely endorsed cashier's checks, for a moment, I want you to consider something curious. You will recall that Mr. Lazia has denied asking Mr. Edlund to endorse cashier's checks in his name. You saw him do that right here in this courtroom. He even claimed that the teller had stolen his money. But how credible is that? Considering Mr. Lazia's reputation in this city, do you think that, if Mr. Edlund had stolen Mr. Lazia's money, he would still be alive to testify about it in this courtroom?"

Walsh shot to his feet jabbing his finger at Vandeventer and shouting, "Objection, Your Honor! That is outrageous and prejudicial! I demand a mistrial."

I was shocked. I'd never seen Vandeventer do anything like that before. Either his blood was up, or he'd done it deliberately. And I suspected it was the latter. My read was, that this was payback for both the accounting records ambush and the reference to Vandeventer's Party affiliation.

Judge Otis convened a sidebar. And he was hot. He sternly admonished Vandeventer, who readily admitted his mistake and apologized to both Walsh and the judge. In the end, the judge denied Walsh's motion for a mistrial. Instead, he gave defense counsel an exception for the record as well as a promise to instruct the jury to disregard Vandeventer's comment.

But of course, everyone knew it was too little, too late. As trial attorneys say, there is no way to un-ring the bell. Vandeventer's outburst had every likelihood of being the one thing the jurors would remember from our closing.

Consequently, when the sidebar broke up, Walsh was still fuming. And he sat at his table with his arms crossed throughout the remainder of the trial. As promised, the judge admonished the Chief in open court and instructed the jury to disregard his "inflammatory" statement.

And with that, Vandeventer returned to the podium to resume his closing. Picking up the chalk, he circled each of the numbered items on the blackboard. "To recap, first, Mr. Lazia has denied receiving over one hundred and eighty thousand dollars in income from cashier's checks endorsed in his name during the years 1929 and 1930."

"Second, he has claimed that a teller at Merchants Bank stole the money from these checks. And third, he has asserted that bank audits for both 1929 and 1930, showing no money missing from his account, were wrong. But Mr. Lazia has offered nothing in support of these empty claims."

"So, I ask you, which is more likely? That these unsubstantiated explanations are true? Or, that Mr. Lazia has concocted this entire story 'on purpose,' to conceal his true income and to avoid paying taxes on it? Members of the jury, I think you know the answer."

With that, he turned and wrote on the blackboard: "Counts 3 & 4: GUILTY" and sat down. After this, Judge Otis read the instructions to the jury. And they filed out to begin deliberations.

For trial lawyers, the hardest part of any case is waiting for the verdict. Vandeventer followed his usual routine. He sat at the counsel table with a stack of daily newspapers and copies of all the current news magazines.

As the jury filed out, Vandeventer picked up the first newspaper and began to read. Meanwhile, Walsh hovered in a corner with Lazia and Carrollo rehashing the trial. But I didn't hang around. I was hot and headed for the stairs.

When I reached reception, I marched straight through it without a word. I stormed down the hall to Costellow's office. And my hands were already balled up into fists. But when I stepped through his door, I saw Costellow wasn't alone. Milligan was standing there. I started to back away, but the Chief stopped me.

"Glad you're here, Mr. Blair," he said coldly. "Come right on in. I was about to call for you."

Milligan was flushed, and his jaw was set. "I was upstairs just now and a more disgraceful bit of sophomoric behavior I've never seen. And I'm talking about *both* of you!"

"Do I have to remind you that we are representatives of the U.S. Department of Justice and that we are in the midst of a criminal trial of national importance? Don't you know that the judge and the jurors have eyes?" We both looked at the floor.

"If you can't put aside, whatever petty thing it is that's going on between you, then you'd better clear out your desks right now. Because I am not going to stand for it!"

"And just so you know, I have a stack of over a hundred qualified applicants for each of your positions, and believe you me, every one of them would be willing to take your place tomorrow. So, either shake hands and put this behind you—or get out. What's it to be, gentlemen?"

I didn't hesitate and extended my hand to Costellow. He

looked at it for a moment like it was a dead fish. Then glancing one more time at the Chief, he took it.

"Good," said Milligan, "I'd hate to lose either of you." Then pointing his finger at us, he added, "But don't think for a moment that I won't fire you both, if I catch even a whiff of animosity between you, going forward. Do I make myself clear?"

We nodded and released our grip.

"Now, Mr. Blair, you can get back upstairs. Mr. Vandeventer may need you. Mr. Costellow and I have a few more things to discuss."

I turned on my heel and headed for the stairs. Milligan was right, of course. What had I been thinking? I would have been a fool to have lost my job over anything so stupid. Costellow and I would never become friends. But from that point on, we ceased working against each other.

The jury did not reach a verdict that evening. And the court recessed until morning. Ironically, the following day was February 14th, St. Valentine's Day. Without much hope, I wrote a valentine to Audrey and put it on her desk.

Throughout the trial, the gallery had been jammed. But understandably, today was worse. Press continued to arrive until no more could be accommodated in the front-row section reserved for them. And there were as many photographers as reporters. Most of them chose to sit on the floor at the feet of their colleagues. That way, they would have an unobstructed shot of Lazia when the verdict was announced.

Lunchtime came and went, but no one left to eat. It was half-past two when word finally came that the jury was returning. Filing into the courtroom, the jurors' faces didn't give anything away. When they were all in place, the foreman stood and handed the verdict form to the clerk, who, in turn, handed it to Judge Otis. The Judge took his time reading it. The clerk then returned the verdict form to the Foreman, who had remained standing in the jury box.

The Judge then asked the Foreman, "Has the jury reached a verdict?"

"It has, Your Honor."

"How do you find on Count One, Misdemeanor Failure to File for the Year 1929?"

"Guilty, Your Honor."

A murmur rippled through the courtroom. Judge Otis banged his gavel and glared down from the bench. "If there's any more of that, I'll instruct the Marshals to clear the courtroom."

Silence returned, but the atmosphere was charged with anticipation. I stole a glance at Vandeventer. He was stone-faced and staring straight ahead.

The Judge resumed, his inquiry of the Foreman, "How do you find on Count Two, Misdemeanor Failure to File for the Year 1930?"

"Guilty, Your Honor."

This time, the crowd merely stirred in their seats. Even so, Judge Otis frowned until everyone settled down. Then he continued.

"How do you find on Count Three, Felony Tax Evasion for the Year 1929?"

I held my breath.

"Not guilty, Your Honor."

My heart sank.

"How do you find on Count Four, Felony Tax Evasion for the Year 1930?"

"Not guilty, Your Honor."

Before the foreman had finished speaking, the gallery had erupted. Scrabbling reporters fled the courtroom fighting with each other as they went. Their single-minded goal was to be one of the first to reach the bank of pay phones at the end of the corridor.

Once they were out of the way, the photogs leaned over the rail and shouted at us. When we turned to see what the commotion was, they fired off a rippling volley of flashbulbs that blinded us. That was enough for Judge Otis; he ordered the courtroom cleared.

We were all stunned by the outcome. Walsh was in shock because Lazia had been found guilty at all. Vandeventer and I were reeling because we had only secured two misdemeanor convictions. It was peanuts.

Once the gallery was cleared, and the doors shut, Judge Otis heard post-verdict motions. Walsh asked for the jury to be polled. And it was. The verdict was unanimous.

Walsh then made the customary motion for a judgment of acquittal, which was denied. Finally, the Judge confirmed Lazia's convictions and set a date for sentencing. Then the court adjourned.

One week later, in front of another packed courtroom, Johnny Lazia was sentenced to twelve months in prison, and for each of the two misdemeanor counts, he received a $2,500 fine. Johnny was jaunty back in his usual sartorial attire. Dolores was at his side in a full-length mink and matching hat. She flashed me a triumphant, contemptuous smile, as they left the courtroom. Lazia was released on bail pending appeal, and I doubted he would serve a single day.

12

JUNE 5, 1934

As expected, Walsh filed a motion for a new trial. In it, he listed over fifty-two reasons why a retrial was necessary. And since Vandeventer was gone, it was all up to me. That meant I had to come up with fifty-two thoroughly researched and argued responses. Fortunately, Wilson and Phelps took pity on me. And so, with their help and plenty of black coffee, I'd managed to file a timely motion in opposition.

In the interim, the city underwent a turbulent municipal election. In March 1934, the Reform Party launched a campaign to assert itself at the polls, and not surprisingly, Lazia resisted. But this time, he took off the gloves. In the resulting mayhem, four people were killed, and dozens injured. But once again, the machine swept to victory.

Then in early May, Charlie Gargotta went on trial for the murder of Ferris Anthon. This time it looked like Sheriff Bash was finally going to put Mad Dog away. But since it was a state court trial held in downtown Kansas City, I figured a conviction was far from certain.

And I was right. When the evidence custodian took the

stand, it was Leonard Claiborne, Jeff Rayen's partner. I remembered the two of them putting their heads together over Gargotta's automatic on the night Anthon was killed. So, I wasn't surprised when Claiborne testified that, according to the evidence tag attached to the murder weapon, Gargotta's gun was not the one that had killed Anthon. With that, Bash's case collapsed, and once again, Gargotta walked.

At the end of May, I was elated when Judge Otis denied Walsh's motion for a new trial. But I knew that this victory was only the first skirmish in what was sure to be a long appellate war. Walsh would certainly appeal Lazia's conviction. But he still had a month to do so, and I could do little until I'd seen his brief.

But that was fine with me since Dolores was getting married on the first Saturday in June. Of course, the newspapers had pestered dad for a statement when the engagement was announced. Finally, he'd been forced to put out a three-line response. All it had said was that the decision to marry Johnny was "Dolores's alone," and that our family was "opposed to the union." The press release concluded by noting that none of us would be attending the ceremony.

Dad had good reasons for this. As a Justice on the Missouri Supreme Court, the Canon of Judicial Ethics required that he avoid any "appearance of impropriety." And just having Johnny Lazia as his son-in-law was going to cause him trouble enough. While I knew dad was right, I just couldn't miss Dolores's wedding. So, on the day of the ceremony, I'd mingled as inconspicuously as I could among the crowd across the street from Visitation Church. Fortunately, the attending reporters were too busy with bigger fish to notice me.

And from the spot I'd chosen, I was able to get a glimpse

of Dolores in her wedding gown when she entered the church. And I'd also seen Johnny and his groomsmen when they'd come out afterward for a smoke. Although, of course for Johnny, that meant a fresh stick of gum. The groomsmen were all longtime Lazia boys, and of course, Carrollo was best man.

As for Dolores's bridesmaids, I only knew one of them, the Maid of Honor. Her name was Gia; she was Lazia's youngest sister. Gia was the one who'd introduced Johnny to Dolores. But I didn't hold that against her.

Later, I read in the *Journal-Post* that one of Johnny's "Uncles," a James Balestrere, had stood in for my Father. Of course, I remembered that Mac had mentioned him as one of the "men of honor." There was a photo of Balestrere in the paper. He was a trim, nondescript man in his sixties looking uncomfortable in formal dress. Or maybe, he just didn't like his picture being taken.

The society pages gave maximum coverage to Dolores's honeymoon. The newlyweds had spent a month in Havana at the National Hotel of Cuba. And there were plenty of photos of them walking on the beach, playing roulette in a casino, and dancing among the palms.

As a wedding present, Johnny bought Dolores a compound at Lake Lotawana. That's an exclusive residential community southeast of the city built on a private lake. The Lazia compound consisted of a sprawling, ranch-style house with a sandy beach and three guest houses. The property also came with two matching speedboats.

When in town, Johnny and Dolores lived at The Park Central. That was a swanky residential hotel on Amour Boulevard near Gillham. They occupied the penthouse. A photo-spread in one paper highlighted its rooftop pool, marble walls, and Art Deco statuary.

In one society-column interview, Dolores had described her typical evening out. She'd said that she and Johnny usually dined at Cuban Gardens or one of the other dinner clubs in the city. And afterward, they would either tour the entertainment district to enjoy the latest Swing or do some gaming on Twelfth Street before heading home in the early hours. It sounded glamorous, and the society columnist had done her best to play it up. But I still had my doubts about Dolores and why she had married Johnny.

I HAD a meeting with Milligan on the Tuesday morning after Dolores's wedding. The new Chief had kept his office the same as when Vandeventer had had it. Even the eight-by-ten of Milligan shaking hands with FDR was hanging in the same spot where the old one of Vandeventer and Hoover had been.

Despite these similarities, there was no doubt that Milligan was a different kind of fish. For one, he was harder to read. For another, unlike Vandeventer, he had political aspirations. And I still wondered whether he was in the Boss's pocket.

When I entered, Milligan was sitting at his desk wearing a dove-gray suit, white shirt, and solid navy tie. His brown hair was slicked down against his head, and there was a scalp-white part on the left. The features of Milligan's long face formed a capital "I." A prominent brow shaded inexpressive eyes, and from its center, a Roman nose ran to a noncommittal mouth.

Milligan gestured with his elevated cigarette for me to take the chair in front of him. But before I could sit, he threw me a question. "What's your take on last March's municipal election?"

"Bloody and rigged," I said, easing myself into the chair.

"Give me your thoughts. And don't spare the detail."

"Okay," I said. "The mayor and nine city council spots were in play. And the Reformers decided the time was ripe for them to make their move. They're a coalition of non-machine Democrats, Republicans, and members of the non-aligned Citizen's Fusion Party."

I lit a cigarette and tossed the spent match into the ashtray at Milligan's elbow. "The mob imported out-of-town muscle. And on Election Day, carloads of toughs roamed the streets looking for trouble. Shooting broke out at one polling station, and four people were killed. That was the worst bit. But dozens of others were injured, eleven of them seriously."

What I didn't tell Milligan was that Audrey's boyfriend, Chandler Brown, had been one of them. He'd been monitoring a North Side polling station when Lazia's thugs had beaten him with a baseball bat. Chandler's back had been broken, and the doctors said he'd never walk again. When Audrey told me about it, my heart sank. I knew I'd never win her back from a guy, who'd been crippled while doing the right thing. I'd paused too long over my thoughts, and the Chief waved impatiently for me to continue.

"Of course, the machine won. They re-elected Mayor Bryce Smith and seven members of the City Council. But surprisingly, it wasn't a total sweep."

"Any actionable evidence of voting fraud?" asked Milligan, as he ground out his cigarette and plucked a stray bit of tobacco from his tongue.

"No, it was mostly circumstantial. The strongest proof was that zero opposition votes were recorded in several districts where we knew reformers had voted. Also, the percentage of ballots voting for machine candidates was way too high. For instance, Mayor Smith received 65% of the total. But none of it was solid enough for a court to act on."

Milligan frowned. "Was there anything this office could have done?"

"Not really. Tackling something like that takes a lot of preparation."

"Do you think the machine will try the same thing in the 1936 Election?"

"I'm sure of it."

"Well then," he said. "This time we're going to do something about it. Any thoughts?"

"Depends on who we're after."

"My preference is the rank and file."

He saw the look on my face.

"I know, I know," he said holding up a hand to placate me. "But we need to start out with a sure win. We should target anyone we can get an easy conviction on such as well-known repeat voters. The machine will have to protect its people. And if we nail enough of them, it'll cost them plenty."

"Do we have the resources for that?" I asked.

"Probably not. But when it gets closer to the time, we'll ask Washington for help. But before we can do that, we'll need a plan of action."

"Can we get the Bureau's help," I asked?

"Sure," he said.

"Good. I've just the man in mind."

13

JULY 10, 1934, 4:10 A.M

The ringing wouldn't stop. And I realized, I'd have to do something about it. So, I fumbled with the phone.

At first, all I heard was sobbing. Then a shaky voice asked, "Sam? Is that you?"

"U-huh."

"Johnny's been shot. It's bad."

"Where are you?"

"St. Joseph's."

"On my way."

I hung up and threw my legs over the side of the bed. Switching on a lamp, I squinted at the clock. It was ten after four. As I stumbled down the hallway to the bathroom, I glanced at the calendar on the wall. It was Tuesday, July 10, 1934.

The street outside St. Joseph's Hospital was lined with cars. And the hospital was all lit up. I found a spot a block away. Even at that hour, folks were coming and going. But the hall outside Operating Room Number 1 was the worst. It was jammed with reporters, police, and wise guys.

Peering over the crowd, I could see Carrollo's moon face on the opposite side. He was leaning against the wall next to a marble statue of Our Lady of Lourdes. Although I couldn't see her, I knew Dolores must be nearby. Since her engagement, she'd never been without a minder.

I launched myself into the crowd and steered toward Carrollo. Jim Wetzel of the *Journal-Post* immediately latched onto me. As usual, he was trawling for a story.

"What do you think, Sam? Was it Lusco, the Chicago mob, or an inside job?"

"I don't even know what happened," I growled trying to shake him. But he stuck to me like tar to the bottom of a shoe.

"Front of the Park Central, two guys from out of the bushes. One with a shotgun, the other a Thompson. Hit Lazia eleven times."

Well, if he was dishing, I was going to take it. "Carrollo?" I asked.

"Driving. Happened when Johnny got out to open Dolores's door. So, what do you think?"

"No idea," I said finally shouldering my way past him.

Sure enough, Dolores was with Carrollo. But not where I'd expected. She was kneeling on the floor hugging Mary's marble feet. And I wondered, what gives?

As soon as she saw me, Dolores jumped up. Her eyes were wide, and she grabbed me by the lapels. "I saw it, Sam—all of it," she blubbered. It was like a line out of a B-movie.

Then I noticed Wetzel was scribbling at my shoulder. I shot Carrollo a glance. Scowling, he put a splayed hand on the reporter's chest and gave him a shove. Wetzel went reeling.

I pulled Dolores in the opposite direction. The policeman outside the operating room gave us a nod and held one of the doors open for us. As he did, the crowd surged forward trying to see inside. But the cop held them back until the door swung closed behind us.

Johnny's labored breathing dominated the operating room. He lay in a circle of bright light, propped up on the operating table, his olive skin, the color of plaster. When one of the nurses stepped away, we could see three glistening holes in his side. Dolores slumped when she saw them, and I guided her to a chair in the corner.

A grim Father Moriarty stood beside the chair. There was a violet stole around the priest's neck, and he held a small tin of chrism in his hand. He was preparing to administer Last Rites.

A matron came through the swinging doors carrying a candlestick phone. Plugging it into the wall beside us, she placed it on a table. Then she went over and whispered to one of the doctors. He looked up and nodded.

The matron returned to the phone and spoke in a low voice to the caller. After a moment, the doctor stepped away from the operating table. Holding up his blood-streaked hands, he waited for the matron to unhook one ear of his surgical mask. Then she held the phone for him.

Speaking into the receiver, the doctor said, "Nigro." After listening for a moment, he replied, "No. No change, T. J." It was Pendergast.

"Certainly—I'll let you know," said the doctor. After the matron hung up, he waited until she re-hooked his mask.

While Dr. Nigro had been on the phone, Father Moriarty had come forward to anoint Johnny. Then making the sign of the cross, he had recited the Apostolic Pardon. Once the priest was finished, Dr. Nigro resumed his place, and Father returned to the corner. There he knelt and took out his rosary.

"Prepare another transfusion," said Dr. Nigro, and a nurse nodded. Opening a white cabinet, she lifted out a bottle of whole blood. Three similar bottles stood empty on a nearby table. As the nurse approached the operating table, Johnny groaned, and his eyelids fluttered.

Dolores rushed past the nurse, but at first, Johnny didn't see her. He focused instead on the doctor, who was leaning over him. Pink foam appeared on Johnny's lips as he struggled to speak.

"Why me—Doc?" he coughed. "Been a friend—to everyone."

Then Johnny saw Dolores, and he gripped her hand. But immediately his eyes shifted to me—beckoning, and his lips moved. Surprised, I stepped forward and bent down trying to hear him. His words were faint and breathy.

"Tell Carrollo—grooms—man's."

With that, Johnny shuddered, and his eyes rolled back. Dr. Nigro felt for a pulse. After a long moment, he shook his head, and the surgical team stopped working.

By the time Dolores and I left the hospital, its corridors were empty. There was no sign of Carrollo. Only a long space at the curb showed where the Packard had been. It looked like Dolores was now all on her own. So, I gave her a lift home.

We didn't talk on the drive to The Park Central. I guess we were both still digesting what had happened. I couldn't imagine Dolores as a widow—and Kansas City without Johnny Lazia.

Then it hit me. The Lazia tax-evasion case was over. There are no appeals for the dead. And I also wondered who would be heading up the mob? Surely, not Carrollo, I thought. The guy was a muscle head.

The eastern sky was pink-and-purple when we pulled to the curb in front of The Park Central. A police van was parked in the circle drive, but no cops were in sight. And there was a large wet spot where someone had tried to wash away Johnny's blood.

Gia Lazia was waiting for us in the lobby—her eyes red from weeping. She and Dolores hugged; then they headed for the elevator. I turned around and went back outside.

Wetzel had said that the shooters had hidden behind the bushes in front. So, I started there. Clicking on my penlight, I looked at the dry ground. Some light scuffing was visible in the dirt, but that was it.

Stepping out of the bushes, I walked to the corner of the building. Training my penlight on the ground, I walked the width of the hotel. There was more evenly spaced scuffing between the clumps of brown grass. It looked like someone had been running.

Then I went over to the trashcans lining the eastern wall of the hotel. Each had an apartment number or abbreviation on it. One at a time, I lifted their lids. Except for a fetid odor, they were all empty. Monday must have been trash day.

A "PH" was painted on the last can. I figured that stood for "Penthouse." As I was putting the lid back on that one, something tucked between it and the wall fell to the ground. It was yesterday's *Daily Racing Form* folded neatly into quarters. I slipped the paper into my pocket to examine later.

Then I walked to the rear of the building and peered around it. An older gent in a gray uniform was sitting on a wooden kitchen chair near the back door. He was hunched over, his forearms on his knees, staring at the ground between his feet. A hand-rolled cigarette smoldered in his fist.

I turned the corner and walked slowly toward him. Seeing me, the man stood up, his eyes full of questions. I extended my hand, "Sam Blair," I said. And by way of explanation, I added, "I'm Mrs. Lazia's brother."

With that, the man relaxed. Dropping his cigarette, he stepped on it. Then taking my hand, he said, "Pleased to meet you, Mr. Blair. Wally Miller's the name—I'm janitor here. Sure am sorry about Mr. Lazia."

I nodded, "Police around?"

"Only a couple now. But they might be at the corner for coffee."

"See or hear anything last night?" I asked.

He scratched the back of his head gathering his thoughts. "Like I told them. Heard a car in the alley. Don't know exactly when—but after eleven for sure." Jerking his thumb at the hotel behind him, he added, "My room's in the basement—here in the back."

When I didn't respond to that, he went on. "After they pulled in, I climbed onto a chair to look out the window. Saw two of them. Thought they were coming to see Mr. Lazia. Often did that. So, just went back to bed."

"Get a look at them?"

"Nope—too dark."

"See how they were dressed?"

Wally rubbed his chin at that, then said, "I'd say hats and suits."

"What happened next?"

"Well, it was real quiet. Then all of a sudden, there was a bunch of shooting. And I rolled out of bed and hit the floor. Then I heard running and car doors slamming. So, I jumped back onto the chair." Gesturing toward the street, he said,

"And they were backing down the alley—real fast—lights off."

"Get a look at the car?"

He nodded, "There's a streetlight at the end of the alley."

"Make?"

"I'm guessing a newish Plymouth." After a pause, Wally added, "And there's more."

"What's that?"

"When they got to the street—another car almost hit them."

Another car, that late at night? I wondered. "Get a look at it?" I asked.

"No—going too fast. But lots of squealing tires," he chuckled.

"Anything else?"

Wally shook his head.

"Anyone else see anything?"

"Nope. Said I was the only one."

Getting out a five-spot, I extended it. But I held on when he started to take it.

"Tell the police everything you told me?"

"Yep. Except for the clothes and make of car." He grinned, "Didn't ask that."

"Just between you and me?"

Winking, Wally pocketed the five. "You bet, Mr. Blair. You bet."

Before leaving, I walked the length of the alley looking at the fresh ruts in the cinders. They were the width of car tires, but something heavier than a car had made them. Walking out into the street, I saw black tire marks—from two separate cars. It did look like a near miss.

Turning back toward the hotel, I slowly walked up the alley scanning the grass on both sides. On the left, near the edge of the cinders, I saw something. It was a blue-tipped kitchen match with its wooden end chewed flat. I put it in my pocket.

When I got back to the car, I sat there for a while—thinking. The police van was gone now. And the wet spot on the drive had dried.

As I was about to start up, an unmarked Fordor rounded the corner on Gillham and swung into the drive. It screeched to a stop in front of The Park Central's double doors. Rayen and Claiborne got out and strolled inside. I frowned. I was glad they hadn't been here while I'd been snooping around.

14

JULY 10, 1934, 9:13 A.M

Stopping at a drugstore on the way home, I bought all the morning papers. I wanted to see what they were saying about Johnny's murder. I put the percolator on and began to read while it slurped and gurgled.

The *Journal Post* carried Wetzel's byline on page one. The headline read, "Wife Witnesses Lazia Shooting." And in the article, Wetzel used Dolores's words to imply that she could ID Johnny's killers.

I flushed. It looked like Wetzel was putting Dolores in the crosshairs—just to get a story on page one, and I didn't like it. But before I jumped down his throat, I had to know if there was anything to it. Maybe, Dolores could identify Johnny's killers.

That meant heading back to The Park Central. So, I called the office and told Ginny I'd be late. After a shave and two more cups of coffee, I got back into the car. When I arrived at The Park Central, I was relieved to see that the Fordor was gone.

I'd never been up to Dolores's penthouse, so I was surprised when the concierge led me to a private elevator and used his key. He must have called ahead because Gia was waiting for me when the elevator reached the top. She led me into the living room; I paused in the doorway to take it all in.

A black terrazzo floor ran to white Carrera walls on which hung primary-color cubist art. In the center of the room, hard leather couches and frail sling chairs were arranged around a chromium coffee table. Along the perimeter, brass nymphs leaped and pirouetted. Only the south wall broke with the room's studied coolness. Multiple French doors opened onto a rooftop patio where a sunlit pool rippled amid potted palms and massed tropicals.

Dropping my Panama onto an end table, I walked over to Dolores. She sat on a couch in the center of the room staring at nothing. A cocktail shaker sat on the coffee table in front of her; next to it was an empty martini glass. As I stood there, Dolores took up the shaker, emptied its contents into the glass and tossed it off.

I wondered how best to raise the subject that had brought me here. Dolores didn't look like she wanted to talk. As I mulled it over, my gaze shifted to Gia who was sitting next to Dolores.

The youngest of the eight Lazia children, Gia was wearing a simple black dress with a gold crucifix. She had Johnny's dark eyes, olive skin and black hair. The latter was in a long bob, pinned up on the sides.

Gia looked pretty good for having just lost a brother. But then, she always looked good. I liked Gia—but I'd kept my distance. The Blair's had enough Sicilian entanglements without me adding to them.

The phone rang; Gia got up to take the call. When she returned, she announced that two KCPD detectives were on their way up. Then she carried the empty cocktail shaker and glass to the wet bar.

I hoped the detectives weren't Rayen and Claiborne. Rayen would tell me to get lost. And I wouldn't hear what Dolores had to say to the questions that I knew were coming. Hearing the elevator and figuring it was my turn, I went to let the detectives in.

I was in luck. The first one off was Lew Hart. He was, of course, the cop who'd helped Mac and I scout out the house on Edgevale Road. Hart's partner, Floyd Thurman, was with him. We shook hands, and I led them into the living room.

With hat in hand, Thurman went over to Dolores. He introduced himself then told her how sorry he was. Dolores nodded her thanks and gestured for him to sit. He did. Hart remained standing.

"Tell us what happened last night," said Thurman.

Dolores rubbed her hands, as she began to talk. "I hadn't been feeling well. Johnny said it was the heat, and he thought I'd feel better out at the lake."

"Lotawana?" asked Thurman.

She nodded in reply.

"And did you go?"

"Yes—after dinner at the Gardens. Charlie drove us. We went for a swim, and I did feel better after that. So, we decided to drive back to town."

Hart was making notes on the back of an envelope. He licked the lead of his pencil, as he wrote. When he finished, he glanced at Thurman.

"So, Carrollo drove you to Lake Lotawana and back?"

"Yes."

"And you had dinner at Cuban Gardens?"

She nodded again.

"About what time?"

"Between seven-thirty and eight."

"See anyone you knew at the Gardens?"

"The Gizzo's."

"Tony and . . .?" queried Thurman.

"Angelina."

He nodded. "Anyone else?"

"We knew lots of people there. But we ate with the Gizzo's," she said.

"Sure. So, when did you leave the Gardens?

"Around nine."

"And when did you get to the lake?"

"Ten thirty or so."

"And you headed back to town about when?"

"We weren't there long—1:00 or 1:30."

Thurman paused then asked, "And tell us what happened when you arrived at The Park Central?"

Here, Dolores's eyes took on a distant look, and her speech slowed. "Johnny was sitting in front with Charlie. I was in back. When we pulled in, Johnny got out and started to open my door. But then he stopped."

Dolores paused and licked her lips. "Then suddenly he shouted to Charlie telling him to drive away. As we took off, I looked out the back window. Two men were coming out of the bushes—shooting. And Johnny fell." Here she broke down.

We waited while Gia fetched a glass of water from the kitchen. After a couple of sips, Dolores nodded that she was ready to continue.

"What exactly did Johnny say to Carrollo?" asked Thurman.

Dolores spoke in a whisper, "He said, 'Drive Charlie. Get Dolores out of here.'"

"Can you describe the men who shot Johnny?"

She shook her head.

Thurman probed, "Tall—short—fat—thin?"

She shook her head again.

"How were they dressed?"

"Suits."

"What kind of suits?"

"Just suits."

"Hats?"

She nodded.

"What kind of hats?"

"Fedoras," she said, "Pulled down."

"Anything else you can tell us?" asked Thurman pressing her.

"It was dark—and I wasn't looking at them." Then she broke down completely.

With that, Thurman frowned and rose. Hart and I followed him into the entry. Once there, Thurman turned to me.

"Seen the *Journal-Post*?"

I nodded.

"Anything to it?" he asked.

"Just something she said."

"So, she did say she saw it all?"

I nodded.

"And?"

"You know what I know."

Thrusting his chin at me, Thurman grumbled, "Yeah, but what do you think? You know her a whole lot better than we do."

I shrugged. Thurman's eyes searched my face.

"Well, you might want to set Wetzel straight," he said.

"I was thinking the same thing."

"If she remembers anything else—you give us a call, okay?"

"Will do."

They got on the elevator, and it started down.

Something wasn't right. But I didn't know what. So, I started back into the living room to try and figure out what it was. But before I'd gone two steps, the phone rang. This time I got it.

Tony Gizzo was on the line. Carrollo wanted to see me —*now*. Curious as to why, I told Gizzo, I was on my way.

CARROLLO WAS at The Old Kentucky Barbecue at 19th and Vine, in the Negro business district. The armored Packard, with a fresh line of bullet dents across the back, was parked in front. Tony Gizzo and Tano Lococo stood on either side of the door giving me the fisheye as I went in. It looked like Carrollo had doubled up on his minders.

The Old Kentucky was upscale for a barbecue joint. Tables filled the area in front of the bar. Beyond it was a bandstand and dance floor. If you wanted barbecue, you ordered through a window into the kitchen. The meat came wrapped in newsprint and was hickory-laced succulence. Art Pinkard was the pit master here. He'd apprenticed under Hank Perry, the granddaddy of Kansas City BBQ.

There was no one inside the Old Kentucky but Carrollo. Sitting at a table in the center of the room, he was halfway through a rack of ribs. Carrollo's sleeves were rolled up, and his silk tie was neatly tucked between two buttons of his white shirt. Except for the smear of sauce on his chin, he looked the part of a newly minted mob boss.

Charlie started talking as I approached, “Cops grill your sister?”

I nodded pulling out the chair across from him.

“Who?” he asked.

“Thurman and Hart.”

“What’d they want?”

I was puzzled. I thought the police and mob were in bed together.

“The usual. What happened. What she saw,” I replied.

“What did she see?” he asked.

Now, I really didn’t get it. Carrollo was acting like he hadn’t been there. I wondered why.

“Not much. Too dark, she says.”

His eyes narrowed. Then he hit the table with a flat hand. “*Minchione!* That’s not what the paper said.”

“Yeah, I know,” I responded wearily. “But Wetzel’s shooting blanks.”

Carrollo cocked his head at me. “She didn’t make the shooters?”

“Naw. Said she only saw two guys popping out of the bushes. Said they wore suits and fedoras. That was it.”

Carrollo thought for a moment. You could tell it wasn’t easy for him. “You sure?”

“Yeah, I’m sure.”

“Cause, if she can make the shooters,” he jabbed a thumb at himself. “I want to know first. Nobody kills our Johnny and gets away with it.”

I had nothing to say to that. So, we just stared at each other. Then Carrollo lifted his chin, “I hear you have a message for me.”

Wondering where he’d gotten that, I nodded.

“So?” he asked.

I repeated Lazia’s last words.

"*Fangul!* What's that supposed to mean?"

I shrugged.

Scowling, he waved me away like a fly. "*Vattinni!*"

But as I got up to go, he dropped the rib he was working on. Pointing a fat finger at me, he growled, "Listen, *Babbu.* Don't ever mess with me again—like at that trial. Or. . .." And he jerked a flat hand like a knife across his throat.

I stared at him. Then I turned and stalked out—letting the screen door bang behind me. It wasn't much of a response, I admit. But it was the best I could come up with at the moment.

15

JULY 10, 1934, 11:08 A.M

On my way to work, I dropped by the *Journal-Post* at 22nd and Oak. More of a rag than a newspaper, it used splashy photo-spreads and lurid copy to reel in readers. The paper was also a mouthpiece for the machine. And that helped circulation by ensuring frequent spats with the reform-leaning *Star.*

Sure enough, Wetzel was at his desk in the middle of the newsroom still wearing the same clothes I'd seen him in the night before. Wearing a green eyeshade, he was banging away with two fingers on a typewriter. A blue pencil stuck behind his ear.

Wetzel didn't stop typing when I dropped into the chair beside him. But he knew it was me. "Give me something on Dolores, Sam. I need a little filler for the noon edition."

"I'll give you something all right," I snapped. "How about a knuckle sandwich?"

Raising both hands, Wetzel rolled out of range: "Whoa there, Brother! What's the bother?"

"You know damn well!"

Arching his eyebrows, Wetzel gave me a lopsided grin, "Not this morning's lead on beautiful page one?"

"Precisely."

"Not a word's untrue, Sammy."

Sammy? I couldn't believe the guy. "Maybe not. But you made it sound like my sister could identify Johnny's killers. And she can't."

Wetzel just stared at me and didn't deny it.

The newsroom had gone silent, and several reporters were watching us. Jumping up, I grabbed Wetzel by the tie and lifted him out of his chair. I held him there, his pasty face just inches from mine.

"You're going to print a clarification. Got it?"

He nodded.

Pulling Wetzel back to his desk by his tie, I yanked the paper out of his typewriter and told him to reload.

"Here's what you're going to say, and I want it on page one."

The next morning, on page one above the fold, the *Journal-Post* carried the following:

Clarification: Lazia Widow Unable to Identify Killers

Yesterday's exclusive written by Staff Journalist James Wetzel, "Wife Witnesses Lazia Shooting," was factually correct. But the *Journal-Post* has since learned that at the time of the shooting it was too dark for Mrs. John Lazia to identify the two men who shot her husband. A North Side politician, Mr. Lazia was gunned down early on the morning of July 10th in front of The Park Central Residential Hotel at 300 E. Amour Road. He died later that day at

> St. Joseph's Hospital. The KCPD is continuing to investigate Mr. Lazia's death. [See Lazia Obituary page 15.]

I read the correction over a morning cup of coffee at the Liberty Bell. It didn't have everything I'd wanted, but it would have to do. I only hoped Johnny's killers would read it and believe it.

16

JULY 13, 1934

The next day was Friday, July 13, 1934. The crowd outside Holy Rosary Church was estimated at over seven thousand. Holy Rosary stood in the center of Columbus Park, the Italian-Sicilian neighborhood where Johnny had grown up. When the church doors opened at eight-thirty, the crowd surged forward, but a line of police held them back.

Those who craned their necks could see Johnny's casket through the open doors. It was sitting on a bier at the foot of the altar. His body had been received into the church the evening before, and as was customary, members of the Lazia family had taken turns praying over him through the night. Dolores had not been one of them.

At eight thirty-five, ushers began to lead the Lazia family down the aisle; Dolores, Gia, and I were among them. The politicians came next. Pendergast, City Manager McElroy, Senator Reed, and Mayor Smith were there along with every ranking member of the Jackson and North Side Democratic Clubs. After the politicians, came the mob. Carrollo was in front with Johnny's top boys trailing after him. Among them were a few out-of-town hoods, who'd come to pay their respects.

After the mob, came the religious. A large group of nuns in brown habits and sandals shuffled in. They were followed by representatives of other communities, each wearing their distinctive habits. Finally, a handful of neighborhood dignitaries and some members of the press were admitted to fill the pews.

At nine o'clock, the choir began singing the *Introit*: "*Requiem aeternam dona eis Domine....*" And the altar servers, wearing black cassocks with white surplices, started down the center aisle. The leader bore a gold processional cross; the two, who followed carried three-foot candles. Behind them was a fourth with a smoking thurible. Six more servers came in a block after them.

A deacon and sub-deacon followed the servers. They were wearing black-and-gold dalmatics and walking abreast. Father Moriarty brought up the rear. He was wearing a black chasuble, heavily embroidered in gold, over a lace alb. On his head was a black biretta. Holy Rosary was not Father Moriarty's parish, but since he had been Johnny's confessor and had given him Last Rites, the family had asked Father Moriarty to preside at the funeral.

The celebrants processed to the foot of the altar and genuflected. Then they mounted the steps and turned to the congregation. When the choir finished the *Introit*, Father Moriarty made the sign of the cross while chanting, "*In Nomine Patris, et Filii, et Spiritu Sancti.*" In unison, the altar servers responded, "*Amen.*"

Following the *Kyrie Eleison*, Father turned to the altar and kissed it. With his back to the congregation, he lifted his hands and prayed the Collect. "Incline your ear, O Lord, to the prayers with which we entreat your mercy, and in a place of peace and rest, establish the soul of your servant, John Lazia, whom you have called out of this world . . . ."

During the readings, my eyes wandered to a side altar dedicated to Our Lady of Sorrows. Above it was a Della-Robbia plaque of Mary, her exposed heart pierced by the seven daggers of her *"dolors."* The wall around the altar was covered with silver-framed photographs. It was a memorial to deceased members of the mob, and I guessed Johnny's picture would soon be joining them.

After the gospel, Father Moriarty, assisted by the Deacon, Sub-Deacon, and servers, reenacted the choreographed ritual of the Tridentine Mass, as it had been celebrated for centuries. Some in the congregation followed in the missals; others silently prayed the rosary. Bells tinkled, as the consecrated hosts and wine were elevated. Then after the *Agnus Dei*, Catholics among the congregation queued to kneel at the rail, where they received the Eucharistic wafer on the tongue. Gia and I joined them along with most of the Lazia family. Following the Post-Communion prayers, Father said, "*Requiescant in pace.*"

For his homily, Father Moriarty had chosen the story of Zacchaeus from the nineteenth chapter of Luke. "Zacchaeus, you will recall, was a small man, much like me." Here there was some chuckling in the congregation. "Who, because of the crowd, had to climb a tree just to see Jesus passing by. And he was surprised when our Lord spoke to him by name and invited himself into Zacchaeus's home."

"Now, Zacchaeus was a Jew and a tax collector, who worked for the Romans. Tax collectors were despised by other Jews, because they often claimed more tax than was due and pocketed the excess. But after meeting our Lord, Zacchaeus had a change of heart. He promised to quit overcharging, give half of his money to the poor, and repay four times over anything he had extorted."

"So, why am I talking about Zacchaeus? Because like him, Johnny Lazia lived a dishonest life." With that, the church went quiet. Father went on, "Our Lord is drawn to dishonest people. Not just those who break human laws but those who are dishonest with themselves, and especially those who are dishonest with Him. But we should always remember that our Lord never gives up on any of us No matter what we've done. And he didn't give up on Johnny Lazia either. In fact, like Zacchaeus, I believe Johnny experienced a change of heart."

"Why do I say this? Well for one thing, in recent months, Johnny had begun giving generous gifts to the diocese in support of its seminarians. Something he had never done before. And, secondly," gesturing toward the rows of nuns in brown habits, "He'd also become a benefactor to the Sisters of St. Francis giving them significant donations to found hospitals throughout Missouri and Oklahoma."

"Now, what inspired Johnny to do this? We don't know. But in my experience, changes like this are often the result of some encounter with our Lord. After all, we know that He is still living and effective in our world no matter what some people like to say. And He is always on the lookout for those who are looking for Him. Seek and you shall find, knock and the door will be opened to you. Whatever it was that inspired Johnny to do what he did should also give us hope for him."

"And since we know that Johnny received Last Rites with an Apostolic Pardon, if he truly repented of his dishonest life, then according to our faith he has already been received by our Merciful Father in heaven." Here, the priest crossed himself and recited the words of the *Requiem aeternum*:

"Eternal rest grant him, O Lord, and let perpetual light shine upon him."

Despite its hopeful tone, Father's homily had made me think of Dante's *Inferno.* And it was not a comforting thought. According to the poet, if Johnny hadn't repented, then the young *cumpari* was now in the seventh circle of Hell. And there, along with the rest of the murderers, he was up to his eyes in boiling blood.

Father came down from the altar for the rite of Absolutions. As he did, the family rose and removed the pall from Johnny's coffin. Then Father sprinkled the casket with holy water and censed it. As he circled the coffin for the last time, the earthy-licorice scent of myrrh filled the church, and the choir began to sing the haunting words of the *In Paradisum*: "May the angels lead you into paradise; may the martyrs receive you at your arrival and lead you to the holy city, Jerusalem."

After this, Johnny's casket was hoisted onto the pallbearers' shoulders and was carried from the church to the tolling of a single bell. Along with the rest of the Lazia family, Dolores, Gia, and I followed it out. And the congregation came after us. Outside, the sun was beating down on the milling crowd. Later, I learned that the temperature had reached one hundred and six. Even so, it felt cooler as we emerged from the overheated church.

The pallbearers slid Johnny's casket into the back of a glass-sided hearse. Two men, whom I did not know, stood with Carrollo and Balestrere watching. I hadn't seen them during the funeral Mass. The face of one of the men was disfigured. Scar tissue covered the entire right side and encircled his lips, which were unnaturally plump and purple.

I'd heard that, as a young man, Joe DiGiovanni had been

burned in a failed arson attempt. So, I guessed that he was the scarred man. If that was correct, then the other one must be his brother, Pete. Avoiding hard-to-pronounce foreign names, locals simply referred to the DiGiovanni brothers as "the D's."

When the rear door of the hearse was closed, the four men approached Dolores. An unusually subservient Carrollo took his place at the rear. The man who I thought was Joe reached out and took Dolores's hand. She reluctantly let him. There was an Old-World formality to the gesture.

"We are so sorry for your loss," the man said in a thick but distinguishable accent.

"Thank you," said Dolores stiffly. When the men continued to stand there, staring at her, she nodded and slowly withdrew her hand. With that, the four of them backed away.

Dolores, Gia, and I were shown into the back of a Cadillac Lasalle. The Lazia family filled a Lincoln Brougham and two Chrysler Custom Imperials. Behind the limousines were four flatbed trucks. Three of them were heaped with floral arrangements. The fourth carried a single tribute—the size of a parade float.

The latter depicted a two-wheeled cart densely embroidered with fresh flowers. To symbolize loss, the cart was canted to one side, as if it had a broken axle. Suspended between its upright shafts was a black banner with gold lettering. It read: "To Johnny, My Brother and Friend—T. J."

A squad of white-gloved motorcycle patrolmen led the creeping motorcade as it pulled away from the church. A patrolman occasionally sounded a siren letting it wind down to a moan before sounding it again. A long line of cars followed with their lights on. Thurman and Hart in the Hot Shot brought up the rear.

The cortege took a circuitous route through the streets of downtown. It wound past Police Headquarters, City Hall, Jackson County Courthouse, and 1908 Main. Then it turned east passing through the entertainment district including Fourteenth Street.

Everywhere, crowds stood in silence. Whenever the hearse passed a Swing club, the band inside would either fall silent or play a slow-beat tribute. Eventually, the cortege arrived at Mount St. Mary's Cemetery at 23rd and Cleveland.

There was a brief graveside service. And when it was over, the gangsters queued to offer Dolores their condolences. Many kissed her on both cheeks. Some pressed envelopes into her hand. The D's were among them.

While this was going on, I noticed a family marker beside Johnny's grave. The name on it was, "Lazio." That was the name of the province where Rome was located. And I wondered if that meant Johnny's family wasn't Sicilian.

As Dolores, Gia, and I returned to the LaSalle, a quartet among the headstones began to play. And the husky voice of Julia Lee could be heard singing a downbeat version of *St. James Infirmary*. It was a song she, and her brother's orchestra, had recently recorded for the Brunswick label.

After the internment, the cortege returned to Holy Rosary Church for the traditional funeral lunch. We sat at long tables in the relative coolness of the church basement. Dolores removed her hat and veil; without them, she was painfully pale and wooden.

Those, who had not already done so, queued at this time to offer their condolences. There was a noticeable stiffness to many of these expressions of sympathy. And it seemed to me unlikely that the Italian-Sicilian community would ever accept Dolores as one of their own.

Following Father Moriarty's blessing, the women of the parish served up hearty bowls of bucatini and sugo. Baskets of crusty white bread also circulated. And men wearing the red-and-yellow sash of the *Unione Siciliana* poured out *russu* wine from unlabeled bottles.

Ostensibly a fraternal organization, the *Unione* was a secret society with mob ties. One could be a member of the mob and not join the *Unione,* but not the other way around. The bi-colored sash and rosette were the *Unione's* public symbols. The *trinacria* was its private one.

The word, *trinacria,* is Greek for "three-pointed." And when Sicily was given that name in ancient times, it referred to the island's triangular shape. But the trinacrian symbol predates the Greeks. It consists of three human legs running in a circle around the head of the Medusa, a gorgon with writhing snakes for hair. Her glance was said to turn men to stone.

Members of the *Unione* were required to have the trinacrian symbol tattooed somewhere on their bodies. And the *Unione's* initiation rites were said to include the burning of holy cards and blood oaths. One of the oaths was the *omerta*; another was the promise to kill anyone, who broke it.

As lunch progressed and the wine flowed, conversations around us grew more animated. They were conducted in a polyglot mixture of Italian, Sicilian, and English. There were even some outbursts of laughter, but not at our table. Glancing around, I noticed that the D's were not present.

As the dishes were collected, Balestrere, wearing a *Unione Siciliana* rosette, stood and raised his glass. "*In Bocca al Lupo*," he said. To which everyone responded, "*Crepi il Lupo.*"

Gia explained that the words of the toast meant, "Into the wolf's mouth," and the response was something like, "May the wolf die—by choking." It was sort of a joke meant to wish everyone good luck. After Balestrere sat down, Father Moriarty rose and gave the final blessing. Then the luncheon broke up.

It was around two when we returned to The Park Central. A patrol car was sitting across the street in the shade of an elm. There were two uniformed policemen inside, and they watched, as we entered the hotel.

When the elevator stopped at the Penthouse door, Dolores said, "I need to be alone now."

"Why don't you let Gia spend the night," I asked. But she shook her head. "Then how about lunch tomorrow? It's Saturday, and I'm off at noon."

Dolores reluctantly agreed. Brushing my cheek with her lips, she turned and hugged Gia. Then she stepped inside. After giving us a final wave through the small window in the Penthouse door, she was gone.

I pushed the lobby button. The elevator lurched and began grinding down. Alone together, Gia and I were suddenly self-conscious.

"Sorry—about your brother," I said lamely.

"He knew what he was doing."

"Yeah, but . . .."

"'*Cui mali accumensa, peju finisci,*'" she said. "'A bad beginning makes a bad ending.' That's all there is to it."

"But he was your brother," I protested.

We'd come to the bottom. But the elevator doors hadn't opened yet. Gia reached out and flicked the switch to "stop."

"Quit being such a sap," she said.

Reaching up, Gia took my face in both hands and ground her lips against mine. I pulled her to me in a tight embrace. Ten minutes later, we came up for air. After fixing her makeup, Gia snapped her compact shut. Pulling out my pocket square, she wiped the lipstick from my face.

Then giving me a saucy wink, Gia flipped the switch to "on." When the doors opened, she strode out of the elevator without giving me a second look. She crossed the lobby with her hips swaying. And I couldn't help following her with my eyes.

Then I noticed the concierge and doorman. Not surprisingly, they were watching Gia too. When I caught them looking at her, they quickly glanced away. And that's when I felt a twinge of guilt.

Though unrequited, my feelings for Audrey were as strong as ever. But I was as red-blooded as the next guy, and Gia was a desirable woman. So, what's a guy to do?

17

JULY 14, 1934

Despite the leisurely flow of Saturday traffic, I made it to The Park Central by half-past twelve. The patrol car was still out front. I parked my Model-A sedan at the curb and went inside.

The concierge said he didn't think Dolores's phone was working. But he was pretty sure she was in. I told him she was expecting me, so he used his key to send me up. When I reached the top, though, the Penthouse door was unlatched. I stepped into the entry and noticed that the phone was off its cradle.

"Dolores?"

No answer.

Walking into the living room, I said louder, "Dolores? It's me, Sam."

I heard muffled voices and walked toward the sound. Down a short hallway, another door was ajar. I rapped lightly on it. Getting no response, I pushed it open. As if on cue, organ music surged from a Philco console radio to my left. A pitch for Fels-Naptha Soap followed. I switched off the set.

I was in the master bedroom. Sunlight filtered through sheer curtains on two east-facing windows. Another pair of windows faced north. Through the open sashes, I could hear the mummer of traffic on Gillham ten floors below.

Turning around, I quickly walked through the rest of the Penthouse. There were three bedrooms, including the master, two bathrooms, a study, and a kitchen, not to mention the living room and entry. There was no sign of Dolores.

Back in the living room, I opened a set of French doors and walked out onto the rooftop patio. The pool glittered in the sunlight. But no Dolores.

Going back inside, I started to get miffed. Where was she? She knew we were going to lunch. Then I thought of the concierge and patrol car out front. They both thought Dolores was here, but if she wasn't . . .?

My first thought was that Johnny's killers had snatched her. But there were no signs of a struggle, and Dolores wouldn't have gone quietly. Besides, how would they have gotten past the locked elevator door?

Of course, they could have been someone Dolores knew, and she might have let them in. But even so, how could they have walked her out again without either the hotel staff or the police knowing?

So, I decided to take another look around. I returned to the master bedroom and started with Dolores's closet. There were empty hangers among the summer dresses, more among the slacks, and two gaps in a line of shoes. A purse was missing from the top shelf.

I turned to the chest of drawers. But when I opened it, there were so many clothes I couldn't tell if anything was missing. Moving on, I opened the drawer of Dolores's nightstand. There was a sleeping mask in it, earplugs, and a brown bottle of pills. The pills were a prescription for Luminal dated six months earlier. It looked like Dolores had been having trouble sleeping.

On the nightstand was Gide's *Lafcadio's Adventures.* It was bookmarked at the passage where the main character, Lafcadio, pushes a stranger to his death from a speeding train—just because he can. Gide's admirers had hailed this episode as a gratuitously free act—because Lafcadio had not been restrained by any moral compunction.

Dolores had made a note in the margin. It was a quote from *The Brothers Karamazov*: "Without God, everything is permitted." I didn't like it. And I put the book back where I'd found it.

Contemplating my next move, I decided to give Johnny's dresser and nightstand a pass. I wanted to stay focused on Dolores. But I couldn't help myself when I came to his closet.

It was a walk-in. In it were suits in every shade of navy, brown, and grey. And there were rows of monogrammed shirts to go with them. As for ties, his collection rivaled the display rack at Woolf Brothers. I wondered how the guy had gotten dressed in the morning, with so many decisions to make.

One thing about Lazia's closet bothered me. A shoulder holster hung from a peg inside the door. It was small and flat, just the size for a thirty-two automatic. But it was empty.

Next, I turned to the bathroom off the master bedroom. Its medicine cabinet had four shelves. Only two of them were occupied, and those contained men's toiletries.

I wandered through the remaining bedrooms, second bath, and kitchen. Everything in them seemed to be, as it should be. The beds were made. The second bath was spotless, and the kitchen looked like it had never been used.

The last room was the study. It contained a mahogany desk suite. Above the credenza was a framed photo of a turn-of-the-century racehorse named "Climax." It had a garland around its neck. Across the bottom of the print was scrawled: "To My Best Friend, Johnny. How It All Began —T. J."

The picture was a reminder that another Pendergast had been a political force in Kansas City. During the early years of the Twentieth Century, Boss Tom's older brother, Jim, had dominated the city's First Ward with his fists and geniality. It was Big Jim who'd taught Tom the niceties of machine politics.

Tom's older brother had owned a string of East Bottom saloons. And it was said, he'd bought his first one with winnings from a lucky bet on the horses. If that was true, then the photo was probably a shot of the speedy nag.

I had a feeling something was behind the picture. And sure enough, when I looked, I found a wall safe. Thinking I might get lucky too, I tugged at the handle—but no dice.

Needing a cigarette, I strolled back into the living room. Taking one from a silver box on the coffee table, I tamped it on my thumbnail. Then I lit the cigarette with a table lighter.

As I smoked, I thought about the results of my search. It looked like Dolores had gone off on her own. The missing clothes and toiletries were proof of that. But how had she slipped away without the police and hotel staff noticing?

I heard the elevator startup. So, I strolled into the entry to see who it was. Maybe, it was Dolores. She might have been visiting someone in the hotel. But I didn't think so. And proving me right, when the elevator arrived, Thurman and Hart stepped out of it.

Thurman said, "We'd like to talk to Mrs. Lazia."

"So would I."

His brow wrinkled. "The man downstairs told us she was here."

"That's what he told me too. But she isn't."

"How'd you get in then?"

"The door was open."

"Mind if we look around?" asked Thurman stepping forward.

"Since I don't live here, that's not for me to say."

He stopped and frowned. "We can always get a warrant."

I didn't say anything.

Thurman snorted, "Okay, wise guy." He poked a finger into my chest and looked me in the eye. "Just so you know, I have a long memory, Bub."

It wasn't an idle threat. Still, I didn't say anything. The two of them turned and got back on the elevator. I could see Thurman's cold eyes staring at me through the little window until they dropped out of sight.

I knew I was making trouble for myself. But there was something I wanted to check out before the cops started poking around. I walked back into the master bedroom and drew the curtains from the north-facing windows.

Sure enough, the sash on one of them was up, and the hook on the screen was unlatched. When I pushed the screen open, I could see a metal ladder bolted to the bricks two feet to the left of the window. It ran down to the fire escape on the floor below.

Dolores had been smart. And she'd been gutsy too. Sometime in the night, she'd climbed down this ladder and then down the fire escape without anyone seeing her. And she'd probably carried a suitcase with her too.

I wondered if I could do it in broad daylight—without a

suitcase. So of course, I had to give it a try. It was a dumb idea.

Crouching on the windowsill, I ducked under the screen and gripped the ladder. Stretching out my right leg, I placed a foot on a rung. Then I tried to swing myself over to the ladder. As I did—my foot slipped. Damn leather soles! I dangled there suspended by my left hand. My eyes locked on the ground ten floors below.

That was when the urge hit me. It was as involuntary and irresistible as bile rising in your throat. And even though there were no words, I could read their meaning. *Let go.* It demanded. *Let go!*

I should have grabbed the ladder with my free hand. But I didn't. Instead, I tried to resist by tightening my grip.

The urge responded with a pulsing vision. Images of the car wreck and boardinghouse fire rocked me. And I saw other things—confusing things—from the day of Midge's death.

Then for some reason, I just let go.

As I fell, a hand snatched my wrist. "Gotcha!" a voice said. And the urge vanished.

Glancing upward, along the arm from which I dangled, I could see Thurman's flat face looking down at me. He was leaning over the edge of the roof. Hart was planted behind him, holding onto his belt, leaning back to counterbalance our combined weight.

"Look what I've caught, Lew," Thurman chuckled.

"Big one, Floyd."

"Shall we throw him back?" the detective teased giving me a shake.

"Naw—think he's a keeper," said Lew playing along.

With that, Thurman swung me over to the ladder. And I got both hands and feet onto it.

"Where'd you come from?" I gasped.

"Can't get rid of us that easily," Thurman said the steely look coming back into his eyes. Then squinting at me, he asked, "What was going on just now?"

I fumbled for an explanation. "I was trying to figure out how Dolores left—without anyone knowing."

"Yeah?" he said.

"When I tried to swing over from the window to the ladder—I slipped."

"Good thing we doubled back," he said. But I could see he hadn't bought it.

"Okay, if we look around now?" he smirked.

"Be my guest," I said still clinging to the ladder while I recovered.

Hart hauled his partner back onto the roof. When he got there, Thurman looked down at me and asked, "Are you going up or down?"

"Down—I think."

"Well, don't try winging it again," he chuckled, "You're no Lindbergh."

I smiled wanly, and he disappeared.

After a few minutes, I began my shaky descent. Reaching the fire escape, I paused to catch my breath. As I stood there, I tried to recall the memories that had come to me before I'd let go. But they were gone.

And I vaguely remembered something similar happening before the boardinghouse fire and car accident. But that was all there was. So, I turned and trudged down the fire escape.

There was a drop ladder at the bottom. It sank under my weight but still ended ten feet off the ground. Working my way down to the bottom rung, I hung there for a moment, then let go.

I watched the creaking ladder swing back up out of reach as I knocked the rust off my palms. Then I gazed up at the window I'd climbed out of. Crossing myself, I said a *Te Deum* in thanksgiving.

Entering the back door of the Park Central, I crossed the lobby and went out the front. The Hot Shot was parked in the circle drive. Two police cars were now under the shade of the elm across the street. I got into my sedan and drove home. One of the patrol cars followed me. It parked across the street from my house.

18

JULY 23, 1935

The remainder of 1934 whirled away like the rows of fruit on a slot machine. During that time, Mac and I put together a plan for the 1936 Election. We realized that, if we were going to get everything done, we would have to divvy up our tasks. So, Mac chose to focus on how the machine rigged elections. While I would search for some expert witnesses to explain our yet-to-be-determined evidence to the jury.

And of course, after work in the evenings, I continued to plug away on Midge's case. But it wasn't going well. Not only were both Nash and Anthon dead, but I soon learned that Nuggie LaPalma had also bought it. Someone had stuffed him, still alive, into a burning incinerator.

Carrollo's boys were the most likely culprits. They were working overtime knocking off any members of Lusco's gang they could find. Publicly, Carrollo had pinned the blame for Johnny's death on Lusco. But the smart money figured he was just using that as an excuse for whittling down the competition.

With LaPalma gone, there were now only six suspects on

my list. They were Gregory, Denning, Keeling, Limerick, Pabst, and Weissman. Of the six, the only one I was likely to get a shot at interviewing was Gregory. The KCPD wasn't going to be protecting him, since he was one of Lusco's boys. But that also meant he might not live long enough for me to talk to him.

As far as Denning, the rumor was that he'd gone back to Nebraska to work with a local gang up there. So, I'd sent the Omaha PD his name along with the three others: Keeling, Limerick, and Pabst. And I'd asked them to give me a call if they took any of the four into custody. Who knew if they would?

Weissman was the only one of the six I'd drawn a complete blank on. As I've said, he was one of Johnny's boys, but he hadn't been seen in a while. Did that mean he was really gone or just hiding out here in town? It was anybody's guess.

In early January, my parents received a postcard from Dolores. It had been mailed from San Francisco. In it, Sis said that she was fine and not to worry. However, I didn't buy it. I suspected Dolores was still somewhere close to home, but I didn't know where. She'd disappeared, so she wouldn't have to answer any more questions about Johnny's murder. And that meant, she knew more than she'd been willing to say. But I'd have to wait to get my answers until she turned up again.

In March 1935, Roosevelt signed a bill reorganizing the Department of Justice. He merged the Bureau of Investigation with the now obsolete Bureau of Prohibition. To avoid confusion, he'd given the new entity a different name. He'd called it the Federal Bureau of Investigation. One advantage of this merger was that it had added some seasoned lawmen with experience fighting bootleggers to the Bureau's roster.

But the jury was still out on whether the new FBI could do any better than the old Bureau had at locating Miller's accomplices at Union Station.

According to Mac, there had been no new developments in the case for some time. Not surprisingly, the press had turned up the heat, and Hoover was itching to get it resolved. He was now fixed on Pretty Boy Floyd and Adam Richetti as the likely culprits. But so far, the FBI hadn't been able to dig up enough evidence to prove they'd done it.

July 10 marked the first anniversary of Johnny Lazia's death. And it was clear that the KCPD had washed their hands of the case. For whatever reason, they were leaving it up to Carrollo and his boys to settle the score—however, they wanted.

Ten days later, Hoover elevated Maurice "Blondie" Denning to the status of Public Enemy Number One. And I had another famous criminal on my suspect list. But it only made me worry that Denning's new notoriety might mean that he wasn't long for this world. And I worried that, if all my suspects kept getting bumped off before I had a chance to question them, I would never solve Midge's murder.

On Monday morning, July 23, 1935, I was sitting at my desk researching the leading members of the Reform movement.

Mac stuck his head around the corner and shouted, "Come on!"

"What?"

"Got a break in the Union Station case!"

And without another word, he took off down the hall. Grabbing my hat and coat, I dashed after him. Ginny looked up wide-eyed, as we ran through reception.

Pausing at the door, I said, "Tell the Chief, I'll be out the rest of the day."

She nodded, as I charged after Mac still trying to get my coat on. The elevator was too slow, so we took the stairs two at a time. Mac's Desoto was double-parked in front of the courthouse. We hopped in, and soon we were heading south.

Mac talked as he drove. "Heard of Needles LaCapra?"

"He's one of Joe Lusco's boys, isn't he," I said.

LaCapra had nearly made my suspect list. He fit the age and description of one of Midge's killers. But I'd rejected him because, despite his long rap sheet, he'd never been accused of robbing a bank.

"That's right," replied Mac. "Though looking at him, you'd never know LaCapra was a tough guy. Pudgy with wavy brown hair," he shook his head.

I nodded just to keep Mac talking.

"Runs small-time prize fights, con games, and sells dope. Why they call him 'Needles.'"

"Uh-huh," I answered. I was having trouble concentrating on what Mac was saying. He was tearing through traffic like we were on fire. He swerved through the intersection at 12th Street against the light. And I had to place one hand on the dash and the other on the door just to stay in my seat.

Of course, Mac's three-window coupe didn't have a red light or a siren. But that didn't keep him from driving as if it did. And all the while, he kept on talking.

Raising his voice above the din of protesting horns, Mac said, "Looks like Carrollo thinks LaCapra was part of the Lazia clip."

"Oh, yeah?" I said.

"Yeah. Remember last summer when Carrollo's boys jumped LaCapra on Independence Avenue?"

"Uh-huh."

"At the time, we thought it was just more turf war—like the Anthon shooting. But now, we think it was because Carrollo had pegged LaCapra as one of Johnny's killers."

"No kidding."

My eyes widened, but not because of Mac's story. We were rapidly approaching a stalled cement truck. The oncoming lane was full, and it looked like we were going to rear-end the Ready-Mix. I braced myself for the impact

But then Mac slowed down, mounted the sidewalk, and scattered a crowd of pedestrians. As soon as he was past the cement truck, he veered back into the street. I exhaled in relief at our own near-miss and that we hadn't flattened anyone.

Mac went on talking as if nothing had happened. "Of course, Carrollo's boys didn't get LaCapra. Even though, they shot up Independence Avenue plenty. And Needles split town. But no one knew where he'd gone. Still, you know Carrollo. He never stopped looking."

We zipped through a red light at Union Station and sped up Main past Liberty Memorial and St. Mary's Hospital. But at 39th Street, we hit another jam. Here, Mac's solution was to hammer on his horn, while swerving into the on-coming traffic. The cars scattered before us like cockroaches when you turn on the light.

Somehow, we made it. And soon, we were ripping down the hill toward Brush Creek; the Plaza shops were off to our right. Crossing the creek, we took the curves of Brookside at speed. Here, Mac steered with his knees while he lit a cigarette. Once it was going, he resumed his story.

"Know Jack Gregory?" he asked.

"Nope," I said, even though Gregory was on my suspect list. I wanted to hear what Mac had to say about him.

"Gregory, or Griffins, take your pick," said Mac. "He goes by both. Gregory's LaCapra's pal. And Carrollo must think he was the second triggerman."

"Something happen to Gregory?"

"Yep. A couple of days ago, three guys jumped him outside the Buckingham Hotel."

"How'd that go?"

Mac snickered and shook his head, "More lousy shooting. Three of them let loose, but they only hit Gregory once. And that was in the leg."

We'd reached the shops in Brookside. And once again, traffic came to a crawl. Naturally, Mac jumped the snarl by taking to the opposite lane again. And after a near-miss, we were through it.

Reaching Meyer, Mac rolled through the stop sign and went right. And at Ward Parkway, we took the eighty-foot-wide traffic circle, with the seahorse fountain in the center, skittering on two wheels. Swerving down 63rd Terrace, we headed toward State Line. There we turned south again.

It wasn't long before the city limits were behind us. And we were cruising at speed past open fields and newly platted subdivisions. Mac then worked his way west until we linked up with Kansas Highway 10.

Mac told me our destination was Wellington, Kansas. And I located it on the road map. It's about two hundred and fifty miles southwest of Kansas City, and not far from the Oklahoma border. Mac told me the route he wanted to take, and soon, we were roaring south on U.S. 73E. Once again, Mac resumed his story taking up where he'd left off.

"The folks at the Buckingham Hotel heard the shooting

and came running. They scared the gunmen off, and somebody called an ambulance. It took Gregory to the hospital."

"Lucky for him," I said. And for me, I thought. I might get a chance to interview him yet.

"You'd think. But after they'd dug out the bullet and put a cast on his leg, Rayen and Claiborne showed up. Rayen flashed a warrant and took Gregory into custody."

"On what charge?" I asked.

Mac snorted, "Witness to a shooting."

We both cackled at that.

We hit a flat stretch of the highway, and I held on as Mac put his foot to the floor. The coupe's six-banger screamed as we barreled and bounced down the two-lane road. We blew past a creeping grain truck and climbed a ridge. After that, we hit a series of hills swooping up and down like we were on a roller coaster. It made me queasy. Finally, we hit a series of S-curves, which slowed us down enough for Mac to talk.

"So, where's Gregory now?" I asked.

"Dead for sure—probably with an ice pick in his brain. I'm betting his remains are either at the bottom of the Missouri River, or he's laid out in that new cement lining Brush Creek."

Damn it, I thought. Wasn't I ever going to get to question any of my suspects? Because of my frustration, I lost patience with Mac.

"Okay," I said. "Can you just spit it out? Why are we going to Wellington anyway?"

"Keep your shirt on," growled Mac, "It takes some telling."

Shaking my head in disgust, I shook out a cigarette, lit it, and tossed the match out the window.

"Like I said," repeated Mac. "Since LaCapra blew town, he's been outta sight."

But because he wasn't giving his full attention to the road, Mac took the next curve way too fast. At first, we just skittered sideways on some gravel. But then we hit something slick and spun out of control. Somehow, after a lot of hard braking, swearing, and wheel twisting, Mac brought the car to a stop—right on the edge of a steep shoulder.

We sat for a moment in silence. Then after crossing myself, I flicked my mashed cigarette out of the window and brushed the still glowing embers off my lap. Mac quietly put the coupe into gear and steered us sedately back onto the road.

Eventually, Mac resumed his story. This time he cut to the chase. "Got a call this morning," he said. "Three of Charlie's bozos tried to bump off Needles last night."

"Where?" I asked.

"A spot in the road near Wichita—called Argonia. Where Needles grew up."

"What happened?"

"LaCapra was out for a joyride with a couple of skirts. Sedan pulled around him like it was going to pass. But instead, the guys inside start throwing lead." Mac grinned then said, "And if you can believe it, the palookas missed—again. Carrollo needs to give his boys some target practice."

"So, LaCapra got away?"

"He did. But the funny part is, the dopes doing the shooting didn't. They ran their car off the road and wrecked it." He snickered.

That wasn't so funny to me after our near miss. But I just nodded and asked, "So, what'd LaCapra do?"

"Last thing you'd expect. He made a beeline to the Kansas Highway Patrol. Told them what happened. And

Bingo! The Patrol catches the three chuckleheads hoofing it along the highway."

I snorted.

"Yeah," he replied. "And the goofs must have mouthed off or something. Cause the troopers roughed them up, plenty."

"Nice."

He nodded. "The Patrol didn't care much for LaCapra either. Told him to scram." At this point, Mac shot me a look.

"What?" I asked, unable to read it.

"LaCapra's so scared, you see, he doesn't want to leave the Patrol's office. And he starts begging for, get this, police protection."

"Go on!"

"Honest to God. The troopers tell him, 'No dice,' unless he gives them something juicy. So, LaCapra starts spilling."

"About what?"

"Says he knows the whole scoop on Union Station. Who the shooters were and the skinny on how it went down."

"For sure?"

"Yep," nodded Mac smugly. "Kansas Patrol called the Bureau. Vetterli tells me to get my rear-end down to Wellington and pronto."

He grinned, "Course, I ask if I can take a certain worthless Assistant U.S.D.A. with me. And you know the rest."

"Think LaCapra's on the up-and-up?"

"Beats me—but we'll soon find out," he answered.

HIGHWAY 73E SHIMMERED in the mounting heat, and it wasn't long before we'd shed our coats and ties. The windows and wings were wide open. But it still felt like we were sitting in front of a bonfire. By mid-afternoon, we'd sweated through our shirts. And it was too hot even to smoke.

When we stopped for gas, we kept the engine running fearing vapor lock. The uniformed attendant carefully loosened the radiator cap with a shop rag—to prevent the boiling water from spewing out and scalding him. Then he topped it up. As he worked, we stood in the shade guzzling sodas watching as he pulled the dipstick, checked the tires, and scrubbed at the bug splatters on the windshield.

We were in Dust Bowl country now. The edge of the horizon had a brownish tint to it, and powdery silt lay in drifts against the south sides of buildings. Foreclosure notices were tacked to the front doors of most farmhouses we passed. They fluttered like yellow leaves in the hot wind.

The few people we saw were on the move. Occasionally, we overtook a sputtering sedan laden with furniture, roped-on bedding, and pans. The pale faces inside stared blankly at us as we swept by. No one waved.

One stretch of U.S. 54 South ran parallel to some train tracks. In mid-afternoon, a highballing Missouri Pacific freight overtook us. The long black-and-silver locomotive trailed a plume of coal smoke. Its linked wheels were nothing more than whirling blurs.

An engineer crouched in the window of the locomotive. His eyes fixed on the track ahead. Beside him, two glistening firemen labored rhythmically to stoke the boiler. Clusters of bums rode on the rolling stock that followed. They lounged in the doorways of empty boxcars or perched on the railed tops of tankers. They stared at us, and we stared back.

The train, traveling a good twenty miles-per-hour faster than we were, slowly pulled ahead. Eventually, all we could see of it was the caboose. And it got smaller and smaller—until it vanished in the distance.

As always, Mac ignored the speed limit, and we made good time. It was late afternoon when we rolled into Eldorado. And after dinner, we skirted Wichita. Around eight, we passed a sign that said Wellington was only five miles ahead.

When we arrived, a trooper led us to an interview room. It had three chairs and a table. It wasn't long before a sweaty Needles LaCapra came through the door. His eyes were bloodshot, and his hands trembled.

We introduced ourselves and told him that we'd heard he had some information on the Union Station Massacre. Needles began talking even before Mac was finished. The story poured out of him like dried beans from a ripped one-hundred-pound bag.

Needles was too keyed-up for questioning. So, we just let him run with his story. Mac took notes for a written statement, while I jotted down questions for follow-up. The following is the gist of what LaCapra had to say.

> Pretty Boy Floyd and Adam Richetti were on the lam, and they came to Kansas City looking to hide out. When they arrived, they contacted Dominic Binaggio, who agreed to help them for a price. Binaggio then called Johnny Lazia and got the okay for Floyd and Richetti to hide out in town. Then Binaggio set them up in the West Bottoms.
>
> Later that afternoon, Vern Miller called on Lazia. He told the mob boss his pal, Jelly Nash, had been arrested in Hot Springs, Arkansas. And that Nash, in the custody of four lawmen, would be passing through Union Station early the next morning. Miller wanted help in freeing Nash, and he asked for the loan of a couple of Lazia's boys.

> But the mob boss declined instead suggesting that Miller contact Floyd and Richetti.
>
> When Miller did, Floyd and Richetti agreed to help him, and the three of them put together a plan. Both Miller and Floyd would carry Tommy guns. Since Floyd already had one of his own, Miller would borrow one from Lazia. They thought that the sight of two Tommy guns would scare Jelly's escort enough that there wouldn't be any shooting. Then after disarming the lawmen, the three of them would free Nash and make their getaway.
>
> The next morning, Miller, Floyd, and Richetti succeeded as planned in getting the drop on Jelly's escort. But then, somebody fired a shotgun, and all hell broke loose. When it was over, Nash and four lawmen were dead. And Floyd had been wounded in the shoulder.
>
> That evening, Miller met with Lazia to apologize for what had happened. But Lazia had been understanding. He had told Miller that "it couldn't be helped." After that, Miller had skipped town. And Lazia had arranged for Floyd and Richetti to get away too.

When LaCapra finally quit talking, I tried to question him. "So, you were at the meeting with Miller and Lazia?"

"No, I wasn't."

"Then how come you know so much about it?" I asked.

"My brother-in-law, Sam Scola was. He told me all about it."

I remembered Scola. He was one of the two men Sheriff Bash had blown away on the night Ferris Anthon was murdered.

Seeing by my expression that Scola wasn't going to cut it, LaCapra quickly said, "Look, I had the same story from Lazia himself. And others can tell you the same."

Of course, Lazia was dead too. "Who else, besides Lazia and Scola?" I asked.

"Wilhite, Speedy Wilhite," Needles said.

"A buddy of yours?" asked Mac.

"Yeah, he'll tell you, just ask him," said LaCapra.

"Still in the Iowa State Pen?" asked Mac.

LaCapra nodded vigorously. Mac made a note.

I switched gears. "You one of the guys who knocked off Lazia?"

LaCapra jumped like he'd stuck a finger in a light socket. "I had nothing to do with that, I swear."

"Some think you did," I said.

"Well, they're dead wrong, I'm telling you."

"If it wasn't you, then who?" I asked.

Raising his hands, Needles replied, "I don't know nothing about that," he whined.

I was inclined to believe him.

The door to the interrogation room swung open, and a man by the name of Marcum joined us. He was the local prosecutor. I got up and gave him my chair.

Marcum said to LaCapra, "Got a guy outside. Wants me to hand you over to him."

"What guy?" LaCapra asked his eyes getting wide.

"Kansas City Police dick by the name of Jeff Rayen."

LaCapra started whimpering, "If you do, I'm a dead man!"

"Well, he's got a warrant," said Marcum coolly. "Looks all right to me. Old drug charge, but still good."

Appealing to Mac and me, LaCapra said, "You got to help me. What else do you want to know?"

Marcum got up and motioned for us to join him in the hall. We left LaCapra jiggling a leg and running his fingers through his greasy hair. After closing the door, Marcum spoke in a low voice.

"Frankly, I don't care much for this Rayen character. Know anything about him?"

"Too much," said Mac.

"Thought so," nodded Marcum. "I can release LaCapra to you if you want. You were here first."

"Sounds good," said Mac.

Marcum went down the hall and through a door. Shortly afterward, we could hear raised voices. Someone snarled, "And I'm telling you, he's committed crimes against the organization in Kansas City. And you'd better hand him over!"

I would have known that voice anywhere.

We couldn't make out Marcum's response. But the cursing and slammed door that followed told us everything we needed to know. After a bit, Marcum returned.

"That Rayen character is definitely no good. And there's another detective with him, who isn't any better. Still want LaCapra?"

"You bet," said Mac, "Let's do the paperwork."

The next morning, just to poke a finger into the eye of the KC "organization," a Kansas Highway Patrol car, with LaCapra onboard, followed us to the Missouri state line. A fuming Rayen and his wheelman, Claiborne, stuck to us the entire way.

As prearranged, Sheriff Tom Bash met us at the border. And he took LaCapra into custody. Needles would be safe in Independence with the Sheriff's deputies watching over him. He wouldn't have stood a chance downtown.

Mac and I dissected Needles' story during the drive back to KC. But we had come to different conclusions. I hadn't bought it. It seemed too pat to me. Not that I'm saying

Needles had made it up himself. No, he wasn't smart enough for that. But I suspected somebody had fed him a line. Who and why was the question?

Mac, on the other hand, had swallowed it hook-line-and-sinker. And he couldn't wait to get back to KC to forward a copy of Needles' statement to Hoover. It was, of course, just what J. Edgar had been looking for. And we both knew that it would shift the hunt for Pretty Boy Floyd and Adam Richetti into high gear.

19

AUGUST 1, 1935

It was Wednesday morning, August 1, 1935. Even though the 1936 Election was over a year away, our plans were already falling into place. That said, we still needed Milligan's approval on several parts of it. I was working on drafting those sections when my intercom buzzed.

"The Chief would like you to come to the conference room, Sam," said Ginny. And I wondered what he wanted.

When I got there, I saw that Milligan wasn't alone. A polished guy in his mid-forties was with him. This turned out to be Special Treasury Agent Rudolph Hartmann. Cleft-chinned and T-shaped, Hartmann fit the public persona of a G-man.

After introductions, we sat across from each other at the table with Milligan at the head.

"Mr. Hartmann, tell Sam what you've told me," said the Chief.

"Call me Rudy, please," said Hartmann. Turning to me, he said, "Bear with me, Sam, there's a bit of background."

Hartmann began by explaining that in 1930 the fire

insurance companies operating in Missouri collectively proposed a seventeen percent rate increase. And the Missouri Insurance Commissioner, by his authority under the state constitution, had rejected it as too high. Following this denial, all one hundred and thirty-seven insurance companies had sued the state.

At the outset of this litigation, the plaintiffs had sought and obtained an injunction that prevented the Insurance Commissioner from interfering with their collection of the rate increase. While the court granted the injunction, it ordered that the disputed funds be held in escrow until the matter was resolved.

The fire insurance companies quickly realized that the state wasn't going to back down. Wanting to avoid the expense of protracted litigation and the creation of an unhelpful precedent, they'd decided to try and settle the matter. By this time, the amount in escrow had grown to over nine million dollars.

"Sounds like the insurance companies didn't do their homework before filing suit," I said. "Didn't they anticipate that the state would reject such a large rate increase in hard times like these?"

"You'd think so," said Rudy. "Of course, there are some who believe that it was intentional. It may not be widely known, but litigation settlements have been used in the past to cover for bribery."

"Really?" I said, starting to get interested.

Rudy resumed his narrative. The fire insurance companies tapped Charles R. Street to chair the committee charged with negotiating a settlement. Street was a Vice President of the Great American Insurance Company of New York.

The committee worked with private counsel, Robert

Folonie, to put together a proposal. They came up with a draft that met the approval of the companies. Street and Folonie then presented it to the Missouri Insurance Commissioner and the state's attorneys. The proposed settlement divided the escrowed funds into three parts. Fifty percent would be paid to the companies. Twenty percent would be returned to the policyholders. And the remaining thirty percent would be placed in a trust fund to cover all the party's attorneys' fees and expenses. The proposal also designated that Street and Folonie would be appointed trustees of this trust fund.

Further, the proposed settlement stipulated that, once the party's attorneys' fees and expenses had been paid, any money remaining in the trust fund would be divided equally among the fire insurance companies. The Governor and the State Attorney General signed off on the proposed settlement. And the agreement was submitted to the trial court for approval.

"That's a pretty sweet deal for the companies," I observed. "Fifty percent of the premium plus whatever was left over after fees and expenses."

Hartmann nodded in agreement. "Now, it starts to get interesting."

And he resumed his story. Without telling anyone and before submitting the settlement agreement to the trial court for approval, Street inserted some language of his own into the proposed settlement. This new language stated that no accounting would be required for the thirty-percent trust fund.

The judge approved the settlement agreement, but not as written. He added a phrase of his own to the language Street had inserted. This new wording specified that no accounting would be required for the thirty-percent trust fund, "unless the court desired it."

"The only reason I can think of for not requiring an accounting of a trust fund is that you're hoping to hide something," I said.

"That's probably what the judge thought as well," said Milligan.

Hartmann nodded and resumed his narrative. Once the settlement was approved by the court, the money was paid out. And it was then that the division of funds became public knowledge. Not surprisingly, there was an immediate outcry.

No one could believe that, even though the state had been squarely within its rights to reject the entire premium increase, only twenty percent of the disputed money had been returned to the policyholders. Further, it was widely rumored that some of the escrowed money had been siphoned off as a bribe.

"So, is that when Treasury got involved?" I asked.

"No, that didn't happen until later and quite by accident," said Hartmann.

He went on to explain that shortly after the settlement had been paid out, one of Folonie's law partners had suddenly died. The law firm's finances were so complicated that the partnership had asked Treasury to assist them in calculating the deceased partner's taxes. And when the assigned agent examined the firm's books, he'd noticed a curious transaction.

The firm had received a sum of $100,500 on one day and had immediately paid it out on the next. No explanation was given in the records for the purpose of this transaction. And when asked about it, Folonie had simply said that the sum was "not taxable income" to the law firm.

Not satisfied with this response, the agent had asked to see the transaction's underlying documentation. When it was shown to him, he discovered that the $100,500 had come from fourteen separate checks, each of which had been received from a different fire insurance company. But the money had been paid out in a single check made payable to Charles R. Street.

When the agent had again asked Folonie about this transaction, he had invoked the attorney-client privilege. The agent then tried to arrange a meeting with Charles R. Street to discuss this transaction. When this failed, Treasury had assigned Hartmann to investigate the matter. Eventually, Rudy had succeeded in scheduling a meeting with Street, which was set for later that day in our offices.

"Other than providing you with a conference room for your meeting, is there anything else we can do?" asked Milligan.

"Yes," answered Hartmann. "I would like for one of your people to join us. If things turn out as I suspect, you'll want to be in at the beginning."

Milligan nodded and looked across the table at me.

"Sure thing," I said.

That afternoon, Hartmann and I were back in the conference room. Across from us sat Charles R. Street and his counsel, Robert Folonie. Audrey was also there to take notes.

Street was a man whose age was hard to read. He might have been fifty or seventy. At six feet two, with a thick head of white hair and a pencil mustache, he had that sinewy weathered look usually indicative of a dedicated tennis player or yachtsman.

Street wore a slate-gray double-breasted suit with a crimson-and-navy regimental tie. On the third finger of his right hand was a heavy university ring. And his French cuffs were fastened with monogrammed gold medallions.

Folonie wasn't as photogenic as his client. His pear-shaped frame was topped by a shiny bald head. And his expression was so dour, I was certain his motto must be: "Expect the worst, and you'll never be disappointed."

We talked baseball while getting a measure of each other. Folonie was from Chicago and feeling guardedly optimistic about the Cubs. But they weren't doing nearly as well as the St. Louis Cardinals, who were pegged to take the National League pennant. The real question was whom the Cardinals would face in the World Series? Would it be the Detroit Tigers or the New York Yankees? Hailing from Manhattan, Street was all-in for his hometown team.

Gradually, we got down to business. Hartmann walked Street through the details of the $100,500 transaction. Throughout, Street sat politely listening his hands clasped in front of him.

Gesturing toward Folonie, Hartmann said, "Your counsel tells us that this money was not taxable income to his law firm."

"That's correct," said Street. "And I am willing to provide you with an affidavit to that effect."

Our visitors had clearly prepared for our meeting. And Folonie slid a document across the table toward Hartmann. The latter picked it up, read it, and passed it to me. The affidavit was already signed, dated, and notarized.

At this point, Street pushed back from the table and started to rise. He thought our meeting was at an end. But he paused in mid-air when Hartmann asked his next question.

"So, why did the fire insurance companies pay you this money, Mr. Street?"

Our guests' surprise was evident. They thought, not without good reason, that all we were interested in was resolving the status of Folonie's deceased partner's estate. But Hartmann's question had raised the specter of a broader, more unwelcome inquiry.

Without answering, Street sat back down and turned to his lawyer. The two of them conducted a whispered conversation behind shielding hands. When they finished, Street turned and smiled disarmingly at us. He said with a chuckle, "To be perfectly honest, I'd rather not say."

But Street's demeanor was communicating something different than his words. It was as if he were saying, "Come now, boys. We don't want to get into *that* do we?"

But Hartmann wasn't going to be fobbed off. "Okay," he said. "Then let me ask you another question. Was the $100,500 you received taxable income to you?"

Street repeated himself—this time without the smile. "I'd rather not say."

"You do realize, Mr. Street, that we can ask you these questions under oath?"

"Of course," he said flatly.

"And?" asked Hartmann.

Street swallowed and answered, "Then I will have to exercise my rights under the Fifth Amendment." Folonie stared directly at us and lifted his chin in approval at his client's response. And it looked as if we were at an impasse.

But then, as so often happens during the early stages of an interview, things took an unexpected turn. Street's demeanor suddenly softened. And his features took on an almost apologetic look.

Glancing at Audrey, Street asked, "Could we talk, uh, . . . more informally?" Folonie glanced at his client in surprise.

It looked like Street was off-script, and another whispered conversation took place.

While this was going on, Hartmann excused Audrey with a wink. She smiled and left the room. When she was gone, he looked over at Street, who had finished his conversation with Folonie. The lawyer's face was furrowed, and he sat with his arms tightly crossed staring straight ahead.

"Was there something you wanted to say, Mr. Street?" asked Hartmann.

Street cleared his throat, "Hypothetically speaking, what if, the money was income to me?"

"Then you'd be expected to pay taxes on it," Hartmann answered.

Street nodded, "And what if, the money went to someone else?"

"Then they'd be expected to pay taxes on it."

"Even if the money was a gift to them?"

"Yes."

"What if it was a—donation?"

"What kind of donation?"

"Say—a political one?"

"Political donations are not tax-deductible—if that's what you're asking," said Hartmann. Then he immediately followed up, "Did you give this money to a politician?"

With that, Street clammed up, and Folonie glared at him. This was followed by the now-familiar refrain, "I'd rather not say." And after that, we made no further progress.

The meeting ended with Hartmann telling Street that he had a week to reconsider his answers. If Street were not more forthcoming by the end of that period, our only recourse would be to bring him before a grand jury and question him under oath. And if we later learned that he had lied, he would be prosecuted to the full extent of the law. When they were gone, Hartmann asked me what I thought.

"Well," I said, "It sure looks like the money was a bribe. And that Street was the intermediary."

Hartmann nodded. "But we're still missing something," he said.

I gave him a quizzical look.

"The $100,500 isn't enough."

"You think the bribe was for more than that?" I asked raising my eyebrows.

He nodded. "If our information is correct, the total was closer to half-a-million dollars."

My jaw dropped in disbelief. I could only think of one Missouri politician who would warrant a bribe of that size. But even for him, such an amount was unimaginable.

"The way things stand," Rudy continued, "Street might still wriggle off the hook. He could claim the $100,500 was income to him and pay taxes on it. Then if he took the Fifth, we would be up a creek."

I nodded.

"So, we've got to find the rest of that money—and fast too. If we could confront Street with evidence of the total amount, he might crack."

"Sure," I added. "But the only way you're going to get that is either through a co-conspirator or getting your hands on some incriminating documents. And how likely is that?"

"I know," admitted Rudy with a long face.

20

AUGUST 4, 1935

It was August 4 and a steamy Saturday afternoon. I'd just picked up some resoled wingtips from a shoe repair on the Plaza. That's a cluster of shops on the north side of Brush Creek. The Plaza was the brainchild of J.C. Nichols and had been built ten years earlier to serve the South Side subdivisions he'd created.

The Plaza shops had been purpose-built for customers arriving by car, the first of its kind in the country. And the businesses themselves were housed in buildings reminiscent of 17th Century Seville. There were lots of towers, domes, and courtyards. And it worked because of the abundance of authentic detail such as wrought iron, tiled fountains, and period statuary.

As I passed the display window of Bennett Schneider Books, I spotted Ernest Hemingway's *Death in the Afternoon*. It was a nonfiction book on Spanish bullfighting. I'd read both of Hemingway's novels, *The Sun Also Rises* and *A Farewell to Arms,* and I'd liked their laconic realism. Hemingway also had a local connection; he had briefly worked as a crime reporter for the *Star* when he was only in his teens.

Interested, I decided to pick up a copy. But when I got to the cashier, I saw another title on display. It was Dr. Karl Menninger's, *Man Against Himself.* The blurb on the back described it as "a landmark in explaining the impulse toward self-destructiveness." I put down the Hemingway book and bought Dr. Karl's instead.

I started to read it as soon as I got home. But I could see it was going to be a slog. The book was four hundred pages long and in fine print. Nevertheless, I settled down and started working through it.

The book started with some statistics. Suicide was more common among men than women. And more single people killed themselves than married. Further, suicide occurred more frequently in urban rather than rural areas. Dr. Karl then turned from fact to fiction.

He noted that, despite the multitude of detective stories printed every year, few used suicide as their solution. His explanation for this was that "popular analysis" often thought of suicide in simplistic terms. It was commonly considered to be a means of escape. Usually from some intolerable life situation such as "ill-health, disgrace or poverty." However, Dr. Karl maintained that the real causes of suicide were much more "complex and unconscious."

There was a knock on my screen door, and I got up to see who it was. I couldn't believe it. Dr. Karl was standing on my front porch looking sheepish.

"Mr. Blair," he said quietly, "Please forgive this intrusion. I know I should have called first but . . .."

"Not at all, Doc, not at all. Come in," I said standing back and opening the door wide.

"If this isn't a good time," he continued, still lingering on the porch.

I brandished the book in my hand. "I'd say we're on the same wavelength, Doc. I was just reading your new book."

"Really?" he replied. "I didn't know it was out yet."

"Just picked it up on the Plaza."

I ushered Dr. Karl into the living room and relieved him of his hat. He took a seat in one of the armchairs by the fireplace.

"Can I get you anything?" I asked.

"Oh no, I'm just fine," said Dr. Karl. "I want you to know, I don't usually pester my patients at home, but you've been on my mind lately."

"Really?" And I sat down in the armchair across from him.

"Well as you can see from my book, your case is of particular interest to me."

"Actually, I've just started reading it. I picked it up because I'm still trying to figure out what you were trying to tell me at the Sanatorium."

"Oh, I thought you'd dismissed the whole thing. And that's why I hadn't heard from you."

"Oh no, I haven't quit thinking about it." After a pause, I added, "In fact, to tell you the truth, I've had another incident."

Dr. Karl's face turned serious. Pulling a notepad and fountain pen from his inside coat pocket, he said, "Tell me about it. And if you don't mind, I'd like to take some notes."

"Go right ahead," I said. And then I told him about what had happened on the ladder. I explained that I'd had an intense urge to let go. And if a policeman hadn't caught me —I would have died.

"So, this time you had an urge to harm yourself?" he asked softly.

"I have a confession to make. This wasn't the first time I've felt urges like that. I had them before the boardinghouse fire and the roadhouse accident too. I don't know why I didn't tell you about them before."

"Tell me about them now, Sam."

"Well, they're visceral. And when I try to resist them, I'm hit with a barrage of memories."

"What kind of memories?"

"That's the hard part. After the urge passes, I can't remember anything specific. But I think they have something to do with the day Midge died."

Doctor Karl made some notes. When he looked up at me again, his face was grave. "You need to do something about this, Sam."

"I know. But I just can't go off to the Sanatorium for God knows how long. Things are happening—in my job—and in my personal life. I just can't drop everything now and go for a cure."

He just stared at me. And I felt bad. Especially, because I knew I needed his help now more than ever.

"Since you're already here. Maybe you can answer some questions for me. What do you say?"

When he didn't immediately respond, I begged, "Come on, Doc, help me out."

He bit his lip, then said reluctantly, "All right."

"Thanks, Doc. I appreciate it. First, why have you been telling me about Charles Nungesser?"

"Because he's—an extreme case."

"An extreme case of what you think I have?"

Dr. Karl nodded. Then he seemed to make some sort of decision. And he began to talk more freely. "Charles

Nungesser has been studied in the field of psychiatry for some time. Numerous papers have been written about him including a famous one by W. H. R. Rivers. In the literature, Nungesser is seen as an archetypical man in psychological distress."

"We know little about his childhood, except that he was born and educated in Paris. But the evidence suggests something traumatic happened to him during this time. He seems to have responded to this event in a classic manner—by repressing his memories of it. And that's probably because he felt somehow responsible for whatever had happened."

"When he came of age, Nungesser left France and traveled to South America." Here, Dr. Karl felt compelled to explain Nungesser's actions. "This was probably a typical flight response triggered by the previous trauma. But of course, changing one's location doesn't work. We can't run away from ourselves."

At this point, Dr. Karl stood up and started pacing. "While we can't be sure, we suspect that, at this time, Nungesser's condition became worse. That's because he began to race cars on the international circuit. And he made a name for himself, as a result of the risks he took. But then, war broke out in Europe, and Nungesser returned to France to enlist."

"From the perspective of the French Army, Nungesser would have appeared to be an ideal recruit. He was young, athletic, and fearless. But what wasn't apparent to those recruiting him was that Nungesser harbored a death wish. And this made him a danger not only to himself but to those around him."

Warming to his subject, Dr. Karl's lecture became a story. "Initially, Nungesser was recruited into the cavalry. And in the first year of the war, he undertook a series of high-risk missions. In the most famous of these, he led a raid behind enemy lines. Nungesser's patrol ambushed a staff car and killed a German general. Then, he singlehandedly drove the staff car back to the French lines through a heavy cross-fire."

"But soon, the ground war bogged down, providing limited opportunities for the kind of risk he craved. So, Nungesser asked for a transfer to the flying corps. This was readily granted because there was a shortage of pilots. Their life expectancy on the Western Front at this time was just two weeks."

"Nungesser learned to fly quickly. And soon, he was posted to the Western Front. There he flew multiple sorties daily. And because he was fearless, he shot down many opponents. But he also took extraordinary risks. As a result, he was often shot down and had numerous crashes. Despite it all, he survived."

"Then one day the war ended. And for him, peace was a catastrophe. During the war, the constant risk of death enabled him to keep his internal demons at bay. Now, they had nothing to feed on—but him."

Here, Dr. Karl paused and looked at me. "You see, Sam, repressed guilt has to be addressed. Otherwise, the internal conflict only builds until it becomes unbearable. And usually, the patient can see only one way out—suicide."

Then Dr. Karl raised a finger, "But once again, Nungesser's case is instructive. It revealed an exception to this pattern. That's because suicide seems not to have been an option for Nungesser."

Dr. Karl's lecturing tone returned, and he again started pacing. "Nungesser showed us that a subset of individuals exists among this clinical group. Those who, for some reason, find the act of suicide unthinkable. This could be because of a religious conviction concerning the sanctity of human life or because they think suicide is cowardly. Whatever the reason, there is only one option left for such individuals: ultra-high-risk behaviors. These are the kind of extreme endeavors where death is almost, but not quite, a certainty."

Finishing his footnote, Dr. Karl returned to his story. "When the war ended, Nungesser sought relief from his worsening condition by traveling the remotest and most dangerous parts of the world. He climbed the Himalayas, trekked the Sahara, and paddled up the Amazon. But from each of these perilous expeditions, he emerged alive.

Dr. Karl stopped pacing. "Then Nungesser learned of the contest to be the first to fly the Atlantic nonstop. This was exactly the kind of risk he craved. And he immediately threw his hat into the ring."

"But true to form, he wasn't satisfied with the long-shot odds, as they existed. In a nod to his wartime past, he had his superstition-flaunting insignia painted on his plane. And he chose to fly the most difficult route, east-to-west against the prevailing winds."

"Raising the ante further, he refused to fill his fuel tanks to the top. He argued counter-intuitively that less fuel would mean less weight and that, consequently, he would be able to fly farther. Finally, he arranged to jettison his landing gear upon takeoff, for the same reason."

"By all these measures, Nungesser had reduced the odds of his survival to a knife's edge. And only then, was he satisfied. If anything went wrong, he would die. And on this occasion, his wish was finally fulfilled."

When Dr. Karl finished, I understood what he'd been trying to tell me. Nungesser and I had much in common. Even though my risk-taking behavior was on a lesser scale, my actions and his were a lot alike. Particularly my failure to seek treatment—even though I knew that I needed it. And now I also suspected that I'd somehow sensed Thurman's potentially saving presence—a split-second before letting go of the ladder.

Dr. Karl picked up my copy of *Man Against Himself* and thumbed through it. Finding what he was looking for, he handed the book back to me pointing to a passage. Then he went to the door.

"I can't make you seek treatment, Sam. You must want to get well. And I hope you will come to us—before it is too late." With that, he put on his hat and left.

Looking down at the book in my hands, I saw that it was open to a chapter entitled: "Purposive Accidents." My eyes went to some lines near the beginning, which Dr. Karl had indicated. They explained that in many "accidents," the damage is inflicted not on someone else but on oneself. And the circumstances, which initially appeared to be entirely fortuitous, could be shown through psychoanalysis to fulfill the victim's own unconscious desire to harm himself. Or as the expression goes, such mishaps happen "accidentally on purpose."

21

AUGUST 22, 1935

During the second week of August 1935, Milligan approved our plan for the 1936 Election, and we immediately set to work. Mac put together a list of professional "repeaters" by using informants and names drawn from complaints filed in past elections. These were individuals, who on Election Day were chauffeured around to various polling stations, where they cast ballots using the names of phony registrants.

However, Mac soon discovered that this pool of repeaters had recently proven inadequate to meet the machine's appetite for blowout wins. Consequently, on Election Day, orders would go out to boost the machine's totals by pressing ordinary citizens into service. Carrollo's thugs, and even the KCPD, would accost individuals on the street in what was styled as a get-out-the-vote effort.

Those who resisted these efforts were roughed up. But those who complied were handed a list of bogus names and marched to the nearest machine-controlled polling station. Once there, they would be watched while they voted a straight-machine ticket for each of the names on their list.

And when they were finished, they were told to keep mum —or else.

We planned to have Bureau agents shadow the professional repeaters on Election Day. We would keep track of how many times they voted, and in which precincts. Then when they were finished, we would arrest them. If we were lucky, they would still have the list of phony names that they had used on them.

We also put out the word, through Reform circles, that we wanted to hear from anyone who had been coerced into voting for machine candidates. We hoped to persuade these citizens not only to identify those who had strong-armed them, but also, to file charges against them.

Unexpectedly, Mac's investigation turned up a promising line of inquiry. Informants told him that many of the machine's ward heelers thought that relying on repeaters and the strong-armed vote was too much trouble. They preferred more direct methods for meeting their voting quotas.

These informants told Mac that, after the polls closed, some precinct captains simply discarded a portion of the opposition ballots, replacing them with an equal number of new ones, which had been marked for machine candidates. Other precincts didn't bother creating new ballots at all. They merely "corrected" the old ones by rubbing out the "wrong" votes and replacing them with the "right" ones.

Then there were those precinct captains who couldn't be bothered with ballots at all. They simply made up the totals. Mac learned that in recent elections the final tally had often far exceeded the number of registered voters in the city.

We realized that, if we subpoenaed the ballots of machine-controlled precincts after they'd been certified, we should have the evidence we needed. If we found "corrected" ballots, the fraud would be clear. If the number of certified votes was significantly higher than the number cast —ditto. Even in the unlikely event that original ballots had been destroyed and replaced by new ones, we were hopeful that machine carelessness and overconfidence would still give us the evidence we needed.

While Mac worked on the election-rigging angle, my job was to get to know the leading members of the Reform Movement. I was looking for individuals knowledgeable about the history of election fraud in the city. We needed background for our briefs and data to support our applications for subpoenas. And we were also looking for expert witnesses to testify for us at trial.

Ideally, these individuals would be informative, well-credentialed, and articulate. We also wanted them to be tough enough to withstand the abuse they would certainly get from the machine's attorneys. Not surprisingly, I found few who fit the bill.

I'd begun my expert-witness search by looking into the backgrounds of likely candidates from the National Youth Movement, Citizens Fusion, and Reform Parties. Then I'd attended rallies where my best prospects, were speaking. In this way, I could evaluate them unobtrusively from the audience. If after this they still seemed promising, I would set up a meeting and try to convince them to help us. While my methodology was sound, I'd had little success.

Even though many Reform movement speakers were knowledgeable enough, they tended to be dry or otherwise unappealing. Of the five, whom I'd already approached, only two were willing to give us affidavits. But they had both shied away from testifying at trial. They naturally feared mob reprisals, and I couldn't blame them. So, I was still looking.

Another reform rally was slated for this evening, August 22. It was at Convention Hall, only a short walk from the office. When I arrived, there must have been over seven thousand people inside the Hall. That was nearly half the building's capacity. The crowd filled the horseshoe-shaped floor in front of the stage and spilled over into the surrounding tiered seating.

As I walked down the ramp, a brass band was playing "You're a Grand Old Flag." At the bottom, members of the National Youth Movement and Citizens Fusion Parties were passing out programs.

As I looked around, the crowd was more diverse than usual. Children were playing in the aisles near their parents, and groups of seniors filled the lower seats. It looked like support for the reform movement was growing. Previously, most of the attendees at these rallies had been college students, young professionals, and businessmen.

Scanning the Hall, I noted some KCPD detectives in plain clothes. Thurman and Hart were there, but not Rayen and Claiborne. Some rough-looking characters were also sprawled in the upper seats. They were probably Carrollo's boys. If they were there to intimidate, their presence didn't seem to be having much of an effect.

I found a spot in the first tier and settled in. And it wasn't long before the lights dimmed. A young man with slicked-back blond hair and a new suit took the podium. He introduced himself as Joe Fennelly, President of the National Youth Movement. Welcoming the crowd, he explained that his organization had a citywide membership of over four thousand "and growing." Simply put, its mission was to end bossism and machine politics in the city.

Fennelly listed the night's speakers and plugged the sponsors. Then he ended with a bit of warm-up. Thumping the podium, he proclaimed, "This is our city. Only legitimate votes should count. It's time to throw the machine out!"

Even this light rousing was greeted warmly showing the crowd was primed. The heads of the local branches of the Citizens' Fusion Party and the American Student Union followed. They also spoke enthusiastically about reforming local government and cleaning up KC.

The first speaker of substance was Russell Greiner, an earnest man with a square chin and high forehead. He was a prominent businessman, who was also President of the Helping Hand Institute. Greiner gave us an overview of machine politics in the United States from the Nineteenth Century to the present.

He talked about Tweed in New York, Thompson in Chicago, and Curley in Boston. In each, he drew direct and unfavorable comparisons to Pendergast and his machine. Greiner explained that every boss-run city suffered from cronyism, corruption, and voter fraud. It was, he said, endemic to bossism. But he asserted, that times had changed, and the days of the local political machine were over. Federalism was the wave of the future. And it was time for Kansas City to kick the Boss out.

Greiner had provided lots of information. But he had generated little enthusiasm. I seriously thought about slipping away. But then, I took another look at the program and saw that there was only one more speaker. And he was someone I'd heard a lot about but had never seen. So, I decided to stay a little longer.

The last speaker was Rabbi Samuel Mayerberg, from Temple B'nai Jehudah. He had been one of the Boss's earliest and most vocal critics. This had earned him a spate of death threats and at least one attempt on his life. But

Mayerberg had not been deterred. If anything, the threats had only made him more forceful in his attacks.

Fennelly introduced the Rabbi by reading a short but impressive bio. Then the lights went down, and a wavering spot tried to keep Mayerberg in its circle as he strode to the podium. There he waited for the applause to die down.

Slender with glistening black hair, Mayerberg wore round horn-rimmed glasses that emphasized his intense eyes. His voice was low and melodious. And he was a practiced speaker pausing periodically to let the echoes die in the Hall.

Using no notes, Mayerberg began by thanking the organizers. He also thanked everyone present for taking this "weighty issue of local governance seriously." Then he surveyed the Hall.

"Friends, I would like to begin with my favorite quotation. It is by an unknown author. I know some of you have heard it before, but I think it bears repeating, particularly in this context. 'Of all the evil done in the world, one third is due to the vicious who do it, and two-thirds to the good people, who let it be done.'"

Again, his eyes scanned the audience. "My friends, for too long, we've let the vicious run our city. For too long, we've looked the other way. It's easy to say we're not politicians—or that it's someone else's business. The truth is we've been afraid."

"We've seen what happens to those who speak up. The beatings and deaths of the 1934 Election were plain enough. They were intended to frighten us. But intimidation is a funny thing. Often, instead of keeping us down—it makes us want to stand up!" This was met with a surge of applause.

"And my friends, the sufferings of the 1934 Election were not wasted. For each person mocked, beaten, and killed, ten more have come forward. Because of the violence, our ranks are swelling. And there are too many now for us to be silenced!" Another round of applause welled up.

Speaking softly, he said, "And so, we have begun to hope. But hope alone is insufficient. For hope to be realized, there must be action." Leaning forward, he struck the podium for emphasis, "And now, my friends—*now* is the time to act!"

He again waited for the applause to die away. "Our efforts are beginning to bear fruit. Recently, as you may already have heard, we've gained the majority on the city's election board. A special thanks go to Mr. Edgar Shook for his willingness and courage to serve." The applause was loud and sustained. A spotlight found Mr. Shook in the front row. A thin man with a shock of white hair, he stood briefly, waved in acknowledgment, and resumed his seat.

Again, Mayerberg waited for the applause to die away. "When we took over the election board, we sought to accomplish only one thing—to purge the electoral rolls. This is essential if we are to ensure that only honest votes count."

"First, the names of the dead were removed. Next, those registered more than once. And finally, those registered at false addresses. It has taken time, but the rolls *have—now—been—purged*!" There was more sustained applause.

This time he spoke over it. "And how many fraudulent voters, my friends. How many ghosts do you think we have spirited away?" He paused and surveyed the crowd again, his glasses glinting in the spotlight. The hall suddenly became quiet.

"Twenty thousand? Fifty thousand? Eighty thousand?" Lifting a sheaf of paper above his head, he shouted, "*Over 88,000 fraudulent voters have been struck from the roles!*" An echoing cheer went up.

The crowd was on its feet now, and I arose with them. Again, he shouted over the roar, "This is only the beginning. We *can* take back our city, and we *will* take back our city with courage and honest votes!" And with that, he waved once, wheeled, and left the podium.

I'd heard it said, even by his admirers, that Rabbi Mayerberg was a dangerous man. Now, I knew why. And I also knew that he'd make a terrific expert witness.

The lights came up, and the band broke into, "Happy Days Are Here Again." I glanced around as scattered applause continued, and the crowd started moving toward the exits. The plain-clothes men were gone, and the upper tiers were empty.

22

AUGUST 25, 1935

It was Friday evening, August 25. Budge had dropped by the house after dinner. I gave him a bottle of beer, and we sat on the front porch. We talked about baseball, politics, and the weather. Then Budge casually let drop that Dolores was back in town.

"What?" I said, sitting up. "When?"

"She came in this afternoon by train."

"Thurman know?"

"Yeah. But he's not interested."

And I wondered why the KCPD had lost interest.

"Is she back at the Park Central?"

He nodded.

"We need to talk to her," I said starting to get up.

"It'll keep—until tomorrow," Budge replied taking a swig.

"You're right," I said sitting back down. I needed some time to think about what to ask her. And how to weigh her likely answers.

At two the next day, Budge and I met as planned in front

of the Park Central. I'd called ahead to let Dolores know we were coming. And she'd left the Penthouse door unlatched.

The place looked pretty much the same, as the last time I'd been there. The same cubist art hung on the walls, the same Art Deco nymphs leaped and pirouetted. And the pool glittered as always in the bright sunlight.

A couple of things were different, though. Dolores's wedding pictures no longer lined the mantel. And there wasn't a drink in sight. I wondered if, during her absence, Dolores had gone somewhere to dry out. But if she had, it hadn't improved her mood. Because I could see she was going to be as prickly as ever.

We sat across from each other. And by way of conversation, I asked, "So, how was Frisco?" That turned out to be a mistake.

She made a face. "You *knew* I wasn't there," she said. "And yeah, I should have told you I was leaving. But I'd had it with the press, the police, and the whole damn thing."

"Okay," I said holding up my hands in surrender.

But she gave me the second barrel anyway. "And *you* had decided to start in on me too! I just couldn't take it."

This time I kept my mouth shut. But still, I wondered where she'd gone—and who with. Trying to be sympathetic I asked, "So, how are you now?"

"Better," she said. "But don't think I'm over it."

Dolores reached into the cigarette box in front of her. She took out a smoke and lit it with the table lighter. Exhaling heavily, she crossed her arms and glared at me.

"Well, I'm glad you're better," I said slowly. "But I still have to know what happened when Johnny died."

Her eyes sparked. "Look," she spat, "You were there when I told Thurman all about it."

"I was," I conceded. "But this time I want to hear *all* of it."

She opened her mouth to say something but thought better of it. Instead, she took a long pull on her cigarette and spewed smoke at the ceiling. I wasn't going to give up, and she knew it. So, we sat there and let the silence grow.

Then for no reason that I could tell, the wind went out of Dolores's sails. She leaned forward and ground out her cigarette in the ashtray. Then she said, without looking at me, "Okay, you're right. I didn't tell Thurman everything."

I was shocked at my success. But I tried not to show it. "Okay. So, what didn't you didn't tell him?"

Dolores licked her lips. She was thinking about what she was going to say—and what she wasn't. So, I waited some more, and after a while, she began to talk.

"When Johnny yelled for Charlie to drive away, we only went a couple of blocks before we doubled back."

Damn right, I thought. No matter what Johnny had told Charlie to do driving off while Johnny was being gunned down wasn't going to sit well with the men of honor.

Dolores went on. "We raced back to the hotel. And when we were nearly there, another car shot out right in front of us."

"Where from?" asked Budge.

"Behind the Park Central."

"That was the shooters' car," I said. "What make was it?"

"I don't know cars," she whined.

"What happened next?" asked Budge trying to keep Dolores talking.

"Charlie swerved. So did the other car. And somehow, we missed each other. But when we swerved," she said, "I was thrown against the window. And as the other car went by—I could see the letters on its door."

"Letters?" I asked.

She nodded.

"What letters?" asked Budge.

"KCPD."

"KCPD?" I repeated stupidly. "It was a police car?"

Dolores nodded.

"No wonder you didn't tell Thurman," I said.

"I know," she whimpered.

"But—I thought the mob and the cops were one and the same."

"Not quite," said Budge.

"What do you mean?"

"When Lazia became police liaison," Budge said. "He weeded out guys like me, who wouldn't go along with what he wanted. But he couldn't get rid of all of us."

"Why not?" I asked.

"He had to keep some—just so the department could function."

"And?" I asked, still not getting his point.

"So, every cop isn't a crook."

While I mulled that over, I turned back to Dolores. "Besides the letters on the door, was there anything else you remember about the shooter's car?"

"I don't know. It was just different."

"How different?" I asked.

"The front-end had things like blinds on it. And there was a gizmo in the windshield."

"A gizmo?"

"I don't know what to call it. A circular dingus—with a metal flap over it."

Budge and I looked at each other. Then we spoke in unison: "The Hot Shot!"

"What's that?" asked Dolores.

"It's the KCPD's fast pursuit car," I explained. "It's armored. There are metal louvers, not blinds, on the front. They're there to protect the radiator. And the Hot Shot's bulletproof windshield has a circular gun port in it, covered by a metal flap. The car's designed to take and return gunfire without getting knocked out."

I remembered riding in the Hot Shot when Mac and I went with Hart to check out the house on Edgevale Road. It was a new Plymouth. That's exactly how the janitor at the Park Central had described it. Why hadn't I made that connection sooner? Then I remembered the ruts in the alley's cinders.

"With the armor plating and bullet-proof windshield, the Hot Shot must be pretty heavy," I said.

"You bet," agreed Budge.

"But why would the shooters use the Hot Shot? Didn't they think somebody might recognize it?"

"Could have been a spur-of-the-moment thing," said Budge.

"Not likely," I said.

Then I remembered Hart saying that the Hot Shot was always assigned to the two most senior detectives on the force. Before the Union Station Massacre, that had been Grooms and Hermanson. Now, it was Thurman and Hart.

So, I wondered: Did that mean Thurman and Hart had killed Johnny? Or had someone just used the Hot Shot to make it look like they had? I didn't even know if that was possible. And it was just one more question to add to my list.

ON MONDAY AFTERNOON, August 28, I had a meeting with Rabbi Mayerberg at his home in Hyde Park. And the Rabbi had been even better in person than he'd been on the stage. So, when we finished, I popped the question: Would he serve as an expert witness for us in "unspecified future litigation?" Thankfully, he'd said "yes."

I'd intentionally kept the object of our engagement vague. But the Rabbi was a savvy guy. And from the drift of our conversation, he had to have known what kind of litigation I was talking about and against whom.

As I was getting up to go, Rabbi Mayerberg asked a question, which showed that he'd been doing a little research of his own. "I hear your father's a Justice on the Missouri Supreme Court."

"That's right."

"And I also hear you have a phenomenal memory."

"Not really, I just know some memory techniques."

"What kind of techniques?"

"The ones originally developed by Cicero, Quintilian, and Aquinas. Of course, they've been refined some over the years. As you probably know, memory training was at the core of a classical education."

"Because books were hard to come by before Gutenberg," he said.

"Precisely. So, people had to rely on their memories much more than we do. For example, in the Middle Ages schoolboys routinely learned all one hundred and fifty Psalms by heart as well as at least one of the gospels—just to train their memories. And that was before the Bible was divided into chapter and verse."

"And you say these techniques aren't difficult to learn?"

"Not really. Once you've got the method down, it's just a matter of practice and concentration."

"Would you mind giving me a demonstration?"

"Not at all. Do you have a deck of cards handy?"

"I do," said the Rabbi with a smile. Opening the top right-hand drawer to his desk, he produced a well-thumbed pack. "I confess to having an obsession for Solitaire."

"Would you mind removing the Jokers and shuffling it?"

"Not at all."

When the deck was ready, I took the top card, glanced at it for a long second, placed it face-up on the discard pile, and turned over the next card. I repeated this procedure until I had gone through all fifty-two cards. Then I turned the deck over and placed it upside down in front of the Rabbi.

"Okay," I said, "Before you turn over the top card, I'll tell you what it is. The first card is the King of Diamonds." And the Rabbi turned over the top card to reveal the same. We went through all fifty-two cards in this manner. And I named each of them correctly.

"How on earth did you do that?" exclaimed the Rabbi in astonishment.

"It's not hard once you know how. If you'd like, I can go back through the deck in reverse."

"No, I'll take your word for it," he laughed. "But really, it's quite amazing."

"Not once you've learned how. Our memory is like a muscle. It just needs training. You've heard the expression that we only use ten percent of our brains? Well, I think that was meant to refer to our memories."

"Are you interested in puzzles, Mr. Blair?"

"Sure, always have been."

"Cryptograms? Cyphers?"

"Probably, although I'm not sure I know exactly what you mean by those terms."

"I've got a new book," he said, "That explains what they are."

The Rabbi went to his bookcase and pulled out a thin volume. It was *Elementary Cryptanalysis* by Helen Gaines. The Rabbi said I could keep it for as long as I liked. He also loaned me an issue of a magazine called *The Cryptogram* to which he was a regular contributor.

I left not long afterward feeling pretty good about finally having the expert witness we needed. Then I realized we still had to get the machine's poll workers and repeaters into court before Rabbi Mayerberg could do his stuff. And I hoped that we would be able to pull that off.

THAT EVENING there was a bar-society dinner in honor of the Chief. He was receiving an award and giving a speech. Because such occasions were typically snoozers, I usually avoided them. But this time, Wilson had insisted that all Assistant DAs be in attendance. So, I'd resigned myself to going. Later, I was glad I had.

The dinner had been as dismal as I'd feared. The roast beef was rubbery, the green beans stringy and the gravy gelatinous. While the Chief's speech had been admirably short, every bar society functionary had felt compelled to add some remarks of their own. Consequently, the dinner had dragged on until well after eleven.

I'd been so tired afterward I'd forgotten that I'd driven my car to work that day. Usually, I commute by trolley. But that morning, I'd been running so late, I'd had to drive. Parking my car in a two-hour zone on Grand, I'd promptly forgotten about it. And of course, I hadn't fed the meter all day. Following the dinner, I'd fallen back into my usual routine and taken the trolley home.

Around three a.m., I'd been awakened by a hammering

on my front door. When I'd opened it, Thurman and Hart were standing there. They'd brusquely told me to get dressed. Then they'd taken me downtown to police headquarters. When I'd asked what it was about—all I'd gotten was silence.

Thurman and Hart had put me in a windowless eight-by-eight room in the basement. There was an odd name painted on the door: "The Goldfish Room." They'd questioned me about where I'd been that evening, who I'd been with, and what I'd been doing. My answers had been received with stony skepticism and jotted down.

After that, they'd left, and I'd spent the next eight hours cooling my heels. That gave me plenty of time to smoke an entire pack of cigarettes and inspect my surroundings. Some curious items were hanging on pegs along one wall of the interview room. These included an assortment of leather belts, lengths of sisal rope, some rubber hoses, and a large canvas sack. The latter I suspected was a head-bag.

But the most disturbing part of the room was the utility sink in the corner. It was black with grime and chipped like a bad tooth. And it didn't take much imagination to figure out what it had been used for. I realized Thurman and Hart had put me in the Goldfish Room to soften me up psychologically. And I also realized that I must be a suspect for something serious. That's when I began to worry.

And yet, when Thurman and Hart finally showed up, the air had gone out of them. And they told me why I'd been picked up. After my car had been sitting at an expired meter all day, collecting parking tickets, it had been towed to the police garage. There it had been searched. And that's when an attendant had found Jim Wetzel's body under a blanket behind the front seat. His neck had been broken.

Since Wetzel's body was in my car, the police had naturally assumed that I had killed him. And when they'd learned of our altercation in the *Journal Post* newsroom on the day of Johnny's death—they were certain of it. However, they had one problem—the timing of the crime.

At the estimated hour of Wetzel's death, as determined by the city coroner, I'd been dozing away among the city's legal practitioners. And at the end of his speech, Milligan had pointed me out, to general merriment, as "a prime example of how the Department of Justice never sleeps." Even Thurman and Hart had to admit it was a pretty good alibi. And they'd released me.

But as I drove home, I realized it had been a close call. The trap had been well laid and perfectly executed. All that had remained was for the city prosecutor to put me away for Wetzel's murder. Only dumb luck had saved me from the noose.

It made me realize that now Johnny was gone, the mob and machine were no longer fooling around. And if I'd had any sense, I would have packed my bags and given Milligan my notice. But of course, I didn't. And why? Because the scare had left me strangely elated. And my reaction had made me wonder if Dr. Karl had been right all along. Maybe, I did have a death wish.

In the end, I'd laughed it off. Heck, I told myself everybody relishes a bit of danger. That's why there are roller coasters and Ferris wheels. And the mob and machine didn't scare me. So, I just put my head down and kept plugging away.

On the following Saturday, a soiled envelope appeared in my Brookside mailbox. There was no return address on it. Inside was an undated, hastily written note.

> Blair,
>
> If you're reading this, then I'm already dead. I know why they killed Jelly Nash, and they're gunning for me. I'm sending you what I've got. Make them pay.
>
> Wetzel

I stared at the note and shook my head. Even dead, Wetzel was going to be a pain. What had he gotten me into now?

23

AUGUST 31, 1935

It was Friday, October 19, 1935. At half-past noon, I was sitting on a stool in the Liberty Bell waiting for my hot roast beef sandwich to come up. Hank and Louise had recently installed a jukebox, and it was playing a new song by Andy Kirk and the Clouds of Joy. Pha Terrell's reedy voice was wailing his way through, "Until the Real Thing Comes Along."

The bell over the door jangled; I turned to see who it was. And Mac was waving wildly at me. Then he dashed back to his idling Desoto.

I slapped a fifty-cent piece on the counter and called out, as I scrambled for the door, "Sorry, Lucille, got to run!"

As soon as I opened the car door, the coupe began to roll. Hopping along on one foot, I eventually managed to get myself inside.

"What's the rush?"

"Pretty Boy Floyd's cornered in the Ohio sticks. And the police are closing in."

In July, FBI agents, led by Melvin Purvis, had hunted down and killed John Dillinger outside a Chicago movie theater. With Dillinger's death, Hoover had boosted Pretty Boy Floyd to Public Enemy Number One. Feeling the heat, Floyd and Richetti had taken to the road searching for a place to hide.

They'd stuck to the upper Midwest, and for a time, they'd succeeded in staying out of sight. But their luck had run out near the small town of Wellsville, Ohio. They'd skidded on a slick road and slammed their car into a tree.

Floyd and Richetti had decided to send the two molls they were with to a local body shop to get the car repaired. The plan was for them to lay low on the edge of town, while the car was being fixed. But local police had become suspicious of the pair and had gone to investigate.

This had resulted in an exchange of gunfire. And the half-drunk Richetti had managed to get himself captured. However, Floyd had slipped away into the thick woods surrounding the town and had escaped.

The local police had quickly identified Richetti and realized the man with him must be Floyd. They then organized a manhunt before alerting the Bureau. Getting the news, Hoover had sent every available agent to Ohio. The Kansas City office had designated Mac and two others for the job. And Mac had gotten permission to bring me along.

We rolled through a red light on Broadway. But instead of turning left, we went right. And I wondered why we weren't heading for Union Station.

"What's up?" I asked.

Mac's face broke into a grin. "Just following Hoover's orders, Sam. Time is of the essence."

My jaw dropped, "We're flying?"

"You-bet-cha. Vetterli's hired a charter flight to Pittsburgh. Wellsville's not far from there."

We crossed the Missouri River on the upper deck of the

Hannibal Bridge. And on the other side, Mac took a sharp left. We swung into the drive of the redbrick terminal with a green cupola tower.

I made a quick call to Ginny from a pay phone. I told her to tell Milligan where I was and why. I was pretty sure he would be okay with it since if Floyd and Richetti were captured, our office would likely handle their prosecution.

While we waited for the others to arrive, I climbed the stairs to the observation deck. A silver Transcontinental and Western Douglas DC-2 was standing outside the hanger being serviced. And I wanted to see it.

The Transcontinental and Western Airline was based in KC. It ran the forty-eight-hour route from New York to Los Angeles. There was only one layover on the flight, here in Kansas City, where the passengers spent the night.

As soon as the other agents arrived, we walked across the tarmac to a gray Ford Trimotor. I marveled at its corrugated aluminum skin. While not nearly as slick as the DC-2's stainless steel, the Trimotor's all-metal construction still felt more secure than doped canvass on a wooden frame.

We settled into our wicker seats, and one-by-one the three rotary engines coughed into life. Cleared for takeoff, we rolled down the runway gradually picking up speed, and after a couple of bounces, the Tin Goose lifted into the air. Then we banked east over the river and turned our nose towards Pennsylvania.

It was my first flight. Puffy clouds dotted the fair-weather sky, as harvest fields glided beneath us. I followed the distant loops of the Missouri River until they disappeared into the haze.

Before long, Mac nudged me to get busy. He handed me the Bureau's files on Floyd and Richetti and told me to start reading. So, I lit a cigarette and flipped open Floyd's folder.

Charles Arthur Floyd had been born in Georgia, but he had grown up on a red-dirt farm in Oklahoma. In the black-and-white booking photo, he had a flat sullen face with full lips and a thick head of hair. Floyd was five-foot-eight and stocky, weighing in at one hundred and fifty-five pounds. A note warned that he was muscled and could be mean.

After a stick-up early in his career, a teller had described Floyd as "a mere boy with apple cheeks." Upon hearing this, the tabloids had started calling him "Pretty Boy." And of course, the label had stuck.

In 1925, when he was just twenty-one, Floyd had been sentenced to five years in prison. Afterward, he had vowed never to serve time again. Upon release, Floyd had bee-lined it to Kansas City. Initially, the KC mob had taken him under its wing. But Floyd was too much of a loner to become one of Lazia's boys.

It was his nickname more than his exploits that had made Floyd famous. And the papers had breathlessly followed his every move. But the moniker had also soured him. Floyd hated it because he thought it implied, he was soft. Consequently, no one dared call him "Pretty Boy" to his face.

Maturing as a criminal, Floyd joined the Harvey Bailey Gang. Bailey was one of a new breed of bank robbers, who'd learned to play it smart. For instance, they cased banks ahead of time looking for exploitable weaknesses instead of just barging in with guns blazing. They also mapped out escape routes and even conducted dry runs using a stop-watch to ensure quick getaways. And to avoid confusion, they assigned specific tasks to each gang member, such as lookout, lobby man, or driver.

And that wasn't all. They saw that the nation's improved network of roads meant that they could work in larger geographic areas. And by using fast cars, powered by V-8 engines, they could minimize the likelihood of effective pursuit. They also realized that armed with the latest automatic weapons, they were more than a match for the local police, who were trying to stop them.

Finally, this new type of bank robber learned to exploit the nation's decentralized system of law enforcement. They saw that state lines were jurisdictional roadblocks beyond which local lawmen were powerless to act. That made locations like the tri-state Kansas-Missouri-Oklahoma region perfect for plying their trade.

But of course, no plan is foolproof. And from time to time, gang members still got caught. It was Floyd's turn in 1930. He was arrested in Ohio quickly tried and sentenced to fifteen years in prison. But before he could be transferred to the penitentiary, Floyd broke out of jail and hightailed it back to Kansas City. Like many before him, he'd vanished, until the frustrated authorities quit looking for him.

For whatever reason, Floyd became more violent following his Ohio arrest. Shortly after returning to Kansas City, he was the prime suspect in the brutal murder of two bootleggers, whose bound and charred bodies were found inside a torched car. Shortly after that, he was also linked to the murder of an unarmed Ohio policeman. It was around this time that Floyd began carrying a Thompson.

In 1931, a couple of Prohibition Agents got the drop on Floyd during a raid in Kansas City. After they'd relieved him of the Thompson and an automatic, he'd suddenly whipped out a second handgun, which had been tucked in his rear waistband. With it, Floyd had killed one of the agents and critically wounded the other. While making his getaway, Floyd had also shot a policeman and an innocent bystander.

It was this incident that had put Floyd on the Bureau's Public Enemy list.

The file confirmed that Pretty Boy Floyd had been in Kansas City on the day of the Union Station Massacre. And of course, Needles LaCapra had said that Floyd had been one of Miller's accomplices. Further, according to the file, Alvin Karpis, a former member of the Harvey Bailey Gang, had also claimed that Floyd had told him that he had been one of the shooters at Union Station.

Contrary to this evidence, usually reliable underworld sources had denied Floyd's involvement. And no credible eyewitness had placed Floyd at the scene. This included all the surviving lawmen. Finally, the Bureau had received a postcard, reputedly from Floyd himself, in which he had asserted his innocence in no uncertain terms. And privately, many in the Bureau believed him.

So, the evidence for Floyd's involvement was mixed. However, there was one yet-to-be-determined fact that might prove conclusive. One of the shooters had been shot in the shoulder while making his escape. I'd witnessed this myself, and I'd also seen the bloody bandages in the attic of the house on Edgevale Road. Since we knew Miller hadn't been wounded, then it stood to reason that, if they were his accomplices, either Floyd or Richetti must have been.

Further, there was testimony from Dominic Binaggio, a member of the Kansas City mob and an informant. He'd sworn that he'd seen Floyd's arm in a sling on the day after the Massacre. And of course, Needles LaCapra had made the same claim. If this was true, then Floyd's shoulder should still bear the scars of that wound.

Consequently, a note had been clipped to the inside cover of Floyd's file. It stated that a medical examination of Floyd's shoulders was a "priority." Scrawled across the note in blue ink was a single word, "Agreed." And under it were Hoover's initials.

The hardwood forests and rocky outcrops of central Missouri were passing beneath us when I put down Floyd's file and reached for Richetti's. Despite the roaring engines, Mac was slumped against the window, his hat over his eyes. He was one of those guys who could sleep anywhere.

The file on Adam "Eddie" Richetti was much thinner than Floyd's. Born in Texas, Richetti had, like Floyd, grown-up poor in Oklahoma. His mugshot showed a pale, scowling face with squinting eyes and a high forehead. According to the description, Richetti was five-foot-eight but weighed only one hundred and twenty-three pounds.

There was little information on Richetti's childhood. He'd run away from home at an early age to work for bootleggers and had become an alcoholic by the age of fourteen. When he was nineteen, he was arrested for armed robbery. On that occasion, a judge had taken pity on him, and he had served only two years in an Indiana state reformatory.

Upon release, Richetti had returned to Oklahoma and immediately became involved in a bungled bank robbery. During the attempted heist, a dead-eyed teller had killed one of the gang outright. And he had also wounded the other three—two of them seriously. Richetti was the lucky one. His wound was slight enough for him to get away with the cash. But his luck didn't hold, and he was caught two hours later.

Convicted and sentenced to prison, another judge took pity on Richetti. He was released on bail, while his case was under appeal. Taking advantage of the judge's leniency, Richetti had promptly skipped the state.

It was around this time that Floyd and Richetti met in Kansas City. They'd become fast friends, but no one is quite sure why. Richetti was drunk most of the time and generally hapless. Maybe, it was because they were both Okies. Or maybe, because Floyd, like others before him, had simply felt sorry for Richetti. Whatever the reason, the two became partners.

During the spring of 1933, Floyd and Richetti had left Kansas City and gone on a spree through Oklahoma and Missouri. They'd stolen cars, robbed banks, and even carried out kidnapping for ransom. By mid-June, they'd decided they needed a break, and they'd returned to KC for the weekend.

While they were in town, the Union Station Massacre had occurred. And the next day, they'd skipped town. The combination of their notoriety, their presence in town, and the timing of their departure made them prime suspects.

The following Monday, Floyd and Richetti had tried to pick up where they had left off by robbing a bank in Galena, Missouri. But reports of the Union Station Massacre had so incensed the local police and populace that they had nearly killed the two before they could even attempt the heist. Dismayed by this heated reaction, Floyd and Richetti had fled empty-handed. And the experience had made them so gun-shy that they'd laid low for the next couple of months hoping that the furor would die down.

At this point, the file candidly admitted that there was no evidence Richetti had been at Union Station on the day of the Massacre. In their after-action reports, none of the surviving lawmen had identified him as one of the shooters nor had any other eyewitness. And only limited physical evidence even connected Richetti to Miller. Two beer bottles from the house on Edgevale Road had partial, latent finger-prints on them. The rest had been wiped clean. One of the Bureau's fingerprinting experts thought that the prints belonged to Richetti. But the file admitted that he wasn't certain.

Finally, there was no indication that Richetti had ever been wounded in the shoulder. And in an exercise of bureaucratic box-ticking, a note in the same handwriting as the one I'd seen in Floyd's file, had been attached to the inside cover of Richetti's. It read, "Check for a shoulder wound."

I'd finished Richetti's file in time for our refueling stop in Indianapolis. I got out and stretched my legs on the tarmac. When we took off, I tried to nap, but without success.

We reached Pittsburgh at ten. And I calculated that we'd averaged well over a hundred miles an hour. I'd never traveled so fast. But it took a while for my ears to quit ringing.

Inside the Pittsburgh terminal, we were joined by Bureau agents from across the country. And we immediately climbed aboard a hired bus for our trip to Wellsville. Hoover had ordered us to proceed without delay, and no one wanted to disappoint him.

We drove through the night, and when we got to Wellsville, it was nearly dawn. The situation there was less than ideal. Even though he had led the team that had taken down John Dillinger, local law enforcement was unimpressed by Special Agent Melvin Purvis. And they weren't about to let the FBI take over their manhunt.

Further, they refused to hand Richetti over to the Bureau. Although they did let a local physician examine him. The doctor told us that there was no evidence Richetti had ever been wounded in the shoulder.

The next day the locals resumed their manhunt. But they weren't particularly forthcoming about their plan. As a result, Mac and I missed out on being there when Floyd was flushed from the woods at a nearby farm. He had tried to outrun a line of police and Bureau agents. And he'd been hit just as he was about to reach cover. Wounded, Floyd had fallen on a grassy slope without firing a shot.

Aware of what had happened to the Prohibition Agents in Kansas City, the lawmen had quickly taken away Floyd's forty-five as well as the backup he'd kept in his waistband. As luck would have it, Floyd was without his Thompson. Its stock had been broken during a fall in the woods. And he'd been forced to discard it.

Consequently, a band of rural Ohio lawmen had accomplished what the Bureau, with all its vaunted scientific policing, hadn't been able to do in nearly two and a half years. They'd taken Pretty Boy Floyd into custody, alive. But what happened next is disputed.

A handful of local lawmen later reported that a Bureau agent, whom they did not know, had stepped forward while Floyd lay on the ground cursing his captors. This man, they'd said, had simply raised his gun and shot Floyd to death. Then he'd vanished.

The Bureau, of course, had laughed off this account. They'd said that Floyd had simply died of his wounds at the scene. Always a company man, Mac had accepted this explanation. I, on the other hand, wasn't so sure.

I'd noticed that in the Bureau's recent encounters with Public Enemies, far more had died than had been captured. John Dillinger, Baby Face Nelson, and Fred Barker were three notable examples. And now, Pretty Boy Floyd could be added to that list.

Of course, they were all hard cases. And they might have simply decided not to be captured alive. But I doubted that would account for all of them. Particularly since not long ago, Attorney General Cummings had famously said that his preferred method for dealing with Public Enemies was to

"Shoot first—then count to ten." And it looked like some Bureau agents might have taken the AG at his word.

I only saw Pretty Boy Floyd's body once. It was laid out on a slab in the East Liverpool, Ohio morgue. And when they pulled back the sheet to reveal his upper torso, there was no sign of a prior gunshot wound to either shoulder.

24

JUNE 1936

As anticipated, the Bureau asked our office to prosecute Adam Richetti. And the Chief gave me the job of evaluating their evidence. This led to several meetings with Mac and an earnest young agent by the name of Monty Spear, who took me through the Richetti file. It didn't take long to realize they didn't have much of a case.

Their strongest evidence came from Vivian Mathias, aka Mrs. Vincent Moore. Mathias had been arrested in Chicago shortly after a failed rendezvous with Vern Miller. And the Bureau had wrung a statement from her before convicting her on conspiracy charges.

As Hoover had hoped, Mathias had identified Floyd and Richetti as Vern Miller's accomplices at Union Station. And according to her, Floyd had been wounded in the shoulder during the shootout. That was her explanation for the bloody bandages in the attic on Edgevale Road. Having seen Floyd's body myself, I knew that this was false.

But there was another problem with Mathias's testimony. Since she didn't want to be known as a rat in the underworld, she had cut a special deal with Hoover. She would plead guilty to conspiracy charges and divulge everything she knew, but only if he kept her statement secret. That meant she wouldn't be testifying.

Absent Mathias, the Government's next best witness was Needles LaCapra. But I knew from our little session in Wellington, Kansas that Needles' testimony was based on inadmissible hearsay. And besides that, his twitchy manner and long rap sheet made him unappealing as a witness. And as if that wasn't enough, he'd vanished when we'd released him from Independence Jail, and no one knew where he was.

But the problems with the Bureau's case didn't end there. Nothing had changed regarding two essential pieces of evidence. First, there was still no reliable eyewitness, who could identify Adam Richetti as one of the shooters at Union Station. And second, the two partial latent fingerprints on the beer bottles at Edgevale Road were the only evidence linking Richetti to Miller.

This meant that the prosecution's case would have to be built around Richetti's criminal association with Floyd. On the bright side, there was ample evidence to support this. But without someone to place Richetti at the scene of the shooting, it was a house of cards. And any competent defense attorney would be able to cast plenty of doubt on Richetti's involvement. So, in the end, I recommended we do not take the case.

However, Milligan still wanted to proceed. It would be a high-profile matter with the D.A.'s name all over it. And considering the public's mood, even with weak evidence, we'd likely get a conviction. That made it a tempting prospect. However, if the jury did convict, it was doubtful that the verdict would hold up on appeal. And to his credit,

Milligan knew this. So, he decided to try and strengthen the case by making a counteroffer to Hoover: we would prosecute Richetti—but only if Mathias agreed to testify.

Despite the plea deal Mathias had cut, Milligan thought that, if we offered to significantly reduce her sentence, she would likely take the stand. Part of our offer was that she would only have to testify that Richetti had been one of Miller's accomplices at Union Station—and nothing more. The Chief believed that this, with the remaining evidence, would be sufficient for us to secure a conviction.

I thought putting Mathias on the stand was nuts. Since we knew one part of her statement was false, I had no confidence in the rest of it. Further, it was likely that, despite any agreement we made, the judge would still allow defense counsel to ask her anything they wanted. There were so many ways it could go wrong—I didn't want to think about it.

But it wasn't my call. And Milligan went ahead and made his proposal to Hoover. Fortunately, J. Edgar got his back up at the mere suggestion of such a deal. He'd promised Mathias her statement would remain secret and that was that. So, Hoover gave us the out we needed, and thankfully, Milligan took it.

Of course, by rejecting Milligan's proposal, Hoover had created a problem for himself. Since trying Richetti in federal court was now off the table and the crime had happened in Kansas City, only one jurisdictional option was left open to him. He would have to turn to the Pendergast courts and Jackson County Prosecutor, W. W. Graves. Graves was, of course, the same man who'd overseen the phony acquittal of Mad Dog Gargotta in the murder of Ferris Anthon.

Initially, my assessment of the Bureau's evidence was

confirmed. The Jackson County Prosecutor's office also balked at the weakness of the Bureau's case. But they soon changed their minds. Boss Tom let it be known that he wanted the Union Station case resolved, and so, Graves had reluctantly agreed to prosecute Richetti. And I wondered if he would be able to pull it off.

DURING FOUR DAYS in June 1936, nearly three years after the Union Station Massacre, Adam Richetti was put on trial for murder in the newly completed Jackson County Courthouse. Because of our interest in the case, Milligan had asked me to monitor the trial. My job was to produce daily summaries for our office as well as for Hoover and the Justice Department. I later learned that some of my summaries even made their way to the President.

At first, I was puzzled by the prosecution's case. Despite the five deaths at Union Station, Graves had elected to try Richetti on only one charge of first-degree murder. And this was for the death of Detective Frank Hermanson. Hermanson, of course, was one of the two KCPD officers killed in the Massacre. Presumably, the Jackson County Prosecutor thought that, of the five deaths, this was his strongest case. And since he was going for the death penalty—justice for one was justice for all.

As anticipated, Graves focused on the exploits of Pretty Boy Floyd in his opening. And he emphasized how, throughout their career, Floyd and Richetti had been partners in crime. Graves also described in graphic detail the injuries suffered by the dead and wounded lawmen. This was intended to arouse the jury's sympathies, in the hopes that they would render a guilty verdict.

Graves then began presenting his case. As anticipated, he used the testimony of the surviving lawmen to show that Floyd and Richetti always worked together. First, he focused on their spree through Missouri and Oklahoma before the Massacre. And then, he elicited testimony on their attempted robbery of the Galena bank immediately afterward. While this line of questioning was offered into evidence as a "chronology of events," its real purpose was to demonstrate that, after they'd met, Floyd and Richetti never operated alone.

I noticed that, so far, Graves hadn't asked any of the surviving lawmen he had put on the stand to identify Richetti as one of Miller's accomplices at Union Station. And I wondered if the jurors had noticed this too. But when Agent Joseph Lackey took the stand, that question was finally asked.

Lackey had been one of the three men sitting in the rear of the shot-up sedan. In a well-orchestrated moment, Graves had asked him whether any of the gunmen from Union Station were present in the courtroom? Without hesitation, Lackey had pointed to Richetti.

I'd been stunned when Lackey had done this. I remembered his written statement, which had been taken right after the shootings. In it, he'd said that he had been unable to identify any of the gunmen—because the windows of the shot-up car had been "too dirty." Interestingly, Lackey had said the same thing to reporters at the time.

So, not surprisingly, Richetti's counsel began Lackey's cross-examination with these conflicting newspaper reports. But Lackey had a ready answer. He said that, when he was talking to the reporters, he'd simply been following Bureau policy. According to that policy, an agent was not permitted to name criminal suspects to newspaper reporters without the express permission of his superiors. It was a glib response, but I knew it was baloney.

The Bureau's fingerprint expert came next. Using blow-ups, he showed the jury the two partial latent fingerprints found on the beer bottles at Edgevale Road. Then he compared them to Adam Richetti's showing that they matched. With this testimony, the prosecution had put Richetti in Vern Miller's residence. So, now it had tied Richetti to both Miller and Floyd—the two individuals who were commonly believed to have carried out the Union Station Massacre.

The finale came with the city coroner's testimony. His focus was on Frank Hermanson's head wound. I vividly recalled seeing Hermanson's body cradled in Grooms's arms on the day of the Massacre. And I'd been previously told that the county coroner had determined that Hermanson's head wound had been caused by large-caliber buckshot.

However, on direct examination, the city coroner now testified that Hermanson's wound was the result of a 45-caliber bullet. And further, that the bullet had come from a Colt automatic. This was convenient since Richetti never carried anything but a Colt Forty-Five. The city coroner was the final prosecution witness, and after he left the stand, Graves rested his case.

The defense then called their only witness, and once again, I was surprised. In my experience, criminal defendants rarely took the stand. They were strongly discouraged from doing so by defense counsel because they opened the door to damaging cross-examination. The latter usually consisted of a restatement of the strongest evidence against them. However, if after learning of these dangers, a competent defendant still insisted on testifying, then there was a strong belief among members of the criminal bar that such individuals were likely innocent.

Richetti's direct examination was brief. He denied all the charges against him and stated that he could not have been at Union Station on the morning of the Massacre because he'd been too hung-over to get out of bed. It was not an inspired defense. But it did have the ring of truth to it. And when defense counsel had asked if anyone could vouch for Richetti's version of events, he'd simply responded, "Only Floyd."

Defense counsel then turned Richetti over for cross-examination. And I braced myself for a long afternoon. But Graves, probably wisely, chose not to ask Richetti a single question. So, he left the stand, and the defense rested.

The judge then gave the jurors their instructions, and they retired to deliberate. Returning quickly, they rendered a unanimous guilty verdict. And after denying the defense's motion for reconsideration, the judge had sentenced Adam Richetti to "hang by the neck until dead."

Of course, the defense had appealed, but without much hope of success. And I'd had to admit that, even though he was sleazy, Graves was an effective advocate. He had put on a compelling, if dubious, case, which had completely stitched Richetti up.

Mac and I never talked about the Richetti trial. He knew the file as well as I did, and, if he had been in the courtroom, Mac would certainly have seen what I had seen. But I suspected that his loyalty to the Bureau would not have allowed him to draw the same conclusions that I had.

With Floyd's death and Richetti's conviction, the Bureau had "solved" the Union Station Massacre. And it had also put to rest doubts about its competence. But the methods the Bureau had employed hadn't been reassuring. Call me old-fashioned, but I still preferred due process and a fair trial—even for the most rotten of apples.

THE NEXT DAY I was back in the office. Late for a meeting with Milligan, I rushed out of my door and ran headlong into Audrey. I not only knocked the stack of mail she'd been carrying out of her arms, but I nearly bowled her over.

"Audrey! Oh, I'm so sorry," I exclaimed catching her before she fell. Thankfully, she was laughing. In relief, I hugged her, and she leaned into me.

There was movement at the end of the corridor. And we turned to see Wilson standing there, staring at us. We stiffened when we saw him but didn't move apart. He coughed once, glanced down at the papers in his hand, and headed back in the direction from which he'd come.

We looked at each other and smiled. Then Audrey knelt to gather up the mail on the floor, and I squatted down to help her. But when we stood up, her face had become serious.

"Sam, I wanted to tell you about Chandler. He's gone to Spain—to fight the fascists." Then, feeling the need for more explanation, she added, "He knows he can't fight. But there are other things he can do to help."

I nodded trying to help her along.

Then she said—all in a rush. "He told me not to wait for him. But I said I would anyway. I just couldn't let him go like that, Sam."

I knew my face told her how I felt. But I nodded as if I understood.

Then handing me my mail, she walked away, down the hall. And I stood there watching her go.

That afternoon, I was reading case law in preparation for drafting a brief on an embezzlement matter. Our office had the Eighth Circuit and Supreme Court reporters, but we often had to borrow volumes for the other circuits from the courthouse library. That morning I'd requested a reporter for a Tenth Circuit case.

When the volume arrived, the page on which the case was located had been thoughtfully bookmarked by one of the librarians. They often did that. But when I opened the reporter, I saw that the bookmark wasn't the usual foot-long piece of green card stock. Instead, it was an unaddressed business envelope. Inside was a single sheet of stationery folded into thirds. I unfolded the paper; on it was a table with fifty-two cells.

I knew immediately that it was from Wetzel. I had read enough of the book on cryptanalysis, which Rabbi Mayerberg had loaned me, to know that I was looking at a simple substitution cipher—keyed to a deck of playing cards. Using it, one could convey a brief message simply by passing a deck of cards to another person with the key.

The cipher assigned a playing card from each of the red suits to every letter in the alphabet. It also paired a card from the black suits to each number in the series from one to twenty-five. I noted that Wetzel had changed the meaning of the King of Clubs from the number "26" to a plus sign. This would double the range of numbers, which the cipher could convey, from twenty-five to fifty.

But I could also see that the cipher had one major limitation. If the message was to remain secure, an individual letter or number could only be used once. Otherwise, multiples of the same playing card would have to be inserted into the deck. And this would betray the existence of a hidden message to an alert interceptor.

Similarly, since English has a high frequency of repeated letters, the cipher could only be used for short alphabetic messages. So short in fact, that they might consist of only a couple of words or abbreviations. That told me that the cipher was best suited to communicating numbers.

I didn't know what this meant or where it was heading. But I did know that the biggest risk to any cipher was to leave its key lying around. So, I committed the contents of the paper to memory and burned it.

25

NOVEMBER 3, 1936

About the time of the Richetti trial, Tom and Caroline Pendergast returned to the United States from a European tour. After disembarking from the Queen Mary in New York City, T. J. had held court at the Waldorf Astoria. There, he'd met with national and state politicians making plans for the 1936 election.

Afterward, the Pendergasts had traveled to Philadelphia for the Democratic Party's National Convention, which had, not surprisingly, re-nominated FDR for a second term. However, during the late-night deal-making, Boss Tom had suffered a coronary. Rushed back to New York City, his condition had stabilized, and he had spent July and August recuperating.

But then, in early September, the Boss had suffered a setback. He had to undergo emergency surgery for an intestinal blockage. And afterward, his recovery had been slower than expected. And so, the Pendergast's had returned to Kansas City for a second opinion. And the Boss was taken to Menorah Hospital for further evaluation. There, his physicians had recommended a colostomy, and this was performed. After that, Boss Tom's health finally began to improve.

Throughout this period, members of the Reform Movement had been cautiously optimistic. No one had, of course, wished the Boss ill. But many had hoped that poor health might force him to retire. Everyone knew that Tom Pendergast had never been keen on power-sharing. And while he'd ostensibly groomed his nephew, Jim, to be his replacement, no one thought the latter up to the task. Although competent, Jim lacked the ruthlessness essential to machine politics. And it was widely believed that, if T. J. retired, the machine would lose control of the city.

Initial reports on the Boss's health had encouraged these hopes. They'd said that Pendergast had lost over thirty-five pounds and that he'd visibly aged. While these reports were factually accurate, those who'd seen him told a different story. They said that, while he *was* physically diminished, Boss Tom's mind was as sharp as ever. And more importantly, his will was just as inflexible.

And it turned out that, by the time of the 1936 Election, Boss Tom had fully regained his health. And once again, he took charge of the machine's electoral efforts. But what the Boss didn't know was that this election was going to be different. This time we were laying for him.

And so, on November 3, 1936, the U.S.D.A.'s office was transformed into an evidence-gathering center. Shortly after the polls opened, citizens began to arrive to file formal complaints of voting fraud. The office staff took down their statements, which were typed up so that they could be signed and notarized.

One of the statements I took was from a nineteen-year-old sportscaster for KCMO radio. His broadcast handle was Walter Wilcox, but his real name was Walter Cronkite. A couple of KCPD cops had stopped him on the way to work and had asked if he had voted yet? When he'd said that he hadn't, they'd walked him to the nearest polling station.

Once they were there, they handed him a list of phony names. And they'd told him to vote the Democratic ticket for all of them. And by the way, they'd said, if he knew what was good for him, he would also cast one more vote for the same ticket—in his name. Cronkite hadn't argued with them and did as he was told. But afterward, he'd been so mad that he'd marched right over to the courthouse and filed a complaint. And there had been many like him.

All the Assistant U.S. District Attorneys, except for Otto Schmid, had taken a turn in the conference room. Because of Schmid's known machine ties, Milligan had decided to assign him to the Independence docket for the day. There, while all election plans had played out, he'd handled routine hearings and arrangements.

We'd also previously informed Judges Otis and Reeves of our intent to file multiple applications for subpoenas—in support of election-fraud claims. And so, as the voters' complaints and affidavits had come in, we'd drafted supporting motions. And by three o'clock, we were ready.

Wilson appeared before Judge Reeves, and I went before Otis. And both judges had granted every one of our requests. Then as soon as the polls were closed, we'd served our subpoenas. And with the assistance of armed Bureau agents, we'd seized ballot boxes and voter-registration books from all the machine-dominated wards in the city. And for once, we'd caught the machine with its pants down.

The next day Milligan asked Judge Reeves to appoint a grand jury, and it was duly empaneled in mid-December. But the number of indictments we'd generated was beyond the scope of that body to deal with. And eventually, three more would have to be appointed before all the indictments could be addressed. In the end, four separate grand juries indicted two hundred and seventy-eight individuals.

Voter fraud had existed for so long in Kansas City, that local citizens had considered it a fact of life. And so, they'd been astonished when charges had been brought against the machine. But they'd been dumbfounded when the charges had stuck. And since our cases had been filed in federal, not state, court, there were no Pendergast-beholden judges to go soft on the culprits.

But what had pleased me most was Rabbi Mayerberg's performance. As anticipated, he had provided eloquent and damning testimony on the long history of stolen elections in the city. And his sterling reputation had been simply icing on the cake.

But the final proof of our success had been in the numbers. Out of the two hundred and seventy-eight individuals indicted, only nineteen had been acquitted. And as Milligan had intended, the large number of convictions had proved costly to the machine. Not only did it have to cover the legal expenses of those indicted, but it had promised to pay the lost wages of all who were convicted. Consequently, a hefty surcharge had had to be added to the local skim—just to meet the cost of the election-fraud cases.

Even though we were pleased with this outcome, we knew that our efforts had been little more than a kick in the shins. Despite the voter-fraud convictions, the machine continued to function much as it had. And of course, we hadn't laid a finger on the Boss himself. More worrisome was that the machine had begun to operate more circumspectly. That meant in the future we would have to hit harder and punch higher if we were going to bring down both the Boss and the machine.

On March 4, 1937, I was getting ready for bed after a full day of hearings and arraignments. I already had on my pajamas and was hanging up my suit when I felt something heavy in the outer pocket of my coat. I rarely put anything into my suit coat pockets, not wanting to bag them. So, I wondered what it was.

Reaching inside, I pulled out a pack of playing cards. At some point during the day, someone had slipped it into my pocket. I immediately carried the deck into the kitchen. Sitting down at the table, I took the cards out of their packet being careful to keep them in order.

I sorted through the deck until I came to the red joker. According to the key, that marked the beginning of the message. Then I laid out the cards in sequence face-up on the table until I reached the black joker. That of course signified the end of the message.

When I'd finished, there were eight cards in front of me. They were the 5 of Diamonds, King of Spades, Queen of Hearts, 3 of Clubs, 4 of Spades, 7 of Clubs, King of Clubs, and Queen of Clubs. Remembering the key, I deciphered the message: "R, 13, L, 16, 4, 20, +, 25." It looked like gibberish, and I wondered if I'd made a mistake.

26

MAY 18, 1937

After lunch on Tuesday, May 18, 1937, my intercom buzzed. And Ginny, using her most professional voice, announced that Rabbi Mayerberg was in reception.

"I'll be right out," I said.

When I got there, the Rabbi was chatting with Wilson, who immediately took his leave. Rabbi Mayerberg and I shook hands, and I showed him to my office.

As we went, I said, "I'm sorry, Rabbi, I wasn't expecting you. And I'm afraid I'm short on time this afternoon."

"My apologies, Sam," he said speaking quietly. "This won't take long. I intentionally did not make an appointment. I'll explain why, when we get to your office."

After we were seated, I noticed that Mayerberg was carrying a parcel wrapped in brown paper.

"Sorry to be so mysterious, Sam. But I'm following instructions, and I want to do so precisely. I was told you would understand."

I knew immediately that the Rabbi was referring to Wetzel. Then Mayerberg handed me the parcel and stood up to go. I locked it in my desk. Then, I showed the Rabbi out.

When I returned to my office, I took out the package and snipped the string that bound it. Inside was a new Douay-Reims Bible. I thumbed slowly through it. When I reached the end, I repeated the procedure, but this time going page-by-page checking for anything I might have missed. When that still turned nothing up, I examined the cover, both inside and out, and the binding.

The back sheet was bound to the cover board with adhesive. On the underside edge of the rear cover board, I noticed a five-inch-long strip of a lighter shade of adhesive than the rest. I took out my penknife and inserted the smallest blade into it. Then I'd felt around inside with the blade. Something loose was there. Using the blade, I fished out a thin piece of cardboard.

It was a two-inch-by-four-inch, yellow claim ticket. The diamond logo of the Kansas City Terminal Railway was printed on it. One end of the ticket bore a box with the word "In" printed above it. There was a date-and-time stamp in the box: "June 20, 1935, 1:56 p.m." The opposite end of the ticket had another box with the word, "Out," printed above it. That box was empty.

Turning the ticket over, I read in tiny font on the back: "Daily rate: 5 cents, monthly rate: 50 cents, double the rate for secure storage. Items left for more than two years will be sold at public auction. Union Station Terminal Railway, Kansas City, Missouri, Left Luggage Room. Tel. GRand – 4444."

At this point, I called Budge. Luckily, he was home, and we agreed to meet after lunch. I put the claim ticket into my wallet. Then, I headed for the Liberty Bell.

At one o'clock, Budge pulled to the curb outside the

diner. He was driving his Chevrolet panel van. I got in, and we drove to Union Station, where we parked in the first row of cars close to the eastern bank of doors.

The Left Luggage Room was at the northwestern end of the Grand Hall. When we arrived, the counter was empty. So, I rang the service bell. After a bit, an agent came out of the back. He scratched his head at the ticket and disappeared the way he'd come.

When he returned, another man was following him, wheeling a dolly. On it was an olive-green metal box. It was about three feet long, 18 inches wide, and one foot deep. Yellow letters were stenciled on its side: "Q.M.C. U.S.A." There was a combination lock in the center of the lid and below it, a D-ring latch.

The agent jerked his head at the box saying, "What you got in there, Joe—gold bullion?" He snickered at his joke. I smiled and paid the twenty-three-dollar secure storage fee, hoping it was worth it. Then, the agent time-stamped the ticket and handed it back to me.

"Homer will help you to your car," he said.

So, with Homer in tow, we retraced our steps to the van. There, we lifted the box into the back. And I gave the dolly-man a twenty-five-cent tip for his trouble.

Soon, we were standing in my kitchen in Brookside. The metal box sat on the floor. It was too heavy for the table. And I asked Budge if he had ever seen one before?

"Sure. The 'Q.M.C. stands for Quarter Master Corp." he said. "They used strongboxes like these to pay the troops at the front during the War. Haven't seen one, though, since Belleau Wood."

"So, what do you know about it?"

"Well, it's not called a strongbox for nothing."

"Can we get it open?"

Budge pushed back his crumpled fedora as he thought, scratching his forehead. "Depends on what's inside."

"We don't know what's inside," I reminded him.

He nodded. "So, we can't use nitro or a torch," he said. "If it's currency or paper, it could burn."

Twirling the dial, I asked, "Ever crack a combination lock?"

"Nope," he said. "Too newfangled for me. No way to pick it. And from what I remember, you can't pry these boxes open either. There's a rack-and-pinion lock beneath the dial. But once you've entered the correct sequence of numbers, you just twist the D-ring and it opens."

"So, what do we do?" I asked.

"Figure out the combination, I guess."

We looked at the dial. The numbers ran from "0" to "50." Only every tenth number was in figures. The rest were indicated by hash marks.

"This is like a 50 to 1 lottery," I said. "With fifty numbers in the combination and a five-digit code, there are over two million permutations. It would be a helluva slog using trial and error. And what if there are only four numbers in the combination or as many as six?"

"Yeah," Budge replied nodding. "I get it."

"Wait a minute," I said feeling like a dope. I'd just remembered Wetzel's last message. The eight playing cards had stood for the following: "R, 13, L, 16, 4, 20, +, 25."

Looking at the strongbox, I realized that the "R" had to be an abbreviation for "to the right." And the "L" must stand for "to the left." That would give us the sequence for a four-number combination: Right-13, Left-16, Right-4, and Left-45.

So, I knelt and twirled the knob several times to the left, to clear the lock. Then I went to the right, to the number "13" and back to the left, stopping at "16." Going right again, I turned to the number "4" and immediately back to "45." Then taking a deep breath, I twisted the D-ring handle. The rack-and-pinion lock rotated freely with a satisfying "click."

"How the hell did you do that?" asked Budge amazed.

"Wetzel," I said. "Let's see what we've got."

I lifted the lid. And we looked at each other in surprise. The strongbox contained nothing but bundles of paper. Taking a closer look, we saw that the paper was, more accurately, business correspondence.

"What the heck," I said. "Nash and Wetzel were killed because of this?"

Trying to figure out what we had, we sat down at the kitchen table and started going through it. And it was just what it looked like—business letters to and from people we'd never heard of. In the letters, they were arranging meetings, proposing agenda items, and circulating draft documents.

Then I spotted something. In the "Re" line of one letter were the words: "Fire Insurance Settlement Agreement." And I glanced at the signature. The letter was from, "Charles R. Street." Digging some more, I found blind carbon copies addressed to "T. J."

"Bingo," I said.

"What?" Budge asked not understanding.

"A Treasury Agent I know would kill to get his hands on this stuff."

"Why?"

"If I'm not wrong, these are Boss Tom's papers. The Government thinks a big chunk of money has gone missing from a legal settlement. And they suspect that it's found its way into Pendergast's pocket. But they haven't been able to prove it."

"Will this stuff help?" Budge asked.

"It just might," I said nodding.

Still digesting our find, we grabbed a beer and went into the living room to talk. We decided that, for the moment, the best course was to keep our find secret. Nash and Wetzel had been killed because they'd not only known of the Boss' involvement in the fire insurance scam, but they'd possessed the evidence to prove it. Now, we were in their shoes. And if we weren't careful, we could end up dead too.

But we also agreed that we couldn't sit on this evidentiary time bomb. We had to get it to Hartmann—and soon. But we had to be careful about how we did it. I was already on thin ice with the mob. And they didn't need another reason to kill me.

TWO DAYS LATER, in mid-afternoon, my intercom buzzed, "Special Treasury Agent Rudolph Hartmann is here to see you, Sam," said Ginny. I asked her to tell Hartmann that I'd be with him in a moment.

I wondered why Rudy was in town. He hadn't let me know he was coming. I glanced uneasily at the strongbox in the corner. Budge and I had moved it to my office, figuring it was safer here than at home. Still, we hadn't yet worked out how to give Rudy the cache of documents, without having my fingerprints all over them.

When I got to the reception, Hartmann was standing there, leafing through a *Saturday Evening Post*. Ginny was snapping her gum and sizing him up while pretending to fill out her delivery log. With his John Wayne build and cleft chin, Hartmann was Ginny's cup of tea.

Rudy dropped the magazine as soon as he saw me and extended his hand. "Sam, good to see you."

"Likewise."

We chatted as we walked into the conference room and closed the door. Rudy tossed his hat onto the table and sat down.

"So, what brings you to KC?" I asked getting out a cigarette.

"Same old, same old."

"Still working the Pendergast scam?" I asked, lighting up.

He nodded.

"What's happening now? Did you get Street to cooperate?"

"Well, no. He's dead."

I sat up. "What the hell? I didn't even know he was sick."

"Neither did we," said Rudy glumly. "He went to the doctor a couple of weeks back. And the next thing we know, he's in the hospital."

"With what?"

"Cancer—and pretty far along. The guy didn't last two weeks."

"Whew!"

"Yeah."

"Get anything more from him before he died?"

"Nope."

"That's rough."

"You're telling me," he said, rubbing his chin.

"So, what can I do for you?" I asked.

"Just thought I'd check-in. We had a meeting at Commerce Bank this morning to examine their books on the escrow account."

"Find anything?"

Shaking his head, "Not really. The bank made the distributions as specified by the agreement. The part we were looking at, of course, was the thirty percent that went to the trust fund. In the end, that amounted to about $2.7 million."

Here Rudy paused to light up. As he exhaled, he said, "We wanted to check the bank's books, because we'd come across something else fishy at the Folonie firm."

"Like what?"

"Well, after paying the attorneys' fees and expenses for the state and the companies, an amount equal to eleven percent of the total was leftover. As you'll recall, the settlement agreement specified that any remaining money was to be paid back to the fire insurance companies."

"Yeah, I remember."

"Well, we found a note in the law firm's file saying that instead of sending one check to each company, Street had wanted to issue two. One of the checks was to be for five percent of the total and the other one for six."

"That's odd; did you ask Folonie about it?"

"We did. He said that, at the time, he thought it was funny too. So, he'd asked Street why he wanted two checks. But when he did, Street had gotten angry and wouldn't tell him why. So, Folonie said that he'd put his foot down and hadn't agreed to it. In the end, only one check had been cut and sent to each company."

"What do you make of that?"

"Well, someone, reportedly in the know, has told us that the skim was supposed to be five percent of the total. So, if that's right, it looks like Street might have been planning on having each company endorse the five-percent check and return it to him for the payoff."

"But that didn't happen."

"Yeah, and it's too bad it didn't. The whole thing would have been a lot simpler if it had."

"So, how much money are we talking about?"

"Around $450,000."

I nodded. "So, what did you do next?"

"Well, we applied to the administrator of Street's estate, which was the City National Bank and Trust of Chicago. We asked for copies of Street's canceled checks, check stubs, and bank statements. But we were told there weren't any."

"Really?"

"Yeah. Well, then the City National Bank folks went all funny on us. They weren't exactly obstructive, but they weren't helpful either. So, we just served them with a blanket subpoena for anything and everything related to Charles R. Street."

"Did that work?"

"Yep. They caved and took us down to the main vault. Inside a large lockbox, was a small suitcase containing all of Street's canceled checks, check stubs, bank statements as well as some personal correspondence and other effects."

"Whoop-de-doo!"

Rudy shrugged, "That's what we thought at first too—until we took a closer look. But Street had over-written the check stubs we were interested in so that the recipients were illegible. But we did find one thing."

"What was that?"

Rudy took an envelope out of his inside pocket and handed it to me. "This was among Street's papers."

The envelope was addressed to Street, and it bore a St. Louis postmark, but there was no return address. The following was typed on a blank sheet of stationery inside.

Dear Mr. Street,

I understand that the Governor will be in Kansas City on Saturday, and I am writing to our friend about the arrangements we have made. I wanted him to be familiar with the details when he sees the Governor.

Our man in Jefferson City has informed me that the Governor wants to be certain our friend approves of the arrangement. So, you can see that we have correctly anticipated what was needed. As you know, this could not have been accomplished without our friend's help.

I would also like to add that I am not at all sanguine about Folonie's understanding of this matter. In my experience, attorneys (although I happen to be one myself) do not always understand practical arrangements of this kind, and how best to present them to the courts. They only think in legal terms, and this matter is a little beyond that.

I was thinking I could still drop over to Kansas City and see our friend, just to make doubly certain everything is understood. But since I haven't heard from you, I will assume that this is unnecessary.

THERE WAS no closing and no signature.

"What do you think?" asked Rudy.

I looked at the envelope and letter again. "Sounds like a St. Louis lawyer helped Street put the skim together. Any idea of who he is?"

"Not yet, but we're looking into it."

"Who do you think 'our man in Jefferson City' is?"

"I'm guessing it's Insurance Commissioner O'Malley."

"And you're thinking 'our friend' in Kansas City is Pendergast?"

He nodded.

I handed the letter back to Rudy. "Anything else?" I asked.

Here, Rudy turned serious. "Except for this letter, Sam, we're at a complete dead end. And we're not hopeful."

He looked me in the eye. "I hear you've got something I need."

I stared back at him. "Did you also hear what'll happen to me if I just hand it over to you?"

"I can't help that, Sam. I need those documents. And I need them now."

The friendliness was gone. And I wondered who had ratted on me?

"Come on, Sam. Don't make me subpoena them."

I didn't have any choice. And if Rudy knew, then the mob probably did too. So, I said, "Okay, but on two conditions."

"Such as?"

"Such as one, you take the documents right now. And two, we both catch the next train to Chicago." Then I added, "If you think I going to hang around here and wait for Carrollo to plug me—you're nuts."

"It's a deal," said Rudy snatching up his hat.

"The papers are in my office," I said.

"Let's go then," he replied

As we exited the conference room, I called out to Gin, "Get us a cab to the station, Ginny. And better make it quick, we've got a train to catch."

She nodded and picked up the phone.

27

MAY 27, 1937

Nine days later, I was on the Golden State Limited and headed back to Kansas City. Working around the clock with Hartmann's team, we had managed to mine the Pendergast correspondence and add everything useful to the existing investigative file. When we'd finished, we knew we had enough to indict Boss Tom and several of his pals.

The crown jewel of the cache was a second letter, from our still anonymous lawyer in St. Louis. In this one, the writer had injudiciously laid out the names of everyone involved in the scam, and the bribe each would receive. This letter, like the first one, was undated and unsigned. But unlike the earlier one, it had been addressed to, "Mr. Tom Pendergast, 1908 Main Street, KC MO."

While I was in Chicago, I'd placed long-distance calls to both Mac and Budge. And we'd devised a plan that we hoped would get me safely from Union Station to my home in Brookside. After that, we'd have to figure out what to do next.

I took a seat in the club car and settled down with the

noon edition of the *Chicago Tribune*. Lighting a cigarette, I started reading, as the train pulled away. The front page was dedicated to the opening of the Golden Gate Bridge in San Francisco. As the longest and tallest suspension bridge in the world, it was an engineering marvel.

As I worked my way through the paper, an article at the bottom of the front page of the international section caught my eye. Its title was, "American Killed in Battle for Madrid."

> Chandler R. Brown, a native of Kansas City, Missouri, and a non-combatant member of the Abraham Lincoln Brigade, was killed on May 10 during a Nationalist assault on the outskirts of Madrid. Brown was serving at a Republican Army supply depot when it came under fire. Wheelchair-bound, he was unable to escape. Choosing to fight rather than surrender, Brown barricaded himself inside the depot and took up arms. He singlehandedly repelled several Nationalist attempts to dislodge him. Finally, he was killed by artillery fire. Diplomatic efforts are underway to recover Brown's body and return it to the United States for burial.

I hoped Audrey already knew about Chandler's death. Because I didn't want to be the one to tell her. And I wondered, what effect, if any, it would have on our relationship.

My thoughts shifted to what awaited me in Kansas City. And I lit another cigarette. I knew that Carrollo's boys would come gunning for me. The only question was when. Would they jump me as soon as I got off the train, or hold off until later when they hoped my guard would be down? We knew Charlie was impulsive and usually took things head-on. So, that was what we had prepared for. I hoped that we were right.

When I stepped off the Limited, my palms were sweaty. But Mac was waiting for me on the platform as planned, and that immediately made me feel better. A detail of three Bureau agents and a couple of KCPD detectives I didn't know were with him. The FBI boys were carrying revolvers in their hands, and the detectives were cradling shotguns. Mac handed me a forty-five automatic, which I tucked into my waistband. It felt good just having a little firepower of my own.

Mingling with the arriving passengers, we mounted the stairs from Platform Eight. When we reached the top, Mac held up a hand, and we paused while he surveyed the Transit Hall. We'd timed my arrival for early Saturday evening when we figured the station would be almost empty. And it was. Only a scattering of layover passengers lined the high-backed benches.

Mac put me in the middle of our group. And we set off down the Transit Hall's central aisle. Our feet fell naturally into sync, as we marched along. And I couldn't help but think of Jelly Nash and his detail. Hopefully, we were better prepared, than they had been.

I wondered if Jelly had had any inkling of what was about to happen that morning. Even if he had, he likely felt safe with seven armed lawmen around him. Still, he'd been killed anyway. And that wasn't a reassuring thought.

Up ahead, a few men were clustered under the station clock. There was nothing unusual about that; it was a well-known meeting point. Still, we eyed them as we approached. But we passed them by without incident and continued through the archway into the Grand Hall.

Soon we were past the unmanned Travelers Aid Desk in

the center of the Hall. And my spirits started to rise. Approaching the front of the station, I saw that only two ticket windows were open, and there was no line. That was good. The fewer people around, the better.

I glanced through the tombstone window above the eastern bank of doors and saw that it was getting dark outside. We went through the doors and came to a halt beneath the canopy. For some reason, Budge's paneled van wasn't waiting at the curb, as planned. Then we saw him. He was just pulling into the parking lot, to our left. He was running only a few seconds late. I breathed easier. I was going to make it after all.

Cold steel pressed against the back of my neck. And a voice behind me barked, "Up, up, up!" My heart sank, as I raised my hands. So much for planning.

"Guns on the ground," the voice commanded. "Now, everyone back away." My escort complied.

Mac spoke to the detective behind me. "Easy," he said.

The man reached around and jerked the forty-five from my waistband. Then the shotgun barrel prodded me forward. "Walk," commanded the voice.

Stepping off the curb, I started across the nearly empty parking lot. Budge had pulled to a stop just short of us. There was nothing he could do.

Then I saw the Hot Shot gliding out from behind a moving van parked at the far end of the lot. It purred towards us. The gun port in the Hot Shot's windshield flicked open, and the barrel of a Thompson appeared. It was pointed at Mac and the cluster of lawmen standing under the canopy behind us.

Easing to a halt, the right rear door swung open. Hands reached out and pulled me inside; they shoved me to the floor. The door clicked shut, and we started moving.

"Nice work, Ralphy," a familiar voice hissed. And someone put a foot on the side of my head. It pressed down until my cheek was flat against the floor.

We wheeled out of the station and picked up speed. Before long, the tires made a singing sound. And I guessed we were crossing the river. Reaching the far side, we sped up. No one spoke, and I tried not to think about what lay ahead.

Before long, we slowed and made a series of turns. I heard the crunch of gravel and felt the rear end slide around. Even before we had come to a stop, they were opening the doors. And I was being hauled out.

My guess had been correct. We were at the base of a bluff, north of the river. Across the street was a white-railed fence with an illuminated sign: "The Riverside Jockey-Club Racetrack." Then I was pulled in the opposite direction.

We went up the steps of a pillared plantation house. There was a brass plate next to the double doors. The words, "Cuban Gardens," were etched on it. We went through the doors and were greeted by the burbling sounds of a nightclub. Horns wailed, and I recognized both the players and the music. It was Count Basie's Orchestra, and they were playing their version of Ellington's *Caravan*.

In the entry, we went to the right through a door marked "Private" and down a long flight of stairs. At the bottom, was a paneled room fitted out with gaming tables. It was dark except for a light at the far end. We went toward it.

As we approached, I could see the light hung over a green-felted table. Six older men sat around it playing cards. Joe D faced me. His brother Pete sat to his right, and James Balestrere was on his left. I didn't know the other three.

The men paid no attention to us. They were playing

some sort of card-taking game. And as they played, they bantered in a language I assumed was Sicilian.

When the game ended, everyone, except for Joe, tossed their cards into the center of the table. Then they got up and walked into the darkness. Without looking at me, Joe gathered up the cards and began to shuffle. As he did, he started to talk.

"You see, there was this guy. He had a boil in a very unfortunate place." Joe paused to grab his crotch just to make sure I got the location. "Got so bad—he couldn't sit down. So, the guy goes to the doctor. The doctor says to him, 'Got to lance it.'"

"But the guy says, 'No way, Doc. Just put medicine on it.' So, the doctor puts medicine on the boil. A couple of weeks later, the guy is in the hospital—swollen up like a balloon. He's got blood poisoning, and he's going to die."

"The doctor comes to see him. Guy says, 'Hey Doc, why don't you tell me I die, if we don't lance the boil? The doctor smiles and says, . . . 'I did.'"

The silence that followed was palpable. And for some reason, I was tempted to laugh. But there was nothing funny about my situation.

Then Joe got up and walked around the table toward me. As he came, Rayen grabbed one of my arms and Claiborne took the other. They held me so that I couldn't back away.

Stopping in front of me, Joe's eyes glittered with malevolence. The scar on his face was florid, and his thick lips, moist and reptilian. His hand shot out, and he grabbed my balls. His grip was viselike, and I groaned

"If we were in Sicily," he said thickly, "I would slice these off, feed them to you, then cut your throat."

Then Joe's grip tightened until tears spurted from my

eyes. When he let go, I dropped to my knees—unable to breathe. Waves of nausea washed over me.

Then Rayen and Claiborne picked me up and hauled me up the stairs. They stuffed me, still doubled over, into the back of the Hot Shot. Rayen climbed in beside me, while Claiborne slipped behind the wheel. I felt the prick of the ice pick in my ribs.

"Nothing smart," snarled Rayen.

We took off down the drive with a spray of gravel. Turning left, we followed a road along the base of the bluff, which soon began to climb. Reaching the top, we skirted the edge until the highway turned north. Then we picked up speed racing past dim farmsteads and empty fields. All I could think of was the ice pick and my aching balls.

I'd recovered a little by the time we swerved off the highway and down a county road. We rattled along over rocks and ruts. And it was pitch dark now. The only light came from the glowing dash and the high beams on the road ahead.

I decided I would rather die in the car than take a walk in the dark. So, I readied myself. And when we hit the next big rut, I shot over the front seat.

"Hey!" shouted Rayen, stabbing at my legs with the ice pick.

He nailed my left calf, but it didn't matter. I was already over the seat and pulling down on the wheel. Claiborne fought to twist it back.

But the Hot Shot's left side lifted, and we rolled. Metal banged; glass shattered. I curled into a ball bouncing between floor and dash. Eventually, the tumbling slowed. And we creaked to a stop—upside down.

I lay dazed, on the inside roof. Glass was everywhere.

Something wet and yielding was wedged between the seat and dash above me. It was Claiborne. He wasn't moving.

Glancing towards the rear, my view was blocked by the dislodged seat. But I could see enough to know that the back window and left door were missing. There was no sign of Rayen.

I knew I had to get away from the car. So, I started slithering feet-first through the opening where the passenger-door window had been. Shards of glass cut me as I went. But I kept going.

When my knees were outside, I reached up to grab onto the inside of the door, intending to pull myself through. But instead of the armrest and window crank, I felt something long and metallic. It was the Thompson—still clipped to the inside of the door.

Then I realized Rayen might still be alive. He could have been thrown from the car and be out there somewhere, laying for me. So, I unclipped the Thompson and pushed it through the window ahead of me. Then I pulled myself out of the car.

I sat for a moment on the road, looking around me. The Hot Shot's headlights were still on. They were canted upwards shining into the night sky. The air was thick with the stench of gasoline. And I could hear the ticking of a rear wheel, as it slowly turned.

Using the side of the car, I pulled myself up, swaying unsteadily. Something was badly wrong with my left leg. But I could still hobble on it.

Bending down, I picked up the Thompson. It looked undamaged, and its drum magazine was firmly in place. I remembered Budge telling me how it worked. He'd said that it had to be cocked before it could fire. So, I grasped the lever on the right side and pulled it back—until it clicked. I just hoped it was okay and ready to fire.

Holding the Thompson waist high, I pointed it ahead of me, as I began shuffling up the road. I went in the direction from which I thought we'd come.

"Hold it!" said a voice. And I heard the cocking of a revolver. I froze.

"Turn around," said the voice. "And make it nice and slow."

I rotated unsteadily on my good leg, still holding the Thompson waist-high. But even though my eyes searched for Rayen. I couldn't tell where his voice was coming from.

"Stop, right there."

Then I saw him. He was pinned under the roof of the overturned car. His hands were stretched out in front of him. They clasped a blue-steel revolver, which was pointed at my chest.

"Smell gas?" I said. "Shoot, and you'll blow yourself up." I didn't know if that was true. But it was the only thing I could think of.

"Maybe, maybe not," he replied. "Drop the chopper."

That's when it hit me. *Do what he says,* the urge commanded. *Drop it!*

Instead, I swung the Thompson at Rayen and pulled the trigger. His body jerked as the rounds hit him. But somehow, he still managed to fire. And his bullet struck me squarely in the chest knocking me to the ground.

There was a wheezing flash. And a singeing wave washed over me. After it had passed, I raised my head. The Hot Shot was in flames. I grinned in disbelief; I'd been right after all.

Then pain pierced me, and I gasped for breath. My chest

throbbed and gurgled. I put both hands on the wound, trying to stem the flow of blood.

Resting my head on the road, I looked up at the night sky. It was a swath of black crepe covered with glittering sand. My eyes searched for the familiar patterns. And to the south, I made out Virgo reclining on the ecliptic. She seemed to hold out her frond to me, then everything went black.

After a while, I became conscious of gentle rocking and the sound of a siren. Someone was working on me. But I was too tired to open my eyes. Then the rocking became a fluid motion, and I was being swept along in dark and turbulent water. All around me was bobbing flotsam. The current flowed in a swirling whirlpool, and I was being drawn inexorably toward its center.

As I fought against the current, something long and gray floated toward me. I thought it was a log. But then I realized it was Johnny's corpse! And as it floated by, his vacant eyes opened, and his peeling lips moved. I backpedaled in horror.

Then something heavy glanced off my back. When I turned, I saw that it was the strongbox. Its dialed door was open, and the Boss's papers were being flushed out into the water. I tried to save them, but they dissolved in my fingers. Then I must have reached the center of the whirlpool because I was sucked down into darkness.

But the swirling water became a spinning sky. And I was spiraling to earth in an out-of-control biplane. The jerking motion threw me from the cockpit, but somehow, I managed to grab a strut. And as I clung to it, I saw there was an insignia on the plane. It was a black heart and inscribed on it, in white, were a skull-and-crossed-bones, two candles, and a coffin. Then I lost my grip and tumbled to earth.

But as I fell, the spinning earth became a dark rotating disk, with a grey dot at its center. The dot grew larger until I saw that it was a face. And I recognized it as the Medusa's! Her teeth gnashed, and the snakes of her hair writhed and hissed.

Then three naked, human legs sprang out from behind the Gorgon's head—running counterclockwise around it. The Medusa's mouth opened and grew ever larger until it filled my range of vision. Then it snapped shut, and she swallowed me.

My eyes flew open, and I wasn't dreaming. Two doctors and a nurse were bent over me, working inside my chest. Seeing I was awake, a second nurse placed a mesh cup over my nose and mouth. She dribbled something pungent onto it. And I went somewhere I'd never been before.

I was there for what seemed like a long time. Although time didn't matter there. And a shimmering Midge had come to me. But she wasn't the Midge I'd known. This Midge was exponentially more vibrant and real. She'd leaned down and kissed me on the forehead. And it had burned where her lips had touched me. But the burning was cleansing and pure. And with her kiss, I'd grown lighter and had slowly begun to rise.

When I awoke, it was night, and I was in a hospital ward. Dad was snoring lightly in a chair beside my bed. My left leg was in a cast and suspended by a pulley. But I couldn't keep my eyes open and drifted off.

The next time I awoke it was late afternoon. Budge was at the nurse's station talking to a doctor. They were looking at a chart. A nurse saw that I was awake and called the doctor. He and Budge hurried over.

"Water," I croaked.

The nurse put an arm under my head and raised a glass

to my lips. She only gave me a sip. Budge leaned over and spoke to me. But I couldn't make out what he was saying. And I drifted off again.

When I opened my eyes the third time, it was morning. Audrey was sitting beside my bed reading a book. I stretched out my hand, and she grabbed it.

"Sam!" She beamed.

I tried to smile. But I wasn't sure I was succeeding.

"How long?" I croaked.

She screwed up her face in thought.

"A week, I think. But I've got to get the doctor."

She jumped up, and I watched her go. My head was starting to clear, but I was weak. Audrey led a doctor to my bed. He took my pulse and shined a light into my eyes.

After a moment, he said, "You're one lucky guy."

"Don't I know it."

28

AUGUST 16, 1937

I was in the hospital for six weeks. And it was another five weeks before I could get around on my own. During that time, I'd stayed with my parents in Jefferson City, but now, I was back in town.

During my recovery, I'd done a lot of thinking. And one of the things I'd thought about was the story Joe D had told me. While it didn't always happen, according to the mob's code, a condemned man was supposed to be given a reason for his murder. And presumably, that had been the point of Joe's story. But at the time, it had been too cryptic for me.

During my recovery, I'd had plenty of time to mull the story over. And I'd come up with what I'd thought it was about. But the only way I would ever know for sure was if someone in the mob confirmed my suspicions. And that wasn't going to happen, so I'd just let it go.

Besides, there had been lots of developments while I was out. Federal agents had poured into KC like it was Prohibition again. But my kidnapping hadn't been the reason for the crackdown. They had just given FDR the excuse he'd been looking for. He'd decided Pendergast was a liability, and that it was time to get rid of him.

Consequently, the Justice Department had given Judges Otis and Reeves the green light. And with the help of the U.S.D.A., Treasury and FBI, they'd called multiple grand juries. These bodies had begun investigating long-standing tax and corruption charges against the Boss and his cronies.

Hartmann had called from time to time to provide courtesy updates on the Fire Insurance Settlement case. And the biggest news was that he'd identified the St. Louis attorney, whose unsigned letters had been found in both Charles R. Street's and Boss Tom's correspondence. But it was the Western Union wired-funds log that had finally given Rudy what he was after.

During the settlement of the Fire Insurance Rate Litigation, Street had wired $30,000 to one "A. L. McCormack of St. Louis." McCormack was President of the Missouri Association of Insurance Agents and a former lawyer. And it soon became apparent that, over the past several years, McCormack had spent significantly more money than he had claimed on his tax returns.

During their investigation, Treasury agents had taken a sample from a typewriter in McCormack's office. Its font had matched the type on the two anonymous letters. Investigators had also determined that, on a day when McCormack had been meeting with Street in Chicago, the latter had withdrawn $331,000 from an agency account he'd set up for the Fire Insurance Companies to use. That evening, McCormack had boarded the Santa Fe Chief for Kansas City, where he'd spent the night. The next day, McCormack had returned to St. Louis where he had deposited $31,000 into his brokerage account.

When confronted with this evidence, McCormack had

caved. Meeting with Hartmann and Milligan in Kansas City, he had agreed to appear before a grand jury that was considering a Pendergast indictment. During his testimony, McCormack gave a detailed chronology of the Fire Insurance scam. He also named names and the amounts each had received. Rudy had cracked the case.

While I'd been recovering, Milligan had asked First Assistant Wilson to take over my part of the Pendergast investigation. This was separate from the Fire Insurance Settlement case that Hartmann was dealing with. On Monday, August 16, 1937, my first day back in the office, Wilson and I met to discuss where things stood.

Our office had proceeded along two tracks in our inquiry into the Boss's finances. One track had focused on Pendergast's gambling expenditures and the other on his local investments. Normally, the Boss was careful and only used cash. And since cash left no tracks, this had made it difficult for us to follow his financial trail.

But we'd hoped that the Boss's well-known obsession with horse racing might have led him to be careless—particularly when it came to paying his debts to out-of-town bookies. So, we'd served a subpoena on Western Union for copies of the Boss's wire transfers. And while I was out recovering, the results had come in.

The transfers revealed that Pendergast had, indeed, wired money to bookies around the country. And that he'd wired from one to ten thousand dollars to them nearly every day. During the last three years, these payments alone had far exceeded his annually reported income.

Our second line of inquiry was also bearing fruit.

Pendergast had admitted to holding stock in several local corporations. On his tax returns, he'd reported receiving income from the Ready Mixed Concrete Company, the W. A. Ross Construction Company and the T. J. Pendergast Wholesale Liquor Company.

But we suspected he'd also made undisclosed investments in other local businesses. We'd investigated these businesses and found that they all had one thing in common. Their principal shareholder was E. L. Schneider.

Schneider was in his early forties, married, with one child. A former bookkeeper, Pendergast had given Schneider his first job, and he and the Boss were long-term associates. While on paper Schneider appeared to be a wealthy man, he lived modestly.

Wilson had interviewed Schneider about the stock he reputedly owned. At first, Schneider had stoutly maintained that he, not Pendergast, owned the stock in these businesses. But when Wilson had pointed out the discrepancy between his paper wealth and modest lifestyle, Schneider had taken the Fifth Amendment.

Then we'd had a break. While going through some subpoenaed bank records, Wilson had come across an entry for a dividend check from one of the companies in question. The entry said that the dividend check had been made out to "T. J. Pendergast," not Schneider. Wilson had asked Schneider about this entry, but the latter had claimed that it was simply a clerical error. And when Wilson had asked to see the canceled check, it had, of course, gone missing.

Then Wilson had learned that the issuing bank had recently installed a Recordak system. Recordak was state-of-the-art. It was a form of microphotography used for document preservation. Using Recordak, banks took photographs of the front and back of all canceled checks and retained these images in their files, after the originals had been returned to the account holders.

Wilson subpoenaed the bank's Recordak images for the missing check. When produced, they showed that there had been no clerical error. The check had not only been issued to T. J. Pendergast but it had also been endorsed and cashed by him as well.

With these images in hand, Wilson had again met with Schneider. After seeing them, Schneider had asked for a week to consider his options, and Wilson had agreed. The week was up. And our appointment with Schneider was set for nine a.m. on the following day.

THE NEXT MORNING, Wilson and I met in the conference room to talk about how we would handle Schneider and to wait for him and his attorney to arrive. Audrey had also joined us to take minutes. But nine o'clock came and went—and no Schneider.

At nine-thirty, we received a call from Schneider's attorney. He said that he and Schneider had planned to walk over to our office together. But Schneider hadn't shown up. The attorney had since attempted to reach Schneider, but unsuccessfully. We reluctantly agreed to reschedule our meeting for the following day. But we had warned Schneider's attorney that, if his client didn't show up then, we would seek an indictment against him.

Later, we learned that Schneider had met with Pendergast the previous afternoon. And that the Boss had been sympathetic to Schneider's plight. He'd reportedly told the younger man, "Protect yourself—too many have already suffered." And after that, Schneider was said to have been greatly relieved.

That evening the Schneider's had gone out to dinner at their favorite restaurant. After they'd returned home, Schneider had organized some files for our meeting the next morning. That night, his wife had said, Schneider had slept better than he had in months.

But during breakfast the following morning, Schneider had received a phone call. And afterward, his wife had noted that his anxiety had returned. Still, his wife said, he'd continued to prepare for our meeting, adding more papers to those already in his briefcase.

But Schneider had not left for our meeting at the expected time. Instead, his wife had seen him pacing on the front lawn, smoking as if he was waiting for someone. Later, she heard a car pull up in the street outside their home.

When she'd looked out, Mrs. Schneider had recognized the driver. It was Otto Higgins, Director of Police. Higgins and Schneider had engaged in a brief but animated conversation. Then Higgins had sped off, and her husband had gotten into their car and followed him.

Around midday, Schneider's car was found—parked on the Fairfax Bridge. But Schneider was not in it. His briefcase lay on the front seat. When opened, it contained documents relating to Pendergast's ownership of stock registered in Schneider's name. A typewritten note lay on top of these documents.

The note was addressed to Schneider's wife. It had said, in part, "I can't see my way out of this mess, and I think this will be easier than trying to live it down for the rest of my life. I still say I did nothing wrong." The note was unsigned.

After finding Schneider's car, the KCPD had searched

the shoreline downstream from the bridge. They'd found Schneider's hat floating among some brush along the river's edge. Three days later, Schneider's body was fished out of the river, two miles downstream. The county coroner later ruled Schneider's death a "suicide."

29

MAY 19, 1938

Three months later, the U.S.D.A.'s office and the Treasury Department, filed an indictment against T. J. Pendergast alleging tax evasion for the years 1936 and 1937. The charges were based in part on the Boss's failure to report the money he had received from McCormack as well as the proceeds from the local stock he had registered in Schneider's name. Additional charges were based on the funds he had wired to numerous bookmakers around the country, which, as has already been noted, greatly exceeded Pendergast's annually reported income.

The first Pendergast indictment was filed on April 15, 1938. It was Good Friday. Even though the Boss had pled "not guilty," he'd still been required to appear at police headquarters and be fingerprinted. Then he had to post a ten-thousand-dollar bond.

Predictably, Boss Tom had denied any wrongdoing. He'd even complained to the press. "There's nothing the matter with me. They persecuted Christ on Good Friday too and nailed Him to the Cross."

That was rich. But the Boss wasn't stupid. He had to have

known that he was nearing the end of the line. The Reformers certainly did. The font of the *Star's* headline that evening was as bold as when the country had declared war on Germany in 1917. It shouted, "PENDERGAST INDICTED!"

Despite the indictment, our investigation into Pendergast's finances continued. And almost weekly, we discovered additional undeclared income. Later that month, the indictment was amended to add more counts for 1935 and 1936. And we told the Judge that we anticipated that we would be filing even more.

Despite the mounting evidence against him, Senator Harry Truman had remained steadfastly loyal to the Boss. He had even declared on the floor of the Senate: "My opinion is that the U.S. District Attorney in Kansas City is indicting Mr. Pendergast because of political animus." But Truman was alone in his defense of Boss Tom, and nothing could stop the case against him now.

Our focus wasn't only on Pendergast. Director of Police, Otto Higgins, and City Manager McElroy were also hit with criminal indictments. And both abruptly resigned. It was an open secret that others in the machine were not only under investigation but were likely to be indicted too.

Nor did we ignore the mob. Treasury had fortuitously received a trove of incriminating evidence from an anonymous "concerned citizen." And these papers had pointed its agents to suspect bank accounts that had been opened under several aliases used by Charlie Carrollo.

Along with our investigative efforts, pretrial preparations continued in the Boss's case. And a meeting with Pendergast's attorneys had been scheduled for May 19. Its purpose was to negotiate preliminary procedural matters. And as his second chair, Milligan had asked me to join him.

John Madden was Pendergast's principal attorney. He was a long-time machine lawyer, who'd also represented E. L. Schneider. But we were surprised when we were told that Reginald Brewster would join Madden for the meeting. Brewster was a long-time Republican and a major figure in the Reform movement.

Of course, we had heard the rumors that Brewster had been offered an eye-popping one-hundred-thousand-dollar retainer to represent Pendergast. But we had discounted them. Surely, we'd thought, Brewster would never stoop to representing the Boss. However, it now looked like the rumors were true.

Brewster and Judge Otis were known to be fast friends. So, many suspected that Pendergast had hired Brewster in a transparent effort to influence the Judge. And it was hard to come up with an alternative explanation.

When I entered the conference room that morning, the other three were already there. Milligan introduced me, and I took a seat at the end of the table with my legal pad in front of me. My job was to take notes and fetch anything that the Chief might need.

Before speaking, Madden glanced at Brewster. He, in turn, nodded for Madden to proceed. Looking at Milligan, Madden said, "In light of the new counts that have been added to the indictment and with the prospect of more soon to be filed, we've discussed Mr. Pendergast's options with him."

"What options?" asked Milligan.

"Actually," said Madden, "Only one—the status of his plea."

Milligan's disappointment was palpable. It was evident that he'd hoped for an extended trial with the nation's attention focused upon it—and on him. But if Pendergast pled guilty now, there would be no trial, only a sentencing hearing.

But the Chief wasn't the only one surprised. For years, I'd dreamt of this moment. But now as it was about to happen, I couldn't believe it.

"Mr. Pendergast wishes to change his plea?" Milligan's asked.

"He does," answered Madden. Then, the attorney quickly added, "Contingent, of course, upon us arriving at a mutually acceptable plea agreement."

"Of course," said the Chief. "And what do you propose?"

Brewster was the one who answered, "We are willing to plead to two counts of attempted tax evasion for the years 1935 and 1936."

It was a smart move. By pleading guilty now, and to just two counts, T. J. might get off with only a year or two in prison. But it was also smart for us to take it. Our job was to convict Pendergast. At his age and with his current state of health, even a short stay behind bars would likely finish him. And so, Milligan wisely decided to take the offered plea.

Five days later, on Monday, May 24, 1938, Pendergast appeared before Judge Otis to officially change his plea. The public's interest in this event was so high that by 7:30 that morning the courthouse corridors were already shoulder-to-shoulder. And the spillover crowd extended to the sidewalks and streets outside. When the doors to Judge Otis's courtroom opened at eight, there was a rush for the gallery, which only ended when every seat was taken.

But it wasn't just the gallery that was packed. All the

space allotted to both the prosecution and defense teams was also taken. Even extra tables had been brought in to accommodate supporting prosecution counsel and members of the accused's family. Attorneys for the Treasury sat at a table behind Milligan and me. While Boss Tom, flanked by his son, Tom Jr., and his nephew, James, sat at another one behind Madden and Brewster.

Everyone stood when the Judge entered the courtroom, but only Madden remained standing when everyone else had sat down. Receiving a nod from the Judge, he moved to change Pendergast's plea to guilty. And once that motion had been granted, he made a second one for clemency based on Pendergast's ill health.

In support of this motion, Madden called to the stand Pendergast's physician, Dr. Abraham Sophian. The doctor enumerated Pendergast's many physical ailments. These included, among others, the Boss's recent coronary, his enlarged aorta, and ongoing complications from both his bowel surgery and colostomy.

Doctor Sophian also testified that, in his professional opinion, the stress of incarceration might cause Boss Tom to have another heart attack. And if one occurred, it could well be fatal. Dr. Sophian concluded his testimony by referring to life insurance actuarial tables, which showed that a man of Pendergast's health and age had, on average, only a life expectancy of seven additional years.

After Dr. Sophian left the stand, Milligan rose to read Pendergast's twenty-page plea agreement into the record. One of the conditions of this agreement, which the Judge had specifically stipulated, was that the Government had to include every possible charge it had against Pendergast—even those that were still preliminary. Also at the Judge's insistence, Pendergast was required to admit guilt to these charges and to affirm that the Government's case was supported by "incontrovertible proof."

The plea agreement made public, for the first time, Pendergast's role in the fire insurance litigation scam. It not only revealed that the Boss had taken a $750,000 bribe, but it described his subsequent efforts to avoid prosecution by obstructing justice and suborning perjury. The courtroom grew increasingly silent, as each of the charges against the Boss was read.

To summarize the agreement, Pendergast had pled guilty not only to two counts of felony tax evasion but to all the Government's specified charges. In exchange, the Government had accepted his guilty plea and had relinquished its right to prosecute him further for the listed crimes. Also, both parties had agreed to a single sentencing. And they had stipulated that, whatever the sentence rendered, they would not contest it.

If nothing else, the plea agreement showed that Boss Tom was still a gambler. But the Government was gambling too. Both sides had put themselves into the Judge's hands. And both were hoping that they'd made the right decision.

After Milligan had sat down, Brewster rose to make an argument for a mitigated sentence. The thrust of his motion was that Pendergast's downfall was not caused by a criminal disposition—but a character flaw. Brewster began with some history.

He said that, when Pendergast was a young man, his funds had been limited. And at the time, horse racing was just a local and infrequent pastime. However, that had changed with the advent of the national horse racing wires in the 1920s. The racing wires had made it possible for anyone to bet on any race in the country. And by this time, Pendergast had also become a wealthy man.

At first, Pendergast had seemed to be just a horse racing enthusiast. He'd worked with others in the community to set up the Riverside Jockey-Club Racetrack in nearby Clay County. And they'd organized a series of races to be held annually at the track. Pendergast had even bought a stud farm and had maintained a stable of promising thoroughbreds.

But it wasn't long before it became clear that Boss Tom's interest in the horses was more than a hobby. Pendergast began betting on a weekly, then daily basis. Soon, he installed a horse racing wire terminal in his office at 1908 Main. And with that, he started betting multiple times daily. And the amounts of his bets also increased. Soon, Pendergast was wagering over a hundred thousand dollars a week.

That's when, Brewster said, Pendergast's problems really began. The larger the bets, the larger the losses. And when the legal means available for covering those losses proved insufficient, then the Boss had turned to illegal ones. And for a man, like him, with considerable influence in the city, Brewster said, many opportunities presented themselves. And the Boss took advantage of them.

The defense attorney concluded by saying that Boss Tom was not a bad man. He had done much good for the city. But his weakness had brought him down. As such, he was a man to be pitied, rather than punished. And with that, Brewster had sat down.

Brewster's argument hadn't moved me. Did he think we'd forgotten how Pendergast had sold out to the mob? And the way he'd lorded it over everyone? I certainly hadn't. And I hoped that Judge Otis hadn't either.

The time finally came for Pendergast to be sentenced. When he arose, he was pale but unbowed. Then Judge Otis said he had a statement of his own to make. And we wondered what that meant.

The Judge began by saying that, contrary to the conditions set out in the plea agreement, he had decided that Pendergast's sentence would be limited to the crimes before the court. In other words, to the two felony tax evasion counts. Further, the judge said, he'd decided to consider Pendergast's health in the sentence.

With that, Judge Otis sentenced T. J. Pendergast to fifteen months in prison for count one of the indictment. He then added a three-year term for the second count plus a fine of ten thousand dollars. But then, the Judge suspended the sentence for the second count, substituting for it a period of five years' probation. Finally, Pendergast was ordered to pay over four hundred thousand dollars in back taxes as well as additional fines and penalties.

But that wasn't all. The Judge also imposed three "special conditions." First, Pendergast was forbidden from engaging in gambling "of any kind." Second, for the rest of his life, he was not to participate, "either directly or indirectly," in any type of political activity. Third, during the length of his probation, the Boss could not set foot in his private office at 1908 Grand. Of course, Judge Otis had intended these provisions to be the harshest part of Boss Tom's sentence. And they probably were.

When the Judge finished, there was a momentary silence in the courtroom. Then the gallery erupted, and the spectators rushed forward to encircle Pendergast, who was still standing. Some in the crowd yelled encouragement, others hurled insults. Reporters waved their arms, whistling for attention and shouting questions.

Head up and expressionless, the Boss ignored them all. He linked arms with his son, Tom Jr., and his nephew, Jim.

Together, they forced their way through the crowd and out into the corridor.

The Marshals gave up on trying to restore order. Even Judge Otis put down his gavel and retired to chambers. As the courtroom emptied, calm returned.

We sat at the counsel table still taking stock of what had happened. We'd hoped for more. Putting the back taxes and fines aside, Pendergast had only received a fifteen-month sentence. And under the Federal Rules, he would be eligible for parole after five months in prison. It was pitiful.

Frankly, Judge Otis had let us down. Particularly since he'd been the one to insist that we bundle the Boss's known crimes into a single sentence. Whatever his motives may have been, it was certain that the Judge would be harshly criticized for his leniency.

The sentence's special conditions were the only part that gave us hope. There was always the possibility that the Boss might slip up and be caught violating one of its provisions. If so, he might yet serve his full term. But even that, would be peanuts.

Some of the reporters had elected not to follow the Pendergast's out. They had instead remained in the courtroom to interview Milligan and the defense team. For a while, I watched as the Chief put the best possible face on the plea agreement that we'd struck. You had to hand it to him. He almost made it sound as if it had all turned out peaches.

Since it looked like Milligan was going to be at it for a while, I refilled the two satchels we had brought with us to the courtroom. Then I took the stairs down to our office. A nice surprise was waiting for me in reception—a smiling Audrey Baxter.

30

MAY 24, 1938, 11:35 A.M

Except for the incessant buzzing of the switchboard, the office was oddly quiet for midday. Even the usually reliable Ginny Oakes had abandoned her post. And I couldn't blame her.

Audrey and I walked arm in arm down the corridor to my office. I dumped the satchels on the floor beside my desk and looked around. It was a disaster. Case reporters were stacked in piles around the desk. A tower of green file folders leaned precariously on a chair. And my desktop was six inches deep in paper. But it could wait.

I turned, and Audrey and I just stood looking at each other. God, she was beautiful. And I couldn't believe that after all we'd been through, we were finally back together again. I only hoped that this time, it was for good.

I sensed that Audrey felt the same way. She smiled and threw her arms around my neck. And I drew her close cupping her chin into my hand. But before our lips could meet, there was a movement in the doorway. And we both turned to see who it was.

Dolores was standing there. Her features were hard, her

face pale. In her right hand was a thirty-two automatic. As soon as I saw the gun, I remembered the empty holster in Johnny's closet.

"Get away from that no-good son-of-a-bitch," she growled.

Audrey jumped aside. And I couldn't blame her. But what was going on?

"You bastard," Dolores snarled.

"What are you talking about?" I asked.

"You killed him."

"Who?"

"Jeff."

"Rayen?"

"Of course!"

"You and Rayen," I said in disbelief.

"Yes!" Her face flushed and her eyes welled up. But the muzzle of the automatic didn't waver.

"But what about Johnny?" I stammered.

"He meant nothing to me," she spat.

Then, I got it. "Rayen and Claiborne killed Johnny, and you covered for them."

She smiled. If you could call it a smile.

"But why?" I asked.

"Johnny was pathetic—and he was through."

"But what about the D's and Balestrere?'"

"It was their idea," she snapped.

There was a sound in the hall, and Dolores stiffened.

"Enough talk," she said centering the automatic on my heart.

And I felt the urge stir inside me. But this time, it just waited.

Still, I wasn't going to just stand there and be shot. So, I threw myself at her. And as I did, Dolores swiveled and shot

Audrey. The sound of the shot was deafening in the small office.

"No!" I shouted—freezing in mid-stride.

As Dolores vanished, Audrey crumpled. I ran to her side, scooping her up. A red stain spread across the front of her dress. Her eyes were wide. And blood trickled from her mouth.

I shouted, "Help! We need help! Someone, call an ambulance!" But there was no reply. And as I glanced down at Audrey, I knew any help would be too late. She was growing limp. And her eyes were losing their luster.

"Don't die, Audrey," I pleaded. "Please. Don't die."

I slumped against the wall, clutching Audrey's slack body. And slowly, I slid down it to the floor. Everything whirled around me. And I was somewhere else.

THE SUN WAS SHINING, and it was a crisp October afternoon. Midge and I were walking home from school. She was telling me a story, and we were laughing.

As we approached the Exchange National Bank, the doors burst open. And three men charged out. There were guns in their hands.

One of them, wearing a red bandana mask, raised his and pointed it at me. We were so close, there was no way he could miss. I batted at the gun knocking it away. And as I did, my fingers brushed the mask from the robber's face. And I knew him.

It was Dolores!

Then the robber, behind Dolores, leaped forward, swinging his pistol at my head. I grabbed the gun. And we whirled around, fighting over it. As we struggled, my finger touched the trigger. And the gun went off.

Surprised by the shot—I loosened my grip. And the man wrenched the gun away from me. Then, he knocked me to the ground with it.

Grabbing Dolores by the arm, the man hauled her after him as they raced to the car at the curb. She yanked the red bandana up and over her face as they ran. The other man charged after them.

It was then I realized that I knew the two men with Dolores. Even though they were younger and less hardened, they were Rayen and Claiborne. Rayen was the one I'd fought with.

The three of them leaped into the car at the curb. Claiborne took the wheel, Rayen the passenger's seat, and Dolores dove into the back. As they squealed away, Rayen flicked something at me, from his open car window.

Tumbling through the air, it landed at my feet. It was a blue-tipped kitchen match. Its wooden end chewed flat.

Then I realized something horrible had happened. Midge had been hit. And she lay bleeding on the sidewalk beside me. I scooped her up. Others came running. But nothing could be done. And Midge died. As she did, everything once again whirled around me.

AND I WAS BACK in my office, sitting on the floor. The room was crowded now. An ambulance attendant was kneeling beside me. He was saying something, which I couldn't understand.

I looked down at Audrey's ivory face. And I knew why Dolores had shot her. I'd killed Rayen, so she'd killed

Audrey. It was as simple as that. Only then, did I understand what the attendant wanted; he was asking me to let go of Audrey's body. And finally, I did.

The following week was just a blur. All I can remember of the funeral is Audrey's open casket and my parents, Milligan, Mac, Gia, and Budge were there. Audrey was buried in Forest Hill Cemetery. And I'd stood for a long time beside her grave after everyone else was gone.

The day after the funeral, I'd traveled to Topeka and checked myself into the Menninger's Sanatorium. It was something I should have done long ago. And maybe if I had, Audrey would still be alive.

AFTER THREE MONTHS at Menninger's, I was nearly cured. Although Dr. Karl had refused to take credit for my improvement. It was Audrey, he'd said, who'd healed me. Her death had unlocked my lost memories, and I'd been forced to confront my role in Midge's death. It was then that I realized that the reoccurring face in my dreams was my own. And with that, the dreams had ceased.

But I was still experiencing the urges, although they were much weaker now and more infrequent. Dr. Karl thought that they might resolve themselves over time—with further therapy. But he could say nothing more than that.

Since I was a practicing Catholic, the psychiatrist had consulted with Father Moriarty about my treatment. Along with my sessions with Dr. Karl, I'd begun a program of frequent confession, guided meditation, and spiritual direction. All of which had been designed to aid in my healing.

However, once Dr. Karl said that he'd done everything he could, Father Moriarty had made a suggestion. If a mental health condition is not resolvable by psychotherapy, he'd said, it was the Church's view that its cause might be spiritual. And if so, a spiritual remedy should be considered.

Dr. Karl did not object to the priest's suggestion. Even though he was strictly scientific in his practice, the psychiatrist was also a Presbyterian. And as such, he understood Father's point.

I was surprised, though, when after some research, Father had named the condition, he thought I was suffering from. He'd called it a demonic "obsession." The term "obsession," he'd explained, was used to distinguish the condition from the more well-known, and more severe, demonic "possession." I asked him how the two differed?

In an "obsession," Father said, malign spirits act from outside a person, rather than from within. But the spirits still try to influence their victims by inserting thoughts and suggestions into their minds. Another way to think about it, he said, was as an extreme form of everyday temptation.

For example, he observed, that when we're trying to lose a few pounds, all we can think about is that slice of cake in the cupboard. Or, if we've resolved to pray for half an hour, our devotions are invariably interrupted by distracting thoughts.

We tend to blame ourselves when this happens, Father said. But it's not our fault. The thoughts and distractions that come to us on these occasions are not our own. That's because we're involved in a spiritual war that most people are unaware of.

Returning to the symptoms of a demonic obsession, he noted that the condition had a defining characteristic. Malign spirits always encourage their victims to harm themselves. And that certainly sounded like what had been happening to me.

So, with Dr. Karl's permission, and my own, Father Moriarty had contacted Monsignor Matteo Lorenzo. The latter was a specialist in dealing with spiritual attacks and a roving exorcist for the Church in North America. Father Moriarty soon confirmed that the priest was available and could consult with us. Then he made the necessary arrangements for Monsignor Lorenzo to travel to Topeka.

However, when the Monsignor arrived, he was not what I'd expected. He wasn't wearing the usual, red-trimmed cassock. And even though he was reputedly middle-aged, the priest seemed much older. He was stooped and walked with a cane. Then there were the fingerless gloves on his hands, which seemed to conceal bandages.

Privately, I'd asked Father Moriarty whether Monsignor Lorenzo was up to the task. And he'd told me not to worry. In his experience, spiritual strength was often accompanied by physical weakness.

Dr. Karl spent some time briefing Monsignor on my psychiatric condition, its assumed causes, and the treatment I'd received. And Father Moriarty had told him that he thought I might be suffering from a demonic obsession. After some discussion, the Monsignor agreed with this assessment.

Then he'd said that he had three questions for me. First, had I ever dabbled in the occult? Second, when had my urges begun? And third, what could I tell him about the man I'd struggled with on the day Midge had died?

In response to the first question, I'd told Monsignor that I'd never had anything to do with the occult. And as far as the second, I'd explained that the urges had begun shortly after Midge's death. That left only Jeff Rayen.

I told Monsignor that, although Rayen had been my sister's lover and that I'd killed him in self-defense, I knew little about him. Still, Monsignor pressed me to tell him everything I knew. And so, I'd begun by telling him that, even though Rayen had been a police detective, he had also been a member of the local mob.

Monsignor stopped me there and asked what kind of mob Rayen had belonged to? I'd explained that it was Italian-Sicilian. Next, he'd inquired as to whether the mob had some sort of symbol with which they identified themselves to each other? And I'd told him about the trinacrian tattoo, with the head of the Medusa at its center. This was apparently what Monsignor had been looking for. Because, once he heard about the tattoo, he stopped asking questions.

Monsignor then recommended that we spend three days in prayer and fasting to prepare for the exorcism. And that's what we'd done. During this time, Monsignor had also sought permission to perform the rite from our local bishop. Once he'd received the bishop's permission, we reserved a small chapel at a local Benedictine abbey. The night before the exorcism, I'd had trouble sleeping.

When we arrived at the chapel the next morning, Father Moriarty heard Monsignor Lorenzo's confession, and then, my own. After that, Monsignor celebrated a Mass in which Father, and I participated. Dr. Karl had also joined us in the chapel, but only as an observer.

Following Mass, I'd knelt before a processional cross in the front pew, and Father Moriarty had knelt beside me. He was there to pray for my deliverance. When I was ready, Monsignor came forward. He had taken off his alb and was wearing only a white surplice and a purple stole.

A Benedictine brother joined us at this point. He held the *Rituale Romanum*, which contained the rite of exorcism so that Monsignor could be free to use his hands. Although the latter seemed so familiar with the rite that he rarely glanced at the book.

Monsignor began by dipping his thumb into holy water and tracing the sign of the cross on my forehead while saying, "In Nomine Patri . . .." Then he recited the Litany of the Saints, asking for their collective intercession on my behalf.

Following that, we said the Pater Noster, and then Monsignor read Psalm 54. "God by your name save me, and by your might defend my cause . . .." After that, Monsignor read the passage from the Gospel of Luke about the sending of the Seventy-Two: "[They] returned rejoicing and said, 'Lord even the demons are subject to us, because of your name.'"

Then we recited the Creed, after which Monsignor placed both hands on my head and invoked the Holy Spirit. Leaning down, he breathed heavily on my face. Then taking one end of his stole, he touched it to my neck, while leaving his right hand on my head. With that, Monsignor intoned, "*Ecce Crucem Domini.*" And once again, he made the sign of the cross.

Then from the *Rituale Romanum,* he prayed:

> God, Creator, and defender of the human race, who made man in your own image, look down in pity upon this your servant, Samuel, now in the toils of the unclean spirit, now caught up in the fearsome threats of man's ancient enemy, sworn foe of our race, who befuddles and stupefies the human mind, throws it into terror, overwhelms it with fear and panic. Repel, O Lord, the devil's power, break asunder his snares and traps, and put the unholy tempter to flight.

With that, Monsignor's tone changed from supplication to command,

> "I adjure you, ancient serpent, by the judge of the living and the dead, by your Creator, by the Creator of the whole universe, by Him who has the power to consign you to hell, I command you, tell me through what instrumentality you have infested this man?"

Then Monsignor paused and cocked his head as if he were listening. I listened too, but all I could hear was the buzzing of a fly. Monsignor then looked at my vest pocket. And he gestured for me to take out my watch.

I pulled it out and offered it to him. But instead of taking the watch, he pointed to the fob on the end of the chain. It was a little horn-shaped amulet that Dolores had given me shortly after Midge's death. She'd said that it was a *cornicello* and that it was an Italian good-luck piece.

I unclipped the little horn from the end of my chain and offered it to Monsignor. But he only made the sign of the cross over it and gestured to the brother. The latter came forward with a dish of Holy Water. And he motioned for me to drop the amulet into it. Then the brother quickly carried the dish from the chapel.

Again, Monsignor placed his hand on my head, and made the sign of the cross over me exclaiming,

> "Almighty Lord, Word of the Father, Jesus Christ, God and Lord of all creation; who gave to your holy apostles the power to cast out demons; I call upon your holy name and in fear and trembling I ask that you grant me, your unworthy servant, the power to cast out this cruel demon."

Then Monsignor spoke to the urge.

> I adjure you, ancient serpent, not by my weakness but by the might of the Holy Spirit, to depart from this servant of God, Samuel, whom almighty God has made in His image. Yield, therefore, yield not to my own person but to Christ. For it is the power of Christ that compels you, He who brought you low by His cross. Tremble before that mighty arm. And by His power, I command you now, unclean spirit. Begone from this creature of God! Begone, I say, for it is God who commands you, and not me. Begone and never infest this man again!

If this had been a horror film, the malign spirit would have cast me to the floor. There I would have thrashed about, gnashing my teeth, foaming at the mouth, and howling hideously. But as it was, I merely shuddered and felt something uncoil within me.

Seeing this, Monsignor had leaned down and peered searchingly into my face. And after a long moment, he'd said, "I can't be sure, Sam, but it may be gone." Then he stepped back and gave me a guarded smile. With that, the rite was over.

Afterward, Monsignor had explained that, if the spirit's hold over me had really been broken, we'd been exceedingly fortunate. Conditions like mine typically took years to resolve, primarily because the source of the infestation was so hard to determine. But in my case, it looked like the cause had indeed been the *cornicello*.

Of course, Monsignor added, we would only know that for sure if the urges ceased. Malign spirits are cunning he said. Sometimes, they lie low for a time just to raise false hopes and to outwit the exorcist. In such instances, though, they return, and another exorcism must be attempted. Consequently, Monsignor told me to remain vigilant and to tell Father Moriarty if the urges returned.

Once he'd finished, I'd asked Monsignor what he knew about the demon who'd "obsessed" me. But he'd immediately shaken his head and held up a hand. Then he'd warned me never to speak of "that one" again. Because, even if the demon was truly gone, just talking about him could cause him to return.

The reason I'd raised the subject was that I was aware of a curious astronomical coincidence. Perseus was one of the forty-eight ancient constellations in the night sky. It was named after the Greek hero who slew Medusa and had used her head to rescue the princess, Andromeda, from the sea monster, Cetus.

In drawings of the constellation, Perseus was often depicted as holding Medusa's head in his left hand. And the region of the night sky where her head had been located contained a notable red star, *Algol.* This star was often described as one of Medusa's eyes. Even more curiously, the name, *Algol,* comes from an Arabic phrase meaning "the demon's head." The star also has a Hebrew name, which is similarly translated as "Satan's head."

I knew that during an exorcism the priest can elicit the name of the inflicting spirit, to gain control over him. And I'd wondered if Monsignor had done so and whether my demon's name was possibly *Algol.* But of course, the whole thing had been an unhealthy curiosity, and it was best left a mystery. So, I dropped it.

Before leaving, Monsignor had given me a special blessing and a spiritual-health regimen to follow. The program included the liberal use of sacramentals, especially holy water, and blessed salt. These were to be sprinkled liberally about my home, office, and even my car. Monsignor gave me some liberation prayers too, for regular recitation. And he also recommended that I attend daily mass, pray the rosary often, and frequently go to confession. Finally, he told me to contact him if the urges returned.

I remained under observation at Menninger's for another month. Then after having had no reoccurrence of the urges and with Dr. Karl and Father Moriarty's blessing, I'd prepared to leave. I thanked them for all they'd done and took the next train to Kansas City. Budge met me at the station and gave me a ride home.

While two of the three mysteries at the heart of this story were solved, one remained. Who were Miller's accomplices at Union Station? And now, because so much time had passed with nothing new coming to light, it was unlikely that we would ever know their names.

31

SEPTEMBER 12, 1938

It was a Sunday in mid-September 1938. Gia and I went to noon Mass at Visitation. Afterward, we took a picnic lunch to Swope Park.

We sat on a quilt under a tree enjoying deviled-ham sandwiches, potato chips, and a tin of fruit salad—washing it all down with soda pop. Afterward, we went for a walk. Like always, I was doing most of the talking.

I was telling Gia that it looked like we would never know who Miller's accomplices were at Union Station. She looked away from me at this point and said, "Maybe you're not asking the right person?"

I laughed at that, thinking about the D's and Balestrere. "They're not going to tell me anything."

But when she turned back, Gia's face had a funny look on it. "As I've said, maybe you're not asking the right person."

"Like who?"

"Like me."

"You," I scoffed.

"Try me," she said lifting her chin.

"Okay, who were the two guys with Vern Miller at Union Station? Cause I'm not buying they were Pretty Boy Floyd and Adam Richetti."

"Of course not," she replied. "They were Bill Weissman and Maurice Denning."

My mouth dropped open. The names she'd mentioned were two mugs from my old suspect list in Midge's murder. But before I could ask Gia why she thought they'd been Miller's accomplices; she'd plowed right on.

"Johnny loaned Weissman and Denning to Miller for the job. And since Floyd and Richetti happened to be in town, he decided to lay the blame on them."

"Now, wait a minute," I said. "How do you know that?"

She smiled. "Everyone thinks the mob's so tight-lipped. Of course, it is. But we all have to talk to someone."

"You mean wives and sweethearts?"

"Sure."

I couldn't tell if she was putting me on. But she could see I wasn't buying it.

"Oh, you think I'm blowing smoke—ask me anything."

Intending to call her bluff, I said, "Okay, tell me if you can, whether Jelly Nash cracked Boss Tom's safe at 1908 Main?"

"Of course," she answered. "And it was pretty dumb too. But the stupidest bit was when he tried to sell the fire insurance papers back to the Boss."

"So, Nash *was* the target at Union Station?"

"You bet. Johnny told Weissman and Denning to pretend to free Nash as Miller wanted. But the real plan was to kill him."

There was a-matter-of-factness to Gia's tone that unnerved me. I'd never seen this side of her before.

"So, why didn't they just kill Nash in Hot Springs—and avoid a shootout at Union Station altogether?"

"That was the original plan. But the Bureau nabbed Jelly first. And after that, they didn't have much choice. They couldn't risk Nash talking to the Feds when he got back to Leavenworth. He would have said anything to avoid going to Alcatraz."

"But Weissman and Denning didn't kill Nash—did they."

"No," she said with a snort. "Some greenhorn lawman in the backseat, who didn't know how to use a pump shotgun, blew off Nash's head before they could. And the same blast not only killed Nash but also Caffrey, who was standing outside the car."

"And they weren't the only ones the guy killed, were they?"

"Nope. With his second shot, the goof nailed Hermanson too. Talk about a massacre."

It was all adding up, so I kept going. "Did Johnny give Weissman and Denning a Thompson to use at Union Station?"

She nodded. "Johnny told Higgins to get the Thompson out of the Hot Shot. At first, he was just thinking of making it easier for Miller and his boys—by cutting down on the lawmen's firepower."

"But then he had a better idea?"

"You bet. Johnny decided to give the Thompson to Denning—to give the shooters an edge."

"And what did they do with it afterward?"

"Johnny had Higgins put the Thompson back in the Hot Shot. He figured no one would look for it there."

It all fit. But I didn't stop there. "Nash wasn't the only

target, was he? Johnny told Weissman and Denning to kill Grooms and Hermanson too."

Here for the first time, Gia balked. But after a moment, she nodded.

"But why did Johnny want Grooms and Hermanson dead?" I asked.

"Some cops on the force still don't like working for the mob."

"And Grooms and Hermanson were two of those?"

"More than that," she said. "They were the leaders."

"So, Johnny had them knocked off too?"

She nodded a third time.

At this point, I was ready to shift to Johnny's murder. Even though I already knew from Dolores that Rayen and Claiborne had killed him, I still didn't know why. But I hesitated, not knowing how Gia might react. So, I started with a softball.

"The D's and Balestrere told Rayen and Claiborne to use the Hot Shot when they killed your brother?"

"Un-huh," she said. "They wanted it to look like a couple of disgruntled cops had killed Johnny."

"And that's also why they left the *Racing Form* at the Park Central," I added. "The one with Jack Baxter's phone number on it."

"Sure."

"But why target Baxter?" I asked.

"Baxter was thick with Grooms and Hermanson. And he was a leader among the cops Johnny had fired."

"So, that made him the perfect fall guy."

"You bet."

"But why did the D's and Balestrere target Johnny?"

She shrugged. "It's like I said on the day of the funeral, Sam. '*Cui mali accumensa, peju finisci.*' A bad beginning makes a bad ending. If you live by the gun—you die by the gun."

So, Mac had been right all along. I kept silent for a moment hoping Gia would flesh it out a bit more for me. And she obligingly did.

"Johnny was too heavy-handed in the Anthon hit and the 1934 Election," she said. "Then he started having ideas of his own."

"You mean like balking when they told him to kill me?"

By now, I'd had plenty of time to mull over Joe D's story. The one he'd told me on the night I'd been shot. And I'd guessed that figuratively speaking, I'd been the troublesome boil in the story. And that Johnny had been the man, who hadn't wanted it lanced.

"Yeah," Gia said. "Johnny loved Dolores. Not that she was worth it. And you were part of her family. So, he'd resisted when they told him to kill you."

I frowned, "I still can't believe Dolores just sat in the car and watched Rayen and Claiborne kill Johnny."

"She didn't love him," Gia said grimly. "She would have done the same if it had been you."

And I knew that she was right. I still had one more question. "Why didn't Johnny recognize Rayen and Claiborne the night he was shot? His last words to me were some gibberish about the killers being his groomsmen or something."

"I think you misunderstood him. Johnny was probably trying to say, 'Grooms and Hermanson,' not 'groomsmen.' But he just couldn't get it out."

That made sense. Johnny had been struggling to speak.

"Well, that's it for me."

"That's it?" Gia looked incredulous.

"What else is there?" I asked surprised by her reaction.

"Don't you want to know about the fire insurance papers?"

"What about them?"

"Johnny paid off Nash to get them back. But then, the D's and Balestrere told him to give them to Wetzel—instead of back to the Boss."

My jaw dropped, "Why would they do that?"

"So, Wetzel could expose the Boss—and nail him."

"But that would've ruined everything."

"No-o," she laughed. "That's what they wanted. You see Boss Tom had become such a leach. He kept demanding a bigger cut—to throw away on the horses. And finally, it got to be too much. Besides, because of his health, he was finished."

"So, why kill Wetzel then?" I asked.

"They got impatient. He wanted the whole ball of wax before publishing. He'd started digging around in the Union Station thing and Johnny's murder. And he just wouldn't quit."

"So, they killed him?"

"Sure. Then, they decided to let the Boss's papers go to you. Wetzel had already made plans for that to happen anyway—in case someone killed him. So, they decided to finish him off and set his plan in motion."

"But then, why try to pin Wetzel's murder on me?"

"They knew you'd be suspicious if the papers just dropped into your lap. Besides, they were hoping Thurman and Hart would have a little fun with you—using the third-degree."

My head was spinning. "Well," I said. "At least, we nailed Charlie Carrollo fair and square."

"Not a chance," Gia giggled. "The D's made sure Treasury got the scoop on him too."

"Now, why would they do that?" I exclaimed, in total disbelief.

"Carrollo was never meant for that job. He was nothing more than a placeholder. Binaggio just needed a little more seasoning."

It had been like drinking out of a firehose. And Gia still wasn't finished. She took a step closer, and her tone changed.

"And I have something else to say, Sam." She looked down for a long moment. When she looked up again, there were tears in her eyes.

"I love you, Sam, and I always will. But you don't love me."

I tried to protest, but she put a hand to my lips and stopped me.

"It's a fact," she said. "A girl has to be true to herself—and to who she is." Then she said, "Charlie Binaggio has asked me to marry him. And I've said, 'Yes.'" With that, she leaned forward and planted a lingering kiss on my lips.

Stepping back, she said, "Goodbye, Sam."

Turning, she walked towards a long black Packard, which had just glided to the curb. A goon jumped out of the front seat and opened the rear door for her. Gia slid in next to Charlie Binaggio. Neither of them looked at me, as the Packard silently pulled away.

32

OCTOBER 10, 1938

About a month later, I was at Budge's house on a Sunday morning, after Mass. He lived in a farmhouse on a hill fifteen miles south of town. Budge had fried up some eggs along with thick slices of country ham. There were also buttermilk biscuits that weren't half bad. And we'd washed it all down with black coffee.

Over the food, we'd talked about Richetti's recent execution. Although the latter had been sentenced to hang by the neck until dead, Missouri had just completed a state-of-the-art gas chamber. And so, on October 7, 1938, Adam Richetti had had the dubious distinction of being the first man to be executed in it.

I'd also told Budge about Gia's revelations. But he had been less convinced than I'd been. He'd agreed that the mob could have been eager to get rid of both Boss Tom and Carrollo. And overall, her story was in keeping with the facts of both the Union Station Massacre and Johnny's death.

But there was one part of her account that he'd flatly objected to. And that was the identity of Miller's accomplices at Union Station. While Weissman and Denning had been Johnny's boys and had left the city right after the Massacre, there was nothing else, he argued, to suggest they'd been the two shooters with Miller.

"Why not?" I asked.

"Think about it. The Massacre was a high-stakes gamble. Johnny wouldn't have just tapped a couple of his mugs to take care of it. He would have picked his two best boys. Guys he could count on to make sure it was done right."

"It couldn't have been Gargotta," I countered. "He's too well known."

"I agree," Budge said. "But what's one thing we know for certain about the Massacre and Johnny's murder?"

When I didn't immediately respond, he answered his question himself. "They were connected."

"You mean by the Thompson?"

"Sure. And remember what we originally thought that meant?"

"We thought Miller's accomplices had killed Johnny," I answered. And then it hit me. "Are you saying Rayen and Claiborne were Miller's accomplices? Nah, they couldn't have been."

"Why not?"

"Well, for one thing, Rayen showed up at Union Station right after the Massacre."

"Couldn't he have been dropped off by Miller during the get-away and picked up by a squad car heading to the scene?"

"Maybe," I admitted. "If they'd pre-arranged it. But what about Claiborne? He wasn't with Rayen at the station."

"And why do you think that was?" Budge smirked.

"You mean—because he'd been shot?"

"Bingo," said Budge.

"So, you're saying, the original plan was for Miller to drop off both Rayen and Claiborne during the get-away. And to have them be picked up by a squad car heading to the station?"

Budge nodded letting me chew on it some more.

"Well," I finally said. "I guess that might have been pretty clever. I mean, no one would have expected two of the killers to come back to the station—particularly as investigating cops."

Budge said, "Keep going."

"So, I'm guessing you think that, when Claiborne was shot, Miller only dropped Rayen off. And then he took Claiborne home with him to Edgevale road. After that, he called a mob doctor to treat Claiborne, and that would explain the bloody bandages in the attic."

But it was all just a little too pat for me, and I wasn't convinced. "I don't know. It sounds like something right out of a detective story rather than anything from real life. After all, someone might have recognized Rayen and Claiborne during the shooting?"

"That was a risk for sure," Budge said. "But of all the lawmen, only Grooms and Hermanson, as KCPD detectives, would have been certain to recognize them. But they were slated to be killed anyway. And that might have been one of the reasons why they *were* killed."

"Well, you're right about that," I admitted. "All the other lawmen were either from out of town or new to the city, they weren't likely to have recognized either Rayen or Claiborne."

"And there are other reasons why the risk might not have been as great as it seems. For one, as we both know, eyewitnesses are notoriously unreliable. And that's particularly true when the culprits are police. Even in a place like KC where most coppers are bent, it's still hard for local citizens to think of them as perpetrators."

"And don't forget," he went on, "It's not healthy for anyone in this town to be a witness to a mob crime. If someone had recognized Rayen and Claiborne, it would have been pretty dumb for them to have said so."

He was certainly right about that.

In the end, I was convinced. The only thing Gia had lied to me about were the names of Miller's accomplices. And even though I'd been disappointed in her for that, I also knew she'd had her reasons. After all, she was going to be a mob wife now, and that was where her allegiance lay.

Then it hit me. If we were right, Johnny's murderers and Miller's accomplices were dead now. And justice had been served. Of course, I'd been the one to kill them. But that part had been dumb luck. And I'd nearly died too. Still, it was pretty funny—in an odd sort of way—when you thought about it.

As dusk came on, Budge and I decided to get some air and stretch our legs. So, we took his hounds, Rafe and Moxie, for a walk in the woods. It was a grey November afternoon, and a cold front was moving in.

Once the hounds had figured out what we were up to, they'd taken off nose down into the trees. We could hear them baying somewhere up ahead. We stumbled down a wooded slope and trudged up a ridge. By the sound of it, the dogs were on the other side.

They often chased squirrels and flushed cottontails, but this time their yelping was different. It sounded like they'd treed something big. And we were wondering what it might be. As we crested the ridge, Budge stepped onto a flat rock trying to spot the dogs.

Without warning, the rock gave way under him. And he was pitched headlong down the slope. At first, Budge flailed his arms, for balance. He was remarkably agile for a man of his size and age. Then he spread his legs like he was going to ski down the slope on the fallen leaves and muddy earth.

It might have worked too. Except that his right foot became entangled in some vines that had grown around a medium-sized tree. At first, Budge's downward momentum had just caused the tree to bend. But the moment came when his impetus slowed, and the tree reasserted itself. Snapping back upright, it yanked Budge's foot out from under him. And he was hoisted into the air like a rabbit in a snare.

It had all happened so quickly that I'd been unable to react. But then, the hilarity of what I'd witnessed seized me. And I'd burst out laughing. Budge had tentatively joined in, more from relief than anything.

As I was laughing, I glanced at Budge. The pant leg of his elevated foot had slipped down exposing his unnaturally white calf. And etched on his calf was a blue tattoo of the Sicilian trinacria.

The laughter died in my throat. And when Budge saw what I was looking at, he quit laughing too. Our eyes locked.

"What the hell," I said. "I thought you were my friend."

"I am," he lied giving me the ghost of a smile.

"Cut the crap. You're in the mob."

All the signs had been there, but I'd been too blind to see them. A former member of the KCPD, who'd initially tried to hide his identity from me. Someone who'd always turned up at the right time and seemed to know all the answers. What had I been thinking? Then other things began to fall into place.

“You were the one who sapped me. And then, you hung around to play nice.”

He didn’t say anything to that.

“And you planted that matchstick to make me think it had been Rayen.”

“No,” he said stoutly. “The match was there all right.”

Although Rayen was long dead the thought of him creeping around my house, maybe while I was asleep, gave me the willies.

“And Wetzel—you killed him.”

“No,” Budge insisted. “It was Gargotta.”

I shouldn’t have, but I believed him. “But you helped him put Wetzel’s body in my car, didn’t you?”

Once again, Budge remained silent.

“And when I got the Boss’s papers, you tipped Rudy off that I had them. Then you turned up just late enough when I arrived from Chicago so that Ralphy had a clear shot at me.”

I was suddenly sick of him. And of the whole stinking thing. I turned on my heel and stalked off through the woods. I left him hanging where he was. It was his problem now.

T. J. Pendergast finally surrendered to the federal penitentiary in Leavenworth, Kansas on May 29, 1939. The delay had been caused by the Boss’s poor health and last-minute wrangling by his attorneys. After he was processed, the Boss’s mug shot was leaked to the press. And it had been a shock to many.

The photo was of a haggard old man with a prisoner number under his chin. The image was in stark contrast to the Boss's carefully cultivated persona. Gone was the brassy grin and steely eyes. Stripped of his mask, T. J. was seen for the worn-out political hack that he was.

But despite his fall, few could conceive of Kansas City without the Boss. After all, Pendergast had put KC on the national map. And he had given her vision and direction. Without him, the city seemed rudderless and her future uncertain.

And even though Pendergast had been toppled, the Government had continued to pursue both the mob and machine. On October 20, 1939, Charlie Carrollo was found guilty of perjury, mail fraud, and tax evasion. He was sentenced to eight years in prison and sent to join the Boss in Leavenworth. But since he had never bothered to become a naturalized citizen, once Carrollo's time was served, he would be deported to Sicily.

And Carrollo wasn't the only one. In November 1939, former Director of Police, Otto Higgins, was convicted of tax evasion and sentenced to two years in Leavenworth. In fact, of all the Boss's intimates, only former City Manager Henry McElroy escaped imprisonment. But he didn't get off lightly. McElroy died of heart disease one day after receiving a subpoena to appear before a grand jury, investigating his finances.

Interestingly, only Mayor Bryce Smith was untouched by the spate of investigations. Even though he had been a willing tool of the machine, Smith seems not to have shared in the widespread corruption and to have paid his full share of taxes. When the Boss was indicted, Smith naively offered to switch sides and execute the demanded reforms.

As a demonstration of good faith, the mayor had even

opened the city's books for inspection. These revealed a staggering, and previously unknown, twenty-million-dollar civic debt. Still hoping to ingratiate himself, Smith fired seven hundred and forty-eight municipal employees on the payroll, who had done little or no work. But in the end, despite it all, Smith had to go, and he regretfully resigned.

Now in the majority on the city council, the Reformers forced through a new charter. One of its provisions specified municipal elections every two years, instead of the current four. This, it was hoped, would unseat the machine's remaining adherents or, at least, force them to endure regular public scrutiny.

And just as many had believed, James Pendergast turned out to be an uninspiring political leader. Under him, the machine's formerly unshakeable grip on the city had loosened. And sensing that they were on a sinking ship, many of the machine's former allies had begun to desert it.

The Reformers also reached out to Governor Stark. Working with him, they succeeded in putting the KCPD under state control, with a new police board appointed by the Governor. This reform-minded board immediately hired a new police chief. His name was Lear Reed.

I knew Reed. He was a former colleague of Mac's at the Bureau. A fourteen-year veteran, he was a thorough Hoover man. And he knew the KCPD's problems firsthand. Reed had been involved in investigating the Union Station Massacre, and he'd been one of the agents sent to hunt Pretty Boy Floyd. More recently, he'd served on the voter-fraud task force.

Reed immediately fired half of the police force and tightened the screws on the entertainment district. He set closing hours for the city's bars, shut down the horse racing wires and gambling establishments, and even drove the prostitutes underground. These efforts played havoc with the mob's rackets, and their profits plunged. With the end of the twenty-four-hour clubs, even the musicians started leaving town.

But what hurt the mob most was its fraying relationship with the machine. James Pendergast, smarting from the public airing of his uncle's crimes, had cut all ties with the mob. And with this, the sweet deal in Kansas City came to an end.

As Gia had foretold, in the middle of this turmoil, a young, bespectacled Charles Binaggio had stepped into Carrollo's shoes. And to give him some gravitas and menace, Charlie Gargotta had become Binaggio's shadow. Soon, they were known about town as the "Two Charlie's."

The word on the street was that Binaggio had big plans. He was said to be angling to put the mob back in the political driver's seat—on an even bigger scale. Exactly what that meant wasn't known. But it was known that he was trying to mend fences with James Pendergast as well as building a political base of his own in the city's eastern wards. But what would come of these efforts was hard to tell.

And something else was worth noting too. While the mob had had its setbacks, the "men of honor" had remained untouched. And they were working quietly behind the scenes to rebuild their empire. Although Mac had told me that there were those in the FBI and Congress, who were determined to unmask them, I couldn't imagine it happening.

And finally, there was one last thing. FDR had turned a blind eye to Pendergast's crimes when he'd been a political asset. But once he'd become a liability, the President had unleashed the full force of the law on him. I didn't like this arbitrary use of the legal process. Criminals should never get a pass just because of their politics.

More importantly, FDR had set a dangerous precedent. Heck, one could even imagine a time when a sitting President might use the Bureau to target his political opponents. Or he could even sic the Justice Department onto members of the public, to discourage them from objecting to his unpopular policies, as farfetched as that might seem.

But all of that was old news. And I was back at work, but my heart wasn't in it. With the Boss in Leavenworth and both the machine and the mob on the ropes, there wasn't much of an incentive. Of course, there was always Charlie Binaggio. But I couldn't bring myself to go after him yet. For one thing, he reminded me too much of Johnny. And then, of course, there was Gia. However, once she and Binaggio were married, all bets would be off.

There had also been changes around the office. Wilson had hired a new secretary for the typing pool. Her name was Betty. She was a sweet girl and a hard worker. But every time I saw her, all I could think of was Audrey. And I thought a lot about Audrey these days. She'd left a big hole in my life, and one I thought would probably never be filled.

And then, both Costellow and Schmid were leaving. Costellow had taken a job with Brewster's firm, and Schmid had, not surprisingly, joined Madden's. Considering all the cases against the machine, Schmid was sure to make partner before long. And with his family's money and connections, Costellow was also likely to be a shoo-in.

But it was Charlie Meeks I was the happiest about. He had finally completed night school and received his law degree. Charlie had asked me for a recommendation, and I'd been glad to give it. To my surprise, he was tapped to work for Edgar Shook at the Sebree firm. It was an up-and-coming place. And it couldn't have happened to a nicer guy.

Then, there was Mac. He'd just been transferred to the Department of Justice in Washington, D.C. There he was assigned to the Fifth Columnist Section. Now that war had been declared in Europe, German provocateurs were active on the East Coast, anticipating our involvement on the side of Britain and France. And the FBI was already tracking them.

In Asia, the Japanese were aggressively pursuing their expansionist goals. And this had led to clashes with U.S. interests and even some American blood had been shed. Although no one thought the Japanese would dare to go to war with us. Still, their agents were reportedly operating in California and Hawaii. And so, the FBI was also monitoring them.

Mac, of course, had been raring to go, and I'd envied him his new assignment. But before he left, I'd asked him to run one more trace on Dolores. The warrants on her were still active. But no one had seen her since the day of Audrey's murder. Once again, Mac's request had drawn a blank.

He figured Dolores had skipped the country and was probably living in Cuba with other mob expatriates. But I wasn't so sure. In any event, I suspected that I hadn't seen the last of my older sister. And it was a funny thing, despite all the harm she had done, a part of me still loved her.

Also, as much as I hated to admit it, I missed Budge too. Even though he'd betrayed me, I couldn't help but like him. But I'd only seen him twice since our day in the woods. Once I'd passed his van on the street. And another time, we'd walked by each other without speaking outside the courthouse. I knew he couldn't be trusted but I still missed his company.

From time to time, I took the train to Jefferson City. The family's law practice was booming, and my parents were both in good health. My older brother, James was getting more active in Missouri politics, now that the machine's grip was fading. And although he didn't say so, I thought he would run for governor someday.

Everyone seemed to be moving on—but me. Still, no opportunities presented themselves. So, I'd said a novena to St. Joseph and waited for a door to open.

On a Friday afternoon in late December 1939, I was staring at snowflakes swirling outside my office window and thinking of Audrey, when Ginny Oakes knocked on my door.

"Special Delivery, Sam," she said handing me a long envelope with airmail markings on it.

"Thanks, Ginny."

"It's from Washington D.C.," she said pointedly lingering at my door.

"I'll get to it, Gin," I said winking at her. I dropped the letter into my in-tray and resumed reading the case reporter lying open on my desk. I listened to Ginny's heels retreating down the hall back to reception. Then I retrieved the letter.

Since it was from Washington, I was hoping the letter was from Mac. But it wasn't. The return address was "Department of Naval Intelligence, OP-20-G, Room 1621, Main Navy Building, Constitution Avenue, Washington D.C."

What the heck, I wondered. I slit the envelope open.

There was a single, typewritten sheet inside with only two paragraphs on it. The letter was from a Captain Laurence Safford—someone I didn't know. Captain Safford invited me to travel, "all expenses paid," to Washington, D.C., for "an exploratory conversation regarding matters of mutual interest."

If this was agreeable, the letter went on to say, I should call Captain Safford's office within the week to schedule a meeting. The only clue as to what it might be about was in the final sentence of the first paragraph. It said that Rabbi Samuel Mayerberg had recommended me to the writer

The last paragraph was even more mysterious. It explained that the meeting concerned a matter of "the strictest confidence." Further, it said, that my trip had already been cleared with District Attorney Milligan. And that it was not necessary, and "in fact preferable," that I say nothing to him or anyone else about the meeting. If asked about the trip, I should simply say that I was traveling to Washington to meet with someone at the Justice Department.

I sat back and stared at the letter. While I realized that this could be exactly what I was looking for, there was something about it that I wasn't sure I liked. It wasn't just the letter's secretiveness. It was that it was instructing me to tell a lie—albeit a white one.

I wondered if I was being overly scrupulous. Then I realized I wouldn't be committing to anything if I just went to a meeting. Besides, an all-expense-paid trip to Washington would be hard to pass up. At the very least, I would have a chance to check in with Mac.

So, I strolled out of my office and down to reception. I told Ginny that I'd be back in a minute. Then I walked to the bank of elevators and punched the down button.

Reaching the lobby, I went to the line of payphone booths. Selecting the one on the end, I closed the door, dropped a nickel into the slot, and placed a long-distance, collect call.

After a series of operators and connections, a distant male voice said, "OP-20-G."

The operator cleared my collect call with the person on the other end. And then she left the line. The voice waited until she was gone.

Then it said, "Mr. Blair, would you mind if I asked you a few questions to confirm your identity?"

I was surprised, but said, "Not at all."

"What was your mother's maiden name?"

"Beaujean," I replied.

"And what was your graduating rank in law school?"

"I was second in my class."

"Hold the line, Mr. Blair, while I connect you to Captain Safford. He's been expecting your call."

ACKNOWLEDGMENTS

This book has had a long gestation, and no one knows how long better than my wife, Jane. She has put up with my plot monologues, detailed reports on research findings, and the reading of multiple drafts. Most of all, she has endured countless days of writing during which I inhabited another reality. For this, and for so much more, she has all my love and thanks.

It has been said that all first novels are autobiographical, and that is true of this one. Its origins lie in the family dinners of my youth, when relatives, who lived through the Pendergast era, spun tales of its corruption and gangsterism. Without these memories, this novel would never have been written. A special thanks go to my late Uncle Sanford, the family raconteur.

My youngest daughter Monica, an adjunct professor of composition and gender studies, who has taught at two universities in the California system and a private college, has given me invaluable tips and much encouragement during this project. As always, she has my unfailing love and thanks. My older brother, Jay, also writes. He has little patience with my dawdling, preferring to bang out his books at a rapid-fire rate. I thank him for his love, interest, and prodding. Hopefully, he approves of the final product.

Additional thanks go to my spiritual guide, Fr. Piotr Krezalek, LC. Father is a good friend, deep thinker, and lively conversationalist. He also has a wry sense of humor.

Many of the ideas in this book have come from our discussions and from those with my good friends Andrew Lynch, Bob Northrip, and the late Vince Dittrich. That said, all errors concerning the Church, its doctrine, and liturgy are, of course, mine alone.

Further love and thanks go to my oldest daughter, Leah, her husband Steve, and their children: Max, Anna, Elena, Maria, Sophia, and Lucy. Their ongoing interest in "Papa's project" has kept me on task. A special thanks go to Sophia and Lucy, who during the pandemic endured home-schooling field trips, which somehow always included lectures by Papa on the minutia of Boss Tom's life. I would also like to thank my son, Simon, former-daughter-in-law, Kristin Tilley Peck, and my California grandchildren Tilda and Otto. They were much in my thoughts, and in my heart during the writing of this book.

Four others deserve particular thanks. When I was mulling over possible topics for a writing project, good friends, Margie and Dan Coon gifted me a copy of William Ouseley's *Open City*. The book reminded me of the Pendergast years and made me realize that it was an ideal subject for a novel. Conversations with Tom and Irma Russell, friends from our English graduate school days, convinced me that the topic had broad appeal.

I also want to thank Archivist, Joyce Burner, and the extremely helpful staff at the National Archives in Kansas City, Missouri for their assistance in my review of the original transcripts, motions, and orders from *John Lazia v. the United States of America.* Further, I would like to thank Jeff Sewell, Janet Mckinney, and the law library staff at Shook, Hardy & Bacon for their help in accessing the firm's history archives, particularly regarding Edgar Shook.

Lastly, I want to acknowledge my debt to the following

works: Unger, Robert. *The Union Station Massacre: The Original Sin of J. Edger Hoover's FBI.* Kansas City Star Books, 2005. Burrough, Bryan. *Public Enemies.* Penguin, 2004. Larsen, Lawrence H., and Hulston, Nancy J. *Pendergast!.* University of Missouri Press, 1997. Hartmann, Rudolph H. *The Kansas City Investigation: Pendergast's Downfall 1938-1939.* University of Missouri Press, 1999. Wallis, Michael. *Pretty Boy: The Life and Times of Charles Arthur Floyd.* Norton, 1992. Urschel, Joe. *The Year of Fear: Machine Gun Kelly and The Manhunt that Changed a Nation.* Minotaur, 2015. Driggs, Frank, and Haddix, Chuck. *Kansas City Jazz: From Ragtime to Bebop—A History.* Oxford University Press, 2005. Hayde, Frank. *The Mafia and the Machine: The Story of the Kansas City Mob.* Barricade Books, 2007. Three-period pieces should also be acknowledged one for local color and historical feel, Reddig, William M., *Tom's Town: Kansas City and the Pendergast Legend.* Lippincott, 1947. And two others featured in this novel, Milligan, Maurice M., *Missouri Waltz: The Inside Story of the Pendergast Machine by the Man Who Smashed It.* Scribner's, 1948., and Menninger, Karl. *Man Against Himself.* Harcourt Brace Jovanovich, 1938.

ABOUT THE AUTHOR

Throughout his life, Gene has loved stories of all kinds from the Bible to *The Maltese Falcon* from *The Third Man* to *The Brothers Karamazov*. This led him to study literature and the folktale at university. Later, while pursuing a PhD. in English, he became a teaching assistant in a comparative-literature great-books program. This fostered an enduring appreciation for the classics. Following graduate school, Gene taught classes in the detective story, fantasy, and science fiction. Switching careers, he joined a national law firm where he specialized in identifying and preparing expert witnesses for complex litigation. During this time, Gene and his family spent nearly a decade in London where he served as a consultant in U.S. law. He now lives in Kansas City, Missouri.

ALSO BY GENE PECK

Coming soon: *HYPO*, the second Sam Blair Mystery

Made in the USA
Coppell, TX
17 September 2022

83290996R00204